THE WARDEN'S DAUGHTERS

Anne Douglas

This first world edition published 2011
in Great Britain and in the USA by
SEVERN HOUSE PUBLISHERS LTD of
9–15 High Street, Sutton, Surrey, England, SM1 1DF.
Trade paperback edition first published
in Great Britain and the USA 2011 by
SEVERN HOUSE PUBLISHERS LTD

British Library Cataloguing in Publication Data

Douglas, Anne, 1930–
  The warden's daughters.
  1. Fathers and daughters–Fiction. 2. Widowers–Fiction.
  3. Villages–Scotland–Highlands–Fiction. 4. Youth
  Hostels–Scotland–Highlands–Fiction. 5. Hotelkeepers–
  Fiction. 6. Fishers–Fiction. 7. Love stories.
  I. Title
  823.9'14–dc22

ISBN-13: 978-0-7278-8049-9 (cased)
ISBN-13: 978-1-84751-361-8 (trade paper)

All Severn House titles are printed on acid-free paper.

Severn House Publishers support The Forest Stewardship Council [FSC],
the leading international forest certification organisation. All our titles that
are printed on Greenpeace-approved FSC-certified paper carry the FSC logo.

Typeset by Palimpsest Book Production Ltd.,
Falkirk, Stirlingshire, Scotland.
Printed and bound in Great Britain by
MPG Books Ltd., Bodmin, Cornwall.

One

The letter had come. From the bottom step of the Edinburgh tenement stair, Monnie could see it, lying on the long deal table in the communal hallway. There were other letters, of course, for other tenants, laid out as usual by the postman, but Monnie was sure that the large, buff-coloured envelope she could see was the one her father was waiting for. And not just her father.

Up the stair, in the first-floor flat that had been her home for all the twenty years of her life, she'd left her father, Frank Forester, quietly having his breakfast. Bacon and tomatoes, dished up by Monnie's sister, Lynette, who would also be wondering now what might be in the post. For, of course, they'd been looking every day since their father's interview in Inverness a week ago, always hoping there might be news. Sad thing was, whichever way it went, they couldn't all be happy.

Contemplating that possibility, Monnie stood for a moment without moving, a tall, slender girl with a cloud of dark hair and clear grey eyes, until two cheerful neighbours hurried down the stair towards her.

'Morning, Monnie!'

Mrs MacEwan and Mrs Logan, who worked in a department store on the Bridges, smiled at her as she moved aside to let them pass.

'Looking for letters, dear?' asked Mrs Logan. 'No point me doing that, eh? The day I get a letter I'll fall flat on ma face!'

'You'll get your bills,' Mrs MacEwan told her with a laugh, as Monnie, gaining courage, dived down into the hall and snatched up the envelope she'd spotted.

'It's for Dad. He's expecting it.'

'Nice it's come, then. Bye, dear. Oh, my, will you just look at this weather?'

As the outer door banged behind the two women, not before a freezing January wind had blown in a flurry of sleet, Monnie slowly climbed the stair, feeling the envelope as she went. It was bulky – must contain forms and such – which meant . . . which must mean . . . Oh, help!

Hesitating for a moment, she faced the impact of the news she was certain the envelope contained. Knew that it would present a crossroads, for all of them, all three Foresters. Then she took a deep breath; told herself, Go on, then, get it over with, and went into the flat.

Here was the centre of her home, the main room that was part living room, part kitchen. Warm, comfortable, where life was easier now than in the old days, at least in this tenement, now that an electric cooker supplemented the big black range, and a small washing machine had been fitted in beside the sink. There was a television set, too, and a wireless and bookshelves by the easy chairs grouped in the sitting area. All very modern, all very pleasant, but this was after all, 1959, and some progress had been made since the ending of the war. Enough to make the Forester girls happy in their home. And not want to leave.

Now Monnie, avoiding her sister's questioning look, slid her eyes to her father, still sitting at the scrubbed kitchen table in the centre of the room, though he appeared to have finished his breakfast.

'Dad, it's come,' she said quietly. 'Your letter's come.'

'Has it?' Putting on an air of calmness, he pushed away his plate and raised his eyes.

'How d'you know it's the one?' Lynette asked, throwing aside the apron she'd worn for cooking, her blue eyes very bright on the large envelope in her sister's hand.

'Got the Hostel Association address on the back. Think it's good news for you, Dad.'

A tall, lanky man in his forties, he slowly rose from the table, pushing aside a lock of sandy hair from his high, benevolent brow, letting his eyes – blue like his elder daughter's, but less bright, more deeply set – rest on the envelope.

'Good news? You're a mind reader, Monica Forester?'

'Sherlock Holmes, no less.' She laughed. 'No, it's just that the letter's too big to be a rejection.'

'So, I've got the job, have I?' He gave an uneasy smile as he took the envelope from her. 'Who says I want it?'

'We know you want it,' Lynette said firmly.

'I'm not sure – I've been thinking . . .'

'Why don't you open the letter?' Monnie asked quietly. 'See what they say?'

Lynette nodded. 'Then you can make up your mind.'

Still, he hesitated, looking from one to the other of his daughters. Honey-blonde Lynette, the older by two years; smart and bubbly, always sure of herself, yet not unlike her dark-haired sister, whose manner was uncertain. It was the features, of course – their small, delicate noses, generous mouths, pointed chins – all gifts from their mother, Frank's dear Ellie, gone from them these three years past.

How he still missed her! Especially here, in this flat, this living room, she'd made so much their home. Which was why he'd begun thinking just lately of a move. Had even got as far as applying for a post as a youth hostel warden in the Highlands, and been knocked sideways when he'd been given an interview. If successful, what would happen? Could he do this to his girls? Could he leave them? Take them with him? Maybe it was all too much, far too much . . .

But then he might not have been successful.

'Oh, come on, Dad!' cried Lynette, snatching at the envelope and opening it with her thumbnail. 'Let's know the situation, eh?'

'Sorry.' His smile had become apologetic. 'Think I must be nervous.'

As he took out the folder of papers the envelope contained and smoothed out the top sheet, the girls standing close together, watched. And waited. This was it, this was the crunch. From here, life changed out of all recognition. Or, stayed as it was. Everything depended on what their father was reading now – and what a time he was taking to do it, wasn't he?

Lynette, fiddling with the flicked-up ends of her hair, couldn't help sighing, while Monnie standing very still, appeared to be scarcely breathing.

'Well?' Lynette asked at last, 'what do they say?'

Frank lowered the sheet of paper and shook his head.

'You didn't get it?'

Monnie, astonished, was ready at once to comfort him; ready, as well, to let out her breath in a sigh of relief for herself. Too soon, though, as her father's eyes told her.

'Fact is,' he answered huskily, looking at her and then away, 'I did. I did get the job.'

And, sinking back into his chair, he laid his letter on the table.

'Oh, Lord, lassies,' he whispered. 'What do we do now?'

Two

Lynette didn't waste any time.

'What we do now,' she said decisively, 'is look at the map.'

'We've already looked at it,' Monnie murmured. 'When Dad first thought of applying, we all looked, didn't we? To see where the hostel was.'

Remembering that chill December evening when Frank had come in with the Hostel Association's advertisement in the *Scotsman*, the sisters exchanged glances. At first, they'd thought their father couldn't be serious. Suggesting he might leave Edinburgh for a warden's job in the Highlands? He wasn't serious. Was he?

Seemed he was. Seemed he'd never been more serious about anything since their mother had died, and as they'd returned his level gaze, they'd suddenly understood why. And it wasn't for the reasons he gave them.

Such as, getting out of Edinburgh's smoke into the clear air of the Highlands. Or, maybe climbing hills again as he had climbed in his youth. Or, taking a boat on to a glassy loch and not hearing a single noise except birdsong. No, and it wasn't even the hope of working with ordinary, healthy young people, rather than the difficult youngsters he worked with at present. All these were good reasons, and believable, but the girls could see that what was driving him was none of them.

It was a wish to turn a page in his life. It was a deep desire to move on. Not to forget their mother – he would never do that – but to try to adjust to life without her, as he had never been able to do. That was why he would not put his reasons into words, but then he didn't need to. Because they were so close to him, because they knew him so well, they understood the reasons, anyway.

'Dad, do you really want to apply for this job?' Lynette had asked him straight out, and he had given one of his rueful grins.

'I want to, but I'm not going to.'

'Why not?'

'Because I could never leave you lassies.'

'Dad, I'm twenty-two, Monnie's twenty. We're not children. We can manage.'

'I tell you, I could never leave you. I'd miss you both too much. It was crazy ever to think about it.'

'No, it wasn't, if you want it,' Monnie told him quickly. 'I think you should go for it. And I think Ma would have said so too.'

'You do?' Though Frank's tone was eager, his expression remained unsure. 'You think she would?'

'Yes, because it's time, Dad, isn't it? Time to move on. Ma always knew when it was the right time to do things. So, apply and see what happens.'

'If I got it, though, it'd be too hard to go.'

'Not if we go with you.'

He stared. 'Go with me?'

'Aye, why not? You agree, Lynette, eh? We couldn't let Dad leave on his own?'

After only a fraction of a second, Lynette cried, 'Of course, I agree!' And flinging her arms round her father, she gave him a quick hug. 'Why, it'd be fun, eh? Moving to a new life?'

'No, no!' Frank's face was twisted in protest. 'No, I couldn't ask it. I couldn't ask you girls to go up there, change your whole lives for me. You've no idea what it would be like – well, I've no real idea myself.' He hesitated, briefly touching Lynette's hand. 'And then there's your young man, Lynette, to think about as well.'

'What young man?' She'd laughed a little. 'You mean, Terry Mackenzie? That's all over – didn't I tell you?'

'Didn't even tell me,' Monnie said.

'Well, it's true. We've parted. He's sweet, but you know how it is – we got tired. So, don't worry about me, Dad, and don't worry about Monnie, either. You do what you want to do, and we'll tag along.'

'No, I've decided. I won't apply for the job, and there's an end to it. Subject closed.'

'Let's look at the map,' was Lynette's only reply. 'Let's see where we might end up.'

And that was the first time they'd looked up their possible destination on their father's Ordnance Survey map of Scotland. That same map Lynette was once again pulling out from the bookshelves now, smiling so brightly, so confidently. As though it would do any good, thought Monnie, to look at the map again. As though it could change anything, to see where they would be going.

There was the same lengthy journey they'd already studied, laid out on the map in white, pale green and brown signifying land and woods and hills, with pale blue for lochs, or, at the edge of the land, the sea. There were some roads, of course, and the first time they'd run their fingers along them, just trying to see how they'd lead to the little place opposite Skye which would be their dad's objective.

'There it is,' he'd said, pointing with a long finger. 'Conair, a wee village beyond Glenelg, where the advert says there's a big old house that's now the hostel. To get to it, as we've no car, we'd have to take a train to Kyle of Lochalsh, then bus back down and over the Mam Ratagan Pass. Och, you should see the scenery from there, girls! The Five Sisters of Kintail! Magnificent!'

When had he seen the scenery? He reminded them of his early climbing holidays taken before he was married, when he and friends, one with an old banger, had come up to the Highlands. Camped and climbed and toured about, admiring the views, having a whale of a time on so little money, the girls wouldn't believe . . .

'Still remember that ancient motor boiling over on the top of every hill,' Frank added, laughing. 'Och, we were young, we were lucky – the Highlands gave us memories we never forgot.'

And then he and his girls were silent, thinking of other memories never to be forgotten, and he had put away his map, asking who knew if he'd need it, anyway? He hadn't even applied for the job yet.

Now, of course, he'd been offered the job and out had come the map again, the girls following the railway line – the Kyle line, as it was called, from Inverness. And it seemed to them as long a trek as the road, even though Frank said, no, it was only eighty miles, it wouldn't take more than two hours or so.

Anyway, there was no point in considering it all now. He'd yet to make up his mind what he would do, and in the meantime, had they forgotten that they were all due out at work? Lynette to her job as shorthand typist in a lawyer's office, Monnie to a bookshop which she pretty well ran for its absent-minded owner, and Frank to a council-run centre for disturbed young people.

'Oh, my, mustn't be late for your delinquent boys!' cried Lynette, teasingly, as she and Monnie rushed around, tidying up, piling dishes in the sink, putting on heavy winter coats against the January weather. But Frank's look, as he prepared to leave, was reproachful.

'Now, now, they're not delinquents, Lynette. Just laddies who've had a bad start. We have to do what we can to set them on the right path.'

'Doesn't mean you won't be glad of a change away from them,' Monnie told him, pulling on her winter boots that were warm but not as fashionable as Lynette's. 'I think you're doing the right thing, Dad, getting away.'

'We'll see,' he replied, and then was off, hurrying down the stairs, leaving the girls to lock up, calling back, 'No tea for me tonight, remember, I'm on duty. I won't be back till nine.'

'OK, Dad,' Lynette replied. And in a low voice, said to Monnie, 'You know, when we said we'd go with him, the truth is, I never thought he'd get the job – did you?'

'I'd no idea.' Monnie was frowning. 'Are you saying you wouldn't have said you'd go, if you thought he'd be successful?'

'No! No, of course not.' As Lynette tapped away down the stairs in her smart boots, she was shaking her head. 'I just thought – well, we might not have to go, anyway.'

At the front door, she turned back to look at her sister. 'I mean, I thought they'd be sure to have a Highlander in mind.'

'They chose Dad, Highlander or not, and I'm glad. It's like I said, I think he's doing the right thing.'

'If he goes.'

'He'll go, all right, now he knows he needn't leave us behind.'

'And you're happy about that too?'

'You know how I feel about it, Lynette.' Monnie pulled open the front door of the tenement and shuddered as the full force of the wind met her. 'Exactly the same as you.'

'A wee bit afraid?'

'Apprehensive.'

'Ooh, such a long word!' Lynette laughed, as they banged the door behind them. 'Anybody can tell you work in a bookshop, Monnie!'

'Not for much longer,' Monnie retorted.

Three

As Monnie had predicted, Frank decided in the end to take the warden's job.

'I feel guilty about it,' he told the girls, 'but you've persuaded me. And it seems you really want to come with me as well. That's what's settled it.' He ran his hand through his hair, as he so often did when confronting difficulties. 'I could never have gone without you.'

'No need to think about it any more,' they were quick to reassure him. 'Like you said, it's settled. We all go to the Highlands.'

They'd expected him to smile, to relax, but he still looked as though he was considering difficulties.

'Dad, aren't you pleased?' Monnie ventured at last. 'We know there'll be things to sort out, but we can do that, eh? I mean, Lynette and me, we aren't stupid. We don't think we can just walk out of the door.'

'That's true,' Lynette chimed. 'We know we have to decide what to do.' Her eyes went round the living room where they were sitting. 'About this flat, for instance.'

'Aye, you'll have been thinking about that,' Frank murmured.

He took up the envelope he'd received from the Hostel Association and shook out its contents. 'But let's take another look at what we've got, eh? First, there's this picture of Conair House. Looks pretty grand, eh? Built in what somebody called Scottish Baronial style, I believe.'

The girls studied the photograph of the house that had become the hostel. Scottish Baronial was right. Built of solid grey stone, it was all turrets, cupolas, and narrow windows, with a great studded door as its entrance, and massed shrubs and lawn as its setting. The distant hills of Skye formed a backdrop, and in the foreground, groups of young people, some in climbing gear, were sitting on the grass, smiling into the camera.

'Certainly looks grand,' Lynette remarked. 'At least, from the outside. I'd have thought they'd have turned it into a hotel.'

'My thoughts, too,' Frank agreed. 'In fact, I made that point at the interview, but I was told there were already hotels in the area. Anyway, the owner had gone bankrupt, wanted a quick sale and took the association's offer. Which pleased them no end, as you can imagine.'

He took up another photograph, this time of the outside of a small modern building.

'And this here's the warden's annexe where we'll be living, attached to the back of the main house. Not too bad, eh? Got all we need, I think?'

Two bedrooms, sitting room, kitchen, bathroom.

Yes, sounded OK. There were no pictures of the interior, so the girls would just have to hope for the best, but at least they'd have their own place.

'The main thing is, the rent's very low,' Frank said earnestly. 'Practically what they call a peppercorn. That's a key factor in taking the job. A real plus, like the car, eh?'

'Oh, the car!'

The sisters were all smiles. They'd never expected that the warden would be provided with a car, but as Frank pointed out, knowing what public transport was like in the Highlands, he'd certainly need it. It was only an old Morris, apparently, but a godsend, anyway, and if he had time he'd teach the girls to drive.

'Did ask me at the interview if I could drive,' he added, 'and I was damned glad I'd learned, even though I never did manage to afford to run a car.'

'Was it that guy who took you to the Highlands who taught you?' asked Monnie, and Frank raised his eyebrows.

'Fancy you guessing that. Yes, it was Bobby Gregor. He was

a natural for anything to do with motors. Had us all driving in no time. Of course, it was easier then. So little traffic.'

'Looks like Monnie and me will have to buy ourselves bikes, though.' Lynette said with a sigh. 'I mean, even if we learn to drive, we won't have the car and we'll have to get to work somehow. We are going to have to find jobs, you know.'

'I know.' Frank heaved a sigh. 'That's another reason for me feeling bad – you girls having to give up your jobs here. But seems there might be something going attached to the hostel.'

'Some jobs?'

'One job. I've just found the info about it. The assistant warden is leaving at the same time as the warden himself. They're having local interviews for the post, and I thought one of you might apply.'

'Assistant warden?' Lynette pondered the idea for a moment, then shook her head. 'Doesn't sound my cup of tea. Monnie, how about you?'

'I wouldn't mind having a go. If they don't mind that I'm your daughter.'

'I'd have nothing to do with the interviews, and there's a precedent already,' Frank told her. 'The reason the assistant warden is leaving with the warden is that she's his wife. So, there you are. You'd be in with a chance, Monnie, if you apply. But Lynette, what about you? There may not be much call for shorthand and typing up where we're going.'

'Oh, come on, I might have to travel but I'll find something I can do. No need to worry, Dad.'

'You make life sound so easy, Lynette.'

'It is easy! If you don't make it hard.'

'You're like Ma,' Monnie commented. 'That's just the sort of thing she used to say to me.'

'Well, you're like Dad here. You worry too much.'

'Can't all be the same,' Frank said and sat back in his chair, his eyes travelling round the living room. 'But don't tell me you haven't been worrying about leaving here, eh?'

Lynette glancing at Monnie, said softly, 'We have, then. This is our home.'

'Mine, too,' said Frank.

'What will happen, Dad?' Monnie whispered. 'To all the things?'

Like their father, she and Lynette were looking at their surroundings. At their home. At the furnishings and possessions they'd known all their lives.

Framed Scottish scenes their parents had been given as wedding presents. Books crammed into shelves. Cushions their mother had made; the hooked rug she'd worked during the war with any materials she could find; her jars and bottles, her pots and pans, cups and saucers, plates on the dresser, photographs . . .

'Dad, where will everything go?' Lynette asked. 'I've been lying awake at night, wondering.'

'Into storage?' Monnie asked. 'That'll cost a lot.'

'Can't leave 'em for a new tenant, can we? And there'll have to be a new tenant.'

'Well, we're not giving them up! Dad, we're not doing that, are we?'

'No, we're not giving them up.'

Frank took out his cigarettes and lit one, shaking his head at Lynette who had stretched out her hand towards the packet.

'You shouldn't be smoking, Lynette, it's bad for you.'

'How about you then?' she demanded, tossing back her hair. 'You've been smoking like a chimney lately.'

'That's just because I've had so much to think about. Once I'm away and settled, I'll cut down.'

'So what are you thinking now?' Monnie asked, the look on his face suddenly making her feel hopeful. 'About our flat?'

He paused for a pleasurable little effect. 'That I'll keep it on. You didn't imagine I could let it go?'

'You mean, pay the landlord the rent, same as usual?' Lynette asked. 'But, Dad, you can't afford it! When you'll be paying out somewhere else.'

'Didn't I say the rent of the warden's flat was a key factor for me in taking the job? It's so small, I can afford to keep this flat on and, quite frankly, if I couldn't have done that, I wouldn't be moving. I want to make a new life, it's true, but I'd never part with this place. With all its memories? No.'

As the girls stared, too wrapped up in their emotions to speak, he drew strongly on his cigarette, his gaze far away. Then he brought it back, to fix on his daughters' faces.

'And then you have to think, as well, what would happen if

something went wrong up there in the Highlands and we'd no home of our own.' He shrugged. 'I'm not stupid, either. We had to have a Plan B, eh?'

'Oh, Dad!'

The girls, laughing, ran to him and hugged him, tears stinging their eyes.

'Makes all the difference,' Monnie sniffed. 'To know we're not saying goodbye to everything here.'

'All the difference,' Lynette agreed, blowing her nose. 'But will the flat be OK, Dad, with no one in it?'

'Well, I thought of asking Mrs Logan or someone to come in from time to time and give it a dust etcetera, and then it should be fine in the summer. For the winter, I might get a fellow I know from work to come in as a sublet. I'll have to get permission, but he's a good careful guy, lives with his mother but wouldn't mind a break. Don't worry, we'll sort something out.'

'We can always pack some of the stuff away in our room, I suppose,' Lynette suggested. 'But we will be taking some things with us, eh? I mean, photos and pictures, Ma's cushions, maybe?'

'Oh, sure, we'll want to make the new place homely. I'll leave it to you to sort out what you want to take, and then we'll send them on.' Frank stubbed out his cigarette. 'The main thing is that we're keeping our home here and that you're both happy. You are, eh?'

'We are.'

'And I am, too.' Frank stood up, stretching. 'So, what happens next is, that after I've said goodbye to my boys –' the sisters rolled their eyes. His boys. So keen to see all his geese as swans, wasn't he? Still, those laddies appreciated him and would miss him. Had to admit that – 'I'll have to spend some time at the headquarters on a course, learning my duties,' Frank was continuing. 'But then, with everything settled, it'll be a case of Conair, here we come! Don't forget, we move in at the beginning of March. Just pray it isn't snowing.'

'Let it snow, let it snow, let it snow!' sang Lynette, waltzing round the kitchen. 'Come on, Monnie, let's make a cup of tea!'

Four

There was no doubt that their father's decision to keep on the Edinburgh flat made a great difference to his daughters' feelings over leaving it. At least, for a time.

As Monnie put it to Lynette, it was like having a mattress in the background. To break their fall, if things went wrong, as Dad had suggested.

'Of course, he doesn't really think things will go wrong,' Monnie added. 'But it's as well to be prepared.'

'I agree,' Lynette declared. 'What's in my mind is that if we really can't stick it—'

'Oh, I'm not thinking that will happen, Lynette!'

'No, but it might. You've just said we should be prepared, and if we find we absolutely hate it, we might just have to tell Dad and come back home.' Lynette gave one of her brilliant smiles. 'And here home will be!'

'Might have to ask the tenant to move out, if it's the winter.'

'So, he can move out.'

'Yes, well, let's hope it won't come to that. I'd hate to disappoint Dad.' Monnie's grey eyes were darkly serious. 'And he does need us, Lynette.'

'Oh, I know. I'm not saying it will happen, anyway. It'll be like having insurance, eh? When you take out insurance, you hope you won't need it.'

'Aye, that's the way to think of it,' Monnie agreed with some relief. 'And in any case, it's grand to be keeping all the stuff, eh?'

'Oh, we couldn't have let it go. I feel so happy we don't have to part with any of it. And we can take the best bits with us.'

All the same, as the days of February melted away and the time arrived to pack up the flat, some of the girls' euphoria began to fade. For now, in the strange bareness of their home, they could no longer escape the truth of the matter. Departing for a new life meant giving up the old. Keeping on their home as some sort of insurance in the background was good, was helpful, but it didn't alter the fact that for now they were leaving it. For very good reasons, and as their own decision, but leaving it, all the same.

'Talk about feeling apprehensive!' Lynette said, shaking her head. 'I don't mind admitting, I've got cold feet!'

'After all we said,' Monnie murmured, laughing shakily. 'But . . . me too!'

'And I haven't even handed in my notice yet.'

'And I haven't.'

'I can't think what Old Mr Couper will say to me.'

'Or what Mr Bryce will say to me.'

'Well, everyone can be done without,' Lynette remarked cheerfully.

'I sometimes wonder if that's true,' Monnie answered worriedly. 'I'm sure Mr Bryce won't know what to do, if I'm not there to tell him.'

And Mr Bryce, a thin, grey figure of indeterminate age, was certain, too, that he wouldn't know what to do if Monnie left him. Who would do the accounts, the ordering, the packing and unpacking, the reminding of which customer wanted what, and where everything was?

'Oh, Monnie, are you really leaving me?' he'd groaned when she had given him her news. 'Going up to the Highlands? I can't believe it. What am I going to do?'

'You'll soon find someone else to do what I do,' she told him as confidently as possible. 'You're the one that matters, being the bookman.'

'Yes, Monnie, my dear, but I can't even tie up a parcel. Still, if you must go, you must, and I'll have to grin and bear it. Where did you say you were going, again?'

'Conair, a little place near Glenelg opposite Skye. My dad's going to be warden of a youth hostel up there, and I might be his deputy. I've got an interview, anyway.'

As Monnie reflected on her pleasure at being given an interview for the deputy warden's post, Mr Bryce looked interested. But not about her possible job.

'Glenelg? Now didn't Dr Johnson and Boswell stay there on

their travels round Scotland? A fascinating account. Could you just put your hand on that copy of Boswell's *Journal of a Tour to the Hebrides*, do you think? Maybe I'll read it again.'

'Right away, Mr Bryce,' sighed Monnie, wondering if she should draft out an advertisement for her replacement that very day.

Meanwhile, old Mr Couper was expressing his regret at Miss Forester's departure from his law firm, Messrs Couper, Couper and Anderson, of Queen Street, Edinburgh. Just as young Mr Couper would have also liked to express his regret, only with young Mrs Couper to remember, it was better he didn't look too downcast over the departure of the prettiest member of the clerical staff.

'So efficient,' old Mr Couper sighed. 'So reliable. Our loss will be someone else's gain, wouldn't you say, Miss Millwood?'

But Miss Millwood, stern-faced senior secretary, preferred not to say too much about Miss Forester, only remarking that she might find it difficult to find a post in the Highlands.

'If anyone can find a post, Miss Forester will,' old Mr Couper declared, at which Miss Millwood only shrugged.

Not that Lynette minded. Who cared what Miss Millwood thought? It was well known that she believed Lynette to be far too full of herself – which was probably true, Lynette herself admitted – but that only made it more likely she would find a job. Confidence was what was needed, eh? And it rather pleased Lynette that old Mr Couper had such confidence in her. Young Mr Couper, too, though he never put anything into words. As for Mr Anderson, he was just a name on the letter headings, having been dead for years.

How typical of a law firm that they should keep the name alive of someone dead, Lynette often commented. Maybe, now she had to look elsewhere, she might find somewhere more exciting to work? The thought helped a little – just a little – in making the move less apprehensive, to use Monnie's word.

'When we get there,' she told her sister, 'you'll see, we'll be OK.'

'Think so?' Monnie asked. 'Just got to get there, then.'

'Now that we're definitely going, I can't wait to leave, can you?'

'It's true, I wish we were on our way.'

★   ★   ★

Some days later, after they'd done all that had to be done, they were – on their way. The flat had been cleaned and polished, and Mrs Logan had agreed to keep an eye on it. The packing cases had been sent off. Frank had completed his course. All farewells, to friends, neighbours, colleagues, and the 'delinquent' boys, had been made.

There they were, then, locking the door, trying not to cry, climbing into the taxi they'd recklessly booked to take them to Waverley Station – well, they did have their big cases to carry – and hurrying out on to the platform to wait for the Inverness train. Oh, how cold it was in the draughty station! Enough to freeze the tears the girls were brushing away.

'Here it comes!' Frank cried, as their train steamed in. 'Got your bags, then?'

'Got the kitchen stove, it feels like,' Lynette answered. 'Monnie, did you put our sandwiches in?'

'Sure I did. I'm going to have mine soon as we set off.'

'Comfort food, eh?'

'Could do with a bit of comfort.'

Monnie was already hurrying down the platform after her father, looking for their compartment. 'Found our seats, Dad?'

'Aye, this is us. Give me your cases, then.'

Settling into their seats, watching the platform slide past after the guard had waved his flag, the Foresters were catching their breath.

'Goodbye, Edinburgh!' Frank suddenly called out.

But the girls seemed unable to speak.

Five

Leaving the train at Inverness, they were thankful they were booked in for bed and breakfast and needn't travel on. Already the evening was growing dark and cold. Very cold.

'Why so arctic?' Lynette asked, as Frank led the way grandly to the taxi queue.

'And are we really splashing out on another taxi?' asked Monnie.

'Questions, questions,' Frank laughed. 'Why so arctic? Well, some do think that Inverness has the coldest winters of any city in the UK, couldn't say if it's true. And are we taking a taxi? Yes, we are. This guest house I've booked is a fair step and we've cases to carry. No need to look so worried, Monnie, we're not running out of cash yet.'

'If you say so,' she murmured, as a taxi drew up and they settled into its shelter from the chill of the wind. 'But I'm just so glad you thought of doing this, Dad. Couldn't have faced trying to get to the hostel tonight, could we?'

'No, and we'd have been pretty late, meeting the outgoing warden. The other good thing is that this way we get to travel by daylight on the Kyle of Lochalsh line – and that's got some of the best scenery in Scotland. Wait till you see it.'

After booking into Mrs Danby's comfortable little guest house, they went out for a fish supper and afterwards to the pictures. Monnie's idea, though she admitted before the start of Hitchcock's *Vertigo* that she'd never dreamed her father would come too.

'Thought sure you'd want to go to bed early to be ready for tomorrow,' she told him. 'I mean, it's all any of us can think about, eh?'

'Och, it'll do us good to relax,' he answered easily. 'And this sounds like a good film.'

'The last we'll see for a long time,' Lynette remarked, sighing. 'I bet there's no cinema where we're going.'

'There's a mobile cinema of some sort. Comes round in the summer.'

'Oh, well then!' Lynette laughed, then sighed again. 'Makes you wonder what there'll be to do, though. For entertainment.'

'There'll be dances, I expect,' Monnie said. 'Ceilidhs and such. Kilts flying, eightsome reels, that sort of thing.'

'Can't wait!' Lynette leaped up, rattling coins in her hand. 'There's the ice-cream girl. Who wants one?'

They all had one, and as the lights dimmed and the film began, settled down to enjoy scraping out their tubs with their miniature wooden spoons, while watching the first shots of Jimmy Stewart looking worried in *Vertigo*, their new life for the moment very far away.

Next morning, it was porridge for breakfast, followed by kippers and buttered toast, all eaten in the church-like atmosphere of the guests' dining room, where the only sounds came from the scrape of cutlery and the stout waitress's murmur, 'Coffee or tea?'

'Any chance of us nipping out to see Loch Ness before we go?' Lynette asked, risking a whisper. As her father stared, she smiled and shook her head. 'Only joking. I know we've got to get that early train.'

'You're right,' Frank said, rising. 'Let's get going. I'll pay the bill.'

But in the hallway, out of hearing of the nosey, middle-aged landlady standing ready at her desk, Lynette touched his arm.

'Dad, you don't need to pay for us, you know. We've got some money.'

'Aye, we're grown up now,' Monnie told him. 'Earning money and all.'

'*Were* earning money,' he said seriously. 'Look, it's upsetting to me that you lassies have given up your jobs. I'm not short, I can manage till I get paid, so you hang on to any cash you've got till you're settled.'

The sisters exchanged glances.

'Knew you'd never agree,' Lynette murmured. 'But we both brought some savings, so we could help out.'

'And very thoughtful you were, but let's leave it for now, eh?' He smiled. 'Tell you what, you could pay for the taxi to the station if you like. Hurry up and pack and I'll get Mrs Danby to ring for one.'

Upstairs, in the twin bedroom they'd shared, the sisters rapidly packed their overnight bags, before putting on coats and boots and doing a last check round.

'No snow out there, but it looks bitter,' Lynette remarked from the window. 'Wish I could've worn my red suit, but it's far too cold.'

'Who on earth is going to see you in your red suit?' Monnie asked. 'There'll only be the warden who's leaving and maybe some young folk at the hostel.'

'Why, you never know who you might meet, Monnie. And first impressions count, you know. I always like to cut a dash. Knock 'em dead, as they say.'

'You're best off in that coat you've got on. I'll bet you any money, this Kyle train won't be heated.'

'And I'll not take you on. Folk up here, they'll think it's only softie Lowlanders like us who expect heating.' Lynette pulled on a dark blue woollen hat to match her winter coat and gathered up her cases. 'Still, Dad said the scenery's lovely, so come on, let's see it.'

It turned out that Monnie was right about the heating on the Kyle of Lochalsh train, but then Frank was right, too, about the scenery. Yes, the train was cold, so cold that the passengers never attempted to remove coats or even gloves on the two-hour journey, and if the carriages were clean enough, they were somewhat spartan where comfort was concerned. But directly the train had left Inverness and begun its journey towards the Black Isle, which was really a peninsula, rather than an island, the scenery was casting its spell.

'You said it'd be lovely, Dad,' Lynette murmured, as they left Dingwall, their first stop, and branched away west. 'And you were right.'

'I was,' Frank agreed, looking towards a distant line of snowy mountains beneath a wide bowl of clear, chill sky. 'And, hey, do you see the deer?'

'Where?' Monnie cried, and smiled as she saw the deer hurrying from the noise of their train. 'Ah, they're so close, eh? Why, there's everything here. Hills and water and wildlife.'

Wildlife to match the wildness of the landscape was the thought that came to mind, as the girls continued to gaze, fascinated, at the country that was so new to them, yet looked as though it had existed for ever. Long, long before Edinburgh had even been thought of, all this would have been here. These hills, these stretches of silent water, this countryside so empty it seemed as if only the deer and the wheeling birds could know it. Beautiful, solitary land.

It was, the girls secretly felt, so different from the streets of home as to be almost alien. How would it compare to the place they were going? As Frank rustled his map, they remained quiet, still keeping their eyes on the views from the train, relieved, in a way, whenever they came to tiny stations. Here, at least, were signs of life.

'I think this is Loch Carron we're looking at now,' Frank said at last. 'Homeward stretch, girls! Not too far now to Kyle.'

'Not the end of the journey, though,' Monnie commented. 'We've still to get a bus.'

'Yes, but we can have something to eat first.'

'And coffee!' Lynette said cheerfully. 'Oh joy! Think I might just make it to the hostel if I get the tank filled.'

'You're like Popeye dying for his spinach,' Monnie said laughing. 'I know, because I'm the same.'

It was a strange sensation to leave the train, which had taken them through such wild and empty country, for the bustle and normality of Kyle of Lochalsh, the base of the ferry to Skye. Here was a large and busy centre, with harbour and pier, lifeboat station and smart hotel, cafes and shops. And people – plenty of them – the sight of which fuelled the girls' spirits almost as well as the coffee and quick snack they had at one of the cafes.

'Civilization,' Lynette said in a low voice. 'I loved that train trip, but – I don't know – maybe I'm a townee at heart.'

'Don't say that,' Monnie answered, glancing at Frank. 'You'll settle in, no trouble.'

'All I want is for you girls to be happy about what you're doing,' Frank said at once. 'It's never going to be too late for you to go back, you know.'

'Who said anything about going back?' cried Lynette. 'Hey, I'm not giving up before I've started. The plan was to come with you, Dad, and that's what we've done. So forget going back.'

'All right.' He nodded. 'Let's go forward, then. It's time we went for that bus.'

Six

It was a very old bus. Maybe even pre-war, with high, faded leather seats rather close together and small, narrow windows. Clean, though, and a pleasant refuge from the wind that had been rattling around everybody waiting at the bus stop.

'Glenelg?' asked the driver, who was tanned and lined and a little grey, as Frank took his turn to pay.

'No, three to Conair, please.'

'Three, it is.'

While he punched out their tickets and gave Frank change, the driver's smile was friendly, his eyes curious – as were the eyes of the other passengers watching as the Foresters took their seats. It was plain everyone on the bus knew everyone else, except for two young men at the back, who were probably climbers, and these three strangers, who probably weren't. So, who might they be? The Foresters could almost hear the question going through the locals' minds.

'Now this bit of the journey, I do remember,' Frank whispered to the girls as the bus set off down the side of Loch Duich making for Shiel Bridge, from where it would turn to the unclassified road to Glenelg. 'We drove all round here with Bobby Gregor. Know what we used to call it? Calendar Land.'

'Calendar Land?' Monnie repeated. 'Why?'

'Why? Just take a look out of the window. Everything on this route looks like a picture on a calendar.' Frank laughed. 'Wait till we get to Dornie and you see Eilean Donan! Don't know how many times I've sent pictures of that castle to folks.'

Dornie? Eilean Donan? As soon as the girls saw the pretty village of Dornie, with the fairy-tale castle of Eilean Donan rising from its little island close by, they understood what their father was talking about. Calendar Land. The words aptly summed up this new part of the world that was different again from the wild countryside they'd seen from the train. Yet there was grandeur here, too, with towering snow-capped mountains on the south side of the glen. Also, when they began to climb Mam Ratagan after the turn at Shiel Bridge, Frank, looking back, pointed out a great ridge of peaks he said was famous.

'The Five Sisters of Kintail,' he told them. 'You'll remember them from the maps?'

'Och, I'm just looking at where we are now!" Lynette cried. 'Talk about switchbacks! I don't envy the driver taking us over this lot!'

'Ah, now, 'tis nothing,' the listening driver called out, smiling. 'I could do it blindfold, so I could, I have been doing it so long. And it's worth it, eh, for the views?'

'The Five Sisters,' Frank agreed. 'Another calendar favourite.'

'They are that! And have a story you should hear. Agnes, why don't you tell it to the visitors?'

Who's Agnes? wondered the Foresters.

She turned out to be a woman sitting just behind them. Heavy-shouldered, with large hands resting on her shopping bag, she had a bold, good-looking face. High cheekbones, straight, thin nose, eyes blue, keen and clear. From a scarf wound round her head, her hair was escaping, in thick yellow strands.

'Me?' she asked, clearly not displeased at the idea.

'You know all the stories,' someone said, and the driver joined in.

'Aye, be telling them, Agnes. 'Twill take their minds off the road, I am thinking.'

'We'd like to hear it, too,' one of the climbers shouted from the back, and Monnie, swivelling round, thought he had rather a pleasant face. She wondered if he and his companion were going to the hostel. Perhaps not. They looked to be around thirty. Might consider themselves too old, even though there was no age bar, as far as Monnie knew.

'Well, then, there's more than one story about the mountains there, but this is the one I know,' Agnes began, her Highland voice soft and lilting.

'Long ago, there were seven sisters hereabouts, daughters of a farmer. Two brothers came visiting from a foreign land and married two of the sisters, which left five, you see, without husbands. So, these brothers said they would return home with their brides but send their five brothers to come back over the sea and marry the sisters who were left. Which, as you can imagine, made them very happy.'

'But guess what happened!' interrupted the driver. 'Ah, 'twas awful sad, eh?'

'Now don't be rushing me, Tim MacLean,' Agnes remonstrated coolly, then relaxed and continued. 'But, yes, it was awful sad. The sisters waited and waited, but no brothers came and in the end they gave up the waiting and went to a local wizard. What they asked him then was very strange, but it was to turn them into the peaks of mountains. Five peaks, you see, for the five sisters, so that their beauty would be preserved for ever.' Agnes raised her large hands. 'Which I think you'll agree, it was.'

'Oh, yes, those peaks are beautiful,' Lynette said quickly, but Monnie was sighing.

'Too sad, though, to think of the sisters waiting and waiting and no one coming.'

'Happens, you know, even today,' a woman near Agnes murmured. 'Remember Maggie Lindsay, engaged to that fellow from Inverness? Borrowed the money for the ring and never came back? Then there was—'

'Ah, now, never mind those miserable tales,' Agnes said quickly, her eyes fixed on the Forester girls. 'Tell me, my dears, are you from Edinburgh, then?'

'We are,' Lynette replied.

'Thought so, could tell by your voices.' Agnes sighed with satisfaction. 'Oh, I love to hear the city accents!'

'On holiday, eh?' the driver asked. 'A little bit early, maybe, for the good weather.'

'Not on holiday,' said Frank. 'I'm Frank Forester, the new warden of the hostel at Conair. And these are my daughters.'

The new warden? There were murmurs of interest from the passengers. Fancy, the warden and his family, on their bus!

'The warden?' Agnes repeated. 'Why, 'tis nice to meet you, then, Mr Forester, and your daughters. We all know Mr MacKay, and his wife, too. Such a lovely couple as they are. And away to Canada to be with their son.'

'I am meeting Mr MacKay today,' Frank said. 'We are on our way to the hostel now.'

'And isn't that lovely?' someone murmured. 'Be watching out for Agnes's boy, then. He'll be delivering your fish.'

'Beautiful fresh fish,' Agnes declared. 'Sure, you'll meet my laddie. But we wish you all the best, Mr Forester, and your girls, too. 'Twill be strange for you, to be in our part of the world after Edinburgh, but anything you want, you've only to ask.'

Voices chimed in. Anything they wanted, they'd only to ask.

'Here comes Glenelg,' the driver announced. 'Your place is next, Mr Forester.'

'How pretty,' Monnie whispered to Lynette, looking out at Glenelg Bay with its direct views to Skye, and the straggling village street of whitewashed cottages. 'Looks like there's a hotel, too, and a little ferry.'

'Seems to be the place to live. Plenty getting out.'

When the bus moved on, however, there were still several passengers left, including Agnes and the two climbers, which made Monnie wonder again if the men were making for the hostel. But when Frank asked with a friendly smile if they were bound for Conair, they said they were going on to the Talisman, the hotel further on. Best of luck, though, to the new warden, they added, wishing him all the best.

'Didn't fancy Conair House yourselves?' Frank asked.

'Not this time.'

So, they'd stayed at the hostel before, Monnie thought. Perhaps fancied a little more comfort now? Not that it was of any interest; she didn't suppose she would see the climbers again.

'Here we are, folks,' Tim MacLean cried, turning his bus off the road into what was no more than a hamlet. A small collection of whitewashed cottages with a shop and post box, a slipway for boats, and a view across the waters, the Sound of Sleat, to the island of Skye.

'There's your hostel, Mr Forester. Conair House, eh? I'll just give you a hand with your luggage.'

Conair House. Their new home. The Foresters, slowly alighting from the bus, stared at the building they could easily recognize from the pictures they'd seen. Yes, it was exactly the same. Scottish Baronial. Victorian. All its towers, cupolas, narrow windows just as they remembered, though now of course there were no young people sitting outside and no sun shone. In fact, the sky was darkening, and the air around the grey stone walls was filled with wintry chill – a chill that the sisters seemed to feel, though their father showed no sign. And Agnes, bouncing out of the bus with the other passengers for Conair, was in high spirits.

'Is it not the grandest place, then?' she cried. 'The grandest place here, of course, for all the rest is cottages. That's mine there, next to the shop, but we're all pretty close. And see – there's Mr and Mrs MacKay coming out to greet you. Best of luck, my dears!'

'Best of luck!' echoed the driver, as he drove away, his last two passengers, the climbers, waving and smiling at Lynette and Monnie.

'Journey's end,' Frank murmured. 'Here we are, girls.'

'Here we are,' they said softly.
And felt suddenly incredibly weary.

Seven

Mr and Mrs MacKay were in their fifties. He, tall, spare, and fit-looking, with a bush of greying hair; she, tiny, with dark, permed curls and darting brown eyes. Energetic people, thought Frank. Ideal wardens, no doubt. Would he be as good? As with his girls, his own energy seemed to be flagging.

'Bill and Rhoda,' Mr MacKay said, as he and his wife heartily shook Frank's hand. 'Good to see you, Mr Forester. Hope you had a good journey?'

'Please call me Frank. Thanks, we had an excellent trip, enjoyed it all. May I introduce my daughters, Lynette and Monica?'

'Your daughters?' Rhoda put her hand to her lips. 'Oh, how silly of us . . . We thought, you know, your daughters were *little* girls.'

Little? The sisters stared.

'Sorry if we're too old,' Lynette said at last, half smiling, though not in fact amused.

'Of course not, of course not!' Rhoda was blushing pink. 'It's just that — well, we didn't think of grown-ups wanting to . . . you know give up their own lives. Oh, dear, am I making things worse?'

'No, we understand.' Monnie was swift to ease the moment. 'But our mother's dead and we just thought we'd like to be with Dad.'

'And that's lovely, dear. Really lovely. Family's more important than anything.' Rhoda nodded her head. 'That's why we're joining our son in Canada — we want to see our grandchildren growing up. But come away into the flat and we'll have a cup of tea before we show you round. You must be exhausted.'

'Won't deny it,' Frank replied. 'A cup of tea sounds wonderful. It's very good of you to take so much trouble.'

'Nonsense,' Bill said robustly. 'We're happy to do what we can.

It can be no joke, running a place like this until you know all the ropes. When we've given you the tour, we'll be taking a taxi to the Talisman Hotel, and tomorrow we're heading for Inverness to stay with friends before we leave.'

'We've sold our house there,' Rhoda explained, leading the way round the main house to the modern extension. 'No ties any more. Gives you a funny feeling, you know, starting completely afresh.'

You can say that again, thought Lynette, as she and Monnie set down their cases in the twin-bedded room they were to share. Not too bad was their verdict, but they didn't linger. Not when tea was in the offing.

The refreshing tea was served by Rhoda with scones and cake in the sitting room of the flat. Empty of all except basic furnishings, this was a pleasant enough room, with fine views of Skye, but would be pleasanter still, the girls decided, when it was truly theirs and had their own things about.

Of course, they should really be looking round the hostel, which was the reason for everything, but just for a while they were content to relax, their father, too. Sit back, admire the view, accept more tea and, perhaps a little more of that excellent coffee cake. 'Made by Ishbel,' as Rhoda told them.

'Ishbel?' Frank repeated.

'Mrs MacNicol, from the shop. She does a bit of baking and I can tell you it's always snapped up!' Rhoda smiled. 'If you're anything like me, you'll use the shop a lot. She has everything – even stamps, though you have to go to Glenelg or Kyle if you want a proper post office.'

'All local info's in a big folder on my desk in the office,' put in Bill. 'I mean, your desk now, Frank. We've listed everything you're likely to want to know. Things like our rules for the hostellers – out after breakfast, back at five or thereabouts, lights out at eleven and single sex dormitories.'

He grinned. 'Well, that goes without saying, we're acting like parents here, have to make sure the real parents can let their girls stay without worrying.'

'Oh, that came over loud and clear in my training,' Frank commented. 'It's where the responsibility comes in.'

'True. But, getting back to the folder, we've given all details of laundry facilities and catering arrangements, etcetera. Sheets can be hired if folk haven't brought any, but we do let them use sleeping bags, provided they're clean. As you know, the young ones do their own cooking and can buy food here – there's a special locked cupboard for that, only used by you. And everybody has to take a turn at the chores. No duty dodging!'

'I can see you've thought of everything, Bill.'

'Well, you can amend things as you like, of course, but we've tried to follow what the association wants and we think it works well.'

'I'm very grateful to you,' said Frank. 'You've certainly made my job easier. One thing I was wondering – how about the cleaning of the hostel? Apart from what the young folk do? Do you have any help, Rhoda?'

'Oh, yes, I've a widow lady who comes in from the cottages. The young people are supposed to sweep out and look after their own dorms and so on, but I get my help to do the basics elsewhere. You'll see her tomorrow. I hope you'll keep her on – she's a treasure.'

'Not the lady we met on the bus?' Lynette asked. 'Agnes Somebody?'

'Agnes MacLeod?' Rhoda's eyes very slightly narrowed. 'No, no, not Agnes. This is Jeannie Duthie I'm talking about.'

'Agnes told us the story of the Five Sisters,' Monnie said with a smile. 'She also said her son sells fish to the hostel.'

'She has two sons. Torquil, who sells the fish, is the younger one. Yes, you'll be seeing him – comes twice a week, usually.' Rhoda stood up. 'Shall we make the rounds, then? And Bill, you could show Frank the car?'

'Grand little Morris,' said Bill. 'Absolute marvel.'

'Can't wait to see it,' Frank said. 'Or, the hostel, of course. Any youngsters about?'

'Och, they'll be cooking at the minute. Can't you smell their sausages?' Bill grinned. 'We've only a handful here at present – dedicated climbers and ramblers, most of 'em, who don't mind the weather, but in the summer there might be thirty or so booking in. Keep you on your toes, Frank!'

'I'll say.'

★　　★　　★

After inspecting the elderly Morris in a rear garage, and finding it as attractive for a warden's car as any Rolls, Frank and the girls followed the MacKays through the studded front door of the hostel and into the spacious hall. It was like stepping back in time.

'Good Lord!' Frank cried, 'it's still got the stags' antlers up!'

'Sure, why not?' Bill asked. 'The family never took 'em, so they just got left. Make a talking point, anyway.'

'Shame they shot so many,' Monnie whispered. 'I suppose they'd nothing else to do.'

'Aye, there'd have been plenty of maids to do the work in the old days.' Bill gestured towards the oak staircase and the lovely woodwork of the floors, now scuffed and marked with footsteps. 'Afraid it's not possible to keep it like it used to be.'

'Och, no!' Rhoda cried. 'Who'd be able to spend the time today? Anyway, it's all been changed. You'll see, as we go round.'

Changed, yes. As they moved from room to room, it soon became clear to the girls and Frank that they were now definitely back in the twentieth century. Though the high ceilings and long windows were still part of the old reception rooms and the warden's office off the hall, there was little idea left of how the original house had been.

The once grand drawing room, for instance, was now a common room with a wireless and ancient piano, while the old dining room, like the bedrooms upstairs, had been partitioned into dormitories. All necessary, of course, and yet . . .

'Sort of sad?' Rhoda suggested in answer to the girls' expressions. 'Yes, you do get to feel sometimes that the old house has been . . . now what's the word I want? Sacrificed. Yet, had to be, of course.'

'I think so,' Lynette answered slowly. 'At least young folk can come and enjoy being in the Highlands now, where once they wouldn't have been able to afford it.'

'Exactly so,' Bill agreed. 'A place like this can give untold pleasure to city youngsters who'd have been totally trapped before.' He gave an easy grin. 'Well, that's enough of the sermon, let's go and see some of these young folk now before their supper's ready.'

In the long, stone-flagged kitchen at the back of the house, the appetizing smell of sausages frying on one of two modern electric cookers met them as they came in the door, and the eight young people preparing their supper looked up and grinned.

'Hi, Mr MacKay!' one called. 'No' gone yet, then?'

'Practically on our way,' Bill answered. 'We're just showing the new warden round – this is Mr Forester.'

The five young men and three young women smiled a welcome, and when Lynette and Monnie were presented, too, were keen to know whether they were staying or not. When they said they were, one young man laughed and said, Wow, maybe he'd not be leaving in the morning, after all.

'Now, now, Craig,' Rhoda said, shaking a finger at him. 'I'm sure these young ladies have got more to do than look after you.'

But after she'd shown Frank the fridge and cupboard where the hosteller's food was kept, she did look a little curious as she took the girls back to their room. What were they, in fact, going to do?

'I might actually be looking after hostellers,' Monnie told her. 'I've an interview next week for the post of assistant warden.'

'Oh, excellent! I've done it for years and enjoyed every moment. I do hope you get it – I'm sure you will.' Rhoda's eyes went to Lynette, who was standing at the window, looking out at the darkness that had now descended. 'And you, dear? Have you anything in mind?'

'Not so far, though I'm sure I'll find something. I'm a short-hand typist.'

Rhoda stood for a moment, looking thoughtful. 'I'll tell you a job I do know about, if you'd be interested.'

'Oh? Tell me more!'

'Well, this hotel where we're spending the night – it's just three miles down the road – very pleasant, very comfortable. They were advertising in the local paper last week for a senior recep-tionist. You could try for that, maybe?'

'Hotel receptionist.' Lynette's brow was furrowed. 'I suppose I was thinking of some sort of secretarial work. But maybe that'd be hard to find.'

'I'd apply, if I were you,' said Monnie. 'Jobs aren't going to be growing on trees round here.'

'I'll find you the advert,' Rhoda promised. 'But then, Bill and

I must be on our way. But I've left you one of Ishbel's ham and egg pies for your supper, and there's milk in the wee fridge and some basic groceries in the larder.'

'Rhoda, you've been too kind!' Lynette exclaimed. 'We can't thank you enough. How much do we owe you?'

'Nothing at all, don't speak about it. Just let us know how you get on. Bill's given our address to your dad.'

After they'd bid farewell to the MacKays and watched them drive off in a taxi ordered from Glenelg, the Foresters turned back to the hostel and cautiously exchanged glances.

'Well?' Frank asked. 'How goes it? How d'you feel, now we're here?'

'Fine,' Monnie answered promptly. 'Now we've seen it, I feel sure we'll be happy.'

'Yes, sure,' Lynette agreed. 'It's beautiful.'

Frank was silent for a moment, looking from face to face.

'That's a relief, then,' he murmured. 'If you think it's OK – so far, anyway. Now, after I've checked that the young folk are managing all right, we'll have that Mrs Whatsit's pie, eh?'

'Ishbel's,' said Lynette. 'I'll just unpack a few things first. But, Dad – hang on a sec, eh?'

'Yes?'

'How do you feel, then? You've asked us. How about you?'

'I love it,' he said simply. 'It's everything I hoped for.'

And the girls, after exchanging looks, were quick to cry, 'That's good!'

When Frank had left them, Lynette, leaving her case still unopened, returned to the window to gaze out at the night.

'How dark it is out there,' she murmured, as Monnie joined her. 'There's not a light to be seen over the water.'

'Maybe no houses at that spot, but there's plenty of life on Skye.'

'Oh, I know, I know. It's just all so different here, eh? From home?'

'Would have to be. Edinburgh's a capital city. This is a dot on the map.'

'Yes.' As Lynette turned aside, it came to Monnie, watching, that this was one of the very few times she'd seen her sister in low spirits.

'Are you all right?' she asked quietly, at which Lynette pushed back her hair and smiled.

'Sure. It was just – you know – seeing the darkness out there, like a great blanket, I felt everything was all so strange. You feel any of that? You're usually more nervy than I am.'

'No, I'm OK. In fact, as I said to Dad, I feel better now I know just what I'm facing.'

Maybe I know, too, Lynette thought, but that's the trouble. But all she said was, 'Let's unpack and have our tea, and if Dad doesn't need any help, maybe we could have an early night. Things will look different in the morning.'

'Sure they will,' Monnie agreed.

Eight

'Oh, what a beautiful morning, oh what a beautiful day!' Lynette sang, back at the bedroom window again, but now the window was open to the clear sweet air from the hills, and everything was bathed in light. As Monnie came in from the bathroom, wearing a coat over her dressing gown, Lynette turned, laughing at the expression on her sister's face, while continuing to sing her favourite number from the show, *Oklahoma*.

'Lynette, for heaven's sake, shut that window!' Monnie cried. 'It's freezing here – feels like snow coming in.'

Lynette stopped singing. 'There's no snow coming in. It's just lovely and fresh. Makes me feel better.'

'Is that what it is? I was wondering what had got into you, singing like that, when last night you couldn't raise a smile.'

'We did say everything would look better in the morning and it does.' Lynette, who was already dressed in sweater and slacks, finally shut the window and ran a comb through her hair. 'I certainly do feel different after a good night's sleep. Last night, I don't mind telling you, I thought I'd just fade away, thought I'd have to tell Dad I couldn't stay, but didn't see how I could . . .'

'As bad as that?'

'Aye, but then you see, today, I feel better. Ready to give it a go here, anyway.' Lynette nodded. 'As soon as I've done Dad's breakfast, I'm going to apply for that job Rhoda told us about.'

'I can smell bacon,' Monnie said, sorting out her clothes to wear. 'I think he's made a start on breakfast himself. Probably found all the supplies Rhoda left us.'

'Never!' Lynette cried, hurrying out. 'This I must see.'

In the flat's modern little kitchen, she found her father at the electric cooker, frying bacon and stirring porridge, and grinning at her amazement.

'Thought I'd have a go and let you two sleep – you were both on your uppers last night.' He handed Lynette his spoon. 'This looks a bit thick, though. Stiff enough for cement, eh?'

'Come on, just needs water.' Lynette gave Frank a quick hug before taking over the porridge stirring. 'Thanks, Dad, it was nice of you to think of us, but we're both OK and raring to go. What about the hostellers, though? Shouldn't we be seeing what they're up to?'

'They're away. One's moved on and the rest have gone climbing. Won't see 'em till this evening. Though I daresay we'll have others coming in later on today, seeing as the weather forecast is good.'

'That means there's always got to be someone here?'

'It does. Which is why I need an assistant.' Frank turned slightly blackened bacon on to a plate and put it to warm under a low grill. 'And I'm hoping it's going to be Monnie.'

'Who's talking about me?' Monnie, coming into the kitchen, dressed in a thick navy jersey and tweed trousers, was rubbing her arms with chilled hands. 'Oh, it's so cold in this wee flat, I can't imagine what it's like in the big house. Isn't there any heating?'

'Storage heaters. Trouble with them is, they don't always come on when you want 'em. Wrap up well, seems to be the answer. Want to serve the porridge, Lynette?'

'Know what this is?' she asked, as they began to eat their porridge, Frank adding salt, the girls, sugar. Monnie, still shivering, answered, Yes, of course, she knew. This was their first breakfast ever cooked by Dad.

'And first breakfast in our new home,' Frank added. 'First of many, I hope, unless you two find yourselves somewhere else to live.'

'Not likely to do that, when we came here to be with you,' Lynette replied. 'Ready for the bacon?'

Their breakfast over, Lynette took out the cutting Rhoda had left her and read it, smiling. 'Listen to this – it's so old fashioned!' She began to read aloud: '"A vacancy has arisen for a lady to work full-time as senior receptionist at the well-known Talisman Hotel, Conair Bay. Must be of good appearance and manner and with experience of working with the public. Some secretarial skills would be an advantage. Please apply in own handwriting and with the names of two referees to the Hotel Manager, Mr Ronan Allan, before March 5th."'

'What's old fashioned about it?' asked Frank.

'Well, asking for a "lady" for a start. And then wanting a handwritten letter of application, when you'd think they'd like people to show off their typing.' Lynette shook her head. 'I bet the manager's some old buffer and heaven knows what the assistant receptionist will be like, but I really do want the job. There might not be anything else for a while.'

'Better get writing, then,' Monnie told her. 'And make it nice and neat. Though I don't know what you're going to say about your experience with the public.'

'Tricky,' Frank remarked. 'You've not had much.'

'Clients came to Couper's, didn't they? Don't worry, I'll make things sound good.' Lynette glanced at the date on the kitchen calendar left by the MacKays. 'But help! I haven't got much time to get this off, have I?'

'Couple of days. Plenty of time if you post it today. Didn't we see a post box as we came in?'

'First, I'll have to get some paper and envelopes. Want to come with me to the shop, Monnie?'

'I have to go to the shop anyway,' Frank said, rising. 'I get supplies in for the hostellers. They buy what they need from me, so I'll have to make my number with the lady cake maker.'

'And I stay here on my own?' Monnie asked. 'Dad, suppose somebody comes? I won't know what to do.'

'You're hoping to be assistant warden, don't forget.' He clapped her thin shoulder. 'Och, you'll be all right. The hostel doorbell rings in our flat, but if you like you can sit in my office and if anybody comes, tell 'em to wait, provided they've got a membership card. If they haven't, move 'em on. It's a strict association rule that only members can use the hostels.'

'OK, but seems like I should be reading that folder,' she said uneasily. 'Remember, I've got an interview this week.'

'Lucky you,' said Lynette. 'Wish I had.'

But Frank was already finding his coat, anxious to be off. 'Come on, Lynette, let's away, so we don't have to leave Monnie too long on her own.'

'She'll be fine, she can do the washing up,' Lynette said with a smile. 'And we'll see if we can bring back something nice to eat, eh?'

'Just hurry home,' Monnie replied. 'I don't want to have to look after a crowd of people without Dad, when I don't know what to do.'

'I've told you, it's still too early for new folk,' Frank told her. 'I guarantee, there'll be nobody knocking at the front door of Conair House just yet.'

Maybe not, but when he and Lynette had left and Monnie, having made the beds and washed up, was in the office, reading Bill's file, someone did come knocking. At the back door.

Oh, Lord! She put down the file and stood up, sighing. Oh, she'd known it, hadn't she? She'd known someone would come.

Well, she'd just have to tell them to wait as her dad had said. No point in being nervous. This was going to be part of her job, after all, if she was lucky enough to be appointed assistant warden. But then if she got that far, she'd know what to do, and now she didn't, and she always liked being sure about what was expected. Unlike Lynette, who could just give a big smile and improvise. Lynette, though, was down at the shop.

Help, there was another knock. She'd have to go, open the door. Hurrying, she made her way to the back door off the kitchen, heavy and old, with a chain and bolts and great iron key.

'Anybody home?' asked a man's pleasant Highland voice.

'Just coming,' she called, struggling with the key.

There. It had turned. She was able at last to open the door. And see the caller on the step.

'Morning,' said a tall young man, touching the plaid cap he was wearing over his straw-yellow hair. 'I'm Torquil MacLeod. Would you be wanting any fish today?'

Nine

He was like his mother, no question about that. The fine nose, the high cheekbones, yes, they were hers. And the yellow hair, of course, and the light blue eyes. Or, maybe not the eyes, which were her colour, but languorous, sleepy, almost, beneath heavy lids, quite lacking Agnes MacLeod's frank inquisitiveness. And then there was the boldness of her manner. Monnie, her lips parted, her heart still beating fast, couldn't, in this young man standing on her doorstep, sense that at all. He seemed very – what was the word? – tranquil.

Suddenly, he was smiling. 'Any fish?' he asked again. 'I always used to bring Mrs MacKay something twice a week, today and Friday. Whatever I'd had the luck with. She told me to call on the new warden, which you see, is what I am doing.'

'Oh – yes. Yes, well, my father's the warden – Mr Forester.' Monnie cleared her throat. 'I'm sure he'll want us to have your fish, but he's out at the minute. Just at the shop, with my sister.'

'Shall I call later then? With what I have? I'm away now for the day.'

'Please do – come this evening. I'll tell my father that you called.'

'Thank you, Miss Forester.' He touched his cap, turning aside. 'Goodbye, then – for now.'

'Goodbye, Mr MacLeod.'

At that, he laughed. 'Now no one calls me Mr MacLeod. Torquil is my name.'

She hesitated. 'People call me Monnie,' she said at last. 'It's short for Monica.'

'It suits you.'

Their eyes met and hers were the first to fall. 'Goodbye,' she murmured again and as he left her, looking back once, slowly closed the door.

For some moments she stood quite still, waiting for her heart to settle down, waiting to feel – what? Herself. To feel as she usually did, not all strung up because a man with blue eyes and yellow hair had come to her door.

What had got into her? She had no idea. Something she'd take care not to be involved in again, anyway.

Still, she stayed where she was, not ready yet to settle back into herself, moving only when she heard footsteps and voices outside and knew her father and Lynette had returned.

'Hi!' she called, opening the back door again. 'I'm in here.'

Rosy with the cold, their eyes sparkling, they joined her in the kitchen, both carrying bags of groceries, which they set down with relief.

'Think we've bought the shop,' Frank said with a laugh. 'But what a nice woman there, eh? So obliging. Monnie, did anybody come?'

'Only the fish man.'

'Agnes's son?' Lynette asked, with interest. 'My, he was quick off the mark. What's he like, then?'

Monnie shrugged. 'All right. Bit like her.'

'Did you buy any fish?'

'Hasn't caught it yet. Said he'd be back this evening.'

'I'll get this stuff away,' Frank said, beginning to unpack bags of flour and sugar, cereals, eggs, cheese, cold ham, bottles of milk and loaves of bread, while Lynette set out a variety of tinned stuff as well as jars of pickle, tomato sauce, more sausages and a selection of vegetables.

'Can't say the hostellers will starve when you look at this lot,' she said with a laugh. 'And that's without stuff from the butcher's van. Seemingly, he calls this afternoon.'

'Well, the youngsters have to pay me for whatever they want, and then I've to keep accounts.' Frank was unlocking the cupboards and storing away his purchases. 'You keeping notes, Monnie. Part of our duties, eh?'

'Your duties, unless I get the job.' Monnie glanced at Lynette. 'Shall we go to the flat and make a cup of coffee? Then you can write your letter and I might walk down to see this wonderful shop. I need some shampoo and odds and ends.'

'OK,' Lynette agreed. 'Dad, you want coffee? We can bring it round.'

'No, thanks. I've some paperwork I want to get on with. You'd better get on with your application.'

'Sure. I'll just grab some of those nice biscuits we bought. Mrs MacNicol's shop really does seem to have everything.'

Back in the annexe kitchen, Monnie put on the kettle and found the jar of instant coffee left by Rhoda, while Lynette opened her new writing pad and uncapped her pen. Then sat back and lit a cigarette.

'Maybe I'll just have a ciggie before I start. Have to sort out what I want to say.'

'Thought you were supposed to be cutting down on smoking?'

'Well, I have cut down, haven't I? You must admit I've been very good since we came here, and so has Dad.' Lynette smiled, as the kettle began to boil. 'Still bought a packet of Players at the shop, though. Maybe we're just on edge, eh?'

'Since when have you been "on edge"?' Monnie, shaking coffee into cups and setting out biscuits, had raised her fine brows.

'Since I decided to apply for this job. Och, I guess we're all a wee bit jumpy. You too, I'd say.'

'Me?' Monnie's eyes flickered. 'I was just a bit worried in case customers came and I wasn't prepared.'

'Oh?' Lynette drew on her cigarette. 'Thought it might be meeting this handsome fisherman.'

'Who said he was handsome?'

'If he's like his ma, he will be. Is that my coffee? Thank goodness – could do with it.'

For some moments the girls, drinking their coffee, were silent, then Monnie set down her cup and stood up.

'I'll away to this shop, then. Let you get on.'

At the door, though, she looked back. 'Can't think why you thought I'd be worked up over that fisherman, Lynette. I didn't say more than two words to him.'

'Come on, you're taken with him, I can tell.'

'That's a piece of nonsense. How can you possibly tell?'

'Because I know you, Monnie. I know just how you are when something special has happened, the same as you know about me.' Lynette shook her head. 'No need to be upset. It's no disgrace to be attracted to somebody.'

'Once and for all, I am not attracted!' Monnie, scarlet-faced, pulled on her coat. 'Look, I'll see you when I get back, OK?'

Outside, the day was fine. Cold, bright, with the sort of air Ellie Forester used to describe as 'a tonic', and ideal for walking. Skirting the side of the hostel, Monnie strode out through the grounds between leafless trees and evergreen shrubs, glancing back when she reached the village street, to wonder why anyone had actually built Conair House.

At least, built it where it was, seeming so out of place with only wee cottages for neighbours. Maybe the original Victorian family had just wanted a tranquil site, with splendid views of the Sound and the opposite island of Skye. And mixed only with the folk from big houses elsewhere, who would all have kept horses and carriages and organized shoots to go stalking the deer.

How things had changed . . . But as Monnie moved on, the hostel left her mind, for her eye was caught by the slipway, some way down from the village street. Next thing she knew, without conscious effort, she was standing at the edge of the water, looking out for a boat.

Looking out for a boat. Well, there was another piece of nonsense, if you like. It wasn't as though she was interested in Torquil MacLeod, or his boat, which wasn't even there. Not as far as she could see. Perhaps he'd already moved on, out of sight, or, hadn't even come yet? What did it matter? She was on her way to the shop.

For another moment or two, she studied the calmness of the Sound, and the majesty of the hills of Skye. Nothing dark about them now, for the morning was so beautifully bright, the water so glittering, the sky so clear, it might almost have been summer. Except that it was still only early March and the air that was a tonic was really quite intensely cold.

Better get going, she told herself, get to the shop. And turning up the collar of her coat, began to hurry back up the slipway to the street.

Here it was, then, Mrs MacNicol's famous shop, a whitewashed cottage with an upper storey, not so different from its neighbours, except that it had a plate glass front window and a door covered in advertisements. As Monnie went in, the bell jangled fit to wake the dead. Or, to summon the owner from her comfortable back room.

Ten

'Mrs MacNicol's shop really does seem to have everything,' Lynette had said, and heavens, she was so right.

Never had Monnie seen a shop with so much to offer, and in such apple-pie order. Nor one so lovingly looked after, with spotless wooden floor and polished counter, and everything that could be made to shine, shining – why, even the few plants for sale in the doorway looked as though they'd just been sprayed.

As she stood staring round at the ranks of tinned goods, bags of flour and sugar, boxes of eggs, packets of cereals, tins of biscuits, ham and bacon, dairy foods in a cabinet, vegetables and fruit in paper lined cases, toiletries set out separately, she was greeted by a slim woman who came out from the back. Mrs MacNicol, of course. And wasn't she nice looking?

'Nice looking' would be the way to describe her, rather than 'good looking', perhaps, for a good-looking woman could have Mrs MacLean's boldness, and that was completely missing in Mrs MacNicol. Probably in her forties, her face was faintly powdered and unlined, her eyes hazel, her hair fair – and, again, you wouldn't call it blonde, Monnie thought, for 'blonde' sounded quite different. Her main attraction was the sweetness of the smile with which she welcomed her new customer.

'May I help you?' she asked, and her voice was exactly in keeping with the rest of her, soft and musical, a Highland voice.

'Thanks, I'm Monnie Forester, from the hostel,' she answered, in her own clear Lowland tones. 'My dad's the warden – he was in earlier with my sister.'

'Oh, yes, of course,' Mrs MacNicol exclaimed, her eyes brightening. 'Mr Forester, the new warden! And your sister – Lynette – well, I'm very pleased to meet you too, Monnie – if I may call you that? I was hoping you'd be coming in, so that I could meet the whole family. I knew the MacKays very well.'

'They spoke very highly of your shop,' Monnie told her. 'And we all think it's lovely.'

'Oh, well.' A blush rose to Mrs MacNicol's cheeks. 'That's very nice of you to say so. But what can I get you now, then?'

Monnie was beginning to say, 'Just a shampoo and some toothpaste, please,' when the door gave its strident jangle and, blowing in, with a rush of cold air, came Agnes MacLeod, large and stout, in a blue mackintosh.

'Morning!' she cried. 'Morning, Ishbel! Oh, and is that young Miss Forester from the hostel at the counter? Good morning to you, my dear – everything all right for you?'

'Fine, thank you.'

Seeing Mrs MacLeod today, hatless and with her thick yellow hair loose around her face, Monnie was deciding she really was quite good looking. And with his mother again before her eyes, it was more than ever clear that the son was like her. Except, of course, that, even if his face was as handsome, his nature might be different; somehow Monnie was sure it was.

'And has my boy been round yet about the fish?' Agnes was asking. 'He said he'd call before he went to his boat.' She laughed merrily. 'See, I was teasing, telling him to look out for the new warden's daughters. Two lovely girls, one blonde, one brunette. They'd be keen to want to cook some fish, I said, and I'm sure he was planning to call.'

'Agnes, will you excuse me?' Ishbel said a little coolly. 'I have to serve this young lady.'

'Of course, of course, do not be minding me. I'm not going anywhere.' Agnes sniffed a little. 'Not like Jeannie Duthie, I might say. Haven't I seen her, hurrying along to the hostel as though she was in a race, just in case anybody gets in before her? Now why is she the only woman in this village supposed to be good at cleaning, I ask? Why has she got that reputation?'

'Because Jeannie is very good,' Ishbel replied, hurriedly moving from her counter to the far end of the shop. 'She cleans for me once a week and I am very happy with her. Monnie, would you care to look at the shampoos, then? All the toiletries are over here.'

'Please,' Monnie said, reflecting, as she followed Ishbel, that life in a Highland village seemed not to be too different from that in an Edinburgh tenement. Och, folk were always the same, eh? Watching and criticizing, thinking they'd been passed over, treated unfairly. At least, there'd be no rows over cleaning the stair here, as there were at home, there being no shared stairs to worry about.

'But did my boy come?' Agnes was persisting, coming to stand close to Monnie as she looked at the shampoos on offer. 'He's away to his boat, got to put out his nets, or I'd have asked him how he got on.'

'He did come,' Monnie answered, finding herself reluctant to speak of him. 'I told him we'd probably want to take his fish, but that my father wasn't in. He said he'd come back this evening.'

'And is there no mother, my dear?' Agnes asked softly. 'Is there just you girls and your father?'

'Agnes . . .' Ishbel murmured, but Monnie answered swiftly that that was true, her mother was dead.

'Ah, so I thought. And you two lassies came here to support your father? Ishbel, isn't that lovely, then?'

'Shall I take those to the till for you, dear?' was Ishbel's only reply, made to Monnie, and when the little transaction was over, she gave a kind smile and said she'd look forward to seeing her again.

'Oh, I expect we'll be coming in all the time,' Monnie told her. 'To a useful shop like this. Goodbye, then, and thank you. Goodbye, Mrs MacLeod.'

'Goodbye, dear!' Agnes called breathily. 'Look out for Torquil this evening. He'll be sure to have something nice for you, he's been doing well lately, with his catches. Ishbel, have you any of your little almond tarts today? I could just fancy a bit of your pastry.'

Outside the shop, Monnie, ready to return to the hostel, saw Lynette in the distance, waving and hurrying.

'Lynette, how come you're back again?' she asked, as her sister came up, wearing her heavy coat and woollen hat, and breathing hard.

'Got my letter to post, of course. You know I want it to go as soon as possible.'

'You've written your application already?'

'Sure I have, I don't hang about.' Lynette, giving her letter a swift kiss, dropped it into the post box. 'There, that's for luck, eh? You finished shopping? What did you think of the shop, then?'

'I'd say we were lucky to have it. But don't go in, Lynette – Mrs MacLeod's there.'

'Oh, Lordy – but I'm not going in anyway.' Lynette took Monnie's arm. 'Come on, you should get back, you've missed all the excitement.'

'What excitement?'

'Why, we've gone up in the world, eh? We have a cleaning lady – at least, for the hostel. Little Mrs Duthie's arrived and Dad's taken her on – she's already scrubbing out the kitchen. Not the size of a sixpence but fizzing with energy like a bottle of pop, and worth half a crown an hour, Dad says, and so do I. Saves us having to do it, eh?'

'And that's the big excitement?' Monnie asked, smiling, as they walked fast up the village street.

'Oh, no, there's more. And you should have been there, not me, because half a dozen guys arrived and I had to help Dad book 'em in and show 'em where to sleep, check they'd got sleeping bags or wanted sheets and all the rest of it. And I'm not the one wanting to be assistant warden!'

'Help!' groaned Monnie. 'I just knew somebody would come this morning. Sorry about that, Lynette. Where've they gone now, these new customers?'

'Out. Not climbing, just doing a recce, they said, but they're loaded up with maps and boots and waterproofs and they've asked Dad to be sure to get 'em something to cook for tonight. He said, chops, seeing as the butcher's van comes this afternoon.' Lynette smiled slyly. 'But we'll be having fish, eh?'

'Maybe.' Monnie shrugged. 'If the fish man comes back.'

Eleven

He did come. But not until after six o'clock, when it was already growing dark and the hostellers were back, grilling chops and roaring with laughter in the old kitchen, while Lynette and Frank were saying they were starving and where was this fisherman?

'He did say he'd come,' Monnie said quickly. 'Maybe he's not been able to get back?'

'The weather's not too bad at the moment,' Frank commented. 'He might at least have called to speak to me.'

And then there was the knock on their back door and the fisherman was on the step, carrying a covered basket and taking off his cap.

'Mr Forester?' he asked, his light blue eyes glancing from Monnie to Lynette and then to their father.

'That's right, I'm Frank Forester, the warden.'

'My name's Torquil MacLeod. I am sorry to be late with your fish – I was delayed at the hotel.'

'We'll forgive you.' Lynette smiled. 'I'm Lynette – sister of Monnie you met this morning. We're all hoping you've got something in that basket for our supper.'

'What I have is hake.' Torquil, removing the cloth cover from the basket, displayed several glistening white fish. 'These are good – like haddock, if you do not know them.'

'Oh, no, they've got heads on!' Lynette cried. 'Dad, what do we do?'

'Bet they'll be to clean as well, eh?' asked Frank, grinning, as he took the fish, wrapped in paper from Torquil. 'I'm afraid my girls are city girls, Mr MacLeod, not used to seeing fish straight from the sea.'

'I'll clean them for you,' Torquil offered, his well-shaped mouth quivering in a smile he tried to hide. 'Will not take me a minute.'

'That's all right, son, I did my share of cleaning fish for my mother when I was a lad, I can manage. How much do I owe you?'

'Settle with me on Friday. I'll be calling again then, if that's all right.' Putting on his cap, Torquil's eyes went to Monnie and back to Frank.

'That'll be fine, Mr MacLeod.'

'Please, call me Torquil.'

'Unusual name, eh? At least, to me.'

'It's a MacLeod name. From Old Norse, I believe. Means kettle of Thor, the god of thunder.'

'Wow, we'd better watch our step with you, then,' Lynette said, mischief glinting in her eyes. 'God of thunder, eh? Might smite us one.'

'Do I look like smiting anyone?' Torquil's tone was light. 'Anyway, my brother's name is similar – Tormad. Mother called us after the sons of Leod, whose father was the King of the Isles.'

'King of the Isles – wow again! Still, I think it's nice that you have these fine old names, eh?'

'Except Tormad calls himself Tony. Suits him better, he says.' Torquil touched his cap and slightly inclined his head. 'Good night to you. I will see you on Friday.'

With one last look towards Monnie, he melted away into the dusk, his basket swinging on his arm, and Frank closed the door.

'Come on, girls, let's get started, then.'

'Do you really know how to clean those fish?' Lynette asked.

'Of course I do. And cook 'em as well. All you need is some butter and grated cheese and a hot grill. Very tasty.'

'You're a man of hidden talents, Dad. First, porridge and bacon, now grilled fish. What next?'

'Och, that's my lot. Tomorrow, you girls can cook the chops we got from the butcher. Look, if I go and clean the fish, will you do the rest? I'll have to be looking in on the hostellers pretty soon.'

'And later on, can go you through what I might get asked at the interview?' Monnie asked, taking potatoes and tomatoes from the vegetable rack. 'I'm beginning to get nervous.'

'Found your voice, though,' Lynette whispered. 'Thought you'd lost it when your Torquil was on the doorstep.'

'My Torquil? He's not *my* Torquil.'

'He's very handsome. I can see why you're interested.'

'Listen, all I'm interested in is getting through my interview on Thursday.'

'OK, so maybe he's interested in you. Certainly looked at you a lot. Still, like I said, you might have to watch your step. Seeing as he's the god of thunder.'

'Oh, Lynette, you're impossible!' In spite of herself, Monnie was laughing. 'I'm going to find somebody to tease you about, but in the meantime, I'll put some water on for these tatties. Think tomatoes would be nice as well?'

'Sure, and I'll grate some cheese. So, who are you going to find to tease me about, then? That old manager chap at the hotel?'

'How do you know he's old? He might be young and handsome.'

'In my dreams!' Lynette shook her head. 'You know what, I probably won't even get an interview, so it won't matter what he's like.'

Monnie, finding a potato peeler, said nothing. She knew she had an interview, all right, and it was true she was keen to do well. But was it true to say it was all she was interested in? No, she had to admit, every time she thought of Friday she felt a sort of heady excitement which was quite new, and as much disturbing as pleasant. But that was the last thing she'd ever admit to Lynette.

Twelve

When Thursday came, however, the exciting thought of Friday had to go to the back of Monnie's mind.

This post of assistant warden she was trying for, it was important. There wouldn't be too many jobs around up here in the Highlands – at least, not for girls like her, without specific qualifications. Lynette had her shorthand and typing, she would have better opportunities, even if she didn't get the hotel post, whereas Monnie could only offer her experience in the bookshop. Still, she'd make the most of it, and the truth was, she'd really run the business for Mr Bryce, doing the accounts as well as everything else, and her dad had said that that would be worth stressing at her interview.

They'd had a long session, she and Frank, the evening before the interview, going through all the duties of a warden, which would be hers too, at least to know about and be prepared to take over if need be. And heavens, what a load of duties there were! When her eyes went over the list, Monnie felt her brain reeling.

Paying bills, working out budgets, booking in hostellers and telling them all they needed to know, preparing their accommodation and organizing catering and laundry arrangements, providing recreational facilities, dealing with enquiries and emergencies, providing tourist information and details of walks and climbs with advice on safety precautions, proper clothing, and so on.

'Anything else?' she'd cried. 'Don't tell me that's all?'

'Oh, yes, keeping discipline – suppose that goes without saying,' Frank answered, pulling at his hair in the way he had. 'And knowing first aid. That's very important, Monnie. Be sure to tell 'em tomorrow that you once did a course.'

'That was just from school, Dad!'

'Never mind, everything counts.' Frank had sat back, smiling. 'But I think, quite honestly, it'll all come down to personality. Don't want to blow my own trumpet, but I think that's why they appointed me.'

'Personality?' Monnie's heart sank. 'Lynette, you'd better go instead of me. I'm no great shakes as a personality, am I?'

'Come on, you can put yourself across if you really try.' Lynette nodded her head. 'Just be definite, that's the trick. Cut out all the "I thinks" and "not sures" and just say what you want to say with no messing about.'

'That'll be your technique if you get an interview at the hotel?'

'You bet.' Lynette sighed. 'But you were right to say "if". I'm sure they'll want a Highland lassie.'

Whether or not that was true remained to be seen, but just before Lynette left with Monnie, to keep her company on the bus to Kyle, she took a telephone call. A woman's cool and rather haughty voice asked if Miss Forester would care to attend for interview, at the Talisman Hotel on the following Tuesday morning at eleven o'clock? Would she not! Oh, yes, Miss Forester would be there, and thank you, thank you very much.

'Monnie, Dad! Guess what?' Lynette had called out. 'I've got an interview at the hotel! Next Tuesday!'

They were as delighted as she, and whirled her
office where Frank had his telephone, until she breathle
free and asked, now wasn't this an omen?

'An omen?' Monnie repeated.

'A good omen. For you. You'll get this job now, Monnie. I
know it.'

'Oh, what a piece of nonsense! You can't know it, Lynette.'

'I do, then.' Lynette's eyes were dancing. 'Just as I know I'm
going to be wearing my red suit for my interview, even if it's
blowing a blizzard.'

'And even if there's only the old manager there?' Monnie asked
wickedly.

'Why, didn't you say he might be young and handsome?
Whatever he's like, I want the job and I'm going to get it. And
so will you get yours, Monnie. Just wait and see.'

'She won't even make the interview if you two don't catch that
bus,' Frank told them, cheerfully, and away they ran, down the
drive and out of the grounds of Conair House, just in time to
flag down Tim MacLean's bus to Kyle of Lochalsh as it wheezed
towards the stop.

Afterwards, Monnie was to say that Lynette must have had second
sight or something, for after her first interview with the people
from the Hostel Association, she was called back for what she
thought would be a follow up, only to be offered the job.

At first, she couldn't believe it, and stared at the kindly man
and woman who'd conducted the interview as though they must
have made a mistake.

'I-I thought you'd be writing to me,' she stammered. 'I mean,
when you'd studied all the candidates.'

'We have studied all the candidates,' they told her. 'And you
were the most suitable.'

'I was?'

'Yes, that's what we decided. You had a positive approach that
we liked, and you've had experience in handling money and
general business which will be useful. We did not take into account
that there was a family relationship involved, but we believe you'll
be a great help to the warden, father or not.'

After Monnie had recovered from her surprise and accepted

the post, there'd been smiles and discussion of formalities, the promise of an official letter to come, and, finally, a shaking of hands and good wishes all round. Only then had she been able to leave the office and smile, in a rather embarrassed fashion, at the unsuccessful candidates still in the waiting room, and make her way to the café where she'd arranged to meet Lynette.

'Well?' Lynette asked at the door of the café as Monnie came bounding up, scarlet in the face and smiling. 'Why does something tell me that you got the job? Could it be that Cheshire cat's grin you're wearing?'

'It's amazing, Lynette, but I did get it and I still don't know why, but d'you know what they said?'

'No, what?'

'They said I had a positive approach. Me!' Monnie flicked back her dark hair and shook her head. 'I did just what you told me to – said everything as clearly as possible, with no ums and ahs, and all that – and it worked!'

'That and all the rest you could offer. You just made it plain you could do the job. Oh, well done, Monnie!'

The sisters hugged each other, smiling, until Lynette led the way from the chill of the outside air to a table.

'You see any other candidates?' she asked.

'Some. Apparently, quite a few were interviewed this morning, but there were several women with me this afternoon.' Monnie sighed. 'They'll be feeling disappointed, eh? There's so little going in the job line. I reckon I've been lucky.'

'Not lucky,' Lynette said firmly. 'You were the best. Come on, let's order tea and cakes before the bus goes. Dad'll be dying to hear how you got on.'

'Your turn next, Lynette. You were right about me, you'll be right about yourself.'

Lynette, selecting a pastry from the cake stand the waitress brought, dabbed sugar from her fingers. 'Hope so. I want to earn some money and as quickly as possible. The last thing I want is to be a drain on Dad.'

'My feelings, too. He's so happy here, eh?'

'Early days, though.'

'But we can be happy, too, can't we? I feel better about it, now that I know what it's like.'

'And now, of course, you've got your job.'

'As I said, your turn next.'

Lynette poured more tea and raised her cup. 'And I'll drink to that.'

'Here's to us,' Monnie said happily and as the girls chinked teacups, they collapsed into laughter, before paying the bill and once again running for the bus.

Thirteen

Friday was a lovely day.

There was Frank bustling around, like a dog with two tails, as he put it, because Monnie had been successful and would be working with him. There was Lynette, deciding what to wear with her red suit for her interview – the cream shirt, or the black? The black one was very striking and would go with her bag and shoes, but then might not hit the right note with the manager, he, of course, being an unknown quantity. So, why not just wear her plain white blouse and look smart, but demure?

And then there was Monnie, booking in new arrivals, making it clear what they could and couldn't do, handing out bus time-tables and leaflets about the local area, while appearing every inch the assistant warden, though she wasn't due to start work for a fortnight. All the time simmering inside, of course, with that strange excitement which no one knew about, but would be with her, she knew, until the evening. When the fisherman called.

Early in the afternoon, Jeannie Duthie, the cleaning lady, arrived for another battle with all that needed doing at the hostel, and, oh, yes, Monnie could see what Lynette had meant about her. 'Not the size of a sixpence, but fizzing with energy like a bottle of pop.' Yes, that was Mrs Duthie, flying round the house with her mop and dusters, clicking her tongue over the way the young hostellers had left their dormitories, flinging open windows, pushing furniture around, and sweeping down the staircase like a minor hurricane. Until Monnie called up that there was a cup of tea ready in the warden's kitchen.

'Well I will not be saying no,' Mrs Duthie remarked, washing her hands at the sink and drying them as though her life depended on it. ''Tis nice to take a break, then.'

Sitting at the table, her raw little hands grasping her cup, she was only partly at rest for her dark brown eyes were busy, moving from Lynette who was now pressing the skirt of her red suit, to Monnie, who was taking shortbread from a tin.

'Sisters, eh?' she said, after her scrutiny. 'One fair, one dark, but still alike. And come up to the Highlands to be with your dad? Very nice, that is, but what are you young ladies going to be doing, then?'

'I've just been made assistant warden,' Monnie told her, offering the biscuits. 'I'll be helping my father.'

'Is that right?' Mrs Duthie bit hard on her shortbread. 'That is a very fine thing to be doing, then.' Her eyes moved back to Lynette. 'And are you looking for a job too, my dear? There's little enough round here.'

Monnie, watching, knew that Lynette was not taking kindly to the interrogation, but she replied politely enough that she was trying for a post as receptionist at the Talisman Hotel.

'At the Talisman ? Working for Mr Allan? Oh, my!'

'Oh, my?' Lynette repeated. 'Oh, what, then?'

'Not my place to speak of the manager, my dear, seeing as I once used to do some work at the hotel.' Mrs Duthie was shaking her frizzy dark head. 'But if you get that job – well – you will have to see how it goes.'

'Of course I'll see how it goes!' Lynette cried. 'I wish you wouldn't talk in riddles, Mrs Duthie.'

'There will be no riddles if you get to work there, that's for sure,' Mrs Duthie declared, rising. 'All will be plain before you've been there five minutes. Mr Allan – he's not an easy man.'

She crossed to the sink, rinsed out her cup and again washed and dried her hands with fierce energy. 'Handsome, though,' she said from the door, snatching up her dusters again. 'Very handsome.'

And with that she went out, leaving them to listen to her clattering back to the main house, and exchanging wide-eyed stares.

'Well,' Lynette said softly, 'that was interesting. First, she says she'll say nothing, then she says plenty.'

'Oh, Lynette,' Monnie murmured. 'Do you think you should still apply?'

'Whatever do you mean?'

'Well, if the hotel manager is like Mrs Duthie said, would you want to be working with him?'

'I'd want to be working with him more than ever!' Lynette tossed her head, her blue eyes glittering. 'It'd be a challenge, eh? See if he could be difficult with me!'

'But why work in an unpleasant atmosphere? I should think you'd rather look for something else.'

'I've said, it'd be a challenge, and I like challenges. Can't wait for that interview now. Think I'll wear my black blouse, after all. Cut a dash, eh?'

Monnie, shaking her head, took her cup to the sink and glanced at the kitchen clock. Time was moving on. When would Torquil call? How soon? How late? Why was she so interested, anyway? He'd probably just hand in the fish and that would be that. Except he'd need to be paid.

'Think I'd better check with Dad about the money for the fish,' she said aloud, and Lynette, dabbing a crumb from her lip, grinned.

'Oh, yes, do that. Better have the cash ready, if you're going to answer the door.'

'Why, I don't know who's going to answer the door,' Monnie retorted. 'Doesn't matter, does it?'

'Not to me,' Lynette said smoothly.

In the event, it was Mrs Duthie who answered the door. Torquil was early. A whole hour earlier than on Tuesday, and Mrs Duthie was only just leaving, tying a headscarf over her hair, when his knock came at the warden's door. Monnie, who had been hovering in the kitchen, wishing Mrs Duthie would be as quick at departing as she was at everything else, ran quickly forward. But Mrs Duthie was ahead of her, flinging open the door and fixing Torquil with a cold stare from her dark brown eyes.

'Oh, it's you, Torquil MacLeod. Got yourself in here, have you? I thought you would.'

'Good evening, Mrs Duthie,' he replied politely, his look already going to Monnie. 'I am not sure of your meaning, but I am here, yes, with my fish, for Mr Forester. Just as for Mr MacKay. Why not?'

Mrs Duthie shrugged. 'I'm away,' she cried to Monnie. 'See your dad next week.'

And with that, she squeezed her little body past Torquil's tall frame and hurried away, while he stood with his fish basket, smiling.

'Hello there, Monnie,' he said softly. 'I see your father has taken on the little dragon.'

'Little dragon?'

'That is what we call her – Mrs Duthie.'

'She wasn't very nice with you.'

'Ah, 'tis nothing she has against me. My mother's the one. They do not get on.'

'I see.' Monnie stood, looking at the basket Torquil was again swinging on his arm. 'Er – what have you brought us, then?'

'Something good. Today, I have been lucky. Threw out my line as well as my net and caught some cod for you.'

'For us?'

'Cod will be a fish you'll know, in the city, I mean, but you will not know others that I catch.' He laughed a little. 'Coalfish, pollack, skate – all manner of things arrive sometimes in the Sound and might not suit.'

'I see.'

Monnie would have liked to laugh with him but did not dare, she didn't know why. Or, in fact, why, after waiting all day to see him, she kept looking away. She had the feeling she must be careful. Not let him see so soon what she was thinking – as though she even knew herself! Och, she was like a straw in the wind, blowing she didn't know where, when this man stood before her, having an effect on her she had never known with any man before.

And there had been some men in her young life, fellows she'd gone out with a couple of times, then parted from by mutual agreement. One she'd even thought she might care for – a student who'd kept coming into the bookshop for days before asking her to go out with him. She'd agreed, too, and they'd got on well, but she'd soon realized he wasn't the one. He'd never made her feel as she felt now.

'Want to see them?' he was asking her gently.

'What?'

'The cod.'

'Oh – oh, yes. I'm sure they'll be fine.'

Her eyes met his and this time did not draw away, but stayed to read something in their blue depths that set her heart beating like a hammer in her chest. Would he say something? He must speak. He couldn't just go away, couldn't leave without putting into words what she had read in his eyes. Couldn't do that, could he?

His lips had parted, he seemed about to speak, when suddenly they were no longer alone. Frank had come into the kitchen, was standing close. And everything changed.

It was like a light being switched off, a shutter coming down. However she cared to describe it, Monnie knew the moment was over, the chance gone. She couldn't have felt more devastated if something she'd been promised had been snatched away. But of course she'd never been promised anything.

'Hello, Torquil!' Frank was saying jovially. 'What have you got for us tonight, then?'

'Good evening, Mr Forester,' Torquil answered with a ready smile. 'I have some very nice cod.'

'Cod, eh? Well, that's something the girls'll know how to cook. A good standby in Edinburgh, is cod. But of course, yours'll be nice and fresh.' As Frank opened the wrapped packet Torquil gave him, his eyes widened.

'Why, you've prepared 'em! Taken off the heads, and cleaned 'em and all. You'd no need to do that!'

Torquil shrugged. 'I told you, 'tis no trouble, and the ladies are not keen on the cleaning.'

'I'd have done it, but still, it's good of you. We appreciate it, eh, Monnie? Run and fetch a plate, then.'

'It's very kind of you, Torquil,' she said in a low voice, when she'd brought a plate for the fish. 'Thank you.'

'My pleasure.' He bowed his straw-coloured head and replaced his cap, as Frank took a handful of coins from his trouser pocket.

'So, how much do I owe you?'

'Seven and six, if you please, sir. Four shillings for the cod, there being two pounds of that, and three and six for the hake, there being a little less in weight.'

'Fine, fine.' Frank counted out the money into Torquil's hand. 'See you next Tuesday, then.'

'Tuesday,' he repeated, glancing at Monnie.

'Tuesday,' she echoed, bravely returning his look. But there was no longer anything to read in his eyes and as he left them, walking fast away, she wondered if she might have been mistaken ever to think there might have been.

Fourteen

Tuesday morning. Interview Day.

Lynette, early out of bed, was studying her face in the dressing-table mirror, groaning at what she said were bags under her eyes, while Monnie, watching, laughed and kept her own thoughts about Tuesday to herself.

'You needn't have got up so early,' she called. 'Your interview's not till eleven.'

'I know, but I've got to sort myself out. Get rid of these terrible bags, decide what to wear—'

'The red suit, the black blouse, wasn't it?'

'I think, maybe the white shirt, after all. More appropriate, eh?' Lynette was standing, deep in consideration, before suddenly being galvanized into action and hurrying to the bathroom, pulling her dressing gown around her.

'That'll be it till I don't know when,' Monnie murmured to herself, heaving her bedclothes to her chin again. 'No point in getting up till Lynette's finished – anyway, it's still early.'

And cold. From where she lay, she could see fresh snow on the hills, but guessed it would not be on the roads. Just as well, as her father was driving Lynette to her interview, while, she, Monnie, held the fort. Strange, since she'd been given her label of assistant warden, looking after the hostel no longer held terrors for her. In fact, she enjoyed it. Meeting all the new people, helping them, thinking of ways to improve their stay. For a start, there was the common room – that could do with a rethink, if a bit of money could be found.

She really was interested in what she might do, but knew, too, that she was pushing all her ideas to the front of her mind, so as not to dwell too much on what might be already there. Tuesday. Interview Day. Yes, and Fish Day, too. Would it be third time lucky? For what? There were those thoughts again.

As Lynette returned from the bathroom, smelling of soap and bath salts, Monnie leaped out of bed and said it was time she got dressed, Dad would be wanting his breakfast.

'Seems to have forgotten that he knows how to fry bacon,' Lynette commented, as she shrugged herself into a crisp white blouse and stepped into her red skirt. 'Don't think this is too short, eh?'

'No, it's perfect. You've got good legs, anyway, why not show 'em?'

'Yes, but skirts aren't that short at the moment, are they? And I don't know if this difficult manager will approve.'

'As though he'd know what was in fashion! He'll probably just see a pair of nice legs and that'll be enough for him.'

'Maybe. I'm not sure. Wonder if I should wear my office black? Be on the safe side.'

'If you'd be happier, yes.' Monnie sighed with impatience. 'Have to make up your mind soon, though.'

'The black it is.'

Lynette was studying her face again, patting her cheeks, smoothing the skin beneath her eyes. 'Oh, but help, will you look at me? Better have a good session with my make-up after breakfast, eh? Think maybe I'll persuade Dad not to have bacon this morning. Don't want the smell in my hair.'

By half past ten, all worries about clothes, make-up, and what Frank might have for breakfast were over, and Lynette, beautifully ready, in warm coat over her black suit, her face as perfect as possible, was sitting next to her father in the old Morris, gazing at the Talisman Hotel.

She'd seen it before, of course. They'd come out one afternoon to do a recce, and she couldn't have been more impressed. Such a fine looking building! White-harled, many-windowed, with what must be spectacular views, trees shielding it from the worst of the wind, and its extensive grounds stocked with hardy shrubs.

There was even a tennis court to one side, though at that time of year, it was hard to imagine players on it. Still, summer would come one day and in the meantime there seemed to be quite a number of patrons, anyway, judging from the number of cars drawn up on the hotel forecourt.

'Money,' Frank said now. 'The Talisman reeks of money.'

'Well, that's good,' Lynette replied. 'Need something that can attract money in a place like this.'

'Aye, you're right, I suppose.' Frank glanced at his watch. 'Want to go and make your number now? I can drop you at the main door.'

'Hope I'm not supposed to use the tradesman's entrance,' Lynette said cheerfully. 'Oh, Dad, wish I'd had time for a cigarette.'

'Want to smell of smoke?' Frank started the car's engine. 'And there's me only having an egg for my breakfast because you didn't want to smell of bacon.'

'Sorry, Dad – you'll be back to bacon tomorrow. Listen, drop me here and I'll walk down the drive, eh?'

'OK, if it's what you want. And you'll be all right getting the bus back?'

'Of course. See you soon, and thanks for the lift.'

'Good luck, pet. Not that you'll need it. Bet you any money you get the job.'

'You're hopeful!'

With a wave of her hand, Lynette left the car and began walking quickly towards the hotel's entrance, and after watching for a moment, Frank, wishing her luck, drove away. She wouldn't need it, she was the best.

In the spacious vestibule of the hotel, where a few guests were sitting talking, Lynette, advancing towards the reception desk, was puzzled to find herself facing three women.

Hello, who's leaving? she wondered, guessing that one of the three would be the outgoing senior receptionist – which ruled out the youngest, a good-looking, dark-haired girl with almond-shaped, dark eyes who looked no more than seventeen. All that could be seen of her outfit was a stiff white blouse for she was standing behind the desk, but up bounced Lynette's spirits when she saw that the other two women, one in her twenties, one perhaps forty, were both wearing smart black suits with calf length skirts.

So, she'd made the right choice. Point to me, she thought, and taking off her coat, knew she looked good. Good enough to be confident as she introduced herself as a candidate for interview for the post of senior receptionist.

'Ah, good morning, Miss Forester,' replied the woman Lynette had judged to be the oldest of the three. She was sharp-eyed, sharp-featured, and oozing efficiency from every pore. 'I'm Mrs Atkinson, Mr Allan's assistant and secretary – I believe we spoke on the phone.'

Oh, yes, the haughty one . . . Lynette agreed that they had.

'This is Mrs Burnett, the present senior receptionist,' the secretary continued, introducing a pale, fair-haired young woman at her side who was giving a welcoming smile. 'It's our loss that she is moving to England with her husband – hence the vacancy – but Miss MacLewis, who hasn't been with us very long, is fast learning the ropes.'

'Nice to see you.'

While the young Miss MacLewis politely smiled, Lynette turned to Mrs Atkinson.

'I hope I'm not late, am I?'

'No, indeed, it's we who are running late. But if you'll give me your coat and come with me, Miss Forester, I'll take you to the other candidates. You'll be called for interview very soon.'

Having followed Mrs Atkinson through swing doors at the rear of the vestibule, Lynette was shown to a small room, where two young women, already in easy chairs, were skimming through magazines. Both, Lynette noticed with satisfaction, were wearing dark suits and white shirts.

'Hi, there.' She gave them friendly smiles. 'I'm Lynette Forester. Have you two already had your interviews?'

'We have.' The girls shook hands. One, a slightly built redhead, said her name was Audrey Logan, while the other, tall, with brown hair and sad brown eyes, was Joan Campbell.

'But there's another lassie in there now,' Audrey Logan told Lynette, in a pleasant Highland voice. 'You're the last.'

'I see.' Lynette dropped her voice. 'What's the manager like, then?'

'Oh, lovely!' Audrey cried. 'Isn't he, Miss Campbell? Oh, an absolute dreamboat!'

Joan Campbell shrugged. 'Very good looking,' she admitted. 'Bit cold, I thought. Still, I wouldn't mind the job.'

The door opened and a slim, anxious-looking young woman came in, followed by Mrs Atkinson.

'Miss Forester?' She gestured towards the door. 'This way, please. Mr Allan will see you now.'

Fifteen

Dreamboat? This man? As he rose from his desk at her entrance Lynette didn't think so. Tall, dark and handsome, maybe, but too strong in features, too severe in manner, to have anything to do with dreams. See how the brief smile he'd managed didn't meet his gold-flecked brown eyes, and how his jaw was so firmly set, he looked as though he spent his life getting the better of people.

Oh, but this wasn't the way to begin an interview, was it? Quick, she told herself, give him the benefit of the doubt. Who cared if he wasn't a dreamboat? As long as she could convince him to give her the job.

'Miss Forester, Mr Allan,' announced Mrs Atkinson.

'Thank you,' Mr Allan replied, and as his assistant withdrew, he invited Lynette to take a seat in a voice that sounded more English than Scottish, and certainly wasn't Highland.

'How do you do, Miss Forester? I'm Ronan Allan, the hotel manager. Sorry if we are a little late in seeing you.'

'That's quite all right, Mr Allan.'

While the manager returned to his desk, Lynette arranged herself as gracefully as possible on the chair he'd indicated. Somehow she still had the feeling that she was off to a bad start with this man in his dark, three-piece suit, white shirt and blue silk tie, who had a signet ring on the little finger of his right hand and an expensive looking wristwatch showing beneath his cuff. But why should she already be at a disadvantage? She had hardly said a word.

Looking down at her application, he was silent for a moment. Then he raised his unusual eyes to look at her.

'I see you say you have come up from Edinburgh to live at the hostel in Conair, Miss Forester?'

His tone was cold, almost disapproving.

'That's correct. As I explained, my father's the new warden. He's a widower and my sister and I – we thought we'd like to come up with him.'

'A bit of a contrast for you, from the city?'

Lynette allowed herself a smile. 'You could say that.'

'But you think it will work out?'

'Yes, we do. My sister's going to be assistant warden, and I'm in the process of finding a job.'

'Not so easy in this part of the world.'

'I know.'

'Though you have secretarial qualifications, which are always useful.'

'I am an experienced shorthand typist.'

Mr Allan looked down again at Lynette's application.

'But your experience has been with a legal firm. You'd need to be in Inverness to find something similar.'

'I wanted a change anyway.'

'A change.' He raised his dark brows. 'To come here as senior receptionist would certainly provide that, Miss Forester. I think you'd find the work very different.'

Lynette nodded. 'I'd be prepared, Mr Allan.'

'You'd be working longer and unsocial hours, alternating with an assistant in the evenings, for instance – how would you feel about that?'

'As I say, I'd be prepared.'

'And then you'd be providing customer service to all sorts of guests who all expect miracles. Taking charge of the reception desk, using your own initiative when problems crop up, as they always do. And, of course, supervising your assistant. Think you could cope?'

'Definitely. I'd enjoy it.'

'What makes you so sure?'

'I like meeting different kinds of people, I like making decisions and I'm sure I could manage an assistant.' Lynette gave a confident smile. 'And I even like providing miracles.'

Mr Allan sat back in his chair, clasping his hands together. He did not return her smile, and for what seemed an interminable time, there was silence in his large, pleasant office except for the sound of the wind outside. Finally, he rose again and extended his hand.

'Thank you, Miss Forester. As you'll understand, it won't be possible for me to make a decision on the appointment today, but I'll be in touch by post as soon as possible.'

'That's fine, Mr Allan. Thank you.'

'Now, if you'd care to join the other young ladies, I'd like to offer you all lunch. Mrs Atkinson will take you along.' Looking down at her from his exceptional height, he gave another brief smile and opened the door.

'Goodbye, Miss Forester.'

'Goodbye, Mr Allan.'

'Wherever have you been?' asked Frank, as Lynette finally came from the bus into his office. 'We thought you'd be back about two and now it's half past four.'

'We were beginning to get worried,' said Monnie. 'I mean, did you get anything to eat?'

'Yes, we were given a very nice lunch at the hotel.' Lynette dropped into a chair, throwing her bag to the floor. 'That was about the best part of the day, to be honest.'

'Oh, help – so, it didn't go well?'

Monnie, gazing with sympathy at her usually bubbly sister, was thinking Lynette hadn't looked so low since the evening of their arrival, when she'd looked out at the darkness over the Sound and had thought she wouldn't want to stay.

'We don't know yet who's been successful, but we think it went well for one.' Lynette gave a wry smile. 'That means it didn't go well for three, as there were four of us shortlisted.'

'And one of the three was you?' Frank shook his head. 'You can't know that, Lynette. People can never judge their own performances.'

'I'd like to think you were right, Dad. All I can say is that one girl was nearly in tears, and another said she'd given up soon as she went into the interview – she could tell the manager just wasn't interested.'

'And he wasn't he interested in you, either?'

'What he had against me seemed to be the hostel, I don't know why. When he mentioned my address, you should have seen his expression!'

'The big snob!' Monnie cried. 'What's wrong with the hostel, for heaven's sake?'

'I take exception to folk with views like that,' Frank said grimly. 'Probably doesn't have any idea what a hostel is like, eh?'

'He'd never stay in one himself, you could tell.' Lynette suddenly snatched up her bag and leaped from her chair. 'Och, what's it matter? The only lassie who liked Mr Allan will probably get the job, but there'll be other jobs going. Bound to be. How about a cup of tea next door?'

'I'll put the kettle on,' Monnie said quickly, but Lynette, who never missed anything, even if in a bad mood, had seen her glance at the clock.

'Oh – oh! It's fish day, right? Look, he won't be here yet. No need to worry.'

'Who won't be here?' asked Frank.

'Why, the fish man, of course. Anyway, he'll come to our door, won't he?'

'Torquil, we're talking about? What's it matter which door he comes to?'

'Come on, Monnie, let's go to the flat.' Lynette took her sister's arm. 'I want to change out of this dreary suit anyway.'

'I thought you were happy about it.'

'Can't say I'm happy about anything at the moment.'

'Hey, what's happened to my bouncy sister?'

At that, Lynette smiled. 'Och, you're right. I need to bounce back. Just give me time – first, to get changed.'

But Lynette had not had time to change out of her suit, and Monnie had only just filled the kettle, when the knock came at their back door.

'Anybody home?' came Torquil's voice.

'Coming,' cried Monnie.

Sixteen

'You're early again,' Monnie said, clearing her throat.

'Meant to be,' Torquil returned, his eyes unmovingly fixed on hers. 'One guess why.'

'I've no idea.' Monnie, glancing round, saw that Lynette had left the kitchen, which made things easier. 'Maybe because you've several places to visit yet?'

'Why should I come here first?' He bent his head towards her face. 'Because I want to see you.'

Her colour flamed and she made a pretence of wanting to see what he had in his basket, slightly lifting the cover, staring unseeingly at the paper-wrapped fish it contained.

'What – what did you bring us?' she asked.

'It's hake again. Hope that's all right?'

'Oh, yes, fine. Shall I take them?'

As she put out her hand, he caught it and held it in a warm, strong grasp.

'Let's wait a minute,' he whispered. 'Till I ask you—'

'What?'

'If you'd like to come out with me. Just for a walk, maybe?'

The world seemed to be spinning, spinning so fast, Monnie was glad her hand was still in his. Not that she was in danger of spinning herself, she knew quite well it was all in her head. But still, she felt safer, just holding his hand.

'I would like to,' she said huskily. 'I would like to go for a walk with you.'

'Would be Saturday afternoon. I give myself Saturdays off, but I still sometimes fish in the mornings, if conditions are good. Afternoons, no – I keep them free.'

He was smiling at her, keeping his voice low.

'Free for you, too? If your father can spare you?'

'Of course he can. I shall see you on Saturday afternoon.' Monnie swung round again, thinking she could hear someone coming, but there was no one there, and she sighed a little, finally releasing her hand from Torquil's.

'Where shall we meet?'

'Here. At the front entrance. I shall have my van.'

'You have a van? I didn't know.'

He grinned. 'How do you think I make my deliveries? I cannot be walking everywhere. Of course I have a van and on Saturday we'll drive, then walk.'

'What time shall we meet?'

'Say, two? Or, half past? Make it half past. Come to the front gate and I'll be there. Now, you'd better take your fish. They're all ready for cooking.'

'Oh, Torquil, you spoil us. I'll get some money—'

'No need, your father can pay me next time.'

For some moments they stood very still in the doorway, eyes locked, but no words said, until Torquil stepped away.

'See you Saturday,' he whispered.

'No, Friday.'

'If you can come to the door.'

'I always come to the door.'

When Lynette returned to the kitchen, wearing a sweater and slacks, it was to find Monnie putting fish on a plate and the back door shut.

'Torquil gone, then?'

'Oh, yes.'

Lynette, after studying her sister for a few moments, began to set the table.

'Dad says he'll be along soon, wants to have tea before all the hostellers are back, so we'd better start now.'

'OK.'

'Are you all right?'

'Why shouldn't I be?'

'You look – I don't know – a wee bit dazed.'

'What an imagination!' Monnie said scornfully.

'Imagination, indeed!' Lynette was to comment later, when her sister casually announced that she was to go out walking with Torquil on Saturday afternoon. She hoped her father wouldn't need her.

'Going out with Torquil?' Lynette repeated. 'No wonder you were looking dazed!'

'Going out with Torquil?' Frank repeated heavily, and put his knife and fork together. 'Now I'm not so sure that that's a good thing, Monnie.'

'What do you mean? Why shouldn't it be a good thing?'

'Well, I was in the shop this morning – just getting in extra provisions, on account of more folk booking in—

'Yes, what of it?'

Frank moved awkwardly in his chair. 'I'm just explaining why I was in the shop – not talking about you or anything – but Ishbel—'

'Ishbel? You call Mrs MacNicol Ishbel?'

'It is her name, Monnie. Thing is, she happened to ask if we were having Torquil deliver fish and when I said yes, she said there'd be no problems there, he was good with his fish business, but—'

'But what?'

'But she thought perhaps she should mention that he and his brother were . . . a bit wild.' Frank sat back, not looking at either of his daughters. 'Considered to be,' he added.

'A bit wild?' Monnie's eyes as she stared at her father, were sparkling, her face very pale. 'Considered to be wild? By Mrs MacNicol, you mean? What right has she got to call them that?'

'Seemingly, it's what most of the village folk call them. They've no father, you see. He ran off years ago – drowned at sea, says Agnes, but it's generally believed he got to Australia and set up with another family. So, the lads have had a difficult start, and maybe it's understandable that they've turned out difficult them-selves. To be honest, it sounds as though Tony's a bit more difficult than Torquil.' Frank suddenly lit a cigarette, sighing, as Lynette helped herself from the packet on the table and lit one too. 'Let's not go into all that.'

'Yes, let's!' Monnie cried, breathing hard. 'I want to hear what's being said about Torquil and his brother, because I'll bet it's not true. What's Tony supposed to have done, then?'

'Got a girl in the family way, if you must know,' Frank answered with sudden roughness. 'It's no good playing ostrich, Monnie. The facts are known – the girl was from here and had to move away – went to Inverness, in fact, and Tony never made the slightest effort to help her. And Agnes kept him up in it, from all accounts. Now, are you satisfied?'

Monnie, lowering her eyes, was silent, while Lynette and Frank drew on their cigarettes, exchanging glances.

'Well, that's Tony,' Lynette said at last. 'Can't blame Torquil for what his brother does though, can you?'

'That's right,' Monnie chimed in eagerly. 'What Tony does has nothing to do with Torquil at all. And you can see that he's not wild, Dad. He's quiet and gentle – why do people call him wild?'

Frank shrugged. 'I agree, he's always been very polite to me. I suppose it might just have been high spirits that got him into trouble when he was younger. Going round with other lads, making a nuisance of themselves the way they do.'

'But that's not important, Dad. As you say, it's what lads do, and then when they grow older, they change. Like Torquil must have changed. I mean, he doesn't cause trouble now.'

Very slowly, Frank put out his cigarette and let his gaze rest on his younger daughter. 'Oh, I think he can still cause trouble, Monnie. In fact, he's already caused it. Between you and me.'

'Oh, Dad!' Monnie's face was crumpling, her eyes filling fast with tears. 'Dad, I never wanted that, I never wanted anyone to come between you and me!'

She left her chair and stood looking down at him, until he stood up and held her, and she leaned against him with her hand to her eyes.

'It's all right, pet, it's all right. I'm maybe being a bit hard—'

'Dad, I think you are,' Lynette put in quickly. 'Monnie's not even been out with the laddie yet. Why get so steamed up? I mean, what's one walk together?'

'It's a start,' he answered tiredly, letting Monnie go. 'But you're right. I shouldn't be laying down the law at this stage. It's just that I don't want you getting hurt, Monnie. You can understand that, eh?'

'I'm not going to get hurt,' she declared, dabbing at her eyes with a tissue. 'There's no need to worry, Dad, Torquil's not going to hurt me, and I can take care of myself, anyway.'

Forewarned is forearmed, he wanted to say, but bit back the words. Maybe he'd said enough.

★ ★ ★

It was good that the hostellers began to arrive shortly afterwards. Cold, wet and hungry, they all needed attention, and some supervision, with the young men scuffling in the bathroom queues, while the girls more often than not nipped in quickly under their noses, hurrying to wash and change before skidding to the kitchen to get first use of the cookers.

New guests were arriving, too, and both Frank and Monnie were kept busy, with Lynette being drawn in to find people places in the dormitories, and even after everyone was dry and fed, it still wasn't time for the wardens to relax. Not with the evening to plan, the young folk to be encouraged, and Frank having to call: 'Everyone to the common room – let's have a sing-song!'

'Oh, help,' Lynette groaned, and fled to the flat, while a volunteer gamely played the piano and Frank led the singing. Passed the time, didn't it? Kept uneasy thoughts at bay, and afterwards, there were board games to play and listening to the wireless until the half hour after ten struck and Frank could call, 'OK, that's it, good night, everybody up to the dorms, then. Lights out at eleven, don't forget.'

'Don't worry about Dad,' Lynette whispered, when Monnie and she were finally alone in their room. 'He'll be OK. He was just the same over that guy you went out with who used to haunt the bookshop. And with me and – well, let me see . . .'

'All those fellows you used to go out with.' Monnie smiled a little. 'But I don't think Dad ever minded about them the way he seems to mind about Torquil. It's all Mrs MacNicol's fault. Telling him about Tony and their father.'

'I expect she meant it for the best. She's not a troublemaker, Monnie.'

'Och, I'm taking no notice, anyway. I know Torquil and he's not like she says.'

Lynette, climbing into bed, made no reply. But as she put out their light, the thought was still in her mind. How could Monnie say she knew Torquil? How well did you get to know a guy, just standing talking to him at the door?

On the other hand, of course, she felt she knew Mr Allan, the hotel manager, after only one meeting. But she was absolutely certain she wasn't wrong about him.

Seventeen

Friday came. No letter yet from the hotel for Lynette, but then it was too early, wasn't it? She wasn't in the least disappointed. Rather relieved, in fact, that she didn't have to face bad news yet. There were always the job adverts in the local paper to scan – she could do that on Saturday.

Meanwhile, Monnie was being very practical, getting on with hostel work for Frank, though she still wasn't officially in her job, and trying not to look forward to seeing Torquil when he called that evening. Somehow, she knew her father, understanding though he might think himself now, would block any talk with Torquil at the door, simply by being there himself.

In fact, she didn't get to see Torquil at all.

Had her father intended that? She wasn't sure. But he'd certainly made things difficult, by sending her to the shop just as the time drew near for Torquil's visit. Well, asked her to go, anyway. Needed milk, you see, and the usual hordes would soon be descending.

'Need milk?' Monnie repeated coldly. 'You were at the shop this morning, as usual. Didn't you get milk then?'

'Forgot it,' Frank said blandly. 'And we do need it, Monnie. If you go now, you'll be back before Torquil comes.'

'And supposing I'm not?'

'No harm done, you'll be seeing him tomorrow.'

Once again, the eyes of father and daughter locked.

'Promise you won't say anything to him, Dad,' Monnie said at last. 'No warnings off, or anything, OK?'

'All I'll do is pay him for the fish.' Frank put some coins into her hand. 'There, that's for the milk. Take the big bag, eh?'

With bad grace, Monnie took the money. 'Why can't Lynette go to the shop?'

'She's washing her hair.'

'Bet you suggested that.'

Frank laughed heartily. 'When have I ever told you girls when to wash your hair? Look, you're making too much of this, Monnie.

I'm not going to be able to stop you seeing Torquil when he delivers the fish, am I? This is just a one-off.'

Because he is going to say something to Torquil, whatever he promises, Monnie thought, preparing to run to the shop like the wind. She would do just as he said, though he was hoping she couldn't do it, and be back before Torquil came.

Didn't happen. Even though she was in and out of the shop in a few moments, carrying the bag full of milk bottles which Mrs MacNicol had thoughtfully put aside for the hostel, she didn't make it home in time. For when she came out of the shop, a young man, about to go in, stepped politely aside, then smiled and called her name.

'It's Miss Forester, isn't it, from the hostel?' His voice was mellow, with an Edinburgh accent. 'I'm Paul Soutar, we met on the bus.'

Oh, yes, she remembered. He was one of the two climbers who were going to the hotel; the one with the pleasant face. And here he was, smiling at her, glad to have met again, it seemed. So, what could she do?

Just for a moment, she set down her bag and shook his outstretched hand, still breathing fast.

'I do remember you – I'm Monica Forester.'

'I'm sorry, you're in a hurry, I mustn't keep you.'

'It's all right.' She too was being polite, having given up all hope of reaching the hostel before Torquil. If he hadn't already done so, any moment now, he would be arriving with his basket of fish. Looking out for her, hoping to talk, and she wouldn't be there. But what could she do?

Her eyes went over the pleasant-faced Paul Soutar. Perhaps he was a little bit younger than she'd thought, it was hard to tell. He was tall, but not as tall as Torquil; seeming, even in his bulky anorak, lean and fit, which he would have to be if he was a climber. He had light brown hair, and light brown eyes to match. Uneven features, so, not particularly handsome. In fact, some might even say, his face was craggy. But then it was so pleasant. The word kept coming back. A good-natured man she felt she couldn't just leave in a hurry.

'Your friend not with you?' she asked, as the wind blew her hair and she pulled it back from her face.

'He's my brother.' Paul Soutar laughed. 'Friend as well. No, he just came with me for a few days' break at the hotel. I've moved in to my cottage now.'

'Your cottage? Here?'

'Yes, it's at the end of the village.' He swung round, pointing in the distance. 'I'm renting it.'

'You'll be staying on, then?'

'Oh, yes, I've got things to do. Won't bore you with all the details. How about you? Are you and your sister staying on at the hostel?'

'As a matter of fact, I've just been appointed assistant warden, and Lynette, my sister, is applying for jobs. We want to keep Father company.' Monnie stooped to pick up her bag. 'Perhaps I'd better get back now. We'll be needing this milk.'

'Can't tell you how nice it's been to meet you. Miss Forester . . .'

'Monnie, please.'

'Monnie. Perhaps we'll meet again. In the meantime, I've got my little Ford right here. Let me run you up to the hostel – that bag looks heavy.'

'Oh, I couldn't let you do that.' (Whatever would Torquil think if he saw her driving up in some other man's car?) 'You've your shopping to do.'

'A few groceries. I can pick them up when I've dropped you off. Come on, won't take a minute.'

She had to admit, it was a relief, not to have to carry the heavy bag home, and the little lift back was over so soon, it seemed hardly to have taken place. As Paul handed her out at the main door of the hostel, there was no sign of Torquil, and after a few more friendly words and promises to look out for each other again, Paul was gone and she was sighing with a different kind of relief. Until she saw Torquil at the side of the house, swinging his basket.

'Torquil!' She ran to him. 'Oh, I'm so sorry I missed you! Dad made me go for the milk.'

'I know.' Even in the shadowy dusk, the light in his blue eyes seemed intense. 'Who was the fellow driving the Ford?'

'You saw him?'

'Saw the Ford.'

'He was just someone giving me a lift.' Monnie's tone, meant to be casual, sounded forced, even to herself. 'When he saw me outside the shop, he thought my bag was heavy. Very kindly offered to drive me up.'

'You took a lift from a man you did not know?'

'I did know him – sort of – we met on the bus that time we arrived. The same time we met your mother, Torquil. He and another man were going on to stay at the hotel.'

'The Talisman? What is his name, then?'

'Paul Soutar.'

'Paul Soutar?' Immediately he heard the name, Torquil relaxed. 'Ah, yes, I know him. He asked me if I would take him fishing sometime, as a change from the climbing. I said I would.'

'He's nice, isn't he?'

'Seemed very pleasant.' Gently, Torquil put his hand on her arm. 'But let's not waste time. I shall see you tomorrow, as we said? Outside the gate at half past two?'

'Yes, of course, I'll be there.' Monnie removed his hand from her arm and held it. 'Torquil, did my father say anything to you?'

'He asked how much he owed me.'

'Nothing else?'

Torquil pressed the hand in his. 'I know what you are thinking, but, no, he said nothing else. Though it seemed to me that he wanted to. Several times he looked at me, as though he would speak, but he did not.'

Good old Dad, he'd kept his promise. Monnie withdrew her hand, smiling. 'Till tomorrow,' she said softly.

'Till tomorrow.'

As he walked away, looking back, she called after him, 'Where's your van, then?'

'Down the street. Did you not see it?'

'I don't know what it looks like.'

'Tomorrow, you will know.'

Turning down the drive, he waved his hand and was swallowed up into the shadows, leaving Monnie to hump her bag of milk bottles into the hostel, feeling a delightful warmth stealing over her at the sound of just the word 'tomorrow'.

'Dad, I've got the milk!' she cried, hurrying into his office, where her father jumped up to take the bag from her.

'Och, this is too heavy, I shouldn't have let you go for it, Monnie. I'll take it to the kitchen, anyway. Oh – and Torquil brought the fish. Some nice plaice.'

'I saw him outside, Dad.'

'You were just in time, then.'

No thanks to you, thought Monnie.

Eighteen

Letters only came to Conair by a small red post office van, and not until the afternoon.

'No question of expecting post in the morning,' Lynette complained at breakfast on Saturday morning. 'Means I have to hang about all day, waiting.'

'The hotel might ring up,' Monnie suggested, only half listening. Saturday mornings, she'd discovered, were always busy with people deciding to book in for the weekend, and she should really be on her way to help her father, already at reception. Be as helpful as possible to please him, seeing as her meeting with Torquil was now only hours away.

'Half past two . . .' The words had taken over from 'tomorrow' in keeping her filled with secret happiness, but a part of her still wanted to do her job and do it well. She was used to that, she supposed. Less used to being dependent on someone else for feelings of content.

'There's nothing in the local paper,' Lynette was continuing. 'Dad brought it up early from the shop, but there are only two vacancies for laundry maids at the Kyle Hotel, and some shop assistants' jobs. I'm beginning to think you were lucky, getting that assistant warden's job.'

'Speaking of which, I'd better go and help Dad. Will you wash up?'

'Sure. Give me something to do.' Lynette stood up, her expression softening. 'Not long now, Monnie, till half past two?'

'Think so?' asked Monnie.

★　★　★

Suddenly, though, it was time. The morning was over, lunch was over, everything at the hostel quiet, with all guests gone until five.

'I'm away, Dad,' Monnie said quickly, looking in at his office. She was wearing her winter coat over her best dark blue sweater and skirt, a bright scarf at her neck, and seemed to Frank's eyes, very young. Or, did he mean vulnerable?

'When will you be back?' he asked, rising to go with her to the door.

'I can't say when. We're just going for a walk.'

'In a van?'

'We're setting off in the van, that's all.'

'Take care, then.'

'Have a good time!' Lynette cried, appearing at the office door. 'Maybe I'll have some news when you get back. And maybe not.'

But Monnie was already on her way down the drive, suddenly worrying – would he be there?

He was there, leaning against the passenger door of a battered little blue van which had his name painted on the side. 'Torquil MacLeod – Purveyor of Fresh Fish – 3, The Cottages, Conair'.

Though the clouds were threatening, he wore no coat, only a grey jersey and jeans, but even in the poor light, his yellow hair shone as gold, and when he ran a hand through it, Monnie's heart lurched. She still couldn't quite believe that it was happening, that she was getting what she wanted. Going out with Torquil. Life wasn't like that, was it?

'So, this is the van?' she murmured, as he smiled down at her. 'It's . . . very nice.'

'No need to be polite.' He opened the passenger door for her and helped her in. 'This van is one of the oldest in the Highlands, I swear. Only keeps going because my brother does the repairs. He works for a garage in Kyle.'

'That's lucky.'

'True, but then I am known for my good luck.'

As she settled into her seat, he touched her hand.

'Notice anything? Or, should I say, not notice anything?'

'What? What do you mean?'

'No smell of fish!' His eyes were alight. 'I spent the whole morning, scrubbing out this poor old vehicle – and all for you, dear Monnie. Every day, I scrub myself, for I hate the smell of fish, but I'll have to admit, I don't bother about my van. Unless, I'm taking out a visitor.'

As he slowly drove off, Monnie stared straight ahead at the road. 'You often take out visitors?' she asked.

Though she didn't look at him, she sensed he was grinning. 'I will not deny, I have taken out one or two.'

She shrugged. 'Well, why not? I didn't think I would be your first passenger.'

'I am twenty-four years old. I'd be a strange fellow not to have had some lady friends, as my mother calls them. But they've not been important.'

'The same for me,' she said hastily. 'I mean, I've been out with people. Oh, heavens, how did we get on to this? I'm sorry, Torquil. Can we start again?'

He laughed. 'We can. Shall I tell you where I have in mind for us to go?'

'Oh, yes, please!'

'Well, if you have not seen our Pictish towers, I thought we'd start with them.'

'The Pictish towers? No, I haven't seen them. I've read about them, in a booklet at the hostel. They're very old, eh?'

'From the Iron Age, a couple of thousand years ago, maybe. Called the Glenelg Brochs, and not far from here. Before we get to the village, we take a turning off to Glean Beag, and there you will see them. Everyone has to see them sooner or later, so, you understand, I am helping to instruct you.'

As she turned to look at him, she could see amusement in his eyes.

'Are you not surprised, that I would do that? Come on, you never thought I would even be interested, did you?'

'I never thought about it,' she answered honestly, but didn't add that now she was thinking about it, yes, she was surprised. And yet the truth was, they had neither of them any idea what the other was like. One object in going out with someone was to find out. Unless, of course, you were only interested in other objects, but Monnie's mind veered away from those. She was close enough to trembling as it was.

'Weren't we supposed to be walking, though?' she asked, trying to collect herself.

'We shall just drive to the turning, then we can walk. 'Tis a nice spot, where the towers were built.'

So it proved to be, a sheltered, wooded valley, where a few people could be seen moving about, studying the two strange and ancient circular towers. Each was constructed of dry stone walling, and as Torquil and Monnie drew nearer, they could see doorways leading to passages.

'Well, what do you think?' Torquil asked.

'I'm amazed. I've never seen anything like them before.'

'So, we have something Edinburgh has not?' He laughed. ''Tis said they are only found in the west and the north of Scotland, and these two are some of the best preserved. Though they've lost their roofs and would have been much taller.'

'How do you know so much? Have you been reading the booklets?'

'Me, reading? No, we were brought along here from school. I was always bored to death then.' He flung back his head and stared up at the towers. 'Now, I sort of feel something for those builders so long ago.'

'I feel something, too,' she ventured. 'I mean, it's so recognizable, what they did. You don't think of folk two thousand years ago building something you might know.'

Torquil's gaze had moved to the other visitors now leaving the interior of one of the brochs, and taking Monnie's hand, he said they should look inside themselves.

'This one is called Dun Telve, in better condition than Dun Troddan, which is the other. Quick now, before the rain comes.'

'Oh, no, is there rain coming?'

'Trust me, there is. And the tower has no roof, remember.'

Inside the stone walls of the broch, they stood very close, marvelling at the way the interior had been so well constructed, with a long low passageway and inner courtyard, a hearth and stairway, and galleries aloft, all, of course, open to the sky.

Very conscious of his closeness, Monnie made an effort to seem her usual self, and asked Torquil why the brochs had been built. Did anyone really know?

He shook his head. 'Some think for defence, some think as shelter. No one is sure. We call them the Pictish towers, but maybe it wasn't even the Picts who built them.'

'At least, they *were* built. That's what's important.'

'True.'

He stood, looking into her face, then put his arms around her and brought his mouth close to hers. For a dizzy moment or two, she was certain he was going to kiss her, but he only brushed her cheek with his lips and released her.

'Look up,' he whispered. 'Was I not right? Here comes the rain.'

And as the rain came splashing down from the top of the tower open to the grey sky, they began to run from the shelter that was no shelter, making for real shelter instead, which was the old blue van, laughing as they reached it, wet, but uncaring.

'No more walking today,' Torquil gasped. 'Here, I keep a couple of towels in the back – take this and dry your hair.'

'I must look terrible!'

'No, beautiful.'

'Oh, please.' She took a comb from her bag and pulled it through her thick dark hair. 'You don't need to pay me compliments, Torquil.'

'I never pay compliments. I only say the truth.'

Still keeping his eyes on her while towelling his own hair, he seemed so in earnest that she blushed and wished she knew how to handle this sort of talk.

'Where shall we go now, then?' she whispered.

'To Glenelg,' he answered promptly. 'I know just the place for tea.'

'That'd be wonderful,' Monnie murmured, feeling strangely weary, she didn't know why, for she had done very little. Strain, perhaps, yet why should there be strain, when she was so happy?

Nineteen

Once in the little café Torquil knew, the weariness vanished, anyway, and all she could feel, sitting opposite him at a window table, was a blissful sense of well-being. Even in his damp jersey, with his hair sticking to his brow, he was so handsome, she couldn't take her eyes off him, yet was thrilled that his light blue gaze was just as firmly fixed on her. How did he see her? He had called her beautiful, but that was the sort of thing men said without at all meaning it. She felt it wasn't true, but maybe to him it was? She wished she could know what he was thinking. Seemed he was wishing the same about her.

'Is this where I say penny for them?' he asked, as a waitress, smiling at Torquil, brought a pot of tea and a plate of toasted teacakes.

'My thoughts?' She poured their tea. 'I was wondering if you knew that waitress.'

'Went to school with her sister. She's called Nina, her sister is Jill. And that's all that's in your mind?'

'Well, I was hoping you wouldn't take harm, sitting there in your wet sweater.'

'Catch my death?' He grinned. 'You don't know how tough I have to be. I cannot afford to worry about a shower of rain.'

'Don't you have waterproofs for the boat?'

'Sometimes get caught out – never take any harm. What about you, then?'

'I had a coat.'

'Sensible girl.'

'Not always.' She flushed a little, but he made no comment, only passed her the teacakes, and she said quickly that her mother used always to be worrying about her and her sister getting wet and catching cold and so on. Mothers were like that, eh?

'Oh, mine has given up worrying.' He looked at her with sudden sympathy. 'But I am very sorry that you have no mother now.'

'Thank you. She's been gone a while.'

'Like my father. He died at sea.'

'That's very sad,' she said carefully, not minding that he was giving her the version he would prefer of what had happened to his father. It was possible, of course, he didn't know the one the village gossiped about, but that didn't seem likely.

'Must have been hard for your mother, managing on her own, with two boys to bring up.'

'Yes.' He leaned forward, his eyes darkening. 'That is what people here do not remember. They blame her for being difficult, but she's the one who's had the difficult life. Where is their sympathy?'

'I'm sorry, Torquil, it's been hard for all of you.'

He sat back, relaxing, his look softening. 'For you and your family, too. How did your father manage, for instance, after your mother had gone?'

'He still hasn't got over losing her — that's why we came here, to start a new life — but my sister and me, we're lucky to have him.'

'Two lovely daughters,' Torquil said softly. 'He was lucky, too. Tell me, did you have jobs in Edinburgh?'

'Of course we did!' Monnie laughed. 'We're not exactly in the private income class! Lynette worked for a lawyer, I helped to run a bookshop.' She hesitated. 'I suppose you think that sounds dull?'

'No, I'm impressed. And will you look for that sort of job here?'

'I've already got a job. I'm assistant warden to my dad. I start officially next week.'

His eyes shone. 'Monnie, that is wonderful. Why did you not tell me earlier? Now you will be able to decide about my fish yourself.'

'Torquil, we always take your fish,' she said gently. 'It's for us, not the hostel.'

'Of course it is.' He pressed her hand in his, then glanced at his watch, large and weather-stained with a thick strap, and shook his head. 'Time we were going. Must get you back home before your father becomes anxious.'

'Back home? Now? But it's quite early.'

Though she was trying not to show her dismay, her face had paled a little and her eyes had widened. 'I'm not fifteen, Torquil, I don't have to be home to a curfew.'

He laughed and held her hand. 'No, no, but this is our first time out. It's best you are not late. And then I did say I would go over to see Tony in Kyle tonight.'

'You are going to see your brother? I thought you wanted to see me.'

'I do. But, the thing is, I said I'd go over tonight before I arranged to meet you. And then, I've explained, I do not want you to be late home.'

'I'm not likely to be late home when it's still teatime,' she said stiffly and stood up to find her coat. 'Let me get the bill.'

But he had already waved to their waitress, who came up running, all smiles for Torquil.

'Are you wanting your bill, then?'

'Please, Nina.' He was smiling, too, and as he paid, continued to smile, while taking Monnie's arm and leaving the café.

'As though I'd let you pay for our tea,' he whispered. 'But you only offered because you were cross with me. Is that not so? Why be cross?'

'I'm not cross.' The rain had stopped, the evening smelled fresh and sweet, and she had begun to feel better. 'Torquil, I've had a lovely time. Thank you for showing me the brochs, and for giving me tea. I'm sorry if I wasn't very understanding.'

'You were very sweet,' he told her, helping her into the front seat of his van. 'I have had a wonderful time, too.'

From his own seat, he looked at her, then turned his head and looked up and down the village street. No one in sight.

'Just time for this,' he said quietly and kissed her on the mouth, drawing back very soon as though to judge her reaction. 'You don't mind, Monnie?'

'No, I don't mind.' Heavens, no! How could she mind? She had been waiting for this moment all afternoon.

'Home, then. You see, it is getting dark. It will not seem so early.'

'And you are to drive all the way to Kyle? Take care, Torquil.'

'I am taking the bus, I should just be in time,' he said cheerfully. 'I am staying overnight, anyway.'

'Oh,' said Monnie. 'Staying overnight?'

'Much easier. Tony can drive me back tomorrow. He is coming to see Mother.'

They did not speak again until they reached the hostel gate, when they looked up the drive to the lighted windows. They were too far away to hear voices, though probably all the hostellers would be back and in the kitchen.

'Goodnight, Monnie,' Torquil said, touching her face for a moment. 'I've got to get the van home and make a dash for that bus. Shall I see you on Tuesday? You will not be going to the shop?'

'I shall not be going to the shop.' Monnie was already fiddling with her door, but Torquil leaned across and opened it for her and she climbed out. From the gate, she called, 'Goodnight, Torquil, and thank you again.'

'See you Tuesday!' he called back, and then the van went roaring away and after standing watching for a moment she turned and walked slowly up the drive.

'Monnie, is that you?' came her sister's voice, as she opened the main door of the hostel and Lynette came rushing to meet her. 'Oh, Monnie – amazing news! I've got the job! The letter came this afternoon.'

'Lynette, congratulations – that's terrific!'

'It is, eh?' But Lynette's face was puzzled. 'Dad,' she called over her shoulder, 'Monnie's back!'

'Already?' asked Frank, coming out of his office, and kicking aside a pile of boots still waiting to be put away. 'Well!'

'You're awful early, aren't you?' Lynette asked, fingering the still damp sleeve of Monnie's coat. 'Is everything all right?'

'Of course. We had a lovely time. Went to see those ancient towers – the brochs – then had tea in Glenelg.'

'The brochs?' Frank glanced at Lynette. 'Torquil think you're interested in ancient monuments, then?'

'He says everyone has to see the towers.'

'Not exactly romantic,' Lynette commented.

'That's where you're wrong, there was something very romantic about them. You should see them yourself.'

'If you say so. But why are you back so early?'

Monnie looked away. 'Torquil had to go over to Kyle to see his brother. He'd arranged it earlier.'

'The famous brother? Fancy.' Lynette shrugged. 'Shall we go and make something to eat, then? We've been having a pretty busy time, haven't we, Dad? Quite a load of folk came booking in. I had to help again.'

'I'm not really hungry – too much teacake – but I'll give you a hand.' Monnie, feeling she was appearing too subdued, smiled at her father. 'Be ready soon, Dad.'

'Fine. Glad you enjoyed your outing, Monnie.'

Later, in their own kitchen, Lynette, sliding a large dish of macaroni cheese under the grill, asked, 'Mind if I ask, but did you really enjoy it?'

'My outing? Yes. Yes, I did.'

'Just thought you seemed a bit down, when you first came in.'

'Did I?'

'Bit of an anticlimax, was it, coming home so early?'

Monnie sighed. 'Suppose it was.'

'Don't blame you for being upset, when Torquil was only going to see his brother.'

'It wasn't seeing his brother that upset me, more he didn't seem to mind. I mean, he thought it was all right to leave me early. Said he didn't want to upset Dad by making me late.'

'I suppose that might have been true, as it was your first time out together. Things could be different next time.'

'Do you think so?' Monnie brightened. 'Well, you may be right. Next time could be better.'

'And you do want a next time, I take it?'

'Oh, yes.' Monnie's tone was soft. 'Yes, I do.

For a long moment, the sisters were silent, busying themselves cutting up tomatoes, slicing bread for toast, until Lynette asked, 'Things aren't so bad, are they? After all, you've got your job, I've got mine, and you're been out with Torquil. I reckon we've made a pretty good start to our new life, eh? Even if I do have to work with Mr Difficult.'

'You'll soon sort him out.'

'Too right, he won't know what's hit him.' Lynette shook her head. 'Och, wish we had a glass of wine or something to celebrate, don't you?'

'We don't need any wine to celebrate. Come on, let's make our tea.'

'The only people ever known to celebrate with macaroni cheese, eh?'

As the sisters began to laugh, Frank came in and began to laugh himself, seeing his girls so happy. Things were working out, then, just as he'd hoped. Life in the Highlands – it had been a gamble, and he was no gambling man, but now, seemed he'd hit the jackpot.

'Should be having a wee dram,' he said, smiling.

'Whatever for?' asked Monnie.

'To celebrate.'

'Just what I said,' Lynette cried. 'We should have been celebrating our new jobs, shouldn't we?'

'Not just new jobs.

'What, then?'

'You know, don't you?'

'Of course we do,' Monnie declared. 'You mean, being here, together.'

'And being happy. You are happy, eh?'

'Dad, I think you've asked us that before,' Lynette told him lightly.

'Well, is the answer still the same?'

'It is.'

'More so,' Monnie murmured. 'If you see what I mean.'

Frank gave a little sigh. 'That's nice to hear, then. Thank you, girls.'

They were giving him quick hugs, when Lynette cried, 'Help, the macaroni! Still under the grill! Quick, the oven gloves!'

'Thought I could smell something,' Frank said cheerfully.

'It's OK,' Monnie told them, bringing the dish to the table. 'Just caught on a bit.'

'I like things caught on.' Frank was in his place, knife and fork at the ready. 'As a matter of fact, I like pretty well everything at the moment.'

And the girls agreed.

Twenty

Lynette managed only a week into her new job at the Talisman before she crossed swords with Mr Allan.

That might have been, she reflected afterwards, because she'd scarcely seen him after his polite welcome and had spent all her time being shown round by Mrs Atkinson and young Fionola MacLewis, Joanna Burnett having already departed. Quite pleasant that had been, for though there'd been a lot to learn, Mrs Atkinson had turned out to be a good teacher and Fionola much more efficient than Lynette had expected.

'But how old is Fionola?' Lynette had felt constrained to ask Mrs Atkinson in private, who had smiled and answered that she was nineteen.

'Nineteen? I thought she might only be seventeen.'

'No, no, she'd have to be older than that to take charge when you're not here. Don't forget you spell each other for evening duty and weekends.'

'She's a beautiful girl.'

'She is, and that could have caused trouble if we'd had a lot of young men as guests, but luckily, most of our clientele are a little on the elderly side. This isn't a hotel for the active, more for folk wanting a nice relaxed holiday.'

So, those two young men the Foresters had met on their first bus trip to Conair weren't the usual types for the Talisman, a fact which was certainly borne out by the guests Lynette saw in her first week at work. Retired, well to do, not too sprightly, but fit enough to sit in the lounge or conservatory, and enjoy excellent meals in the dining room. Maybe take short walks to the shore, or drives out to admire the scenery, but as different from the young folk at the hostel as it was possible to be.

Ah well, no one could stay young for ever, but Lynette couldn't help feeling a little oppressed from time to time, by the atmosphere of comfort and effortlessness that hung over the whole hotel. Apart from the reception desk, and behind the scenes, where the young staff worked flat out to provide all the lovely comfort.

It soon became apparent to Lynette that the place she liked best in the hotel was the kitchen. Buzzing with vitality, everything zipping along to a certain goal and coming together with efficiency and confidence, it was exactly where she could feel at home. Just as the staff there were her sort of people. Young, friendly, hard working and full of fun, she guessed at once that they took their tone from the top and the top was a lanky young man with carroty hair and a good-natured, freckled face. Scott Crosbie was his name, Mrs Atkinson told her, when she introduced him.

'And he comes from your neck of the woods,' she added, as Lynette and Scott shook hands. 'Yes, Edinburgh.'

'Edinburgh?' Lynette's eyes shone. 'Whereabouts?'

'Och, no' the New Town,' he answered with a laugh. 'Wee flat in Dalry. How about you?'

'Old Town tenement.' She too had laughed. 'We're not New Town, either.'

He'd grinned at that and then Mrs Atkinson had whisked her away, saying they'd lots more to see, but Lynette had known she'd be going back. Maybe to pretend she wanted to collect the day's menus, really to soak up the atmosphere, smile at Scott and his three assistants – Hamish, Fergus and Brigid – and give herself a reminder that there still was a real world outside the comfort zone.

'How's it going?' Monnie asked her at the end of the week. 'Are you enjoying it?'

'Sure. It's a nice little number.'

'Work no problem?'

'None at all. Mrs A. says I'm a natural, whatever that means. Working the switchboard, being nice to the guests, or whatever, she seems to think I'm good at it, anyway. And Fionola's sweet, and good at her job, which I was surprised about, though maybe I was just prejudiced because she's so pretty.'

'And how abut Mr Difficult?'

'Never see him. In fact, he's away this weekend at a managers' conference, Mrs Atkinson will be standing in. She's a bit sharp, but quite friendly, and very efficient.'

'So, everything's all right for you, then?'

'For now.' Lynette gave her sister a considering look. 'And for you too, I take it?'

'Me? I'm just working for Dad.'

'I wasn't thinking of work. I mean, seeing Torquil. You told me he'd asked you out again when he came on Tuesday.'

Monnie eyes were very bright. 'That's right. But not for this Saturday. He has to go to Inverness for some part for the boat's engine.'

'At least he's not going to see his brother. So, when did you say you were going out, then?'

'Wednesday week. We're going to Kyle for a meal. Torquil's going to try to finish early.'

'And you'll be coming back late. That's better than last time, eh?'

'Look, I just wish you'd stop going on, Lynette. Are you taking over from Dad, or what?'

'Sorry.' Lynette smiled apologetically. 'I don't mean to act the bossy sister. It's just that I want everything to be all right for you. You understand?'

'I suppose I do.' Monnie smiled back. 'I'd probably be the same with you, if you were going out with someone new.'

'Nothing like that to worry about on my horizon at the moment. Only Mr Allan, coming back on Monday.' Lynette yawned and stretched. 'But I'm certainly not worrying about him. Maybe we'll get on better than I thought.'

When Monday came, however, she changed her mind on that.

Twenty-One

Monday morning shone with such bright April sunshine, Lynette, taking out her dark suit again, decided to put it back.

'Now, why should we all look like we're going to a funeral?' she asked Monnie, who was hastily dressing, ready to check on the hostellers at breakfast. 'I mean, there's Mrs Atkinson in black, Fiona in black, and Mr Allan, probably in black, too. Why don't I bring a bit of spring into their lives, eh?'

'And do what?' asked Monnie, then stared as her sister took a familiar suit from the wardrobe. 'Why, you're never going to wear that red suit to work, are you? After all you said about being on the safe side?'

Lynette, fondly holding the suit against herself, was smiling. 'I told you, I want to bring a bit of spring into the hotel, a bit of colour. I bet it'll cheer the old buffers up no end.'

'Put it on quick, then, or you'll be missing your bus.'

'Wish I could drive and had a car,' Lynette said with a sigh. 'Or, even a bike. Maybe I'll get a second-hand one when the summer comes. Put a wee card in Mrs MacNicol's window.'

For the present, she had to catch the old, lumbering bus, wearing a raincoat over her suit. She knew all the drivers now, Tim Maclean being one and on duty that day. He smiled and waved as he put her off at the hotel and she ran in through still cold air, even if the sun was shining.

'Good morning, Lynette!' called Mrs Atkinson, pausing on her way to her office. 'You don't mind my using your first name, now that you're part of our family, so to speak?'

'No, no, Mrs Atkinson,' Lynette answered, noting that the other woman didn't offer her own first name, which was known, in fact, to be Ailsa. 'I prefer it.'

'And you're quite happy to be in charge of the desk now?'

'Quite happy, thanks.'

'That's excellent. Please don't hesitate to ask, if you need any help.'

'Thank you, I won't.'

How well we're getting on, thought Lynette, but as she slipped off her raincoat, did not miss the flash of surprise in Mrs Atkinson's eyes as she took in the red suit. Surprise, was it, or disapproval? She made no comment, however, only nodded briefly as she moved away, leaving Lynette to speak to Fionola, who had just arrived at Reception.

'Shan't be a tick, I'm just going to hang my coat up.'

'That's all right.' Fionola smiled. 'Lynette, I like your suit. What a lovely colour.'

'Think so? Hope everyone agrees with you.'

In the staff cloakroom, Lynette hung up her raincoat and combed her hair at the mirror, observing before she hurried back to Reception that she looked well, with a high colour and a sparkle to her eyes. Not as striking as Fionola, of course, but who was?

'Is the boss in yet?' Lynette asked, straightening the register, putting things in order as she liked.

'Mr Allan? Oh, yes, I saw him going into his office.'

With no one around at that moment, most of the guests being still at breakfast, Lynette, perching herself on a stool, studied her assistant.

'Listen – haven't asked you before – but is he really as tough as he seems?'

Fionola's lovely eyes widened. 'Tough? No, he's very nice. At least, he's always been nice to me.'

'Must be just me, then, that brings out the worst, eh?'

'Why, you've hardly seen him, Lynette! When you get to know him, you'll find out he's OK.'

'Hope you're right.'

Suddenly, the entrance doors opened, as Ken and Barty, the day porters, appeared with luggage, followed by three new guests making for Reception, just as the phone began to ring, and an elderly man limped from the lift, asking for his bill.

Oh, joy, the day's begun, thought Lynette, I think this is the way I'm going to like it, nice and busy.

'If I can ask you to wait for a moment, sir, I shan't keep you,' she said to the elderly gentleman, picking up the phone and assuring the caller that she had confirmation for a Saturday booking. 'Certainly, madam, I have the details right here—'

'My bill is supposed to be ready,' put in the elderly party. 'Mr Rowlandson is my name.'

'And it is ready, sir,' Lynette told him, while Fionola booked in the new guests. 'If you'd just like to check it through? And book you a taxi? Of course, sir. One moment . . .'

Nice and busy, Lynette had said she liked it, but really that Monday morning was almost too hectic, and when a slight lull did come, she was glad to take time to stretch and walk up and down the corridor, after shooing Fionola away for a coffee break. It was then that she saw Mr Allan's tall figure moving deliberately towards her, for all the world like some sort of policeman.

Oh, Lord, what was he going to say? Hallo, Hallo, what have we here?

All he said was, 'Good morning, Miss Forester. Having a quiet moment?'

'Good morning, Mr Allan. As a matter of fact, it's been very busy until now. I'm just snatching a moment while Fionola's at coffee.'

'I see.' For some moments, his eyes rested on her, taking in the red suit as Mrs Atkinson had done, though with no flicker of reaction. 'I'm sorry I haven't been able to speak to you before about your work here. Are you enjoying it? Finding it easy to cope?'

'Yes, thank you, Mr Allan. I'm enjoying it very much. Haven't found any problems so far.'

'Good, good.' He seemed to be hesitating, was even a little ill at ease. 'I notice, Miss Forester, you have a change of outfit today from last week.'

'Thought I'd provide a spot of colour.'

'It is a colourful suit, certainly.'

Guessing what was coming, Lynette felt irritation rising. 'You don't think it's appropriate?'

Again, he hesitated. 'Perhaps I should just explain, here at the Talisman we have a staff dress code – everyone presenting a rather similar appearance, rather than being strikingly different.'

'No one told me about a dress code.'

'Perhaps it didn't seem necessary. What you were wearing was exactly right.'

'And now it's exactly wrong?' she flared up, turning scarlet. 'Honestly, Mr Allan, I take exception to that!'

'No, no, I'm not saying there's anything wrong with what you've chosen to wear. It's most attractive, would be perfectly suitable for one of the smart London hotels, for instance, but we're just a rather old-fashioned place with perhaps an older clientele—'

'Who might just like to see a spot of colour. Please answer me this, Mr Allan, are you telling me not to wear my red suit again?'

He slightly shook his head. 'I'm just saying I'd prefer you to have the look of the rest of the staff who serve the public directly.'

'No dress code for the porters, I take it?'

The manager tightened his lips. 'I think you understand me, Miss Forester.'

'Perfectly.' Lynette, breathing hard, stared at him with glittering eyes. 'May I go for my coffee now? I see Fionola has returned.'

'Certainly. I don't wish to keep you.'

Turning on his heel, Mr Allan left her, and Lynette, trying to contain her simmering anger which was in danger of boiling over, ran, not to the staff dining room, but the kitchen, where she cried, 'Quick, you folks, give me a strong coffee, before I explode!'

Twenty-Two

As his three assistants looked up with interest from their chopping, peeling and stirring, Scott Crosbie grinned and poured a strong black coffee from a pot on the stove.

'Here, this'll sort you out,' he told Lynette, who took the coffee gratefully. 'But what's up, then? Has one of the guests been causing trouble?'

'No, just the manager. Listen, would I be allowed a cigarette in here?'

'A cigarette?' Lanky young Fergus laughed. 'Are you joking?'

'No ciggies,' Scott said firmly. 'How about one of the breakfast croissants?'

'With butter and jam? Oh, yes please!'

'So what's misery guts Allan been up to, then?' asked Hamish, as Brigid left her chopping board to bring Lynette a large flaky croissant with butter and jam. 'We all know what he can be like if he's in one of his moods.'

'Trouble is, we never hit it off from the start.' Lynette was buttering her croissant with a sigh of pleasure. 'This looks delicious – thanks very much. No, he seemed to take against me, just because I'm from the hostel. I ask you, why would he be like that?'

'Do you not know?' Brigid's sweet Highland voice was becoming a squeak. A round-faced and apple-cheeked girl, with short black hair and dimples, she was clearly bursting now to tell Lynette all she knew. 'He used to live at Conair House! It was his family home.'

'Conair House was his family home?' Lynette, brushing crumbs from her mouth, was incredulous. 'You mean, he's one of the folk who shot all those stags stuck up in the hall? I don't believe it!'

'No, no, it was the people who built the house did that and they were the MacDonalds. But they'd no heir and when old Miss MacDonald died in the thirties, Mr Allan's father bought the house.' Brigid, delighted to be the centre of attention, nodded her dark head.

'I know all this because my mother used to be parlour maid at the house before she married, and she remembers Mr Allan's family moving in. 'Course Mr Allan was only a laddie then. Later on, he went away to school.'

'But what happened?' asked Lynette, deeply interested. 'I mean, how did the house come to be a hostel?'

'Why, Mr Allan's father went bankrupt!' Brigid answered. 'Lost all his money in the war when his business went under. Think it was something to do with exporting stuff – or, was it importing? Anyway, he had to sell the house, and that's when the hostel bought it.'

'And Mr Allan's had a dirty great chip on his shoulder ever since,' Hamish remarked, returning his attention to a pan of stock bubbling on the stove. 'Hates even to think of young folk tramping round his old home. So, I've heard.'

'Aye, but what's all this past history got to do with you?' Scott asked Lynette, when she rose, dabbing her lips and preparing to leave. 'Has Mr Allan said something today?'

'Has he not!' Lynette was flushing again, remembering her grievances. 'Only told me I oughtn't to wear this red suit, but dress for a funeral like everybody else. Well, wear dark colours, I mean, because that's the dress code. As though it was 1909 instead of 1959!'

'Told you not to wear that lovely suit?' Brigid cried. 'Why that's ridiculous. I was just thinking how nice you looked!'

'Very nice,' Scott said seriously. 'Very nice, indeed.'

'I don't know about that,' Lynette murmured. 'All I know is that I'll have to do what he wants, or kiss my job goodbye, eh?'

'It wouldn't come to that. I'm sure he'd never sack you.' Scott's craggy face was still serious. 'You're too efficient.'

'And how do you know that?' she asked, laughing a little.

'Och, I can tell. I can always tell. And so can Mr Allan. If it came to a showdown, I bet you'd win.'

'I'd better not risk it. There aren't many jobs around for people like me.'

'You any good at cooking? Poor old Fergus here has to do his national service pretty soon. We could do with some temporary help.'

'Macaroni cheese is my speciality.' Lynette was laughing again and the kitchen staff laughed with her. 'No, but I wouldn't mind learning how to cook. Give me a few lessons, eh, Scott?'

'Nothing I'd like better,' he told her cheerfully. 'Feeling OK now?'

'Much better. After all the chat and that terrific croissant. Many thanks, all. I'd better dash.'

'Gorgeous girl,' Fergus murmured. 'Bet she doesn't stay. You can tell old Allan really puts her off.'

'It's right what she says, though, there aren't many jobs around for people like her,' Scott said quickly. 'I think she'll stay.'

'You hope,' Brigid told him, smiling, at which spots of red appeared on Scott's freckled cheekbones.

'Finished slicing those julienne carrots?' he asked shortly, and, still smiling, she obediently went back to her chopping board.

Back home that evening, Lynette had plenty to say, not only about her battle with Mr Allan, but also about his connection with Conair House. Naturally, both Frank and Monnie were indignant over the manager's veto of the red suit, though fascinated to learn more of the history of the hostel.

'I think your manager's nothing better than a tyrant,' Monnie exclaimed. 'Telling people what to wear, indeed! As long as you look smart and neat, why shouldn't you wear what you like?'

'Does seem hard,' Frank agreed. 'Though it's true, firms do have dress codes, sometimes you've just to go along with them. Though I can't see any harm in a receptionist wearing a bright outfit, I must admit.'

'The kitchen folk were saying Mr Allan has a tremendous chip on his shoulder because his family lost this house,' Lynette muttered. 'But why should he take his troubles out on other people? Really annoys me.'

'You won't leave though?' her father asked, and she shook her head.

'Not while there are so few jobs around. I'd better stick with it and get some experience for the future.' Lynette suddenly smiled. 'And it's not all bad news. I get on well with everybody else and really like the work.'

'That's the spirit!' cried Frank.

'Guess who I met in the village again,' Monnie said to Lynette as they were preparing for bed. 'One of the chaps we saw on the bus – Paul Soutar.'

'Oh, yes, I remember. You met him at the shop, too, didn't you?'

'Well, he lives here now, and it's a pretty small village. You know what he asked? If I'd like to go for a walk with him.'

Lynette paused in hanging up the rejected red suit, and turned to give her sister a long look of surprise.

'And what did you say?'

'I didn't know what to say. I mean, I couldn't tell him I'd better not, because I was going out with someone else. That would have sounded as though – I don't know – as though Torquil and I . . . well, you know how it would have sounded.'

'So, you said you'd go?'

'Yes, I thought it would be nice, anyway, to get to know the countryside. We're going out on Friday afternoon. Dad says I can take it off.'

'Monnie, I'm pleased. I'm really pleased.'

'I can't think why. I'm going to tell Torquil about it and if he's not happy, I'll say I can't go again. That'd be only fair.'

'Oh, what a piece of nonsense!' cried Lynette.

Twenty-Three

Monnie wasn't exactly disappointed that Torquil appeared not to mind about her going walking with Paul Soutar. No, disappointed would be the wrong word. Surprised, maybe. Surprised that when she told him about it on Tuesday evening, he should just fix her with his limpid blue eyes and say, 'Fine.'

'So I won't be here on Friday when you come,' she went on carefully. 'You won't mind?'

'Well, of course, I would like to see you, but I shall understand.'

'Understand I'll be out walking with Paul Soutar?' She felt she sounded rather desperate, but still heard herself adding, 'And not with you.'

'Sweet Monnie, do you think I should be jealous?' He put his hand to her cheek. 'Mr Soutar – he's a nice guy, eh? What you'll have with him will be a walk, and that is all. I think you will enjoy it.'

And with that they exchanged a hurried kiss on the doorstep, before he handed over their fish as usual and then was away, touching his cap and smiling. Clearly, he regarded Paul Soutar as no rival, which did still surprise her. And, yes, why not admit it – disappointed her, too.

Early on Friday afternoon when she went to meet Paul at the front of the hostel, she was relieved that the weather was fine. Still cold, of course, but bright, and she was really looking forward to the afternoon, until with a sinking heart, she found Mrs Duthie busy sweeping at the open main door.

Oh, trust her to be around when she was not wanted! And putting two and two together when she saw Monnie's anorak trousers and stout shoes, and making more than four.

'Going on another walk with Torquil MacLeod, Monnie?' the little woman asked at once. 'Is he finishing early from his fish round, then?'

When her question was answered by Paul Soutar's sudden appearance at the front door, it didn't take her long to revise her guesswork and turn with glinting eyes to Monnie.

'What a surprise then, 'tis Mr Soutar you are seeing, not Torquil! Now he is one of my clients, you know. I clean his house twice a week. And very tidy he keeps it. Oh, if only some of the young people here could keep their dormitories the way you keep your home, Mr Soutar, my life would be a lot easier!'

'Good afternoon, Mrs Duthie,' Paul said pleasantly. 'Hope I'm not in your way. Miss Forester, shall we go?'

'Yes, I'll just say goodbye to Dad – he's in his office.'

'No, I'm here,' Frank said, coming out with papers in his hand and giving Paul a smile of recognition.

'So, we meet again – Mr Soutar, isn't it? Haven't seen you since we first arrived on that dear old bus!'

'How are you, Mr Forester? How are things going with the hostel?' As Paul and Frank shook hands, Mrs Duthie watched with interest while Monnie stood at the door, just wishing that she and Paul could be on their way. But her father was eagerly talking.

'Oh, it's going well. We're really enjoying the life here, aren't we, Monnie? My assistant, you know, Mr Soutar, and a great asset.'

'I'm sure. But this is a wonderful part of the world, isn't it?'

'Absolutely couldn't agree more. All we want is to get to know it better.'

'One reason why I suggested your daughter might care to do some walking with me.'

'Good, good.' Frank spoke with genuine approval. 'Monnie will love it, I can tell you. Well, mustn't keep you. Enjoy your walk.'

'Thank God, away at last,' Monnie murmured, as she and Paul made their way down the drive. 'With Mrs Duthie's ears flapping over every word, I couldn't wait to get away.'

'Oh, she's not too bad,' Paul said cheerfully. 'Sorts my cottage out pretty well.'

'I'm not saying she isn't good at her job, just too keen to live our lives for us.' Thinking she might be complaining too much, Monnie suddenly relaxed. 'Sorry, Paul, let's talk about our walk.'

'Well, we're cheating a bit to start with.' He laughed, as they came to the village street and he halted her beside his car. 'Yup, here it is, my trusty wee Ford. Like to hop in?'

Raising her eyebrows slightly, she took the passenger seat, and Paul, in the driving seat, assured her it was OK, they weren't driving far.

'I just wasn't sure how many miles you were prepared to do, so I thought we'd go part of the way to Loch Hourn, then walk by the water. What do you think? Do you know Loch Hourn?'

'No, but I've heard of it. Look, I'm prepared to do some walking. I've got suitable shoes, I hope.'

'I noticed. Fine for today, but if you're interested in hill walking, you'd need good, stout boots.'

As they drove away, Monnie turned her head to look at him, as Torquil's comments came back into her mind. 'Mr Soutar, he's a nice guy, eh? What you'll have with him will be a walk and that's all . . .'

How right Torquil had been, how well he'd recognized the

sort of man Paul was. Trustworthy, loyal, sincere – all those wonderful words would be right for him. Never in the world would anyone call him wild. Even though she'd spent hardly any time with him, she was feeling safe sitting beside him, safe, and tranquil, if that was not too strange a word to use. Certainly, it wasn't one she'd ever use to describe the way she felt with Torquil. Oh, God, no!

Perhaps feeling her eyes on him, he gave her a swift glance, before looking back at the road.

'Monnie, mind if I say, I hope I'm not acting out of turn, asking you to walk with me? I didn't know that you were . . . seeing young Torquil.'

'Young Torquil?' She tried to speak lightly. 'You're not much older than he is.'

'I feel a lot older. But you haven't answered my question.'

The truth was, she didn't know what to say. To tell Paul that Torquil had given his permission, so to speak, for her to walk with him, would not, she felt, go down well. Good-natured though he was, Paul would hardly want to be told that she'd felt the need to have another man's OK. On the other hand, she couldn't let Paul think there was nothing between herself and Torquil, for that wouldn't be true. They might have had their differences, but there was that spark between them, that spark she cherished. The sort of spark she would never share with Paul himself, though why she was thinking he might want that when they scarcely knew each other, she didn't know.

'I am seeing Torquil,' she said at last. 'It doesn't mean I can't meet other people. Other . . . friends.'

'Friends,' he repeated, smiling. 'I'd like to think we could be that.'

'Well, why shouldn't we be? After all, we're neighbours.'

'We are, aren't we?'

Still smiling, he drew up as the winding road turned east and they came to the shore of Loch Hourn, the long sea loch flowing out to the Sound of Sleat, with magnificent views to the Knoydart Peninsula.

'See the land across there?' Paul asked. 'It's what people call Britain's last wilderness. Still unspoilt because it's so remote and hard to reach, except by boat or a great trek over rough country.'

'The last wilderness,' Monnie repeated. 'Nice to think there still is one.'

'My thoughts exactly. If it weren't completely impossible, it's where I'd like to live. But, being in the real world, I'm looking for somewhere not too far from Conair.'

'You're going to buy a house round here? Sounds interesting.'

'Not just a house to live in – somewhere I can make into a centre for my school.'

'A school? You're a teacher?'

'No, a journalist – I write on climbing for Scottish papers and magazines.' He grinned. 'So, my school won't be teaching the three Rs. My brother and I had some money left us by our parents and I'm going to spend mine on a school for mountaineering and hill walking. That's why I'm here, looking for a property. Think it's a good idea?'

'A wonderful idea.' She smiled. 'Hey, I could be your first pupil.'

'Perfect! Only I haven't found my house yet. Want a bit of walking practice first? We'll leave the car off the track and follow round the loch to Arnisdale. We can have a rest there.'

As they began to walk around the shores of the loch, Paul asked Monnie if she'd already seen something of that area.

'No, I haven't. There are so many places we want to see, but the problem is finding time away from the hostel.'

'I can imagine. I stayed there once or twice, when the MacKays were in charge. Always on the go, it seemed to me.'

'It's true, but Dad says we must try to organize time off, and he's been very good, letting me . . .'

She hesitated, letting Paul finish the sentence for her.

'Letting you come for a walk with me, not to mention Torquil. He's quite right, you both need time off.'

'Torquil doesn't get much,' Monnie said, after a pause. 'But he told me that he keeps a rowing boat at Arnisdale – not the one with an engine he uses for fishing – and sometimes he just likes to row out on the loch by himself and enjoy the peace and the scenery.'

Her eyes on Paul as she talked were serious, as though she wanted to press home the point that Torquil was not just an uncaring young man, but had a side to him that not many knew.

'He's not really wild,' she finished. 'That's just what people say, you know, because of his brother.'

'I didn't know they said that of Torquil,' Paul answered mildly. 'He's been very helpful with me, taking me fishing. Not that I'm any good at it.' He gave a rueful smile. 'Don't like taking the fish off the hooks.'

'I'm the same,' she told him. 'But it's a bit hypocritical, eh? When I eat fish twice a week caught by Torquil.'

Laughing, they continued their walk to Arnisdale, which was really two tiny hamlets a mile apart, each with a few cottages overlooking Loch Hourn, and breathtaking views of mountains towering everywhere.

Twenty-Four

Surely, thought Monnie, sitting with Paul on a narrow shore at Arnisdale, there could be no more peaceful place than this? There were cottages behind them, smoke from their hearth fires drifting upwards, but their eyes were only for the waters of the loch, so unruffled in the pale sunlight, so unstirred by wind, they reflected every contour of the mountains around.

This was where Torquil came, then, the Torquil no one knew, to sit in his boat and find the peace he seemed to seek. How right she had been, Monnie decided, to tell Paul that the young man some called wild had different sides to his nature.

Hard to recognize, perhaps, for even she had been surprised, to know that the man who could stir her own emotions so deeply, should feel the need for solitude. Not that she could tell Paul of her surprise, or of Torquil's effect on her. Those were secrets for her heart alone.

Suddenly, Paul, the companion she had forgotten about for the moment, broke into her thoughts with mention of Torquil himself.

'Sorry, what were you saying?' she asked, her eyes on him wide and startled.

'Only that if Torquil likes to come here for tranquillity, he'll be aware he won't always find it. Know what the name Loch Hourn means in Gaelic, Monnie?'

'I've no idea.'

'Loch of Hell.'

She stared. 'Why? It looks like heaven at the moment.'

'True. On a fine day, it's beautiful. But when the gales blow, it can be a killer. Capsizing boats, causing great waves with terrible spindrifts – that's when the spray is blown from the surface of the sea by the wind.' Paul shook his head. 'Come here in different kind of weather, and you'll find a very different Loch Hourn.'

She shivered a little, trying to picture the loch before her as he had described it, but its present calmness defeated her.

'You make it sound frightening,' she murmured.

'Forgive me, I don't want to spoil your views of it now, only things can change and quickly in the Highlands.'

Paul looked back at the quiet hamlet behind them. 'There've been changes here, too, in Arnisdale, only they're more permanent. Would you believe that this was once one of the biggest herring fisheries in the area? Everybody at work, bringing in the catch, sorting, salting, preparing. So many boats, you couldn't count them.' He shrugged. 'Very different now, but that's the way things go, eh? Fish stocks don't last for ever.'

Leaping up from the old bench where they'd been sitting, he gave his hand to Monnie and pulled her up.

'Shall we walk on now to Corran? It's even smaller than this place. But first, I want to show you something.'

As she moved to stand beside him, he slightly turned her round so that she was looking at the highest of the distant peaks.

'One of the reasons people come to Arnisdale is to start their ascent of that mountain over there, the "hill of scree", as its Gaelic name means. Once you get to the top – and it's pretty stiff going, I'll have to admit – the views are incredible. Over Knoydart and Barrisdale Bay, Skye, the Cuillins – amazing.'

'I wish I could see them.'

'Well, you could, you know. Didn't you say you'd be my first pupil?' Paul's tone was light, his expression serious. 'After some practice, it would be good to try a Munro.'

'That hill's a Munro?'

'Certainly is. It's one of the hills in Scotland over three thousand feet, as listed by a man named Munro back in 1891. I expect you've heard of them?'

'Oh, yes, I've heard of them,' she told him, laughing. 'From the hostellers. They know all about Munros.'

'I bet they do. Probably go Munro-bagging when they can.' Paul's brown eyes were bright. 'Maybe you'll be a Munro-bagger too. I want this one to be your first, anyhow. Like to have a go eventually?'

'Yes, I would. See how I get on. But I suppose I'll need some boots.'

'You can get good ones in Kyle. Maybe I can drive you over some time? I'd like to advise.'

'Thanks, that would be wonderful.'

He hesitated. 'They can be pretty pricey, good boots. Perhaps I could—'

'That's all right,' she said at once, feeling embarrassed. 'I can manage.'

He nodded, equally embarrassed, and touched her hand. 'Listen, you won't regret it, being introduced to hill walking. There's nothing to compare with reaching the summit, being on top of the world, seeing the most sublime scenery all around you. And even if you don't make it at first, the day will come when you will.'

'Paul, you really make me believe that,' she said quietly. 'I think you're going to make a success of your school, you know, just the way you put things.'

Embarrassed again, he looked away.

'How about getting on our way now? I don't know if you've heard, but you can get tea at Corran.'

It was after five when they got back to the hostel and Paul, parking at the gates, said he'd better not come in. He knew how busy it was at that time, with hostellers returning from their day away.

'But I want you to know, Monnie, how much I've enjoyed being with you today. I hope you've enjoyed it too.'

'Paul, I have,' she answered with truth. 'It's been lovely. And you've told me so much, I feel I know so much more than I did.'

'Oh, help!' He rolled his eyes. 'Don't know why, I can't help lecturing. Next time, just shut me up.' He paused for a moment, his eyes anxious. 'There will be a next time, won't there? If Torquil is OK about it?'

'Why, we're going to look for my boots, aren't we? You said we could go to Kyle.'

'True. I'll phone you, shall I?'

'You have a phone in your cottage?'

'No!' He laughed, as he came round to open the car door for her. 'I'll use the village phone box.'

'OK.' She put out her hand. 'Thanks for a lovely afternoon, Paul.'

'Thank you,' he replied with emphasis and after shaking her hand for slightly longer than was necessary, returned to his car and with a last smile, drove away.

Walking slowly towards the house after time spent with a young man now driving away, Monnie had the feeling that there was something of a repeat performance about her afternoon out. How much seemed the same, yet how indescribably different. For if it was true that she had very much enjoyed being with Paul, hearing him talk, being able to relax in his presence, as she reached the hostel door, she was already thinking of Torquil.

'Has he brought the fish?' she asked her father in his office.

'Hey, you're back.' He stood up, smiling. 'Same as all the hostellers. See the boots everywhere?'

'Torquil, Dad, did he bring the fish?'

'Oh, yes. Some time ago. He was early, as a matter of fact. I put the fish in the fridge.'

'I thought I might have seen him.' Monnie was taking off her walking shoes. 'He's not always early.'

'Gave me a message,' Frank said flatly. 'Said he'd look out for you on Tuesday.'

She relaxed. 'He said that?'

'Funny guy, eh? You'd have thought he'd want to know how you'd enjoyed your walk. Wouldn't mind knowing myself.'

'It was lovely, Dad. We went to Arnisdale and looked at the loch, and then Paul asked me if I'd really like to try hill walking one day. Maybe even a Munro. I'm going to have to buy some proper boots.'

'You got on well with him, then?'

Ignoring the hope in her father's voice, Monnie agreed carelessly that she had. But then anyone would get on with Paul.

'I think he might be interested in you, Monnie.'

'Oh, yes, we've already decided, we'll be very good friends.'

'Good friends?'

'And that's all. No matchmaking, Dad.' Monnie picked up her shoes and made for the door. 'I'll go and see how they're getting on in the kitchen, shall I?'

'Wish you would.'

'And then I'll see what fish Torquil's brought us. Better get something ready for when Lynette comes in.'

'Aye, do that,' Frank said, turning back to his office, his shoulders drooping, but Monnie didn't notice, she was already on her way.

'So, how did you get on with Paul Soutar?' Lynette asked as soon as she came back from work. 'I've been thinking about you.'

'Why is everyone so interested?' Monnie asked, checking on her fish pie.

'Come on, he's interested, isn't he?'

'Just what I said,' Frank remarked.

'Well, I'm not,' Monnie declared. 'Except as a friend.'

'Where did you go, then?' Lynette pressed. 'With this friend?'

'Arnisdale. Paul told me all about the way it used to be, when the herring fishing made it so busy, and then he talked about Loch Hourn and how dangerous it was, and asked me if I'd like to try hill walking some time. He's a wonderful talker.'

Lynette raised her eyebrows. 'Honestly, Monnie, can't you get somebody to take you somewhere nice? One fellow wants to show you ancient monuments, the other one lectures you on the herring trade. I'd want something different, I can tell you!'

'Well, you're not me.' Monnie's tone was sharp as she set her fish pie on the table. 'Don't tell me what I should want.'

'That pie looks excellent,' Frank intervened. 'Let's all get on with our tea, eh? D'you have a good day, Lynette?'

'Yes, except for you know who.' Lynette sighed. 'Och, we just rub each other up the wrong way, Mr Allan and me, and that's all there is to it. Even though I'm doing just what he wants and wearing all my darkest clothes for work, he still finds fault.'

'Bet you do, too,' Monnie said, grinning.

'Aye, well, guess we're too much like, that's the trouble. Next week, though, he wants me to do some typing for him when Mrs Atkinson's away. Watch out for sparks, eh?'

'Know what I think?' Monnie asked, serving out the fish pie. 'I think you secretly enjoy it, having these dust ups. Adds a bit of excitement to the day, eh?'

'Are you joking?' Lynette cried, flushing. 'I can't stand the man, and you know it.'

'Well, you know what they say about that sort of feeling, don't you?'

'No, what do they say, for heaven's sake?'

'Better drop this,' Frank ordered, beginning to eat. 'Let's just enjoy our meal.'

'I agree,' Lynette snapped.

'Me, too,' said Monnie.

And the talk turned at last to other things.

Twenty-Five

Some days later, as she had expected, Lynette was called from Reception to Mr Allan's office for secretarial duties.

'Hold the fort,' she whispered to Fionola, as she picked up her shorthand notebook. 'Send in a rescue party if I'm not back in half an hour.'

'Honestly, anyone would think Mr Allan was a tyrant, Lynette! He's really very polite.'

'Even when he's telling you off?'

'Never tells me off,' Fionola retorted sweetly, and Lynette, patting her hair, straightening the skirt of her dark suit, shrugged and stalked off to the manager's office.

'Ah, come in, Miss Forester,' Ronan Allan called, after she'd knocked. 'Please, take a seat. I just have a couple of letters for you.'

'I have my pad,' she told him, and settling herself into the chair opposite his desk, crossed her excellent legs, took her pencil and looked at him expectantly.

Mr Allan, however, seemed far from at ease, keeping his eyes on papers on his desk and shifting his large frame in his chair as though he could not make himself comfortable. Several times he cleared his throat and Lynette put her pencil to her pad, ready to begin, but it was a false start, he said nothing.

What's the matter with him? Lynette wondered, and cleared her own throat.

'OK, Mr Allan?'

He looked up, glanced at her legs, then immediately away. 'Thing is, I'm not very good at this dictation lark,' he said at last. 'Might be easier if I just give you the letters to type.'

'Whichever you prefer,' she said smoothly.

'Seems a shame, Lynette, when you're so experienced with shorthand, not to use your skills.' He smiled as he passed across his handwritten letters. 'Maybe we could try again some other time?'

Lynette? she was thinking. He's calling me Lynette? What's come over him?

'Certainly, Mr Allan,' she answered, casting her eye down the sheets in her hand. 'Oh, excuse me – I think I've spotted something—'

'What?' he asked sharply. 'What's wrong?'

'Just a spelling error. I'll correct it, nae bother, as they say.'

'A spelling error? Let me see!'

Leaving his desk he moved swiftly to stand at her side, his eyes on his own handwriting. 'Where? Where's this spelling error you say you've found?'

'Well, actually, there are two,' she told him brightly. 'See, in this letter here, describing rooms to someone, "accommodation" has only one "m".'

'One "m"? That's ridiculous. Can't you see it's just a slip of the pen?' His brow thunderous, he was looking down at Lynette with flashing eyes. 'Just correct it, for God's sake, there was no need even to mention it. As though I wouldn't know how to spell "accommodation"!'

'I said I'd correct the errors,' she answered calmly, though her heart was bounding at the successful way she had needled him. 'But, if you're interested, further down in the same letter, you say "all the principal rooms have excellent views", but you've spelled "principal" as "principle".'

'My first point applies,' he retorted, breathing heavily. 'I was just thinking of something else – lost my concentration. You don't really believe I could confuse those two words?'

'No, Mr Allan, of course not. You're right, I shouldn't have said anything.'

He stood looking down at her for several moments, then moving back to his desk, sat down heavily.

'Lynette,' he said quietly, 'why do you do this? Why do you seek to upset me? Take such pleasure in it?'

She couldn't believe it. Couldn't believe he had said what he had. To her? As though what she did mattered?

Her eyes widening, she held on to her notebook with slightly trembling hands. 'I could say the same to you,' she answered in a low voice. 'Ever since my interview, you've found fault with me. What I wear, my telephone manner—'

'When did I criticize your telephone manner?'

'You told me I should be more definite – when I'd only been in the job five minutes! Of course I had to check my information before I could give definite replies.'

'I can't believe I ever accused you of not being definite.' He ran his hand over his brow. 'You're just magnifying remarks of mine that were never intended to be critical. I'd never take pleasure in upsetting you. Why should I?'

'I don't know. Maybe because I come from the hostel and you're prejudiced against the hostel, aren't you?'

A high colour rose slowly to his cheekbones and again he put his hand to his brow.

'I see,' he said softly. 'Someone's told you.'

'It was your home, yes. And I'm sorry you had to lose it, but it's wrong to despise the hostel just because it's taken over your old home. Wrong to feel the same way about me, too, because I live there.'

'The same way! What are you talking about? Of course I don't despise you, Lynette. And I don't despise the hostel, either. It's just that – you don't know what it meant to me to have to leave Conair House.'

She was silent, watching him, watching his face change, soften, the gold-flecked brown eyes no longer fixed on her, but looking back to scenes only he could know.

'We weren't gentry, you know,' he said, almost to himself. 'My father was a self-made man from Sheffield, my mother had worked in his first office. But all they wanted was to live somewhere like Conair, somewhere with hills and water and peace. The sort of place they'd never dreamed would be for them. But when my father made his money before the war, they came up here, found the house and bought it.' Ronan Allan's eyes turned back to Lynette. 'When we moved in, I'd never been so happy in my life.'

She looked down at her notebook and the letters he had given her to type seemed already a long time ago.

'Can you imagine it?' he asked. 'Coming to a place like this? Being able to climb hills, go fishing, learn to ride? I thought I was in paradise!'

'What happened?' she asked, at last, though of course, she knew.

He shrugged. 'The war came, Father's business collapsed. Trading with other countries, exporting, importing, none of that was possible. He did what he could but in the end was declared bankrupt. Had to sell up to pay his creditors, I had to leave my school, our whole life changed. Paradise lost, you might say.'

He leaned forward a little, keeping that strange gaze on her.

'I suppose you think I'm complaining too much? There are thousands of people – millions – worse off than me? I know that's true, but when you've been given something that means everything to you and then it's taken away – it's hard.'

'I know, I understand,' she heard herself saying, marvelling at the sympathy she'd never thought she could find for this man. 'Where did you go, then? When the crash came?'

'Back to Sheffield, back to what we were. My parents died and I went into hotel management. Worked in Yorkshire, Cornwall, several places. Then I saw this job.' He smiled a little. 'You can imagine how I felt. Couldn't believe it, a chance to be near my own home. You know the rest.'

Lynette slowly rose to her feet. 'You didn't think it would be too painful, to come back?'

'I knew it would be painful, but the pull of the Highlands was too strong. I'll admit, seeing the old house as a hostel – I suppose

I didn't take it well.' He came to stand close to her. 'Lynette, I'm sorry. You understand how it was?'

'Yes.' She looked down at his letters. 'Yes, I understand.'

'Couldn't we start again?' he asked quietly. 'Become friends?'

'Friends?'

'I'd like very much to be friends with you, Lynette.' He put out his hand. 'Shall we shake hands on that?'

Reluctantly, she put her hand into his and as she did so, feeling the firmness of his fingers clasping hers, something ran through her like an electric current. Oh, Lord, what was happening? Couldn't be, could it, that she was finding in her inner being an attraction to Ronan Allan? That sudden jolt – it was some time since she'd felt anything like it on meeting a man, but she knew well what it was. Oh, yes, she knew what it was, but she couldn't take it in. Or, wouldn't. It was just too impossible to believe.

All the same, as she freed her hand from his and moved towards the door, she was trembling again.

'I . . . must get on,' she murmured. 'Fionola will be wondering what's happened to me.'

He was with her at the door, opening it for her, looking down at her, letting her see the new softness in his gaze.

'I'm glad we've had this talk, Lynette. Or, at least, that you let me talk. I feel we've cleared the air, haven't we? Now, we can start again. You do want that, don't you?'

'Yes, of course. Why not?'

She took a firm grip on herself, returning rather to her old, crisp manner as she left him.

'I'll get these letters back to you as soon as possible, Mr Allan.'

'No hurry, Lynette. And my name is Ronan.'

'I couldn't call you that.'

'When we were alone, you could.'

Alone? Her gaze sliding away, she made no reply but moved swiftly out and he watched her go.

Twenty-Six

Lynette did not in fact return at once to Reception. Whatever was happening there, Fionola would have to cope, for she felt so strange, so at odds with all that was usual, she must have a smoke in the fresh air, or she didn't know what she'd do. Dumping Mr Allan's letters in Mrs Atkinson's little office, she took her cigarettes from her suit pocket and let herself out into the grounds from a glass side door.

Ah, that was better. Inhaling deeply, she gazed at the amazing views, on the one hand across the Sound of Sleat to Skye, on the other over Loch Hourn to Knoydart. Splendid hills, either way, some still peaked with snow, even though this was late April and there was surely a promise of warmer weather soon. But wasn't it said that in the Highlands it could be any season any time?

Her thoughts were running riot, moving everywhere except to Ronan Allan, though she knew she must face the thought of him some time. Something had happened between him and her that morning, something that couldn't be put back, and the question would have to be asked – did she want it put back?

'My name is Ronan,' he had told her. She could call him that when they were alone. Alone? No, no, she didn't feel up to thinking of that, being alone with him, calling him Ronan. No, no, look at the clouds, she told herself, look at the hills . . .

'Ha, ha, caught you!' a familiar voice whispered in her ear and she spun round to find Scott Crosbie smiling down at her, his ginger hair blowing in the wind, a cigarette at his lip. 'Hi, Lynette. You're doing just what I'm doing, eh? Having a secret smoke? Why didn't you come to the kitchen for a coffee?'

'Oh, Scott, you made me jump!' She raised a smile for him and pushed back her own blowing hair. 'I'm really supposed to be doing some typing – just dashed out to clear my head.'

'Clear your head with a cigarette?' He laughed. 'Suppose we should really be giving them up, but, hell, I don't smoke much and I lead a stressful life, don't I? I need a ciggie.'

'Do you?' she asked, as they walked a little way across the lawns. 'Do you lead a stressful life?'

'Sure I do. All chefs do. Goes with the job.' His eyes on her face were suddenly sharp. 'But you look a bit stressed yourself at the moment. What's up? The boss been at you again? Or, have you been at him?'

'You know how we are.' Her smile was bright. 'But, it's funny, I sort of feel sorry for him now.'

'Oh?' Scott looked at the cigarette between his fingers, his mouth tightening. 'First time you've said that.'

'Well, it must have been hard for him, having to leave his home. I mean, when you've had something you love and it's taken away, it can be hard.'

'That what he told you?'

Almost word for word, she thought, but said nothing.

'Trust him,' Scott muttered. 'Pulling the old heart strings. Did you ask if he played the violin? The truth is, there are a stack of folk in Scottish tenements who'd give their eye teeth for his life, eh? He's got nothing to complain about. When did he ever have to worry about the rent, or what the bairns were having to eat?'

'His father did go bankrupt, you know.'

'Aye, but I bet he didn't end up on the dole. Look, let's talk of something else. When are you coming for another cookery session?'

'Oh, soon, Scott, soon. I really enjoy helping with your fancy dishes.'

It was true. The snatched times she had spent with the cooks in her lunch hour had proved completely satisfying to her, though she had no hopes that she would ever be able to make their soups and soufflés, elaborate meat and fish dishes, gateaux and desserts.

'It's kind of all of you to let me help – I do appreciate it. Just hope I'm not too much in the way.'

'Look, you're not getting in anyone's way. We're the ones should thank you, when you're acting as unpaid kitchen maid.'

Scott tossed his cigarette end into the grass and gave Lynette a rueful smile.

'Feel guilty, in fact, that I haven't given you proper lessons yet. Maybe you could get an afternoon free some time? I have a lull about then.'

'I'll try. I could maybe work a split shift with Fionola. Though I might have to clear that with Mrs Atkinson first.'

'As long as it's not with you know who,' Scott said with a grin.

But when they re-entered the hotel, it was to see the tall figure of Ronan Allan walking down the staff corridor towards them, and Lynette's heart leaped in dismay.

'Ah, Miss Forester.' The manager's eyes were flickering between her and Scott. 'Do you have those letters for me to sign?'

'Not yet, Mr Allan. I was just taking a break, but I'll get on with them right away.'

He nodded. 'Thank you. And you, Scott, everything all right with the guests' lunch?'

'Certainly, Mr Allan.' Scott's tone was cheeky. 'Isn't it always?'

'I was just observing that you were away from the kitchens.'

'Having a wee break, like Miss Forester here. If that's OK with you?'

Flushing darkly, Mr Allan made no reply but walked away, his head held high, and Lynette, turning to Scott, touched his arm. 'I hope you haven't upset him, Scott.'

His brown eyes puzzled, he stared. 'You've changed your tune, haven't you? I thought you liked having a go at His Nibs?'

She laughed uneasily. 'Maybe I'm a reformed character.'

'Is he, though? Look, I'd better get back to work. Don't forget what I said about finding afternoon time.'

'I won't.'

She hurried away to descend on Mrs Atkinson's typewriter, rolling in paper and clattering away at Mr Allan's letters with an incredible turn of speed. When she had finished, she read them through and took them, not to his office, but Reception.

'Lynette, where on earth have you been?' Fionola cried, her beautiful eyes stormy. 'I've been rushed off my feet here, answering the phone, booking folks in – I was just about to send out an SOS.'

'Sorry, I had these letters to type. Would you be a sweetheart and take them in to Mr Allan for me? Then go and have your break.'

'Thank the Lord for that. I'm dying for my coffee.'

'Take as long as you like,' Lynette said grandly. 'I'll be here.'

Certainly will, she thought. Facing the manager in his office again was something she just didn't want to do. But, oh God, there he was some moments later, actually at Reception, gold-flecked eyes fixed on her, dark eyebrows raised.

'You didn't need to send Fionola in,' he said softly. 'Am I so terrible, you can't face me?'

'No, no, it was just that I wanted to stay here, let poor Fionola go for her break.'

'I see.' The eyebrows descended. 'Oh, well, I can breathe again. Listen, Lynette, there's something I want to tell you – though maybe Mrs Atkinson's mentioned it already?'

'Mentioned what?'

'Our ceilidh evening at the end of April. Thing is, we pride ourselves on being part of the community, and twice a year we hold a little dance that's open to everyone in the area for a small fee we give to charity. We hire a band, the guests usually join in and everyone has a good time. Have you heard about it?'

'No, I haven't, but it sounds a terrific idea.' Lynette, relaxing, was genuinely interested. 'A ceilidh – dancing – oh, I can't wait!'

He studied her, slightly biting his lip. 'There's something else I'd like to suggest. I was wondering if, this year, we should ask the young people from the hostel if they'd like to join us. They need only make a small donation. What do you think?'

'You're going to ask the hostellers? Why, that would be wonderful! They'd love it. All they get usually is a sing-song! Oh, but are you sure, Ronan?'

Somehow, the name slipped out, but she saw him jump a little and catch his breath, and then he suddenly touched her hand.

'I'm sure. The guests will be happy to see a cross section of the community, and the hostel is part of the community. I think the young folk should be here.'

'I don't know what to say. It's perfect.' She laughed. 'Apart from anything else, my dad can come as well, and he's pretty good at an eightsome reel. Oh, it's good of you. I appreciate it. Honestly.'

'Would you be willing to help Mrs Atkinson, then? You know, organizing it? Sending out invitations, discussing the buffet menus, booking the band, that sort of thing.'

'Of course I'd be willing! I'd be delighted.'

They stood together, smiling at each other, he suddenly seeming years younger, she her most attractive self, until the hotel doors flew open, the porters came in with luggage, new guests following, and as Lynette slipped smoothly into her routine, Ronan returned to his office. As he sat down at his desk, his lips still curved into a smile, he found himself humming under his breath, and recognized the tune – one used for the eightsome reel.

Twenty-Seven

News of a dance for the locals to be held at the Talisman seemed astonishing to Frank and Monnie, who hadn't been expecting anything of the sort from such a superior hotel. And any young folk at the hostel were welcome to attend as well?

'Why, that's grand, Lynette!' Frank exclaimed. 'But I thought you told us your boss didn't like the hostel? How come we're all welcome at the ceilidh?'

Lynette hesitated. 'I suppose he's finally realized the hostel is part of the community.'

'Will you be able to go?' Monnie asked, her grey eyes thoughtful on her sister. 'Can you leave Reception?'

'It's all arranged. The ceilidh won't start till eight and Mrs Atkinson has kindly said she'd stand in for Fionola and me until nine, when George, the night porter, takes over anyway.' Lynette smiled. 'Should be fun, eh? Going dancing again!'

'I'm curious to see your Mr Allan. You getting on better with him these days?'

'I don't know about that.' Lynette's expression was cagey. 'I do sort of understand his feelings, though. Must have been hard for him, leaving Conair House.'

And while her father and her sister gazed at her without comment, she quickly changed the subject from Mr Allan to his chef.

'I'm really enjoying doing a bit of cooking these days, since I managed to get an hour or two free once a week. Scott – he's the chef – has been showing me all sorts of things. Know what I helped to make the other day? A bombe glacée!'

'Fancy,' said Monnie.

'And what on earth is that?' asked Frank.

'An ice cream dessert made in layers in a special mould. Very tricky! But Scott's very good. He trained at the North British Hotel, you know in Edinburgh. Concentrates on French and Scottish, but he can do anything.'

'So, you'll be changing jobs, will you?' Frank laughed. 'Or is it just this chef you're interested in?'

'I'm not particularly interested in anyone,' Lynette retorted.

'Unlike Monnie here,' Frank said with a sigh. 'Seeing Torquil again on Saturday, eh?'

'Why not?' asked Monnie.

No one replied.

'Monnie's seeing Torquil again this afternoon,' Frank told Ishbel MacNicol in her shop on Saturday morning. 'I suppose it's all right, but I can't help worrying.'

'Because of what I told you?' she asked quickly. 'I feel rather bad about that, Frank. I shouldn't have said anything about the MacLeod boys.'

'No, you were right to let us know their reputation. After all, we're strangers here. We couldn't know past history.'

'I still feel I shouldn't have said anything.'

'Don't worry about it. If you'd never said anything at all, I'd still feel uneasy. There's just something I can't put my finger on.' He shook his head, looking down at his shopping list. 'Och, I'm probably just prejudiced.'

'Well, what can I get you, anyway? I've some lovely ham on the bone in this morning, and pork pies. What about sausages?'

One or two people came in as she was helping him with his list and they had no chance of further conversation until she was totalling up his bill.

'These for the hostel account, these for me to pay for now, for myself,' he told her, resting his eyes on her sweet face bent over the counter until she looked up and caught his look, at which he coloured a little. She only smiled and asked if he'd be going to the hotel ceilidh.

'Is it true that the young folk at the hostel can go this year? Mr Allan must be having a change of heart, then. He has never wasted much love over your hostel, Frank.'

'I know, but it's true enough. Anybody who's staying is invited this year. And yes, I'm certainly going myself. Hope you are, too.'

'I wouldn't miss it for the world!'

'So, you'll promise me the eightsome? It's the only one I know.'

'Frank, by the time the evening's over, you'll know them all,' she told him happily, and her other customers, turning round to see who Ishbel was laughing with, were not surprised to see that it was Mr Forester from the hostel. These days, it usually was.

Twenty-Eight

When Torquil came to collect her on Saturday afternoon, Monnie was waiting at the gates to the drive, in anorak and jeans again, for the skies were grey and rain was forecast. As soon as she saw him, it came to her that for what had seemed a lifetime she'd been suffering from withdrawal symptoms. Yes, he called with the fish, but those snatched moments were not enough. She really needed to be with him, just him alone, and to know that he felt the same about wanting to be with her. Of that, she couldn't be sure, but wouldn't let herself dwell on it. How could you ever be sure what someone else was thinking? All you could do was hope.

'So lovely to see you,' she whispered, sliding into the passenger street. 'Have you missed me? I mean, being with me?'

'Certainly have.' He gave her a quick smile as they began to drive away. 'Sorry about last week. But then you had your trip out with Mr Soutar.'

'Yes, it was nice. But I've already told you about that, when you came with the fish.'

'And he's taking you to Kyle?'

'Just to look at climbing boots.'

'Well, you take care when you start running up hills round here. They're not as easy as he might make out. I've done enough to know.'

'I didn't know you were a climber, Torquil.'

'Sure, I am. We all grew up climbing and hill walking. If you live in the Highlands, you do.'

'Why, then you could have taken me hill walking!'

He shrugged. 'Mr Soutar's the one with the time. You're best off with him.' His eyes slid to her and away. 'For that.'

She smiled and settled herself into her seat. 'Where are we going today, then?'

'Thought we'd just walk a bit. There is woodland off the Glenelg road where we can be on our own.'

His words might have been an answer to her prayer and her heart lifted, as he drove fast away from Conair.

'Have you heard about the ceilidh at the Talisman?' she asked after a pause. 'You'll be going, won't you?'

'Always do.'

'It's a regular thing?'

'Sure. We look forward to it.'

'Who – who do you dance with?'

'Everybody!' He laughed. 'That's what you do at that sort of dance. Do not need just one partner.'

'I see.' How quickly her spirits could fall . . . She must pull herself together, not droop like a flower out of water the minute Torquil indicated she was not the only person in his life . . .

'As a matter of fact, I do know about ceilidhs,' she said quietly. 'We have them in Edinburgh, as well as ordinary dances.'

'And you will have been in demand, then. Just as you will be at the hotel. Promise you will dance with me some time?'

'If you dance with everybody, I'm sure to be included.'

He whistled and shook his blond head. 'Oh, Monnie, you are sharp today. Am I in disgrace again?'

She shrugged. 'Where's this wood you were talking about?'

'Coming up. We turn here for the road we took to the brochs, then turn again. It's just what you might call a copse, but pretty in the spring.'

Oh, yes, it was pretty! So many trees in new leaf – birch mainly, but ash and oak, some old, some saplings, with a faint sun coming through their branches as the rain clouds moved on. Best of all, there were no people. When Torquil had parked the van and they walked together, hand in hand, there was no sound but the leaves rustling in the breeze and their footsteps moving through the grass.

'This is wonderful,' Monnie said softly. 'Thank you for bringing me here.'

'Tis difficult to be alone, even in the Highlands. Just when you think you are the only people in the universe, suddenly, someone appears.'

'I hope no one appears now.'

'So do I.'

Slowly, he took her into his arms, and they kissed, at first gently, gradually more fiercely, until their mouths meeting seemed to be all that mattered and they clung together under the trees as though they would never part. They had to part, of course, and stood staring into each other's faces, murmuring each other's names, taking breath before they kissed again. And then Torquil was unzipping Monnie's anorak and she was unfastening his shirt, as they sank to the grass, caressing and fondling, never letting go. Until Torquil suddenly sprang away, leaving Monnie bereft.

'Oh, God, this grass is wet, sweetheart – can't let you catch pneumonia. Up you come, up you come . . .'

'Oh, Torquil, Torquil . . .'

He was helping her back into her anorak, shrugging himself into his own jacket, glancing at his old watch.

'Hell, we'd better go!'

'Go where? Torquil, go where?'

'Back to Conair. I said I'd take you to my mother's. She wants to see you.'

'Your mother's?'

A great cloud was descending over Monnie, blanketing her rapture, blotting out the sunlight coming through the trees.

'I don't understand, Torquil, why does your mother want to see me? It's not as though—'

She stopped, but he swiftly took her meaning.

'Not as though we were engaged? No, we are not, but we are going out together and she just wants to be friendly. You are not from the village, so she'd like to get to know you.'

'To see if I'm suitable?'

'Suitable? Are you joking? A lovely girl from Edinburgh? You are suitable, all right.' Torquil took Monnie's arm and they began to retrace their steps to his van, Monnie glad to have his support, for she felt dazed, as though she were struggling up from some dream. 'And then Tony's coming over this afternoon. I thought you'd like to meet him.'

'Tony? Your brother? Yes, yes, I would.'

But back in the passenger seat of the van, Monnie smoothed her hands over her face, and ran a comb though her hair, frantically trying to make herself look as though she hadn't just been passionately kissing Agnes MacLeod's son in the local woods.

'I wish you'd told me about this before,' she murmured. 'I could have worn something smarter.'

'Come on, you know my mother's not one to care about smart clothes. You look beautiful, anyway.'

The words tripped easily from his lips and glancing at him it seemed to her that their first real kisses had not had the effect on him they'd had on her. Perhaps they didn't mean as much? Don't, don't, she told herself, don't go down that road. He cares, he does. And he was taking her to see his mother . . . She would soon find out what that meant, if anything.

'Here we are!' he announced jauntily. 'The home of the MacLeod's, Lords of the Isles, ha, ha! Our cottage, at least, and there's Tony's old jalopy at the door. Not to mention my mother, all ready and waiting. Come meet my folks, Monnie.'

And she was being welcomed in.

Twenty-Nine

'Come in, my dear, come in!'

Agnes MacLeod, her yellow hair drawn up with combs and her good-looking face filled with excited curiosity, was drawing Monnie over the threshold of the cottage with all the delight of an angler catching a prize fish. Not only that, was enclosing her, too, in a warm, soft hug that sent a great burst of lavender over her hair and made Monnie move guiltily aside to free herself.

'It's really nice to meet you again, Mrs MacLeod,' she said politely, as she tried not to be too obvious in looking round Torquil's home.

The low-ceilinged room was small, with one tiny window and an old fashioned kitchen range, roaring away. A table laid for tea stood against the back wall and a settle, piled with cushions, papers, knitting and pieces of sewing, took up most of the floor space. Staring at her with suspicious eyes from a basket by the range was a large ginger cat, who eventually slid away and disappeared through a door to what looked like a scullery.

'Yes, off you go, Toffee!' Agnes cried merrily, and moving some knitting from the settle invited Monnie to sit down.

'Oh, 'tis lovely to meet you properly at last, Miss Forester, or may I call you Monnie?' Agnes's clear eyes were busily going over Monnie's flushed face as she sat beside her. 'I first saw you on the bus, with your family – do you remember? How you all looked so worried! And then I've seen you around the village, but not really to speak to, so I am looking forward to a nice talk. Give me your coat, dear, and we'll hang it up. There are pegs behind the door.'

'Mother, Monnie hasn't met Tony yet,' Torquil murmured, as he hung up Monnie's anorak, along with what looked like all the coats of the household, on the back of the front door. 'Tony, come and meet Monnie Forester. She's assistant warden at the hostel.'

A tall blond young man rose from a chair by the kitchen range and shook Monnie's hand, murmuring it was nice to meet her.

At first, she'd thought she was seeing a second Torquil and her heart had jumped a little, but she soon recognized the differences. Yes, there was the same colouring – yellow hair and blue eyes, and also the same look of Agnes – but there was a certain foxiness about this man's manner that was missing from Torquil's, and he seemed to make it plain that he was not out to charm. Still, he was handsome. Monnie could imagine him attracting the girls, especially if they liked a spice of danger.

'How'd you like it here, then?' he asked politely.

'Oh, I love it, thanks. We all do. The Highlands suit us very well.'

'Now, isn't that nice?' asked Agnes. 'And you've got your own things in the warden's flat, have you? That always makes a difference.'

'Yes, they've arrived and we've made a very nice home of it.'

'I'm so glad. Well, now we're all here, we'll have our tea.' Agnes waved to her boys to pull up chairs. 'I will put on my kettle and find a plate for my girdle scones. They're just a touch caught on, but not burnt.'

As Tony and Torquil exchanged glances, Monnie asked if she could do anything to help.

'Oh, no, dear, it's all in hand. I've just the tea to make and Ishbel's coffee cake to cut.'

'Ishbel MacNicol, are you meaning?' Tony asked curtly. 'Why you patronize that woman is beyond me. She is nothing but a gossip and a troublemaker.'

'Now, Tony . . .' Agnes began, casting a hasty look towards Monnie. 'I don't like to hear you talking like that. Ishbel can be very sweet.'

'Sweet at spreading rumours, I'd say.'

'We are not meeting to speak ill of people, Tony, and Monnie's father gives Ishbel a lot of custom, from the hostel, you know. They get on very well, don't they, my dear?'

'Do they?' Monnie raised surprised eyes. 'Dad just does his shopping at Mrs MacNicol's. It is the only shop, after all.'

'Of course it is, which is why I don't want to open up old wounds, something Tony does not have to worry about. I mean, where else would I shop?'

'All right, Mother, you've made your point.' Tony's face had settled into sulky lines. 'Let us have this tea you said was ready.'

They moved to sit at the table which was covered with a linen cloth that made the MacLeod boys stare – clearly it had been brought out specially – and thick white china. Agnes seemed to be in her element, passing round her 'caught on' scones, all thickly buttered, and cups of strong, sweet tea, before handing out Ishbel's coffee cake, which Tony, everyone noticed, did not refuse.

'No point in wasting it, if you've bought it,' he muttered. 'I just wish you didn't have to go to her shop in the first place. You could always get Torquil to run you into Glenelg.'

'Oh, yes?' Torquil asked. 'And when would I have time to do that?'

'Of course you have no time,' Agnes declared. 'No, no, Tony, you leave the shopping to me. I have to get on with Ishbel, whatever we think of her. And now, if we've all finished tea, what about you two laddies splitting some wood for me out the back? That stove just eats fuel, eh?'

'Want us out of the way?' Torqil asked, glancing at Monnie,

who was feeling too hot and too full, and perhaps looked it.
'Monnie and me should be moving on.'

''Twill not take you but a moment,' Agnes said, whisking off
the tablecloth. 'I just want a nice little chat with Monnie on her
own. Off you go, then!'

'Perhaps I could help you with the washing up?' Monnie asked
faintly, but Agnes said she wouldn't hear of it and led her back
to the settle.

'Now, dear, you will not be minding that I want to say a few
words to you between ourselves?'

'Not at all.' Monnie sighed, as Agnes fixed her with her piercing
blue eyes and for a moment laid a plump hand over hers.

'Seeing as Tony has already spoken of Ishbel, you see, I wanted
to make it plain that there are people in this village – and she is
one – who talk against my boys with no justification whatsoever.
No doubt, you have already heard the things that are said?'

'Well . . .' Having no idea how much she should say, Monnie
paused, but Agnes was not waiting for any answers, only wanting
to press on with her own case for the defence.

'Now, what folk like to tell you is that my boys are wild, which
of course they are not. A little mischievous, perhaps, when they
were young, but you will know Torquil – there is no harm in
him, eh? No harm at all.' Agnes smiled winningly.

'And Tony's the same, but he is always blamed for that business
with the foolish MacDonnell lassie, who was simply no better
than she ought to be and led him on. I mean, can you blame
him, if there was a baby in the end? He never said he loved her,
he never promised to marry her, he told me so himself, and what
I'm saying to you, Monnie, my dear, is that he was not to blame.
You see that, don't you?'

'I heard that the girl had to move away,' Monnie ventured at
last. 'That seems a shame.'

'She only had to do that because her parents were so strict.
Oh, terrible religious, they were – still are – and would not
have her in the house. So, she went to a cousin's in Inverness,
but that was not Tony's fault, was it? And things turned out
well, for she met some man who accepted the baby and now
she is happily married. So why has everyone got their knife
into poor Tony?'

'Seems strange,' Monnie agreed.

'And you do see, dear, that you've nothing to worry about where my boys are concerned?' Agnes went on softly. 'Both Tony and Torquil are lovely laddies, very kind to me, who's had to bring them up all alone, seeing as their dad died at sea.'

And again the plump hand was laid over Monnie's.

'Has not been easy for me,' she whispered. 'But I am proud of my boys and only want their happiness. That's why I am talking to you like this now. For I think Torquil could be happy with you. I can tell, you see, I know him so well. And I think I know you too, my dear. You care for him, eh?'

Monnie, unwilling to answer, heard herself answering all the same. 'Yes, that's true.'

With a sigh of relief, Agnes sat back, her eyes alight.

'Ach, I am so glad we had this little talk, Monnie. Everything will be all right now, you will see. I'll just give the boys a call. They should have finished out there now.'

It seemed to take an age for Monnie and Torquil to get themselves out of his mother's cottage. So many farewells, embraces, pressing of hands – heavens, Agnes was like a great feather eiderdown, wrapping herself so tightly round the leave-takers they could scarcely breathe, while Tony lay back in an armchair, smoking and grinning.

Finally, they were out of the door, waving to Agnes, who was crying, 'Come again soon, Monnie! Torquil, be sure to bring her.'

'OK, OK,' he called back, then hooking Monnie's arm into his, led the way down to the little jetty that lay behind the cottages.

'You're looking pale, Monnie. Like some fresh air?'

'Oh, please!'

'Mother's place gets a wee bit warm, 'tis true.' He gave an indulgent smile. 'She likes to pile up that range with wood and get a real old heat going. Too much for most of us, even Toffee, our cat.'

'Didn't see Toffee again. Where did he go?'

'Ach, he will be away mousing. Great mouser. And would not want to be with you, seeing as you are a stranger.'

'I don't think your mother wants me to be a stranger,' Monnie said after a pause. 'She made me very welcome.'

Torquil, studying her face, drew her gently towards a bench from where they could sit and look out across the Sound to Skye. Everything was very still, very beautiful, the water pale beneath the rise of the facing shore and the great dark silhouetted hills. No one was about.

His arm around her shoulders, Torquil suddenly held Monnie close. 'What did my mother say to you?' he asked, lightly. 'While we were chopping the wood?'

'It was more about Tony, really.' Monnie's eyes were fixed on a boat moored at the jetty. It was covered with tarpaulin, but she could see the hump of an outboard motor and, where the cover did not quite fit, a painted name. "Lord of the Isles". She turned her eyes on Torquil.

'How the things people say about him aren't true, and the girl who had the baby was to blame for leading him on.'

Torquil sighed and loosened his arm from her shoulders. 'I can tell from your voice you do not believe that.'

'I don't know what to believe.'

In fact, Monnie felt strangely unwell, as though she had fallen through a great hole and could not regain herself. For all that Agnes had said to excuse her sons – and it wasn't possible to exclude Torquil – had seemed to have had the opposite effect from what Agnes had wanted. The more she described their virtues, the less Monnie felt convinced.

'A little mischievous', she had said of them when they were young. But how mischievous? There seemed nothing particularly mischievous about Torquil now, so perhaps it was true, he'd only behaved as boys do and had now become an adult and sensible. That was how Monnie had defended him already, but the odd thing was that when his mother defended him and his brother, it seemed to make it more likely that the two MacLeods were as wild as everybody said.

'It may be true that the girl was partly to blame,' she said slowly. 'Who knows? But when the baby was on the way, Tony should have supported her. Don't you agree, Torquil?'

'Hell, I don't know the truth of it any more than you do.' Torquil was staring at the clouds streaking the evening sky, his fine mouth set in severe lines, his shoulders drooping. 'But I am not going to run down my own brother. You would not be expecting that?'

'No, of course not.' She was beginning to feel she must salvage something of their evening together, must not go home on a low note that would ruin her days until she saw Torquil again.

'Let's talk of something else,' she whispered, taking his hand. 'I was wondering, is that your boat down there?'

His face lit up. 'It is, then! I keep it here mostly, though there's a boat house I could use further along the shore.'

'I like the name,' she laughed. 'Suits you, eh?'

'Sure, it does.' He was laughing too. 'But 'tis my little joke. No one believes Tony and me are the Lords of the Isles.'

'Why haven't you taken me out in the boat yet? The water's so calm, it would be lovely, to have a trip.'

'It is not always calm, and that boat – not like my van – does smell of fish.'

He was drawing her into his arms again, and she was surfacing from the dark hole where she had been trapped, finding solace from the thoughts that had been troubling her, melting into an embrace so exquisite she wanted it never to end.

'But I will take you out in my boat,' Torquil was whispering. 'If you promise not to expect too much.'

'As though I would. But when shall we go? Next Saturday?'

'Have you forgotten? Next Saturday is the hotel ceilidh.'

But she couldn't really think of next Saturday while they clung together, kissing, exploring, not minding that the evening was darkening and growing colder, that the lights were coming on in little dots of brightness across the water, and the wind was rising.

'Time to go home,' Torquil said, releasing her at last. 'And how I wish we could just stay here!'

'Oh, so do I! Or, that we had places of our own.'

'If I had a place of my own, I could never invite you back. And do not look so startled. You know why that would be.'

'Why?' she still asked, as they turned to leave their little haven.

'You would be too much of a temptation, I would never risk it.' She saw him smiling in the dusk. 'I am not my brother.'

And afterwards, much later, when she could think straight again, she realized that that was the closest Torquil had come to telling her his true feelings about Tony. Oh, but who cared about Tony? Lying in her bed, listening to Lynette's even breathing in sleep, only one man was in Monnie's thoughts. And always would be.

Thirty

Lynette did not always sleep so soundly; sometimes, she lay awake, thinking against her will of Ronan Allan. Since that extraordinary day when he'd seemed to open his heart to her over his boyhood trauma, he'd said very little to her. Mrs Atkinson had returned from leave, there had been no need for Lynette to do secretarial work for him, and she had the feeling that he was keeping out of her way. Except, when they did meet, those unusual eyes of his never seemed to leave her face. While her own eyes kept looking away.

And now there was the ceilidh to occupy everyone's minds. So much to do, Mrs Atkinson kept reminding them, to organize and plan.

'And, oh, isn't she enjoying herself?' Fionola had sighed. 'But we shall all be roped in.'

Lynette's own problem was what to wear. She discussed it with Monnie over her usual hasty breakfast, the day after Monnie's tea party with Agnes MacLeod, but took only a short time to decide that her sister was still half asleep.

'What's up with you?' she asked sharply. 'Your eyes are glazed, you look as though you're a hundred miles away.'

'No, I'm not!' Monnie retorted. 'I'm thinking about my plans for improving the common room. It's time we made some improvements, isn't it, Dad?'

'Talk about quick thinking!' Lynette exclaimed. 'Bet you've just dreamed that one up.'

'No, Monnie and I have already discussed what we could do,' Frank told her. 'Problem is funding. One idea is to put up more bookshelves, make a little library for paperbacks and such, and that wouldn't cost much, but then we think we should have a new record player, plus records, of course, and a snooker table.' He shook his head. 'We'll have to see what we're allowed.'

Scarcely listening, Lynette was watching Monnie.

'You've kept very quiet about where you went with Torquil yesterday. 'What did you get up to, then? Go looking at more historical sites?'

'As a matter of fact, we had tea with Mrs MacLeod.'

'Tea with Agnes?' Frank repeated, staring.

'Tea with Torquil's mother?' Lynette cried. 'Monnie, what's happened? Are you engaged, or something?'

'Of course not! She just wanted to meet me and have a talk.'

'But for a chap to take a girl to meet his mother, that usually means something.' Frank's eyes were bleak. 'What's going on, Monnie?'

'Nothing. It wasn't Torquil who wanted to take me, I tell you, it was his mother who wanted to meet me.' Monnie stood up, gathering the breakfast dishes, her grey eyes mutinous. 'Why are you trying to see something that isn't there? What Agnes wanted to do was make excuses for Tony, that was all. She thought I might have heard gossip.'

'Which we have,' said Lynette, helping to clear the table.

'Yes, from Mrs MacNicol.' Monnie glanced at her father. 'Tony was there yesterday and he was rather bitter about her. Said she was a troublemaker.'

'He said what?' Frank was flushing scarlet. 'What the hell gives him the right to talk like that about Ishbel? She was only speaking the truth about him and if I see him, I'll give him a piece of my mind, I can tell you!'

'Dad, calm down,' said Lynette, surprised. 'Better not get involved with Tony MacLeod, I'd say. He's the troublemaker.'

'I've got to go,' was all Frank replied, and pushing back his chair, he left the table and strode out.

'Why so steamed up?' Lynette asked Monnie. 'I've never seen him get mad so quickly.'

Monnie shrugged. 'You'd better go for your bus, if you don't want to be late.'

'Yes, and we haven't even discussed what we're going to wear for this ceilidh.'

'Oh, nothing special. I don't suppose it matters what we wear.'

'It does to me,' Lynette said firmly. 'We did bring our old

sewing machine, didn't we? I think I might see if I can get some material in Kyle and run something up.' She put her hand on Monnie's arm. 'Before we go, what did Agnes say about Torquil? She must have said something.'

'Just that he was a bit mischievous as a boy.'

'Somehow, I can imagine that.'

Monnie's face was expressionless. 'Shouldn't you be off now?'

'I'm on my way. Want to come with me to Kyle, if I can get the time off?'

'No, thanks, I'd better wait and go with Paul.'

Thank goodness she at least wants to do that, Lynette thought, running for her bus. Clearly, Paul Soutar would be better in every way for Monnie than Torquil MacLeod, but there was no point in telling her that. You couldn't tell people who to love. Lynette's pretty mouth twisted a little. Couldn't even tell yourself.

At the reception desk, when she slipped quietly in – not late, after all – she found Fionola stifling a yawn as she stood behind Mrs Atkinson, who was already declaiming from her clipboard.

'Just checking on the arrangements for Saturday,' she informed Lynette. 'To make sure you're both au fait with what we have to do.'

'As though she hasn't done that already half a dozen times,' Lynette heard Fionola mouth under her breath, and managed to hide her smile.

'First,' Mrs Atkinson was continuing, 'there'll be the guests to advise on the change of dinner plans. Tables will be set in the conservatory for those wishing the usual meal, but quite a lot of people have already opted for the buffet at the ceilidh, so we need to finalize numbers there. And then I need one of you to tell Scott to let Mr Allan have his menus as soon as possible, so that he can go through them—'

'I can do that,' Lynette volunteered, and Mrs Atkinson gave a little smile.

'Oh, yes, you get on well with Scott, don't you, dear? I expect coming from the same city is quite a bond for you. And then I hear he's been giving you a few cookery lessons – isn't that right?'

'Only in our free time,' Lynette said hastily. 'Which reminds me, would it be possible for me to be away tomorrow afternoon? I really need to buy some material to make a skirt for the dancing.'

Mrs Atkinson looked dubious. 'I think you'd better clear that with Mr Allan.'

'Oh, couldn't you just give me the OK? I really don't want to be bothering him—'

'You could ask him now, he's just coming over.'

Her heart sinking, Lynette turned her head to see the manager approaching, looking, as he so often did, like some very tall officer of the law, and making Lynette feel, as he so often did, that she'd just been found out in doing something wrong. Oh, well, if he wanted to turn down her request, so be it. Maybe she wouldn't go to the ceilidh, after all, if he couldn't be more cooperative . . .

'Mr Allan, Lynette would like to take a few hours off tomorrow afternoon,' Mrs Atkinson said crisply. 'Is that all right?'

'A few hours off?' The gold-flecked eyes rested on Lynette's defiant face, and a slight smile transformed the manager's face. 'I don't see why not. Is there some special reason, Lynette?'

'Just want to go to Kyle for some material,' she answered huskily. 'To make something for the dance on Saturday.'

'Don't tell me,' he said lightly. 'You haven't a thing to wear. By all means, go to Kyle, Lynette. I'm sure Fionola will look after things here.'

'Oh, yes, Mr Allan,' Fionola said quickly. 'No trouble at all.'

'Fine, fine. Mrs Atkinson, I was just coming to look for you – could we go through your arrangements for Saturday again, in my office?'

'Certainly, Mr Allan.'

'Hey, what's your secret?' Fionola asked Lynette. 'How d'you manage to get Mr Allan do what you want? And make a joke as well?'

'Well, didn't you say he was really very nice?' Lynette countered. 'To you, anyway. So, why not me?'

'You used not to like him.'

And as Fionola's almond-shaped eyes slid away, it dawned on Lynette that she might be interested in Mr Allan. Interested, though not in love, for she didn't give that impression and usually you could tell if that was the case. Love will out, and so on . . . No, maybe she just wanted to set her cap at him? Maybe he had in fact, shown himself attracted to her, and she'd thought he might be quite a good catch? The idea that he liked to keep his eyes on Lynette herself might be purely a product of her imagination. All the same, it was plain enough that the younger girl was jealous of Lynette's apparent power over him, which was a piece of nonsense, if ever there was one!

'Are you bringing anyone to the ceilidh?' she managed to ask in between work on routine tasks. 'Any boyfriends, for instance?'

'I have no boyfriend,' Fionola answered shortly.

'Don't tell me there aren't some fellows hanging around you in Shiel Bridge.'

Lynette knew, of course, that though Fionola had to live in at the hotel, her home being too far away for her to travel in every day, she did return there quite regularly. And for a girl of her looks, there must surely be a queue of young men somewhere in her life? Unless, she didn't want them. Unless, she had her sights set elsewhere?

'I'm not interested.' As the telephone began to ring, Fionola took the call, her lovely face serene, and Lynette, turning to find a guest's key, knew she would say no more.

Later, having coffee with Scott in the kitchen, Lynette told him she'd be out the next afternoon, shopping in Kyle. Mr Allan had said she could have a few hours off to buy material for a new skirt, for the ceilidh.

'Oho, getting more and more pally with His Nibs, are we?' Scott asked coldly, as his staff weaved around the kitchen, busy already with the lunch menu. 'To think there was a time when you said you couldn't stand him.'

'I'm still not sure what I think of him. He can be quite friendly.'

'If you ask me, he lives in a straitjacket, invented by himself. As I always say, what's he got to complain about? In the meantime, spare a thought for me at the ceilidh, stuck at the buffet. Story of my life.'

'Oh, Scott! You'll get some time off, surely.'

'Enough to have a dance with you, I hope.'

'You've only to ask me.'

'As long as you know who doesn't get in first.'

'I'm wondering if he won't be dancing with my assistant,' Lynette said lightly, as Scott topped up her coffee.

'Ah, our resident beauty.' Scott shook his head. 'Bet there'll be a line up to dance with her.'

'And you'll be in it?'

'No' if you're around,' he said seriously, and finishing her coffee quickly, Lynette said she must be getting back to work.

On her way back to Reception, she found herself hoping Scott wasn't getting interested. He was a great guy, someone she really admired and felt at ease with – not because, as Mrs A had suggested, he came from her own city, but because he was who he was. The last man, you might think, to be a chef, considering the reputation chefs had for being touchy, temperamental, even fiery, for Scott was quite the reverse. Not in the least touchy, or volatile, or likely to blow up if the soufflé went down, but just a likeable fellow you could always trust, with no hidden depths to worry about.

On the other hand – she felt guilty thinking it, yet knew it was true – he was not the type to fall in love with. And who was the type? Lynette drove the question from her mind, thankfully finding that the desk was busy when she got back and she had no more time for uncomfortable musings.

Thirty-One

Finally, it arrived, the night of the Talisman ceilidh.

Oh, the excitement! You could feel it before anyone even set foot in the long dining room cleared for the dancing, or the lounge beyond, where there were little tables and chairs, balloons and streamers, Scott's buffet trestle at the end of the room and flower arrangements on corner pedestals.

But when the band – two fiddlers, an accordion player, a bass player, a guitarist and a pianist – took their seats round the dining-room piano and the first guests began to appear, Lynette felt things had really reached fever pitch.

'It's because we're so starved of any entertainment here, we're all ready to go mad just because we have a ceilidh,' she whispered to Scott, who had surfaced from the kitchen for a moment. 'I know I can't wait to get on to that floor!'

'Know how long it took the guys to polish it?' he asked, just wanting to look at her in her thin white blouse and full scarlet skirt, clinched at her waist with a scarlet belt, her blue eyes sparkling, her lips parted, the image, it seemed, of youth, vitality and beauty.

'Lynette, you look so terrific tonight,' he said in a low voice. 'How am I going to leave you?'

'You know you're just dying to show off that buffet of yours,' she answered, her eyes now on the door, searching for Frank and Monnie, and after a moment or two, Scott had no choice but to take himself away.

Still no sign of them, thought Lynette, hoping her father's car hadn't broken down. She had been all day at the hotel herself, only changing into her dancing clothes in Fionola's room after kind Mrs Atkinson had relieved them shortly before eight o'clock. Och, they'd surely be along in a minute, and she was already, in spite of herself, looking out for someone else. Someone she'd seen quite recently, still in his dark suit, looking just the same as usual, would you believe? What a death's head at a party . . .

'Good evening, Lynette,' a tall man in a dark red kilt said quietly, adding, as she stared, 'don't you know me?'

'M-Mr Allan?' she stammered.

'Ronan.'

Of course, of course. His face was the same, his eyes were the same, his voice, his height . . .

'It was just the tartan . . .'

'The MacDonald of Clanranald, I am entitled to wear it. I hope you approve?'

'Oh, yes, yes – it's fine . . . suits you.'

'Thank God you think so. You don't know what it costs a fellow who's not used to it, to show his legs.'

He laughed and she laughed too, but he was soon serious.

'Lynette, you won't need me to tell you that you're looking most attractive tonight.' He hesitated. 'Most attractive . . . Is that the skirt you made from the material you went to buy?'

'It is. Do you like it?'

'I'm wondering if it's meant to make a statement?'

'A statement?'

'Well, it's red, isn't it?'

Her eyes widened. 'You're not serious? Comparing this skirt to that red suit you told me not to wear? I never gave it a thought!'

'I'm so glad,' he said earnestly. 'That was a bad disagreement we had. Will you believe me, if I tell you I've been sorry about it ever since. When I saw you in your beautiful red skirt just now, I thought . . . God, I don't know, that maybe you hadn't forgiven me.'

In spite of the guests now swirling around them, the chatter of voices, the tuning up from the band, they seemed suddenly to be quite alone, just two people, making peace, gazing into each other's eyes.

'I didn't even know you wanted me to forgive you,' Lynette said, so quietly he had to lean forward to hear her. 'How could I, when you never said?'

He put his hand to his brow and shook his head.

'You see how hopeless I am? I haven't an idea what to do – how to go on . . . oh, Lynette—'

'Lynette!' came her father's voice and there he was beside them, not only with Monnie, looking very pretty in a blue dress Lynette knew well, but also Ishbel MacNicol, coolly attractive in a pale pink blouse and tartan skirt.

'We've been looking all over for you,' Frank shouted cheerfully above the surrounding noise. 'Sorry, we're late. Had to change a tyre on the way.'

'You didn't!' Lynette groaned, then, smiling, introduced her father and sister to Ronan, who, recovering himself well, welcomed them with ease and surprising charm, saying how delighted he was to meet them and he hoped they'd have a wonderful time.

'Mrs MacNicol, of course, I know,' he added, giving Ishbel a slight bow. 'Sells the best fudge in the whole of Scotland, which is my undoing, I can tell you!'

He tapped his waist, grinning, as Lynette looked on in wonder, and Ishbel, turning as pink as her blouse, told him she'd be firm in future and ration his purchases.

'Don't your dare!' he cried, but then asked if they would excuse him, he had to make a short speech of welcome.

'What a charming fellow!' Frank exclaimed, as Ronan made his way through the crowd to the band. 'I thought you said he was some sort of ogre, Lynette? Why, he couldn't have been nicer!'

'Mr Allan an ogre?' Ishbel exclaimed. 'Never! He's always very polite and pleasant when he comes to my shop.'

'I must say, he's not how I pictured him,' Monnie put in, and Lynette, colouring furiously, threw back her head and said folks had to speak as they found, eh?

'And I have to say that Mr Allan hasn't always been the easiest of people to work with. He can be very nice, I know, but even Mrs Duthie said he was difficult.'

'Speaking of angels, there is Mrs Duthie,' Frank murmured, eyeing his cleaning lady, resplendent in orange blouse and Royal Stewart tartan kilt, chattering to the fiddler in the band, just as Ronan held up his hand for silence.

'Of angels?' Ishbel whispered. 'I am not so sure about that!'

But the room full of people had fallen silent, waiting for the manager to say his few words and let them get on with the dancing, and he did not disappoint them. No sooner had he made his short welcome and reminded everyone that the buffet would be served at ten o'clock, he was turning to the band, waving his hand, and announcing that the first dance would be 'Strip the Willow'. And could he see everyone on the floor – *please!*

'Ishbel, may I have the pleasure?' Frank asked, in courtly fashion, at which she gave him her hand, smiling, and away they went to join the couples already on the floor, while Frank's daughters stood together, waiting.

'Where is he, then?' Lynette asked, while trying to see if a man in a Clanranald tartan was approaching.

'You mean Torquil?' Monnie's tone was casual, as though she wasn't at all concerned if her sister meant someone else.

'Well, I don't mean Tony, who's just come in with Agnes. Oh, get that huge kilt she's wearing! How many yards of tartan has it taken to go round her waist, then?'

'There's no need to be rude about her,' Monnie retorted, but her eyes had begun to take on an anxious look as they raked the faces of people still joining the dancers. Until, suddenly, she saw him. Torquil, on the floor. Torquil, slim and elegant in the dark green MacLeod tartan. Torquil, waiting for the music, preparing to dance, but not with her.

'Oh, God,' she whispered. 'He's with that girl from the café. Oh, I can't believe it.'

'What girl?' Lynette asked, bristling. 'What's he playing at?'

'She works in the tea shop, he was at school with her.' Monnie's lips were so stiff she could hardly speak. 'Oh, I never thought he'd not be dancing with me!'

'Of course he'll be dancing with you. Why, I bet she caught him at the door as he came in!' Lynette's voice was suddenly icy. 'Like someone else I can see from here. Would you credit it?'

'Credit what?' Monnie asked dully, her eyes still watching Torquil and the girl from the tea shop, now smiling at each other and gliding away together as the music started.

'Fionola has asked Ronan Allan to dance. Look, there they are, tripping away down the room. Oh, it's too bad!'

'Why, what do you care who Mr Allan dances with?'

Monnie, just for a second, turned her gaze from Torquil to her sister. 'I didn't think you'd be dancing with him anyway.'

'Oh, I don't care,' Lynette retorted. 'I don't care at all. I just don't want to be a wallflower.'

Wallflowers. There was no chance they would be that. First, Fergus, playing truant from the kitchen, came up to sweep Lynette on to the floor, to be followed by one of the hotel guests who escorted Monnie. Somehow, each sister managed to produce a brilliant smile, and as they progressed through the dance, pretended not even to notice when two young men tried to catch their eyes. It was only when 'Strip the Willow' was over and the two men came to them, that their own eyes flashed fire and the recriminations began.

Thirty-Two

Torquil's blue eyes were innocently clear; his expression puzzled.

'What's wrong?' he asked, trying to take Monnie's hand, which she snatched away. 'What have I done?'

As she made no reply, only turned her head and stared away, her face stony, he groaned and shook his head.

'Ach, it is Nina you are upset about, eh? Because I danced "Strip the Willow" with her? But, Monnie, what could I do? I was late arriving and she asked me the minute I came through the door. I could not refuse, could I?'

'Could not refuse?' Monnie had swung round to face him. 'Why could you not refuse?'

'Well, it would have hurt her feelings. And it was only one dance, because here I am with you.' His smile was disarming. 'Come on, now, give me your hand and let us dance this Scottish waltz they are playing now.'

'Why didn't you just tell her you'd be dancing with me?' she whispered, allowing herself to be led on to the floor. 'You knew I'd be waiting for you.'

'Sweetheart, I was looking for you, but there were so many folk, I couldn't see you.'

She was a little mollified and as they moved into the Scottish waltz, a quiet, gentle dance she had always loved, she began to feel happier. To be with him again, to be close, to feel his hand in hers, was enough to be working familiar magic over her, and already she knew she was surrendering to its spell.

'I am not the only one in trouble,' he suddenly whispered against her face. 'I can see from here that your sister is looking daggers at Mr Allan.'

'Oh? Well, they often have arguments,' Monnie murmured uneasily.

'Aye, he gets on better with the lovely Fionola, eh? Saw him dancing with her in "Strip the Willow".'

The lovely Fionola . . . A coldness hit Monnie's heart, but she tried to smile. 'You think she's lovely? I don't know her, but Lynette has told me she's beautiful.'

'Too beautiful for ordinary mortals.' Torquil laughed. 'Fishermen like me, for instance.'

Instantly, Monnie's forced smile vanished. 'You asked her out, Torquil?'

'Me? No! To me, she is . . . unreal. Besides, I told you, she only has eyes for rich hotel guests. Or else, the manager. Maybe that's what annoyed your sister?'

'My sister doesn't care about the manager,' Monnie answered loftily, but at that Torquil only smiled.

Across the room, Ronan was trying desperately to placate Lynette, who, as Torquil had described it, had been looking daggers at him ever since he'd joined her.

'I appear to be in disgrace,' he was murmuring. 'If so, I'm sorry. All I want to do is dance with you and now the music is playing and we shall soon be too late. Couldn't we go on the floor?'

'If you wanted to dance with me, you might have asked me before,' she answered coldly. 'I did "Strip the Willow" with someone else.'

'Lynette, Fionola asked me and you know I have to dance with people on the staff. I could scarcely refuse.'

'I'm sure that's just what Torquil MacLeod has been saying to my sister.'

'Torquil?' Ronan looked bewildered. 'What's he got to do with it?'

'Nothing. Forget it.'

Lynette was standing, tapping her foot, annoyed with herself for showing her feelings, yet unable, somehow, to conceal them, and then, as Scott Crosbie appeared suddenly in the doorway, wished with all her heart she could have been dancing with him. How easy it would be! How pleasant and painless, not to be all worked up and stressed as she was now! Her gaze reluctantly moving to Ronan's quite anxious face, she sighed and shrugged.

'Well, as I'm a member of staff, I suppose we should dance this waltz before it finishes. What do you say?'

'Lynette, you know it's what I'm waiting for!'

As they stepped together on to the floor, Lynette gave another quick look towards the door and didn't know whether to feel sad or relieved that Scott was no longer there.

After the waltz, there was an eightsome, and as they hadn't really had much time dancing together, Ronan said they might as well stay as partners for that.

'And look who's here!' he remarked with a grin, and Lynette laughed, because opposite her was her father, whose partner was again Ishbel, and as the music began and they weaved in and out in the pattern of the dance, it vaguely crossed Lynette's mind that she hadn't seen Frank look so happy in a very long time. Monnie and Torquil were dancing in another set, but Lynette decided to ask her sister later if she had noticed how happy, and even youthful, their father was looking, and wasn't it strange, that they'd never realized before how much he liked dancing?

The eightsome was followed by 'The Duke and Duchess of Edinburgh', then 'Kate Dalrymple' and 'Petronella', and still Ronan showed no desire to partner anyone other than Lynette, while Torquil stayed with Monnie, and Frank with Ishbel. Was anyone noticing? wondered Lynette. Maybe not. But then her eyes caught Mrs Anderson, who had left Reception and joined the ceilidh, and it was clear enough, from her wry smile, that she had not missed a trick.

What of it? Lynette's lips curved into a smile. One thing was certain, she was not going to stop dancing with Ronan because people were noticing. He felt the same as she did, she was sure. How could he not, when they were both buoyed up by the special, heady excitement of a possible new relationship? When you say yes, this could be it! And climb together to Cloud Nine, or else go dancing to it.

'Buffet time,' Ronan was murmuring. 'Lynette, I'll have to dash – check that Scott's finished setting it all out.'

'I'll go with you,' she said at once. 'But don't worry, it'll be lovely, Scott always knows what he's doing.'

Sure enough, the buffet table looked splendid, the excellent choices beautifully displayed: cold chicken, cold ham, roast beef, salmon on special dishes, decorated with cucumber and mayonnaise to hand, potato salads, green salads, mounds of rolls, curls of butter, cheeses . . .

And behind it all, ready to serve, Scott with his staff, all bubbling with excitement except Scott himself, whose face under his chef's hat was distinctly long and whose reproachful eyes on Lynette made her own gaze fall.

'Scott, this looks wonderful!' Ronan was saying heartily, 'Congratulations to you and your team. Well done, all of you!'

But poor Scott, Lynette was thinking, he's out of all the fun, while we're enjoying ourselves.

'When the buffet's over, you'll come out and have a dance, won't you?' she asked him quietly, but his mouth twisted a little and he shrugged.

'A dance with you? Sure you can fit me in?'

'Oh, come on, Scott! You said you'd dance with me.'

'I'll announce the buffet,' Ronan said, moving off, but Scott was already on his way to the other end of the table, leaving Lynette to stand back before the guests came pouring in.

Thirty-Three

'Oh, my, what a scrum!' Frank said happily, as he and Ishbel sat together with their loaded plates. 'Have you ever seen so many happy faces?'

'The Talisman buffet is the highlight of the year for a lot of people, my son for one,' she told him, laughing. 'I can see him from here – I think he'll be coming over.'

'You son will?' Frank, looking a little put out, laid down his fork. 'Well, I'd better be quick, then. Just want to tell you, Ishbel, that it's a long time since I enjoyed myself as much as I have tonight.'

'I want to say the same thing,' she answered softly, her eyes meeting his.

'So, where's your son, then?'

'Waiting for Sheana – that's my daughter-in-law – to finish choosing.' She leaned forward, touching Frank's hand lightly. 'I do want you to meet them both, Frank.'

'Oh, sure. I want to meet them, too.'

'And the ceilidh's not over yet.'

'That's the best bit, Ishbel.'

As they began to eat again, their smiles on each other very sweet, guests were filling up plates, laughing, talking, sitting at little tables, some even opting for the floor, though Frank and Ishbel weren't watching. Didn't even notice for a time that Monnie and Torquil were close by, with Lynette and Ronan, while Agnes, Tony, Nina and her sister, Jill, were at the next table. Not far away, Mrs Atkinson (now answering to Ailsa) and her husband, John, were sitting with Fionola and a portly hotel guest named Ernest Warner, who was making Lynette smile.

'Oh, my, do you see the way that guy is looking at Fionola?' she whispered to Monnie. 'Maybe he thinks Christmas has come early this year?'

'Ssh,' Monnie whispered back. 'Should you be talking about a hotel guest like that? Ronan might not like it.'

'Och, he's nattering to Torquil about the fishing.' Lynette'e eyes had moved to her father and Ishbel. 'Monnie, have you ever seen Dad looking so happy?'

'Not for a long time. He just loves it here, eh?'

But Monnie, who had been smiling affectionately, suddenly stiffened. 'Oh, help – here comes Mrs Duthie! Hope she doesn't want to sit with us.'

'Hello everybody!' Flushed little Mrs Duthie was already pulling up a chair and sitting down at the table with a plate piled high. 'Is this not grand, then? What a spread! All thanks to you, Mr Allan!'

'No, no,' he was murmuring, but her interest had switched to Monnie and Torquil.

'Now isn't it a shame, Monnie, that that nice Mr Soutar had to go to Edinburgh and miss this lovely do? He said to me, he'd never been so sorry. Still, I expect you knew that, eh? Were you not going with him to buy walking boots?'

'I haven't been yet,' Monnie answered curtly, feeling guilty, in spite of her irritation, that she hadn't given Paul a thought until now.

'Nice though that he's going to help you with hill walking, eh? Torquil, you'll be proud of her, I'm sure?'

'I am always proud of Monnie,' Torquil answered, smiling

tranquilly, at which Mrs Duthie slightly tossing her head, waved to Tim MacLean, the bus driver, who was walking about with an enormous helping of everything, looking for somewhere to sit.

'Over here, Tim! We can always fit in another one, eh?'

As Tim obediently squeezed in beside Mrs Duthie, Ronan excused himself to speak to the band, while Lynette and Monnie said they were just going over to speak to their father.

'Aye, your lovely dad.' Mrs Duthie sighed deeply. 'Sitting with Ishbel, eh? That's her son with her, and daughter-in-law. Son sells fishing tackle, she waits on at the hotel. No children yet. But goodbye, dears, come back soon.'

Interested in meeting Ishbel's family, Lynette and Monnie took particular notice of the young couple sitting with Frank and Ishbel, who were introduced by Ishbel as her son, Niall, and daughter-in-law, Sheana, from Glenelg.

Niall, tall and lanky, had Ishbel's fair hair, but his eyes were dark and deeply-set, while Sheana was red-haired and green-eyed, and on the plump side. They greeted the girls pleasantly enough, but were not, Lynette thought, outgoing people. Certainly, Niall hadn't the social skills of his mother, and very soon rose, saying he and Sheana had better be going back to their own table.

'Nice to meet you,' he murmured, giving a nod to Frank. 'And you, Mr Forester.'

'Perhaps we'll meet again,' he said, rising, as Ishbel, too, stood up, looking apologetic.

'Oh, yes,' Niall muttered. 'We're often over – have to keep an eye on Mother.'

'Whatever for?' she cried indignantly, but the young ones were already on their way, taking their empty plates with them.

'They're a little bit shy,' Ishbel said quickly. 'Not used to talking to strangers, but they've always been very good to me.'

'Of course, of course.' The sisters were already looking elsewhere. 'We'll see you later, eh, Dad?'

'Aye, you'll be wanting a lift back, eh?'

Monnie hesitated. 'Maybe not. I think Torquil will be taking me home. Tony can take his mother, you see.'

'How about you, then, Lynette?'

'I expect I'll be coming with you.'

'Are you sure?' Ishbel asked, smiling. 'Mr Allan has a car.'

'Mr Allan lives at the hotel,' Lynette replied lightly, glad to return with Monnie to their table, where Ronan and Torquil were waiting, though Mrs Duthie and Tim had departed.

'Mustn't miss our desserts,' Ronan told them. 'They look gorgeous – Scott's excelled himself tonight.'

'I really should dance with Scott after this,' Lynette remarked as they helped themselves to chocolate soufflé. 'I don't see him now, but he'll probably appear after the buffet's over.'

But when the buffet was over and the dancing had begun again, there was no sign of Scott, and Brigid rather accusingly told Lynette and Ronan that he was exhausted and had gone off to his bed.

'Poor laddie, he's had so much to do, while everybody else has been having a good time, eh?'

'Not everybody,' Lynette said defensively. 'You were working too, Brigid.'

'Aye, but the buffet was not my responsibility, was it? And anyway, I'm going dancing now.'

As Brigid was whirled on to the floor by a young man who had been hovering, Ronan looked at Lynette.

'Scott's not really exhausted, you know, he loves his work, it never tires him. He's just upset, not to be with you.'

'Oh, look, I said I'd dance with him! I wanted him to join us!'

'I think you know what I mean,' Ronan answered steadily.

'They're forming the sets for the next reel,' she said after a moment.

'Maybe we could sit it out?'

'No, I think we should dance it.'

'You're afraid of people noticing?'

'No! Are you?'

'Haven't shown much sign of it up to now, have I?'

She looked at him with sudden objectivity, setting apart her own feelings. 'I bet some people will be surprised, eh?'

'Why?'

'Because you're the manager. It's your job to care what people think.'

'Not about everything.'

His voice was soft, his unusual eyes never moving from her face.

'I wish I could ask you what you mean,' she began, but he shook his head.

'They're forming the sets, we'll have to go.'

As they ran to take the last places for 'Hamilton House', he managed to whisper, 'May I take you home tonight, Lynette? I have my car outside.'

'Do you have to ask?' Her eyes were shining. 'I'll tell Dad not to wait for me.'

He would only have Ishbel for a passenger, she thought, as the dance began, for Monnie was being driven home by Torquil. How strange, that both she and her sister had got what they wanted. Even stranger, was that what she wanted was Ronan Allan. How had it happened? How had it come about? One thing for sure was that dancing a Scottish reel was not the time to be pondering on it. But the question, she knew, would come back to her and fascinate her, as the handsome face of the man opposite fascinated her now.

The dance ended, and by midnight, the evening had ended, too. Ronan had to make another little speech, drawing the gathering to a close and thanking everyone for coming. 'Auld Lang Syne' was sung, there was applause for the band, then it was over. Except for those looking forward to what would follow. An evening was not over, after all, until the journey home had been made, and goodnights had been said. Particularly, goodnights to certain people.

'All set?' Frank asked Ishbel, helping her into her coat. 'There's just you and me going back. Hope I don't have to change a wheel again.'

'Hope not,' she agreed, with a nervous little laugh. 'I see Agnes is giving Monnie and Torquil a send off.'

'Aye, Tony's taking her home.'

'Now you two take care,' Agnes was saying, smiling broadly. 'And don't drive into the Sound by mistake, eh?'

'Hey, I am not drunk!' Torquil exclaimed, opening the door to his van for Monnie. 'At least, not with alcohol.'

Oh, just let's go, thought Monnie. Let's be on our own, please!

And they did go, followed by Ronan and Lynette in Ronan's large Wolseley, and a little later by Frank and Ishbel, as Agnes waved and murmured to Tony, 'Guess they'll all be taking the long road home, eh?'

'There is no long road home,' said Tony. 'Mind if I squash in Nina, Mother? Means we'll have to go to Glenelg first, but Jill's gone off with some guy she knows and Nina's on her own.'

'Seems like you've found a long way home, anyway,' his mother told him tartly. 'Better drop me off on the way.'

And Tony's battered Morris took its place in the convoy leaving the Talisman, the red tail lights of the cars ahead glinting through the darkness, their headlights picking out the grass verges and hedges, hostellers walking back, and one or two startled rabbits leaping away.

Thirty-Four

There was certainly to be no long road home for Frank, for he had to be back at the hostel to open the door for his young clients – which didn't mean that he couldn't spend a few minutes saying goodnight to Ishbel first.

'I meant what I said,' he told her quietly, as he helped her from his car. 'About this being one of the happiest evenings I've had in a very long time.'

'I meant what I said, too.'

Though her shop window was dark, the light over her side entrance showed Ishbel's face to be as serious as Frank's, her lips slightly trembling, her eyes intent on his.

'I've never been so happy. Never thought I could be – after Robbie died.'

'I feel the same. Never thought, after my Ellie left me, that I could ever want to be with someone else the way I want to be with you.'

'It is not wrong, to feel like that, Frank. It doesn't mean, you're forgetting. Only that—'

'I know what you're saying.' Very gently, he drew her into his arms. 'Time heals, moves on, and we move on, too. The loved ones – they'd understand.'

'I think so.' She slowly raised her face to his, offering her lips for his first kiss, which, when it came, made all words, all thoughts, vanish for the long, long moment it lasted. Even when they had drawn apart, looking at each other just a little self-consciously, they made no effort to speak, until, finally, Frank sighed and released her from his arms and whispered her name.

'Ishbel, Ishbel – how do I leave you?'

'You have to let your young folk in,' she murmured. 'They'll be sitting waiting on the doorstep.'

'I'd like to say, let 'em!'

'But you're too conscientious.' She ran her fingers down his cheek. 'Better go, Frank, before it gets too hard.'

'Hard enough now.' He put his hand on his car door. 'But I'll come to the shop tomorrow, eh? Bring a shopping list as long as my arm so I can spend a good long time with you?'

'It's Sunday tomorrow,' she answered demurely. 'But I could come round to see you tomorrow afternoon?'

'Ishbel, would you?'

'I would!'

They laughed and he got into the driving seat.

'You never know, my girls might be home before me. They could let the hostellers in.'

'Your girls home before you?' Ishbel laughed again. 'You must be joking.'

'Aye, maybe I am. Goodnight, dear Ishbel.'

'Goodnight, Frank.'

'See you tomorrow.'

'Tomorrow.'

Driving the short distance to the hostel after Ishbel had vanished into her own door, Frank found himself shaking with continuing excitement. It had happened. He had declared himself. He'd never believed it possible that he would be able to let Ishbel know what was in his heart, though he'd been pretty sure for some time that her heart was feeling the same as his own. But feeling and declaring – they were two different things. Without the ceilidh that had brought a new intimacy to their meeting together, would they ever have dared to take the risk of speaking out?

Oh, God, I'd have had to, Frank thought, but knew that he might not. Might have been afraid. Of what? Of rejection. But there had been no rejection. As he drove up the hostel drive and parked his car, his spirits rose like birds and his heart was singing.

'Grand party, Mr Forester!' a young voice called, and remembering his responsibilities enough to take notice of what was going on, he saw that Ishbel had been right. Quite a crowd of his hostellers were sitting on the steps of the house waiting for him, all as happy as he was, from the look of them, having been so royally entertained at the Talisman.

'Have a good time, then?' another voice asked.

'You bet!' Frank answered, taking out his keys. 'Am I the first back?'

Well, of course, it was clear that he was, for his daughters would have unlocked the door, but they'd be along soon and in the meantime, he'd bedtime to organize for all his overexcited hostellers.

'Lights out in fifteen minutes!' he called, ignoring groans, only pausing to wonder, after the house finally grew quiet, just when his girls would be coming home.

Both Torquil and Ronan had had the same idea – not to find a long way home, but just to move off the road, park beside trees under a dark velvet night sky; quite away, of course, from one other. Quite away from anyone at all.

'You weren't wanting to go straight home?' Ronan asked quietly, taking Lynette's hand in a firm, dry clasp.

'No, I wasn't wanting that,' she answered, breathing a little fast as she felt the pressure of his hand.

His face, like hers, was no more than a pale blur in the darkness that held them, but they didn't need to see faces; the nearness of their bodies in the cramped seats of the car was enough to drive up an excitement they could hardly contain.

'This is the first time we've been alone,' Ronan said huskily.

'If you don't count your office,' Lynette whispered.

'Don't talk of that.' He slowly drew her towards him. 'I don't want to be reminded.'

'I can't forget.'

'You can't forgive me?' They were very close now, their faces touching, his hand stroking back her hair, smoothing her brow.

'It's not that. Just I can't understand the way we were . . . seeming to hate each other—'

'Hatred is close to love, they say, but there was no hatred, Lynette. Never any hatred.'

His mouth sank to hers, and then for some time there was no more talking. No need for talking, only the longing to kiss and kiss again, to shut out the world, to be as close as possible, until at last they had to draw away, if only to breathe, laugh a little with joy, and sit back, trying again to see each other in the darkness.

'How did it happen?' Lynette asked at last, putting her hand to her lips, as though she could still feel Ronan's kisses.

'How did what happen?' His words were slow, a little dreamy.

'Us. How did we change?'

'We never changed. The way I see it, underneath all that antagonism was something we didn't want to recognize.'

'No, no, I never felt that. I took against you from the first, I don't know why.' She put her hand to his cheek, to soften what she was saying. 'Perhaps because I thought it was you who'd taken against me.'

'Taken against you? I was attracted from the start!'

'You never showed it. You just seemed cold and arrogant – prejudiced, because I came from the hostel.'

'Oh, God, is that true? Is that how I seemed? Lynette – darling – it's not how I felt. I was attracted and – I don't know – angry about it, because I could tell, I suppose, that as you've just said, you'd taken against me.'

Suddenly, he caught her in his arms again, and again they kissed, but more gently, more sweetly, until he released her.

'Let's not talk of it any more,' he said quietly. 'What's past is past. Let's think of now.'

'I want to, Ronan, but I must go. It must be getting very late, Dad doesn't keep tabs on us, but he must be wondering by now what's happened to me.'

'We'll go, as long as you promise me, we'll be together again soon.'

'It won't be easy.' She smiled in the darkness. 'Considering where we work.'

'I'm talking of free time.'

'Free time? Oh, wonderful!'

'It will be, it will be.'

At the gates to the hostel, she turned to him, glad now to see his face in the lamplight, her heart leaping at the expression in those strange eyes of his, knowing her own look reflected it.

'You know when things really changed for us?' she asked softly. He shook his head. 'Tell me.'

'It was when you told me of your life here, at the house, and of how you'd had to leave it. For the first time, I saw another side of you, a human side, and I began to understand.'

'Lynette, that's amazing. I don't know what to say. Even then – you were beginning to care for me, weren't you? You were recognizing what we might have?'

She hesitated, was about to speak, when a horn sounded on the drive and swinging round, she and Ronan saw Torquil's van stopping and both Torquil and Monnie getting out.

'Hi, there!' Torquil cried. 'Seems you are as late returning as we are!'

'Monnie, where've you been?' Lynette asked, stupidly, for what right had she to ask that? Especially when it was so clear from the radiant look on Monnie's face that she and Torquil had been to the same lovers' haven as Lynette and Ronan themselves.

Thirty-Five

Some few days later, Monnie was spending a half day, not with Torquil who hadn't yet fixed up the boat trip, but Paul Soutar. At long last, they had met to drive to Kyle in search of climbing boots, and having found a pair that passed Paul's inspection, had had an argument over buying them, which Monnie had won.

'I'd like to have got them for you,' Paul told her earnestly. 'It was my idea, after all, to take you hill walking.'

'I'm the one who wants to go,' she said firmly, 'and the boots are for me, so I'm paying. But you can take me to tea, if you like.'

'Thank the Lord for that! I'm dying for a cup.'

They walked leisurely through the busy village, conscious all the time of their nearness to Skye just over the water; enjoying the soft early May weather, and, indeed, being together.

Paul was so easy to be with, Monnie thought as she had thought before. So – she searched for the word – undemanding. His first instinct would always be, she felt sure, to fit in, if possible, with whatever his companion wanted, at the same time keeping his own strength of purpose, making sure things would go well. Whatever happened, wherever you found yourself with him, you'd be able to trust him. And how much that meant! More than charm? Oh, yes. More than that something it was impossible to describe, that drew you to a person and held you fast? Oh, no.

Turning her fine grey gaze on Paul's face, Monnie found herself sighing, at which he cheerfully took her arm.

'Hey, no sighing! What you need is tea and cakes, and there they are, right in front of us. I've been steering us towards this tea shop all along – it's my favourite.'

'You're right!' she cried jauntily. 'As soon as I've had my fix of tea and fancies, I'll be as cheerful as you. Or, almost.'

'I was really sorry I missed the hotel ceilidh, you know,' he told her seriously, as she poured the tea in the charming little café he'd found for them. 'You might say, in fact, that I was devastated, but there was no way of getting out of going to Edinburgh. I had a meeting of the backers for my school – couldn't afford to miss it.'

'More important, I'm sure, than dancing all those reels with the local lovelies.'

'What local lovelies?' He laughed, as he passed her a plate of small cakes.

'Well, there's Lynette's assistant for one,' Monnie suggested, rather despising herself for having to bring Fionola into the conversation, as though she had to dwell on the girl's beauty. In spite of her rapturous kissing and caressing with Torquil after the ceilidh the other night, and in spite of the promised boat trip, she knew she was still afraid that she had rivals. Nina, for instance, who had danced with him. And Fionola, he'd described as 'lovely'.

'A very good-looking girl,' Paul was remarking now. 'Same as your sister and both fine dancers, I expect. But if I'd been at the ceilidh, I'd have been hoping for a dance with you.'

'And I'd have been delighted,' she told him. 'Of course I would.'

Paul studied his pastry for a moment, before raising his eyes to her. 'But I would have had to fight off Torquil, I suppose? That goes without saying.'

'I did dance mainly with Torquil,' she admitted.

'As I said, goes without saying. He's your admirer.'

'Admirer? Paul, that sounds so old-fashioned!'

'Does it? Suppose I'm an old-fashioned guy, then, because I'm an admirer, too.'

At that, she looked down at her iced chocolate cake and he immediately reached forward to grasp her hand.

'Sorry, Monnie, sorry! I'm not trying to embarrass you, not trying to spoil things. I do admire you, but as a friend.' His gaze was appealing, his hand, holding hers, very firm. 'OK, then?'

She looked up, smiling with relief. 'OK, Paul. Absolutely OK.'

He sat back, relaxing, loosening her hand from his.

'Glad that's settled, then. Like another cake?'

'No thanks, I haven't finished this one yet. Besides, I don't want to put on weight.'

'Monnie, you'll never put on weight, especially after you've been up a few Munros. We must plan where we'll start.'

'I do want to do that, see how I get on.'

Paul hesitated. 'And it's all right, is it? With Torquil, I mean?'

'Torquil?'

'He won't mind, if you go hill walking with me?'

'Oh, no. No, he's quite happy about it.'

'I see.' Paul finished his tea and set down the cup, his face expressionless, but Monnie's antennae picked up the signals.

Oh, no, she groaned inwardly, he's guessed Torquil sees him as no threat, and he minds. But why should he mind, if he was only a friend? She put the thought aside. Perhaps no man would like to be disregarded in that way? No woman, either, come to that.

Putting on a cheerful smile again, Paul signalled for the bill and they both rose to go.

'It's been so nice, Paul, thank you,' Monnie said. 'For driving me in and helping me choose my boots, this lovely tea, and everything.'

'My pleasure. It's been nice for me, too.'

Driving back to the hostel, Paul said he'd be looking at his maps, picking out the right place to take Monnie on her first outing.

'I'm not sure that Beinn Sgritheall is the best one for you to try as a beginner – you remember, that's the "hill of scree" near Arnisdale I showed you? It's got a few difficult bits, and we might find something easier.'

'Hey, I like a challenge!'

He grinned. 'I daresay, but safety is all in hill walking. That's my cardinal rule, so we'll do some practice runs before we tackle that particular Munro.'

'I'm in your hands, Paul.'

'Sounds good.' He laughed. 'But here's the hostel, already. Monnie, I'll ring you, shall I?'

At the hostel gate, they stood for a moment, gazing in companionable manner at each other. Should she kiss his cheek? Monnie was wondering. Better not. She touched his hand, made her thanks again, and waved as he climbed back into the car and drove away, with one last smile.

'Had a good time?' asked Frank, as she looked in at his office. 'Get your boots?'

'Oh, yes, I'm all set now. Scottish mountains, here I come!'

'Wonderful. Er – Monnie – you'll be on duty this evening, right?'

'Right. Do you want me to do something?'

'Just to be here. Ishbel's asked me for supper.'

'Oh?' Monnie slightly raised her eyebrows. 'Very nice, eh? Bet you'll have a lovely meal.'

'It's OK, then?'

'Sure it is. I'll just go and see what I can rustle up for Lynette and me – she's home early this evening.'

And wait till she hears about Dad going to Ishbel's, Monnie was thinking. Was it surprising, or not? After the way those two had danced together at the ceilidh, maybe not. On the other hand, as she took two chops from the fridge, Monnie decided she was, after all, just a little surprised. Surprised, and not altogether pleased. Dancing in public was one thing, but having a meal together in Ishbel's home, maybe that meant something else? What would Lynette make of it?

★   ★   ★

Seemed Lynette didn't know what to make of it. When she
arrived home, she looked as wonderfully happy as she'd looked
ever since the night of the ceilidh, but when she saw her father
leaving, all spruced up for his date with Ishbel, her face changed.

'Supper with Ishbel, just the two of them?' Her gaze on Monnie
was thoughtful. 'What do you think it means?'

'You tell me.'

'I can't. Don't know what to say. I mean – at their age – it's
odd, eh?'

'What is?'

'Well – being so attracted, and such.'

'They're not as old as all that.'

'Come on, they're behaving like—'

'Like us?'

'Like folk much younger, anyway. And then there's our mother,
isn't there? She meant everything to Dad, didn't she? He couldn't
. . . just forget her?'

Monnie bit her lip. 'That's what I've been wondering.'

The sisters exchanged long troubled looks, until Monnie said
she'd things to do, they'd better get on cooking those chops, and
Lynette sighed with exasperation.

'Oh, it's too bad, eh? Just when things are working out for us,
up comes another worry!'

'Everything all right, then, between you and Ronan?'

'Couldn't be better.' The smile returned to Lynette's face. 'We're
going to go over to a country hotel he knows beyond Glenelg
on Saturday evening. Mrs A is going to cover for him and Fionola
for me till we close down, though they don't know we're going
out together. But I'm so happy, Monnie. Never thought I'd be
so happy!'

'So am I,' Monnie declared quickly. For it was true, wasn't it?
Forget all those thoughts about rivals. In a couple of days, Torquil
would be calling and they'd be fixing up the boat trip. She'd
every reason to be happy.

'If only Dad doesn't go and do something silly,' said Lynette.
'We'll have to keep an eye on him.'

'And Ishbel,' said Monnie.

Thirty-Six

Sweet though Lynette's life had now become at the Talisman, there was just one thing that hurt, and it was Scott's attitude. Ever since the ceilidh, he'd made a point of treating her like a stranger, an unwelcome one at that, with no more friendly coffees being offered if she put her nose into the kitchen, no more chats or smiles, and certainly no more cookery lessons. In fact, she didn't even dare to mention them, and soon learned to keep out of his way, taking her morning break alone in the grounds of the hotel, with coffee from the staff room and yesterday's newspaper to read.

She was on her usual bench one morning, deep in the fashion page, when a hand touched her shoulder and she looked up to see Scott's unsmiling face.

'Scott! What are you doing here?'

He sat down next to her and took out his cigarettes.

'Come to see you.'

'To see me?' She watched him light a cigarette, shaking her head when he offered the packet to her. 'This is a change, isn't it? You haven't wanted to give me the time of day just lately.'

'I know, and I feel bad about it. I've been behaving like a little kid throwing a tantrum.' An uncertain smile crossed his freckled features. 'Will you forgive me?'

'Oh, come on, Scott! Let's not talk like that. All I want is for us to be friends again.'

'Aye, friends.' He blew smoke. 'I want that, too.'

'Well, then.'

'Thing is, it was hard for me, Lynette. Seeing you at the ceilidh with Mr Allan. I thought you didn't even like him and there you were, dancing with him and having supper with him, looking at him all starry-eyed, like he was Santa Claus and Elvis Presley rolled into one. I couldn't take it in.'

Lynette lowered her eyes, drank some cold coffee in an effort to do something, while thinking of what she might say.

'Things have changed,' she said at last, while Scott sat looking at her with hurt in his eyes and his cigarette smoke curling around him.

'I can tell that. You've fallen for him, haven't you? And anybody can see, he's fallen for you, which is no surprise. But Lynette, for God's sake, how did you come to change?'

With two spots of red burning in her cheeks, Lynette stood up. 'I've got to go, Scott. I'm sorry . . .'

'No.' He stubbed out his cigarette and stood up with her. 'I'm the one who's sorry. I promised myself, I wouldn't go on, wouldn't say a word, but you see how I am, it's all come out just the same.'

'Never mind, I understand.'

He shook his head. 'You'd have to be me to understand.'

'I do, all the same.'

Their eyes met, and Scott put his hand on hers.

'Maybe you do,' he said quietly. 'Look, can we no' be as we used to be? You coming in to see us, doing a bit of cooking? Having a coffee?'

'It was you who stopped that, Scott.'

'I know, I know. But I was playing the fool. I've grown up since then. Now I'll settle for what I can have.'

'Oh, Scott!' She reached up and kissed his cheek. 'Welcome back!'

He managed a grin and gave a quick look round.

'Hope there are no guests lurking in the shrubbery, eh?'

Or, a hotel manager, thought Lynette.

As she returned to Reception to relieve Fionola, she felt happier. Losing Scott as a friend, as had seemed to be the case, had upset her more than she could have thought possible. It was terrific, rapturous, to have a relationship with Ronan, something she wouldn't change for anything, but Scott had become very dear to her, she couldn't deny it. True, at one time she'd thought him very easy-going and now she'd found out he was not, but even so, it was good to have him back. Oh, heavens, yes, because she'd missed so much what they'd had together, and wanted it again.

'Mr Allan was looking for you,' Fionola told her, her lovely mouth curving into an impish smile. 'Think he'd like to see you in his office.'

'Oh, yes? Well, I can't go till you've had your break, so you'd better scoot.'

'I don't mind waiting if it's anything important.'

'No, no, that won't be necessary.'

Left alone, Lynette, in spite of her mind half being elsewhere, dealt competently with all she had to do, which was plenty, now that the better weather was bringing in more guests. Just the way she liked things, of course, except that the mention of Ronan's name had set her pulses racing and she couldn't help glancing at the clock and longing for Fionola's return so that she might make her escape. And then Ronan himself appeared, lifting his dark brows at the sight of her, putting on a formal smile for the benefit of any guests at the desk, murmuring, 'Miss Forester, could I see you for a moment?'

'As soon as Miss MacLewis comes back,' she answered coolly. 'Oh, and here she is!'

As Fionola sauntered up, still with her knowing smile, Lynette gathered up a handful of papers and followed Ronan towards his office.

'Won't be long,' she called. 'Just have one or two things to discuss.'

'That's all right,' Fionola called back, and as she moved to busy herself with a new arrival's signing of the register, Ronan opened his office door for Lynette, who slid around it, closed it, and went into his arms.

Only for a moment, before both pulled away, desperate still to be together, yet not at ease to be in Ronan's office, the manager's office, the last place they could display their feelings.

'Crazy,' Ronan whispered. 'That was crazy of me, but I couldn't help myself. I wanted to see you so much, wanted to be with you . . .'

'You think I don't feel like that?' She stroked his cheek. 'Out there at Reception – so near, so far – trying not to mind Fionola's smile.'

'I suppose she'll have guessed why I asked you in?'

'Anybody would've guessed.'

'After the ceilidh, most people will know there's something between us.' Ronan straightened his shoulders. 'But we'll have to be more careful – I will, I mean. Wait till we're really alone.' He drew her to him once again and held her close. 'But, oh, God, it's hard, Lynette, it's just too hard.'

'Let's think about Saturday.' She straightened her hair, trying to look businesslike; the perfect receptionist who had only been with her boss to discuss work. 'It's not far away.'

'A lifetime.'

'A lifetime,' she agreed, giving him one last swift kiss. 'Do I look all right now, to face Fionola?'

'You look wonderful,' he said hoarsely. 'Facing Fionola, or not.'

'Till Saturday,' she said softly.

'Till Saturday.'

At Reception, she was lucky. There was so much activity, Fionola was too busy even to look at her until a lull came, by which time Lynette was her usual cool professional self.

'I'll take first lunch, shall I?' she asked, collecting her handbag. 'Might go down to the kitchen, cadge something nice.'

'What, from grumpy old Scott? Thought he wasn't speaking to you?'

'We're friends again, I'm glad to say.'

'What a charmer you are, Lynette. Wish I had your secret.'

'You've mentioned my secret before, as though I had one. But you don't need any help from me, Fionola.' Lynette was beginning to walk away. 'Think you know that, eh?'

Thirty-Seven

Saturday came and it was special, not just for Lynette, but for Monnie, too. As they were getting ready in the morning, she could hardly stop smiling, for today was the day.

'For my boat trip,' she reminded Lynette. 'I can't wait for this afternoon!'

I don't understand, what's so wonderful about a boat trip?' Lynette asked, studying her sister's radiant face. 'Even if it is with Torquil?'

'It's hard to explain. I think, perhaps it's because I know being in his boat means such a lot to Torquil. Being on his own, I mean. He just likes to be there, alone, on the water, not having to talk, which is why he doesn't share the fishing with anyone. Doesn't take anyone with him at all.'

'But he's taking you?'

'Yes!' Monnie's eyes were shining. 'He's taking me. And I know that means something. I'm different, you see. I must be, don't you think?'

'I suppose so.' Lynette was slightly frowning. 'But if he's such a loner, he's probably—'

'Probably what?'

'Difficult.'

'He's not difficult!' Monnie cried. 'And he's only a loner for his boat. People are attracted to him, aren't they? They don't think he's a loner.'

'OK, but take care, eh? There's just going to be you and Torquil in this boat.'

'And on the island,' Monnie corrected. 'Don't forget, we're going to visit an island.'

'Well, take care, anyway. I mean it, Monnie.'

'And how do I do that?' Monnie was all smiles again. 'I'll have to leave everything to Torquil – and that's just the way I like it.'

As they left their room for their usual hurried breakfast, she gave her sister a quick, speculative look. 'Have a good time tonight, Lynette. Perhaps I should be telling you to take care, eh?'

'Me?' It was Lynette's turn to look radiant. 'You couldn't find anyone more trustworthy than Ronan.'

She did not add that if there were ever to be a choice between going out with Ronan to a good hotel and going out with Torquil in his boat, she knew which she would rather do.

By mid afternoon, she was still at work, her dress for the evening hanging in Fionola's room, for in the end, she had given in and told her assistant where she was going that evening and who with. For what was the point in trying to keep her in the dark any more? It would just get more and more complicated. Besides, Lynette needed somewhere to change.

'I guessed it would be Mr Allan you'd be seeing,' Fionola had commented. 'Aren't you the lucky one?'

'Though you won't admit it, I bet you've got chaps queuing up to go out with you,' Lynette had cried, at which Fionola had shrugged.

'My next date, as a matter of fact, is with Mr Warner.'

'Mr Warner?' Lynette was hard-pressed to know what to say. 'Well, I knew he'd booked to stay on another fortnight, but I never knew you were going out with him.'

'Oh, we've had dinner out once or twice already – at the same hotel where you're going, as a matter of fact.'

'And you're the one who asks me for my secrets!'

Fionola had only smiled, and after a few moments Lynette gave up trying to imagine her with stout old Mr Warner and let her thoughts drift to Monnie. How would she be faring in Torquil's boat on her adventure that meant so much? Just as long as she was all right . . . But why shouldn't she be?

Och, I'm an old fusspot, Lynette decided, and stepped forward to greet yet another new guest being ushered in by Barty.

Not so very far away, sitting in the boat that Lynette had been picturing, Monnie was certainly not worrying about herself, being, as she was, in seventh heaven. Everything was just as she'd always imagined it. Herself and Torquil, alone in his boat, skimming over the Sound of Sleat on a clear afternoon in May. No one around on the shores they were passing, no one to see them from the mountains of Skye, no sounds to disturb them, except, of course, the outboard motor on the boat that was carrying them so swiftly towards their destination which, in fact, Monnie didn't even know. A little island somewhere off the Point of Sleat, Torquil had said, one of several so small they would hardly qualify to appear on a map.

'Not as big as the Sandaig Islands there? We saw them before on the way to Loch Hourn, if you remember?'

'I remember,' Monnie told him.

'Now you can see the Ornsay lighthouse – that's on a tiny island too, not really on Isleornsay.'

'Isleornsay's on Skye?' Monnie was turning her head to follow his pointing finger. 'You know, I haven't been over to Skye yet.'

Torquil raised his fair brows. 'Not even with your admirer?'

She sat up straight. 'You mean Paul? Why d'you call him that?'

'Well, isn't he?'

Sitting back again, Monnie was recalling how Paul himself had used the word, and thinking how astute it was of Torquil to use it too – because it fitted, didn't it? Fitted Paul.

'He's my friend, Torquil. That's all. And you know that, don't you?'

He smiled and nodded. 'I do. No need to worry.'

'No need for you to worry, you mean.'

'Ah, but I am not!' He was looking ahead with his far-sighted blue eyes. 'Because you are here with me and want to be, I think.'

She didn't even answer him, for what could she say? He knew the truth of it, he could see for himself how happy she was.

Before long, they had finished travelling down the coast of Skye and Torquil had switched off the engine and moved to take the oars. 'Here we are, then, Monnie, Gull Island coming up. My name for it, anyway. 'Tis too small, really, to have a name.'

'Why, it's not as small as all that,' she remarked, looking in surprise at the piece of land ahead that appeared to have not only a strip of shore and a few stunted trees, but a sort of miniature cliff on which seagulls were perching and crying. 'There's certainly somewhere for us to sit.'

'Sit? You can even walk.' Torquil laughed. 'Though 'twill not take you very long. Now, I'll just take us in and tie up and then we can have some of that coffee you made us, eh?'

'Oh, yes. I've got the Thermos in my bag, and some chocolate.'

She waited, looking all about her, as Torquil skilfully beached the boat, then tied it to a wooden stump before sweeping Monnie up and carrying her to the strip of shore.

'Your feet!' she cried, as he set her down. 'They must be wet.'

'Sweetheart, haven't you noticed, I'm wearing my boots?'

He was still holding her and looking at her, his gaze intense on her face.

'Your first landing on my island,' he whispered. 'Like it?'

'Love it,' she answered breathlessly. 'But is it really yours?'

'Of course not. You must know by now that I do not own one thing, except for my boats. I think of this place as mine, and the other islands, too, as nobody else wants them, I'd guarantee.' Releasing her from his clasp, he rubbed his hands together and looked up at the sky. 'Come on, let's have that coffee, then. The weather's changing, it's getting colder. We might have to make for the cave.'

'Cave? What cave?'

'It's tiny – just an entrance in that bit of cliff there, but enough to shelter us. Give me your hand.'

They plodded up the damp sand toward the little opening he had pointed out, where Monnie set down her canvas bag and took out the Thermos flask of coffee.

'Come on, it's dry, you can sit down.' Torquil patted space beside him. 'Sit close to me, let me make you warm.'

'Just let me give you your coffee,' she murmured, her hand slightly shaking as she passed him his cup and sipped from her own. 'Oh, that's good, isn't it?'

'Very good, but finish it up and come to me.'

She needed no urging, and casting their coffee cups aside, they went into each other's arms, sliding back against the sand, loosening their clothes, ignoring the cold air coming up from the Sound as they gave themselves up to bliss. Yet, when they paused to take breath from the passionate holding and kissing, Monnie suddenly drew away.

'For God's sake, what is it?' Torquil cried, his face a mask, one she hardly recognized, but then, she supposed, her own must be the same. They were different people, just for that moment and she couldn't help it, she had grown afraid – not of the different Torquil, but of herself. What might she not do in this incredible moment? What so many girls did? What that girl had done, who'd had to go to Inverness?

'Tell me what's wrong?' Torquil was demanding. 'You are not worried, are you? You are not thinking I will make you do something you do not want?'

'I'm worried because I do want it,' she whispered. 'And I know – it would be—'

'Stupid? Crazy?'

'Too much of a risk.'

'And you are not one who takes risks? Monnie, neither am I.' Torquil, now looking his normal self again, sat up, half-smiling, and fumbling in the pocket of the jacket he'd put on again, took out his cigarettes. 'I am not Tony, you realize.'

For some moments, he smoked without speaking, and Monnie too was silent, as she fastened buttons and zipped up her anorak. The moment had passed, the moment of danger; she knew it had only increased her love for Torquil, who was so quiet now.

'That's it!' he cried, suddenly leaping to his feet and dowsing his cigarette in the sand. 'The weather's closing in, I must go for the gulls' eggs.'

'Gulls' eggs?' She stared at him. 'What gulls' eggs?'

'It's the right time to find them and when I come out here, I always look for some for Mother.' He pulled a cap from his pocket. 'I can just put a few in this, they'll be safe enough. Wait here for me, Monnie. I shall not be long.'

'I'll come with you!'

'No, no, that would not do, sweetheart. I can manage much better on my own. Please, just wait here.'

'Torquil, come back! Come back!'

But he was already climbing nimbly around the little cliff away from her and as she stood, searching for a last glimpse of him, uncertain what to do, the mist from the sea began rolling in.

Thirty-Eight

For some time, she stood, waiting, certain he must come back for her, but as time passed and there was no sign of him, she sank down at the entrance to the cave and wondered what she should do. With the coming of the mist, the temperature had dropped, the chill of the air beginning to penetrate her bones, and after tightening her anorak around her, she drank some coffee straight from the Thermos, her cup being full of sand, and ate a little chocolate. For a while, she felt better, or, at least warmer, but the effect soon faded and as Torquil did not return, panic set in.

Where was he? Why had he left her? Was he ever coming back?

Of course he's coming back, you idiot, she told herself. Why would he not? He'd only gone for those wretched eggs, he shouldn't be much longer. But supposing he had tripped, injured himself, was lying somewhere in the mist, waiting for her?

She jumped to her feet, determined to find him, when through the mist, she heard something that stopped her in her tracks. It was the sound of an outboard motor.

Oh, God! She put her hand to her lips. He had left her, he had taken his boat, that was the boat she could hear. What could she do? She was alone on this island. Who would know where she was? Her father and Lynette knew about her boat trip and that it involved an island, but they didn't know where it was and probably wouldn't miss her for hours. Lynette herself, anyway, wouldn't be back home until late.

Shivering with cold and apprehension, Monnie tried to reason things out. Why should Torquil leave her? It would be crazy, wouldn't it? The action of someone with no sense at all, and that wasn't Torquil. Yet, she couldn't forget that he had once been described as 'wild'. Wild enough to go off somewhere and forget all about her, or just play a trick? No, no, she couldn't, wouldn't, believe it. So, why had she heard the engine of his boat?

She decided to run to the little strip of beach, see if she could see anything through the mist which might just be lifting a little. Please God, please God, may she see Torquil coming for her. Please God, may he not have gone away.

How long she stood there, straining her eyes to see him, she couldn't tell, for she had not worn her watch in case of damage by salt water and probably couldn't have read it anyhow. All she knew was that every minute seemed like an hour, until, quite suddenly, as though pulled like a curtain, the mist rose. And coming straight towards the island in his boat was Torquil.

He had switched off the engine to row into shore and in the new light of the May evening was as clear-cut as a statue, raising one hand from his oars to wave to her, while smiling easily and calling her name.

'Hi, Monnie! I got them!'

She was trembling as she watched him bring the boat in, secure it, and step out, very carefully cradling his cap. Trembling, not with cold, not with emotion that he had returned to her, but with an anger that was as strong and bright as a flame surrounding her, an anger so painful, she could hardly speak. But she did speak. She did get the words out that she wanted to say.

'Where have you been, Torquil? What have you been doing?'

'Why, you know what I've been doing – finding gulls' eggs.' He was staring at her with a clear, limpid gaze. 'There weren't any here, so I just took the boat to the next island. Got half a dozen, anyway. Want to see?'

'No, I do not want to see!'

What she wanted to do was run to him and hammer her fists on his chest . . . to take his cap and break the gulls' eggs on the nearest rock. But, of course, she did not. Only stood her ground, her heels sinking into the soft sand, her chilled hands clasped, her grey eyes flashing.

'Didn't it occur to you to tell me where you were going?' she asked, stammering in her eagerness to make him see what he had done to her. 'Didn't you think I might be frightened, left alone on this island, hearing your boat leaving? Were you playing a trick, or did you just not give a damn? I think I know which is true. Oh, God, I know!'

'Monnie, what are you talking about?'

He was shaking his head, his eyes on her still clear and innocent, as she had seen them appear before, his whole manner giving the impression that he was taken aback, quite mystified, by her tirade.

'I do not understand what you're complaining about. I went to look for the eggs, the mist came down and I couldn't see any. What was I to do?' His tone was suddenly cool. 'I knew there was a chance of finding them on Skua Island – that's what I call the one next to this – so I just took the boat and went over.'

'Torquil, you could have come and told me what you were doing! You could have checked that I was all right!'

'Why should you not have been all right? OK, it was misty, but not too bad – I could make things out, anyway. It never crossed my mind you would make such a fuss.'

He turned to set his cap of eggs in the boat, still handling it as carefully as if it were something very precious, Monnie noticed, and then came back towards her, holding out his arms.

'Ah, come on, forget about it. What's done is done.'

She made no reply.

'All I did was take the boat and not tell you. Not exactly a hanging matter. And I wasn't away for long. It just seemed like that to you.'

'Because I was alone and I didn't know if you were coming back!'

'That's ridiculous, Monnie. That's hysterical. Of course you knew I would be coming back. What sort of man do you think I am?'

'One who doesn't care for me,' she threw at him. 'One who cares so little, he doesn't even worry if I'm afraid or not, being left alone on an island in the middle of the Sound.'

A terrible silence descended over them, as they stood quite still on the little shore, and the wind that had perhaps cleared the mist, ruffled the waters of the Sound and behind them bent the island's few stunted trees.

'Think we should go back,' Torquil said at last. 'Come on, I will take you home.'

Refusing his hand, she climbed into the boat, keeping her gaze straight ahead, but seeing very little. All her thoughts were for her own desolation of spirit. She would not recognize that the beauty of the scenery she had studied earlier was still there, for it meant nothing to her without the extra colouring of Torquil's love for her.

And she knew now, in her heart, that he did not feel for her as she felt for him. Perhaps she had always known that secretly, but wouldn't face it until she'd seen that day how little he'd cared that she was upset. So, maybe it wasn't a hanging matter, that he'd left her alone, but wouldn't a man who loved her have wanted to comfort her? To make things right between them? That he had not, had taken away her shell; left her cold and vulnerable to pain. How long before that pain receded? She was not even able to imagine it.

Back at the jetty in Conair, again she refused Torquil's help and left the boat herself, waiting while he tied up and joined her, holding, of course, his cap of gulls' eggs.

'You'll want to get those to your mother,' she said curtly. 'So, I'll say goodbye.'

'I will walk you to the hostel, Monnie.'

'That won't be necessary. Goodbye, Torquil.'

'Wait! Please, wait! We can't just part like this. I thought we would be going out. I was planning to fetch my van.'

'I am not going out with you, Torquil. I am saying goodbye.'

Though she felt a knife turning in her heart, she turned and began to walk away.

'Wait!' he cried again. 'Wait, Monnie! When are we going to

see each other? You can't just leave me like this. It is not fair. I have not done anything, I am not to blame!'

She kept on walking, half-expecting him to follow, catch her up, take her arm, which she didn't want, but still minded when he did not. Showed, didn't it? How little he cared.

Thirty-Nine

There was the usual noise echoing around the hostel, mostly coming from the kitchen, where the young people were cooking, but the warden's kitchen was quite the reverse. Very peaceful, very serene, with only Frank and Ishbel, sitting together over the remains of a meal, talking quietly – though falling silent as soon as Monnie appeared.

'Why, you're back early!' her father cried, leaping up. 'Thought you and Torquil would be going out after your boat trip.'

'Monnie, what is wrong?' asked Ishbel, whose eyes were sharper than Frank's and who was already at Monnie's side, taking off her wet anorak, rubbing her cold hands. 'Why, you're wet through! What happened? Did you capsize, or something?'

'No.' Monnie sat down at the table, resting her head for a moment on her hand. 'We were on a little island, then Torquil went to find some gulls' eggs and the mist came down and the sun went in – I suppose I must have just got chilled.'

'He went to find gulls' eggs and left you on your own in the mist?' Frank asked. 'What the hell was he playing at?'

'I don't know. We had a row, anyway.' Monnie's voice suddenly thickened with tears. 'And I don't want to see him again – it's as simple as that.' She left her chair, grabbing her bag and her anorak, and ran out of the door, calling over her shoulder, 'I'm going to see if there's any hot water for a bath, OK?'

'Well,' said Ishbel, after a moment or two. 'I think I'd better put the kettle on and see what I can find for that poor girl to eat. She looks half frozen.'

'Worth it, if it means she's seen sense about that fellow at last. I was never happy with her going out with him, never.'

'I don't blame you, Frank. I'd feel the same.'

He looked at her fondly and as she moved to fill the kettle, grasped her hand. 'We feel the same about a lot of things, eh, Ishbel?'

She nodded. 'Things that matter.'

'When are we going to tell them – I mean, the family?' he whispered, standing close.

'About us?'

'Of course, about us.'

'I think we'll have to wait a little while. See how Monnie gets on.'

'Better to get it over with, is my view.' He kissed her cheek. 'I'm not worried about my girls, you know – they'll understand. But what about your son and daughter-in-law?'

'Oh, I'm sure Niall and Sheana will be delighted,' Ishbel answered, so quickly Frank guessed she wasn't sure at all. 'They just want me to be happy.'

'As I do. I want to make you happy.'

'It's the same for me, Frank. You've been through a long sad time. We both have. But it's like you said, we should move on, and now I want to make a new life with you.' Ishbel's gaze on him was steady. 'I won't let anyone spoil that.'

'Nor me,' he said huskily and would have taken her in his arms, but she sidestepped him, saying she must heat up some soup for his poor daughter.

'She is like a little ghost, has lost all her colour, did you notice?'

'I noticed,' he said grimly, and glanced up at the kitchen clock. 'Wonder what Lynette will have to say about it. Suppose she won't be home for some time.'

'Oh, no, she will be late, for sure. But you needn't worry about her, Frank. She's with dear Mr Allan.'

For Lynette and Ronan, the evening at the Altair Hotel, some miles inland from Glenelg, had been perfect. The meal, the service, the ambience, everything, had been just as they wanted – and expected – seeing as the manager was a friendly rival of Ronan's and had pulled out all the stops to impress.

'Oh, yes,' Ronan had said, when they were taking coffee on the terrace. 'Deacon's a good chap, very efficient, really cares about his clientele – that's the mark of a successful manager.'

'You should know,' Lynette told him, accepting the cigarette
he had lit for her. 'You are one.'

'You don't think I'm too . . . serious?'

'Not now. That was just an act you put on. You're just as
efficient, but more human. Didn't I tell you once, that I recognized what was under all that starch? A very sweet, vulnerable
man?'

'Hey, you never said all that!'

Ronan, stubbing out his cigarette, was very slightly blushing,
and Lynette, smiling teasingly, covered his hand with hers.

'It's true, anyway.'

'I don't know . . .' He lowered his voice, glancing round the
shadowy terrace. 'But the thing is, I'm glad I'm not in poor old
Deacon's shoes, human or not. He's having to look for another job.'

'No! Why?' Lynette's eyes were wide. 'Why has he to go? He's
doing a wonderful job here, isn't he?'

'Yes, but the hotel is closing. The owner says it's too small and
isn't paying, so he's letting it go.' Ronan gave a rueful grin. 'Maybe
this part of the world is more a hostel and bed and breakfast sort
of place, anyway? Makes me lie awake at night some times,
wondering.'

'Oh, Ronan, the Talisman's a splendid hotel! Near the sea, and
lovely country and with every comfort – it will always attract
people.'

'Hope you're right.' He gave a sigh and looked at his watch.

'Think we should be making a move? I'll call for the bill.'

'It's been so wonderful, Ronan, I can't tell you. I'll always
remember it.'

'Why, there'll be plenty more times like it, won't there? You'll
want to see me again? And I don't mean at work.'

'No need to ask me. I want to see you again.'

Satisfied, he relaxed, waving his hand to their waiter, who
brought their bill followed by the youngish, keen-faced manager,
Mr Deacon himself.

'Everything all right, Ronan?' he asked, glancing quickly at
Lynette. 'Miss Forester?'

'It's been excellent, Stuart,' Ronan told him. 'Lynette and I
congratulate you. Just wish – you know – things were different
for you.'

'Yes, well, c'est la vie, as they say.' Mr Deacon shrugged. 'But I've a few irons in the fire. Possibly in Glasgow.'

'No interest from buyers for the hotel at present?'

'Oh, there's interest, but not for keeping it as a hotel. Not to worry, Ronan, I think you'll be safe enough at the Talisman.'

'Hope so.' Ronan was moving away with Lynette. 'Keep in touch, Stuart, let me know how things go.'

'Sure, I will,' the manager replied. 'I'll tell you what happens to this place.'

'And I'd be interested in that,' Ronan quietly told Lynette.

Forty

As they drove from the hotel, the daylight, that stayed so long on Highland spring evenings was at last beginning to fade, and the darkness, moving to cover the sky, was causing Ronan to sigh.

'What a shame, the light's going,' he murmured. 'Now I won't be able to see you properly when we stop. I mean, to say goodnight?'

'Of course,' she answered, her voice a little tremulous.

'And you look so beautiful this evening, Lynette, in your blue dress, really lovely. Oh, God, couldn't we stop now?'

'Ronan, we've just set off! I think we'd better get nearer home, don't you?'

Their 'goodnight' stop, off the road to Conair but well away from the hostel, was as filled with passion and delight as they'd known it would be. For one fleeting moment, when she broke from Ronan's embrace, Lynette was struck afresh by the wonder of her situation – but then he drew her back again and she gave up wondering, or even thinking, in the pleasure of their closeness.

At last, of course, they had to part. Lynette said she must go, and Ronan, too, had to get back to the hotel. Slowly, reluctantly, they drove down the empty road to the gates of Conair House.

'One day, you must come in,' Lynette murmured. 'You never have.'

'I can't think of that now. Only of you.' Ronan turned to look at her. 'It's so hard, isn't it? Parting. Is it always going to be this way?'

'I guess it's the way things are.'

'They needn't be,' he said eagerly. 'If we love each other. You do love me, don't you? Because you must know I love you.'

Love. It was strange, but now that Ronan had said the word, Lynette realized she had never actually thought about being in love with him. She wanted to be with him, he had come to be the most important part of her life, he stirred her to the depths of her being. And yet, she had never put it into words for herself that she loved him. Of course, she did, though. She must, to want to be with him, as she did.

'You're not answering, Lynette.' He grasped her hands. 'Why aren't you answering? Tell me, you love me, for God's sake!'

'I do, Ronan, I do!'

'You mean it? You're not just saying what I want to hear?'

'I mean it.' She kissed him on the lips. 'I do mean it.'

'Then will you marry me?'

'Marry?' She stared at him, through the darkness. 'Why . . . oh, heavens, I don't know what to say. I hadn't even thought about it.'

'I've thought of nothing else since the ceilidh.'

'Since the ceilidh?'

'Yes, because we're right for each other. We've each met the one that counts, the one they say that's waiting – everybody has one, the perfect partner.'

'We haven't known each other very long, you know,' she said hurriedly. 'It's a big step – a huge change – we'd have to be very sure . . .'

'I'm sure, I couldn't be more sure.' He hesitated. 'But, look, maybe I have thrown this at you too soon. You may need time to think about it?'

'Time, yes, I do need time. It's – you know such a surprise. I'm sorry, Ronan, I don't think I can answer you now.'

'But you're not saying no?'

She shook her head. 'I'm not saying no. It's like you say, I just need time.'

'I won't hurry you,' he told her quietly. 'This is too important to me for that. We'll just keep on seeing each other, and you'll let me know your answer when you feel you can.'

'I will, I promise.' She began to open the car door. 'But I really must go now. I want to see Monnie, see if she's all right.'

'Why shouldn't she be?'

'I don't know. She was going out with Torquil in his boat today and so looking forward to it, I just hope it went well.'

'She'll be fine. Kiss me goodnight, then, Lynette. One last kiss.'

They kissed quietly and then he came round to the passenger door and very quickly they embraced.

'It was lovely tonight,' she whispered. 'Thank you again, Ronan.'

'Thank you, for coming. I'll see you tomorrow, then.'

'Yes. Goodnight, Ronan.'

'Goodnight, Lynette.'

He watched her running up the drive and round towards the warden's flat, but had driven off, of course, before she'd reached her father's door. Didn't know that her father was still up, in the kitchen, waiting for her, or that all her fears for Monnie had been realized.

'Monnie's very upset,' Frank told her. 'She's not asleep, she'll tell you all about it. But she doesn't want to see Torquil MacLeod ever again.'

Until well into the small hours, the sisters talked, with Lynette soothing and comforting, and Monnie alternating between tears and stony-faced misery.

'You'll see, Monnie, it'll all be for the best,' Lynette kept saying. 'Torquil was never right for you, everyone agreed.'

'Some people thought that. Not everyone.'

'I bet his mother was the only one to approve.'

'His mother.' Monnie's lip curled. 'I see now that he cares a lot more for his mother than he does for me. Look how he caused all the trouble, just by wanting gulls' eggs for her! Left me alone, terrified he wasn't coming back.'

As tears welled into her eyes again, Lynette touched her hand. 'He was being very thoughtless, anyone would say that.'

'You think I'm exaggerating? Behaving like a baby? You don't know what it was like at the time, you weren't there. When I heard the boat roaring away, what could I think?'

'It all proves my point that he isn't right for you. No girl wants to be tied to a fellow who can't see how things might be for other people. I'm just glad you've decided not to see him again.'

'Sounds so easy,' Monnie whispered. 'But it hurts so much.'

'I know, I know. Look, let's try to get some sleep now. Things will look better in the morning.'

Monnie's great eyes rested on Lynette as she switched off her light and settled into bed.

'I didn't ask – how was your evening with Ronan?'

'Very nice. Well, wonderful.'

'Strange, how you've changed towards him.'

'I suppose so.'

Lynette was trying to decide whether or not to tell Monnie that Ronan had asked her to marry him. In the end, she decided not to say anything, to Monnie, or to anyone. It would be best kept a secret, until she'd decided what to do.

'I just understand him better, that's all, and he understands me. Goodnight, Monnie. You will feel better soon, I promise you.'

'Maybe,' sighed Monnie.

Forty-One

On Monday, Frank, agreeing to Monnie's request, was preparing to make a trip into Kyle to buy paint for the redecoration of the common room. Their grant for the new bookcases and snooker table had been approved, and Monnie had decided that she would do the painting before these arrived. First, though, she would have to wash the walls and woodwork down with sugar soap and complete all the preparation work, which meant she had plenty to do.

'And that's what you want, I suppose?' Lynette had asked over the cornflakes. 'Well, it'll take your mind off things, but just don't kill yourself, that's all.'

'Get Mrs Duthie to help you,' Frank advised, but Monnie's brow darkened.

'I do not want Mrs Duthie anywhere around me, so don't you

dare suggest it. She'd probably want to know why I've been crying, and I'm not saying.'

'As though you would!' Lynette said roundly. 'But she isn't in today and you've already stopped crying.'

'Have I?' Monnie jumped up and put her dishes on the draining board. 'Think I'll make a start. Just leave the washing up, Lynette, I'll do it later.'

When she had hurried out, toting a pail of water with mop and scrubbing brush, Lynette sighed. 'Oh, Lord, I see difficult days ahead. She's not going to settle down for some time to come.'

'At least she's doing useful work.' Frank stood up, shaking his head. 'Poor lassie. We all know what heartbreak's like.' He turned his gaze on Lynette, who was clearing the table. 'I suppose I don't have to worry about you, do I? Your Ronan seems a very reliable chap.'

'Oh, yes, he is,' Lynette agreed. If also unpredictable, she added, to herself. Who would have thought he would have proposed to her, for instance, when they scarcely knew each other? Although she did feel a certain guilt over not telling Frank or Monnie about that, she was still convinced she was doing the right thing in keeping it to herself. Better not to tell anyone yet, as she was still no nearer knowing what her answer would be, even though her heart was alight at the thought of seeing him again that morning. Oh, poor Monnie, she thought, running for her bus, if only she could be as happy as I am!

The day wore on for unhappy Monnie, cleaning away, quite alone in the house, with the hostellers out on their expeditions, her father away to Kyle, Lynette at work, but she didn't mind. The way she felt, she didn't want people around her; didn't even want the radio on. Mopping, scrubbing, moving furniture, anything that involved physical effort, seemed to be the key to getting through the hours, and when Frank arrived home with the paint, she didn't really want to stop, even for a late lunch.

'Come on, I'll make us a sandwich,' he said cheerfully, when she'd inspected the paint and found it satisfactory. 'You can't work all day without a rest, Monnie.'

'All right, I'll have a quick bite and a cup of coffee, then I'll crack on.'

'I might go down to the shop afterwards, there are one or two things we need.'

'There are always one or two things we need, eh?'

Frank's gaze met Monnie's and dropped. He seemed on the point of speaking, but changed his mind, moved to the sink and noisily washed his hands, before setting out the makings for their sandwiches.

'Cheese, or potted meat?' he asked, clearing his throat. 'It's Ishbel's potted meat and very good. Or, you could have tomato.'

'Anything will do,' Monnie answered. 'Anything at all.'

By four o'clock, the common room was smelling of soap and disinfectant, and looking wonderfully fresh. Frank said they could move the furniture back before the hostellers returned, but had Monnie thought what they would do once the painting was started?

'Can't have everybody in the common room when the paint's still wet, you know.'

Monnie frowned. 'Hadn't thought of that, I must admit. But if it's a fine evening they can sit outside, I suppose, and it shouldn't take long to dry.'

'Maybe we should have got professional painters in. They'd have been quicker and better on ladders than you and me.'

'Painters cost money and we're trying to save it. No, I think we should do as much as we can ourselves. And who says I'm not good on ladders?'

For the first time, she gave a ghost of a smile, and Frank was smiling, too, when their doorbell rang.

Her smile fading, Monnie glanced quickly at her father.

'It's not fish day,' she faltered. 'It can't be him.'

'He's not coming here on fish day or any other day,' Frank snapped and strode to open the door, ready to do battle, while Monnie watched, her hand to her mouth, until she saw his shoulders relax and heard him cry, 'Why, hello, Paul, it's you!'

It was Paul, only Paul, oh, thank God, thank God.

'Come in,' Frank was saying genially, but Paul said he mustn't, he'd been out all day and must get back to write a stack of letters. Looking towards Monnie, he smiled.

'Just called to see if you'd like to fix a time next week for our hill walk, Monnie? I've got one planned for a hill near Glenelg – not big enough for a Munro and not too difficult.'

'That's wonderful, Paul. Could we make it the end of the week? We're going to be painting the common room.'

'Sounds great, I'll help you! How about Friday, then, or Saturday?'

'Saturday,' she answered promptly, and saw in his eyes that he knew something was wrong, for when had she ever been ready to meet him on a Saturday? Saturdays were for Torquil, he'd always been aware of that. And then he must already have noticed her reddened eyelids, her look of strain; must have guessed there'd been a falling out. Not that he would ever comment.

'I'll call for you about eleven – if that's all right? I think there's a little place en route where we can get something to eat.'

'Perfect.'

'That's fixed, then. But don't forget, I said I'd help with your painting. When d'you want me to come round?'

'Och, there's no need for you to do that, Paul,' Frank said easily. 'We can manage and you've probably got plenty to do.'

'No, I'd like to. I'll look in tomorrow.'

Paul was turning to go, when he halted, glancing quickly back at Monnie.

'Why, you've another visitor coming. Is it fish day for you?'

'Fish day?' Monnie whispered, as a voice she knew well called out. 'Hello, Mr Soutar!'

And Paul, moving away, answered, 'Hello, Torquil.'

Forty-Two

He appeared nervous, standing on their doorstep, turning his cap in his hand after Paul had left them. Nervous, yet so heart-rendingly handsome. Although she knew his face as well as her own, Monnie seemed to be seeing it afresh, after a long, long absence. Much longer than two days. Had it only been two days? Though her father's arm was strong around her, Monnie felt herself trembling, dissolving almost, losing all that had kept her strong since she had said goodbye. It was too much. Too much, to see him again. She couldn't take it.

'Torquil MacLeod,' Frank said curtly. 'Just what the hell do you think you're doing here?'

'I came to see Monnie, Mr Forester.'

'She doesn't want to see you. I think she's made that plain. Please leave now. And don't bother bringing any more fish.'

'You do not want my fish?'

'No, we can do without your services.'

Loosening his arm from Monnie, Frank took a step towards Torquil. 'Are you listening to me, Torquil? We want you to go. My daughter has nothing to say to you. You've upset her too much.'

Torquil's eyes rested on Monnie, who had not been able to take her own gaze from his face, and he smiled. 'Monnie,' he said softly, 'what do you say? Do you want to talk to me again?'

'No!' cried Frank.

'I-I don't know,' said Monnie.

'Just to give me the chance to explain?' Torquil murmured.

'How can you explain?' Frank asked desperately. 'You left her alone, she didn't know where you were—'

Somehow, it didn't seem so bad, did it? All right, Torquil shouldn't have done it, he had upset her badly, but had she made too much of it? Monnie's eyes went to her father.

'Dad, I think – maybe I should talk to Torquil. I mean, I want to be fair—'

'Oh, Monnie, Monnie!' he groaned. 'Don't. Don't get involved again. You've done well, you can come through. Just don't leave yourself wide open for more heartbreak!'

'There will be no heartbreak,' Torquil said quietly.

He stretched out his hand to Monnie, who, after a moment's hesitation, took it, feeling such shameful relief she dared not look at her father.

'It's all right, Dad,' she said in a low voice, moving slowly towards Torquil, still clinging to his hand. 'Don't worry about me. I'll just . . . hear what he has to say.'

'You do that,' Frank cried. 'You do that and take the consequences. I'll certainly say no more. If you want to run headlong into trouble, I can't stop you, but just remember, when the wheels come off the cart, I warned you it would happen. Now, I've things to do.'

Turning sharply, he left them, banging doors behind him, which they didn't even hear, for already they were in each other's arms.

'You know I never meant to upset you,' Torquil was whispering. 'I was a fool, but it was a mistake, that's all, a genuine mistake. Tell me you believe me.'

'I believe you, Torquil.'

And it was true, she did believe him. She had to, but then, she wanted to. Just believing him took away all the pain, the great jagged waves of misery that had consumed her since their parting, and though she felt guilt that she was making herself happy at a cost she couldn't calculate, she knew she couldn't help it. Torquil called, and she answered. All her intentions of never seeing him again seemed now to count for nothing; she was helpless to resist.

'Will you come out for a little while?' he asked, smoothing back her hair from her brow. 'Away from this house?'

'Time's getting on, people will be back soon, I'll be needed.'

'Just for ten minutes before they come, then.'

'All right. I'll just get my jacket.'

'You won't need your jacket. It's warm, it's like summer. Come on, give me your hand.'

She gave him her hand and together they ran down the drive, while watching from his office window, Frank shook his head and groaned.

It was evening. The hostellers had had their meal and were sitting about in the sparkling common room, saying, 'Wow, will you look at this' and 'Hey, wonder where we go when the painting starts?' Collapsing into giggles, when somebody answered, 'Out on the town in Conair, of course!'

Meanwhile, Lynette had just arrived home early from work to be met by Monnie, flushed from cooking, who wanted to get a word in before her father.

'You may as well know,' she said quickly, 'I'm back with Torquil. He came round today and we made it up.'

'Made it up?' Lynette's blue eyes were glassy with surprise. 'I don't believe it. After all you said? How can you have made it up?'

'How indeed?' asked Frank, who was sitting at the table, waiting for supper, his face poker stiff. 'Didn't take him two minutes to make her take him back, all forgiven, all forgotten.'

'I don't know about forgotten,' Monnie said quietly. 'But I think now I might've been – you know – a bit hasty.'

'You weren't hasty, you were right,' Frank said. 'But there's no point going over it. You've made your decision, let's say no more about it and have our tea.'

But Lynette was giving her sister a long direct look.

'Are you happy about this?' she asked shortly.

'Yes.' Monnie's face was defiant. 'Yes, I am.'

'OK, I'll just go and wash before supper. What are we having?'

'Gammon and baked potatoes, it's all ready. Don't be long.'

The meal was good; in spite of all the distractions Monnie had done well, and looking at her sister's face now free from strain, Lynette relaxed and thought, All right, she's taken him back. Why not, if it makes her happy? She knows the risks now, it's up to her to look out for herself. We can't do any more.

Her gaze moving to her father, she saw that he too had relaxed, was looking into space, half smiling, and she wondered, Was he thinking of Ishbel? No, she couldn't really believe that Ishbel had become so important to him, even though something – or, maybe, someone – seemed to be making him particularly happy. But then he was happy anyway, up here in the Highlands.

As for herself, she knew she was half smiling too, thinking of seeing Ronan again that day, meeting his eyes, remembering their lovely time together. True, she hadn't decided what to do about his proposal, but for the time being that didn't matter; it could go on hold while they just enjoyed seeing each other. Being happy.

Seemed they were all happy, then, the three Foresters. Happy in their new life, even if the future was uncertain. Happy enough to have a drink and a toast, or at the very least, a cup of coffee.

'Here's to us and staying happy!' she cried, leaping up from the table. 'I'll put the kettle on, shall I?'

Forty-Three

Real summer came to the Highlands the following weekend. No mixing with winter now, even if the locals did say you sometimes couldn't tell which was which, even if there was still snow on some of the higher mountains. In Conair and everywhere around, all was fine and pleasant.

'Just right for your hill walk with Paul,' Lynette commented to Monnie on Saturday morning before she left for work. 'I take it that's still on?'

'Oh, yes,' Monnie answered, but the colour rising to her brow suggested that all was not as straightforward about the meeting as might have been.

'Torquil not happy?' Lynette asked sympathetically. 'Saturday was his day, eh?'

'Look, I've got to check the dormitories.' Monnie jumped up. 'See you this evening.'

'No, wait. I just want to tell you that Dad says it will be fine if I bring Ronan round tomorrow afternoon. It's time he faced up to seeing his old home again.'

'Ronan's coming here? I thought he didn't want to set foot in the place!'

'He's just afraid of stirring up old sorrows, but I want him to see how much pleasure the house is giving to young folk now. I mean, it might make him feel better.'

'And he's agreed to come?' Monnie shook her head. 'You can certainly twist him round your little finger, can't you?'

'Think so?' Lynette was not displeased. 'But I've got to fly. Could you do me a favour and buy one of Ishbel's cakes for tea on Sunday? I can't get to the shop today.'

'Sure, I'll see what she has, but I won't be here tomorrow myself . . .' Monnie hesitated. 'I've arranged to meet Torquil.'

'I see.' Lynette shrugged. 'Oh, well, can't be helped. I should have guessed, if you can't see him today, he'd want to be with you tomorrow.'

'Yes.' Monnie, her face averted, was already on her way to the dormitories. 'See you tonight,' she called again.

'Don't forget the cake!' Lynette called back, and hurried for her bus, a slight frown disturbing her smooth brow.

'Can't see him today', were the words Lynette had used of Monnie's not meeting Torquil, but it wasn't strictly true. As she made her rounds, checking that all beds had been made, and all hostellers had departed for the great outside, Monnie knew that she might have seen him. Might have cravenly backed out of her hill walk with Paul to be with him, if he hadn't said it didn't matter, they could meet on Sunday.

But when she'd first told him she was to go hill walking with Paul, it had mattered. His light blue eyes had flickered, and a coldness she had never seen in him before had descended on him, like a covering of frost.

'So, you meant it, then?' he asked. 'You agreed to go out with him, you meant never to see me again?'

She had stared at him, perplexed. 'You've never minded about me seeing Paul before, why now?'

'I'm saying that to agree to seeing him on Saturday shows you meant to give me up. That is something of a shock.'

'But why, Torquil? You know I was upset. I did think I would give you up, just for a little while. But if you want me to, I'll ask Paul if we can fix another time. He won't mind, it will be no trouble.'

'You'd do that?'

He seemed to be softening – unfreezing, almost – before her eyes, and as she felt a great rush of relief, she knew that she had been for a moment or two very anxious.

'Ah, well, that's good. It was just a mistake, to fix up to see Mr Soutar on a Saturday. You never meant to give me up.' He drew her into his arms at her father's door, where he had come on Tuesday, just as usual, with his fish. 'Let's just forget all this and say we'll meet on Sunday. How would that do?'

'That would be wonderful, Torquil.'

But as she clattered downstairs and sought out her walking boots from the lobby, Monnie was feeling too guilty to be happy. She should never have offered to change her day for seeing Paul;

that had been wrong and only done to placate Torquil, who should not have needed placating, anyway. If only she had been as strong when she was with him, as she felt now! As clear-sighted and firm to do what was right! But if she had managed to put on a show of strength when he had so much upset her, she was very unsure that she could ever do it again.

'Everyone's away to the hills,' Frank said, coming out of his office. 'And they've a grand day, eh? You, too. When's Paul coming?'

'About eleven. I've just got time to run down and buy the cake Lynette wants for tomorrow.'

As her father gave her a quick glance, she knew he wanted to say something about Torquil, but thinking of something to deflect him, she asked quickly if maybe he'd like to go for the cake instead.

'Just while I'm still here, getting ready, Dad, in case anybody wants to book in.'

'Go to the shop?' His face brightened. 'Aye, I'll nip down now. It's for Ronan, eh? What sort shall I get?'

'Oh, leave it to Ishbel. She'll give you something nice.'

'Be back in a tick, then.'

Away went Frank, beaming like a child running out for sweeties, while Monnie concentrated on giving her new boots another protective rubbing and looking out for Paul. When he came, a little early, she was ready with her anorak over her arm, her boots firmly laced, and her small rucksack on her back.

'Paul! Lovely to see you. I've just got to wait for Dad, though. He should be back from the shop any minute.'

'Here he comes now!' cried Paul, waving. 'Nice to see you, Mr Forester. Aren't we lucky with the weather?'

'Och, I'm out of breath,' Frank gasped. 'Sorry, I'm late, Monnie, we got to talking, Ishbel and I.'

'Did you?' Monnie raised her eyebrows. 'Now, why am I not surprised? What sort of cake did you get, then?'

'One of Ishbel's best – the coffee and walnut.' Frank reverently placed a cardboard box on his reception counter. 'Well, you two'd better get off, eh? Have a good climb then. And Paul, the name is Frank, OK?'

'OK.' Paul, grinning, took Monnie's arm. 'And Frank, don't worry. I'll take good care of her.'

'I won't worry,' Frank said simply. 'I know you will.'

Forty-Four

Though she knew she had no need to feel nervous over hill walking, Monnie couldn't help worrying in case she somehow let Paul down. He was so kind, so anxious for her to enjoy the thing that meant so much to him, it had become very important to her to acquit herself well. But supposing she didn't? Found it all too much, couldn't keep up? He wouldn't blame her, of course, but she knew she would feel so bad about it.

In the event, he said she was a natural. The perfect walker to be his first pupil. How had it happened? More by good luck than good management, she'd told him, but he said not at all. She had the right build, the right strength and fitness, and with training, he could see her becoming a very accomplished Munro bagger.

All of these complimentary remarks came at the summit. To begin with, there'd been the easy start, which had involved driving to the little place he knew, no more than a hut, really, on a minor road out of Glenelg, where they could get coffee and rolls and delicious sticky buns.

'Carbohydrates – good for energy,' Paul remarked. 'Like chocolate – but I've got plenty of that in my rucksack.'

He had been watching her, she'd noticed, while they ate, and now he said quietly, 'It's good to see you looking so well, Monnie.'

'Am I?'

'Oh, yes. I was worried about you the other day. You don't mind if I say that?'

'I didn't think you would mention it.'

'We're friends, aren't we? Friends can say if they're worried.'

'You've no need to worry about me.'

'No, that seems true today.' He lightly touched her hand. 'And you needn't tell me anything unless you want to, I'm not asking that. But if you did want to talk, it sometimes helps, you know.'

'Yes, I know. Maybe later.' She raised her eyes to his and tried to laugh. 'Just now, I'm worrying about that hill we have to climb.'

'No, no, we walk it.' Paul laughed too and stood up. 'Better make use of the little comfort station at the back. First lesson in hill walking – don't be worrying about the loo.'

They had left the little catering outpost to cries of 'Good luck!' from the elderly owner and a couple of walkers still having lunch, and taken an overgrown track leading, some miles on, to a tiny loch.

'Don't ask me to say its name,' Paul told Monnie, halting to take off his waterproof jacket, for the day had become very warm. 'It's Gaelic, of course, like the name of the hill we're aiming for – and that's hard to say, too. Really think I'll have to take a few language lessons before I open my school.'

'Found a property yet?' Monnie asked, who was already stuffing her own jacket into her rucksack.

'Not yet. One or two possibilities. What do you think of the view? You can look over to a couple of hills from here, one being ours.'

'The colours are beautiful.' Monnie, shading her eyes with her hand, gazed at the amazing blue of the little stretch of water, and in the distance the vivid greens and browns of the hills Paul was pointing out. 'Don't seem so high, though, do they? Not like that hill near Arnisdale.'

'High enough, I think you'll find, once we get going to ours. It's not altogether easy terrain.'

'Now you tell me!' cried Monnie.

Some two hours later, having made their way up and over rough, muddy country, rising much higher than Monnie could have ever imagined from her distant view, they reached what Paul described as the summit.

'The summit?' Monnie gasped. 'Seems . . . seems more like a plateau.'

'Ideal for resting, then.' Paul grinned. 'Come on, let's sit down – it's fairly dry – and have some chocolate. Water first, though. We need it.'

They both drank long and thirstily from their water bottles, then ate Paul's melting chocolate, until they felt their batteries pleasantly recharged and lay back to rest.

'This is so nice,' Monnie murmured, enjoying the sun on her face and bare arms. 'I suppose I've been lucky. How often is the weather like this?'

'Very rarely. Usually, there are strong winds, rain, mist, snow showers – all good fun.'

Monnie smiled, too, and was silent for a while. Suddenly, she sat up. 'Paul, you know something?'

'What?'

She hesitated. 'I think I would like to tell you what happened between Torquil and me. You know something did, I suppose?'

'I'd guessed,' he answered quietly.

'Yes, well, it's true you're a friend and I don't want secrets from you. Not that it was all that terrible – in fact, I maybe made too much of it, I don't know.'

Paul, chewing a piece of grass, said nothing, though she could sense the intensity of his interest, and hurried on to tell her story, wanting to get it over with, and know his reaction.

Again, in its retelling, she felt she'd magnified her ordeal. After all, what had happened? She'd been left alone on an island, she'd heard Torquil's boat leaving, she was cold and frightened and thought all sorts of hysterical things. Was that all it was? A thoughtless action from him, the wrong reaction from her?

'That's what happened,' she finished slowly. 'Do you think I was in the wrong? Blaming him? He never meant me any harm.'

Paul, his gaze on Monnie steady and considering, threw aside his blade of grass. 'You weren't blaming him because he meant to do you harm, Monnie. You were blaming him because he hadn't thought about you. Isn't that it?'

She took a cotton sun hat from her backpack and pulled it down over her brow before she answered. 'Yes, that was it. It seemed an age to me that he'd been gone, because of the mist and the loneliness. Then, when I heard the engine of the boat, I – I suppose I panicked. I really did think he'd left me.'

'He hadn't told you what he was doing. In the circumstances, you were right to wonder what the hell was going on.' Paul reached over and took her hand. 'I don't blame you at all for reacting the way you did. And when he came back to you, I'm not surprised you wanted to finish with him.'

'But I haven't finished with him,' she said in a small voice. 'Paul, I can't.'

He took his hand from hers and looked away from her, back to the views. 'You're in love,' he said at last. 'That's what being in love means, I suppose. You accept, you forgive. If you can say goodbye, maybe you're not in love after all.'

'I did try, to say goodbye, because I thought Torquil didn't care for me. But then he came to the hostel – and there was nothing I could do.'

'He cares for you, after all?'

'He seemed to want to see me again, and I couldn't say no. That's the way it is, when I'm with him.' She shook her head. 'I don't see myself saying goodbye to him again.'

'Monnie, what are you saying?' Paul suddenly leaped to his feet and pulled her up with him. 'He has a hold over you? You can't think for yourself when you're with him? That's not just being in love – that's obsession. And is Torquil right for you, anyway? He's handsome, he has surface charm, but what's underneath?'

Just for a moment, Paul held her close. 'I'm worried about you, feeling for him as you do,' he whispered, letting her go. 'Forgive me if I'm speaking out of turn, but has he ever said he wants marriage?'

'No, but I'm sure it's in both our minds. Something to think about for the future. There's no need to be worried, anyway. Honestly, there isn't.' She put her hand to his cheek. 'I think maybe I've given the wrong impression. Torquil told me himself, he's not like Tony, and I'm not going to end up like Tony's girl-friend who had to leave the village.'

'You're under his spell, Monnie. You said yourself, you can't think straight when you're with him.'

She pulled off her hat and ran her hands through her dark hair. 'I'm all right, Paul. I can't say more. Shall we go back now?'

'Yes, we'll go back,' he said heavily. 'Better make sure we've left no litter. Chocolate paper, and such.'

'All in the rucksack.' She slung it on to her back and replaced her sun hat. 'Sorry if I spoiled things, talking about myself. You did say you would listen.'

'I always listen.' He swung up his own rucksack and took a deep breath. 'But if I got a bit carried away, let's forget about it, OK? We mustn't spoil things between us, because we've a lot of hill walks ahead of us. You're a natural, you know. The way you've kept up today, I couldn't be more impressed.'

'It was more by good luck than good management, I'm sure.'

'Not at all. You've got the right build, the right strength and fitness. With training, I see you becoming a very accomplished Munro bagger.'

Oh, what a relief it was, to be talking of hill walking and not her love life, thought Monnie. Yet, she had brought it up and wasn't sorry. It was good Paul knew about her feelings for Torquil, even if he had, as he put it, got carried away. Best that he knew how things were for her, for though he'd never told her and probably never would, she knew very well how things were for him. With all her heart, she wished they could have been different, but she had no magic wand. The three of them – herself, Torquil and Paul – must all do what they could with what had come to them. And if Torquil came out best, it was only to be expected, because he cared the least.

Forty-Five

Before she left Fionola in charge after lunch on Sunday, Lynette asked her to do her a favour.

'Yes, if I can. What is it?'

'Well, if you should see Scott, could you not tell him I've asked Ronan over to the hostel today?'

'He'd care?'

'It's just that we're good friends and he might wonder, you know, why I haven't invited him.'

'Surely there's a special reason for inviting Mr Allan?'

'Yes, but I think I'd just as soon not have Scott know about it.'

'Lynette, he must know by now that you and Ronan are . . . well, as good as engaged.'

'That's not true, as a matter of fact.'

Fionola smiled. 'We're all expecting an announcement any day.'

'Same might be said about you and Mr Warner.'

'Mr Warner?' Fionola's smile became a laugh. 'Come on, he isn't even here. He's gone home.'

'Bet he did propose, didn't he?'

'He did, in a roundabout way. And I refused, in a roundabout way. Didn't want to hurt his feelings, poor old chap.'

Fionola hesitated for a moment, then took a small jeweller's box from her bag beneath the desk and opened it. 'Look, he insisted on giving me this. Drove all the way to Inverness for it.'

'Oh, my!' At the sight of the small brooch glittering inside the box in a very expensive way, Lynette's eyes opened wide. 'Fionola, that's beautiful.'

'You think it's valuable?'

'Looks it. Not that I know anything about jewellery.'

'If it is worth a lot, I'll send it back to him. I really don't want to take anything of that sort from him.'

'Then you'd hurt his feelings.'

Fionola shrugged. 'Maybe I'll think about it, then. Oh, look out, here comes Mr Allan.'

'All set?' called Ronan, fast approaching, his eyes on Lynette.

'All set!' she cried, noting that in his off duty clothes of pale blue shirt and light trousers, he was looking unlike himself, and though still handsome, rather strained.

'You'll be all right?' she asked Fionola. 'It's usually pretty quiet on a Sunday afternoon, eh?'

'I'll be fine.' Fionola was deftly slipping the jeweller's box back into her bag, out of Ronan's sight. 'Have a nice time off, won't you?'

'I'll be back by six,' Ronan told her. 'Miss Atkinson will be in charge until then, and she has a contact number, in case I'm needed.'

'Ronan,' sighed Lynette, 'can we go?

In the car, driving the short distance to Conair, she could tell that he was very much on edge, as though he were facing some terrible ordeal. But then, of course, returning to his old home did represent an ordeal to him, as was proved by the fact that he'd never once been back, though he lived so close. Hope he's not going to be really upset, Lynette thought, suddenly recalling that making folk do what was good for them sometimes backfired.

'It'll be all right, Ronan,' she whispered, as they reached the gates to the hostel. 'But if you're really not happy, we can always give this a miss.'

'No, I said I'd come and I meant it.' He gave her a quick glance. 'And now we've got this far, I'm really quite curious.'

'That's good. Let's leave the car here and walk up, shall we? Aren't we lucky, it's another lovely day?'

He did not answer, his attention being only on the old house before them; that Scottish Baronial house Lynette had come to know so well she scarcely noticed its turrets and cupolas and generally 'over the top' appearance any more. But now she saw it through Ronan's eyes and knew he must be thinking of the pride he'd had in his home, of its grandness and distinction, and of how its exterior, at least here, had not changed.

But when they met a few young people just leaving the house, he seemed taken aback, as though these strangers were too much for him, and it was Lynette who spoke to them.

'You've just booked in?' she asked crisply. 'Fine, I expect the warden told you, everyone else is out for the day, but if you like to go exploring, they'll all be back about five.'

'That's right, he did tell us,' they said cheerfully. 'We said we'd be back by five.'

'Enjoy your afternoon,' she called, and when Ronan belatedly called out a goodbye, she sighed and smiled.

'No need to look so worried, Ronan. If you come to a hostel, you'll see hostellers, you know. But, come on, let's go inside. Ready?

'Ready,' said Ronan.

Forty-Six

They stood together at the handsome, studded front door, with its heavy locks and clasps.

'You'll remember this, I expect?' Lynette asked. 'I believe it's the original.'

'Oh, yes, I remember it. This was our door.'

Touching it briefly, he moved through into the entrance hall, then halted, brought up short by the sight of the stags' antlers high on the walls.

'Good God, they've still got those up there,' he whispered. 'I never dreamed to see them again. My old friends.'

'You didn't shoot them, did you?' asked Lynette.

'No, no. The family shot them. We weren't "family", you know. Just people who bought the house.' In a low voice, he added, 'And lost it.'

'Dad's office is just here,' Lynette said hastily. 'That's new, of course. Just been stuck on as an extra.' She called through the open door, 'Dad, are you there? Ronan's here.'

Out came Frank, followed, to Lynette's surprise, by Ishbel who was looking very attractive in a sleeveless summer dress.

Didn't look her age, did she? But Lynette was wondering when her father had invited her. He'd never said a word to her. Seemed these days he was meeting Ishbel more and more.

'How nice to see you, Mr Allan!' Ishbel cried, and Frank, shaking Ronan's hand, said how pleased he was to see him in his old home at last.

'Hope you don't think it's been hacked about too much, Ronan. Some changes had to be made, of course.'

'Of course, I quite understand,' Ronan replied, drawing on his social skills, for of course he didn't understand, thought Lynette, and never had. To him, as a boy, it must have seemed the least easy thing to understand in the world, that his home should be changed. As a man, he'd shown he felt the same.

'I'm afraid the staircase has taken a bit of a beating,' she murmured apologetically. 'The floors too, of course. Need a lot of work.'

'I believe they were always hard work,' Ronan replied. 'I seem to remember seeing the maids polishing and so on.'

'Did you know that Brigid's mother was parlour maid here in the old days?' Lynette asked him, as they moved a little away from Frank and Ishbel.

He stared and flushed scarlet. 'Brigid's mother? Oh, Lord, I should have known that, shouldn't I? Why did nobody tell me?'

'Everyone knows you don't like to be reminded of your home,' Lynette said quietly.

'You've reminded me.'

'I thought it would be good for you.'

'Thank you, Nanny Forester,' he said, relaxing and laughing. 'Where to now?'

'The common room. I believe it used to be the drawing room.'

'Oh, yes,' Ronan agreed, his laughter dying. 'This was the drawing room.'

As he stood, looking around, Lynette pointed out the newly painted walls and woodwork, all done by Monnie and Paul, and explained that new bookcases were on their way, as well as a snooker table.

'And as you see there's a record player, for folk to play the Elvis Presleys and so on, and a piano for the sing-songs.'

'Sing-songs?'

'Oh, yes, there's always a get-together before bed. No telly, of course – can't get the reception.'

'I can see your father works hard for the young people. Monnie, too. She's not here today?'

'Out with Torquil.' Lynette was studying Ronan's expressionless face. 'I know you're finding it changed,' she murmured, 'but it's a nice room still, isn't it? And hasn't lost the plasterwork ceiling.'

'I noticed that,' he agreed.

They moved on, past the long dining room, now partitioned into a dormitory, and climbed the stairs to look in at the dormitories created from the old bedrooms, which Lynette was glad to see had been specially tidied by Monnie.

'All changed again,' she said brightly. 'Partitions everywhere. But new bathrooms, you'll notice.'

'An improvement on my day,' Ronan admitted, and stood for some time looking about him. 'Somewhere or other, there should be my old room. I suppose it's been swallowed up into a dormitory.'

'There is a small room at the end of the landing. I think it was difficult to fit it in, so it's used for storage. Want to see it?'

'Oh, Lynette,' he said huskily, stepping into the little room that had become a store room, 'this is it, this was my room. I can't believe it's still here. My bed was in this corner – and then I think there was a wardrobe . . . and the window – see the window? Looks out to Skye.'

He turned to Lynette, his eyes alight. 'The hours I must have spent here, eh? Often at this window, gazing out at the hills. It was one of the happiest times of my life.'

'Was it?' she asked softly, and came to stand next to him, slipping her arm into his, sharing with him the view that had meant so much. 'You don't mind, seeing it again?'

'No, I'm glad. I'm glad to have seen it. I was wrong, to try to shut everything out, because I'd lost it.' He bent to kiss her gently. 'Thank you, for bringing me back.'

'Oh, Ronan, what a relief! I could tell you were getting more and more depressed . . .'

'No. No, I wasn't. I knew there would be changes, but when I finally saw them, I realized they'd been done as well as possible and – I don't know – I didn't mind them as much as I thought I would. I seemed to be able to look beyond, remembering what we'd had, but not with so much hurt.' He held Lynette close. 'You're a wonder, though, aren't you? How did you guess it would happen?'

'I thought you might have moved on. The way people do.' She put her face to his. 'I'm just glad if I was right.'

After a long kiss, they pulled apart and Lynette said they'd better go down for tea.

'In Dad's flat which is new to you, so no need to worry,' she told him, at which he kissed her again and said he wasn't worrying.

'There's just something I'd like to say before we go.' She gave him a long serious look. 'It's wonderful that you're feeling happier about the hostel, anyway, but the other thing to remember – and I'm always saying this – is that your old home's been such a godsend to the folk who come here. I mean, it's opened up the hills and the countryside for them in a way they could never have afforded if they'd to pay elsewhere.'

She took his hand, leading him back towards the staircase.

'And if you could just see their faces when they come in, after their day away, I know you'd understand what I'm saying.'

'I do understand, Lynette. I'm glad, honestly, that other folk can share what I had.'

'Ah, Ronan, that's nice to hear. Maybe I've been maligning you.'

'Not lately,' he said teasingly, and together they ran down the stairs for tea.

Seeing Ishbel moving easily round their kitchen gave Lynette a rather strange feeling. It was as though she'd already moved in, which was absurd. But she did seem to know where everything was, and it was her coffee cake she was slicing, and her soda scones, she was buttering, and all the time, she was smiling her friendly smile and Frank was watching her as though she was something special.

Still, tea went off very well, with Ronan charming everyone by being perfectly at ease and praising all that he'd seen, the warden's flat included. If only Monnie were here too, Lynette thought, and suddenly there she was, back in time to help with the return of the hostellers she said, but ready for some of that coffee cake first.

'Had a good day?' Lynette asked, when they went together to make fresh tea.

'Oh, yes, it was fine.' Monnie seemed relaxed. 'We just went for a walk, you know.'

'And Torquil was OK?'

'Yes, I said, everything was fine.'

'That's good. And we've had a lovely afternoon here. Ronan wasn't too upset at all, about seeing the house. In fact, he feels much better about it all round.'

'Trust you to be right!'

'He's got to go back soon, though. Might just have time to see our happy hostellers coming home. I hope they look as cheerful as I said they would.'

'They will, they always do. But better get Ronan away before they start their cooking, eh?'

At his car, ready to leave, having seen the 'happy hostellers' arrive back and marvelled at their appearance of health and strength, Ronan's eyes were on Lynette as she stood to see him away.

'Thank you again,' he said quietly. 'For everything.'

'I wanted to see if I could help, that's all.'

'You did help. And there's something else.'

She waited, as he hesitated, trying to find the words he wanted.

'Seeing the house again, thinking of how I learned to love the Highlands – it's made me glad I've come back.'

'You don't mean, just to the house?'

'No, to work. To live here, in this part of the world again.' He shook his head. 'I know I could never live anywhere else, Lynette. Could you? Now that you've discovered it?'

She put her hands to her arms, as though she were cold, and said quickly, 'Oh, it's beautiful, I agree. Really . . . beautiful.'

He nodded, watching her face.

'Suppose I should go. Mrs A will be looking out for me. Oh, God, you will be in tomorrow, Lynette?'

'You know I will.'

Looking round, to see if anyone in the village street was watching, they hastily kissed, pressed hands, and parted, Ronan to his driver's seat, Lynette to stand back, ready to wave. In a moment, he was gone and she was left to walk slowly up the drive to the house.

It had been a good day, she was pleased it had gone well. If only there weren't that cold feeling around her heart that she would not even try to identify.

'Lynette,' Monnie called, catching her as she went into the flat. 'You didn't tell me Ishbel was coming here today.'

'I didn't know. Dad invited her.'

'Hmm. Well, she's gone home now, but she does seem to be here a lot, eh?'

'Or, he's at the shop.'

They looked at each other.

'Suppose we'll find out sooner or later what's going on,' said Monnie.

'Come on, we already know,' Lynette retorted.

But of course they couldn't be sure.

Forty-Seven

Early in July, Frank sprang a surprise on the girls. Not the one they'd been expecting, which wouldn't have been a surprise, anyway, but news of a weekend trip he intended to take back to Edinburgh.

'Edinburgh?' Monnie echoed. 'To see the flat?'

'To see the flat. Yes, it's about time I did a check. I'll only be away two nights, Friday and Saturday. You can cope, Monnie?'

'Of course. It'd be fun, to be in charge.'

'A weekend in Edinburgh,' Lynette was saying thoughtfully. 'Dad, how about I come with you? Fionola's taking Saturday off this weekend, I could go the one following. What do you think?'

'Why, it's a great idea, Lynette. I'd be glad to have you.'

The news that Lynette was to be away for a weekend was not well received by Ronan.

'You're going to Edinburgh?' he asked blankly. 'Why not have checked with me first?'

'Why, it's all right if I go, isn't it?' Lynette asked, frowning. 'I'm entitled to one weekend off every five weeks on our rota.'

'Oh, I'm not saying you can't go, but we might have gone together. Now this date you've booked is when I have some people from Inverness coming over to do a recce for a conference. I can't get away.'

'I'll only be looking round our old flat with Dad, Ronan. It'd be much better if we went together some other time, eh?'

'If you say so,' he sighed, his brow still dark.

Scott's face, on the other hand, when he heard of Lynette's plans, was sunny.

'Tell me the dates again,' he said, when she was taking her coffee in his kitchen. 'Mid July, eh? Well, that's a coincidence, if you like.'

'What is?'

'Why, I'm going to Edinburgh that same weekend! Can you believe it?'

'No,' said Lynette, with a laugh, in which Scott's assistants joined. 'I don't believe in that sort of coincidence.'

'But it's true! I've got an appointment on Saturday morning in George Street, honest.' Scott turned to Hamish. 'You tell her, Hamish. I'm leaving you in charge, right?'

'Right,' groaned Hamish. 'And I'm shaking in my shoes already.'

'Come off it, you're a good chef, you'll be fine. Lynette, you believe me now, eh?'

'I'll have to.' She drank her coffee, smiling. 'So, are you going to travel with Dad and me on Friday? We're just going to check our old flat.'

'I'd like to,' Scott said earnestly. 'But is You Know Who no' going with you?'

'He means Mr Allan,' Brigid put in helpfully.

'I know who he means,' Lynette retorted. 'No, Mr Allan is

not going with me, but if you want to travel with us, that'd be grand.'

'It's a date,' he said, beaming. 'Tell your dad I'll drive us all to Inverness, now that I've got my old banger. We can do the trip in one day, if we take the train from there, and it won't hurt to leave the car at the station.'

To be back in Edinburgh, it seemed so strange. As though, Lynette thought, she'd been away for years, and to somewhere foreign, too. Was her father feeling the same? Was Scott?

Scott said he'd been back a couple of times to see his mother, he'd sort of got used to the feeling of coming home when he first set foot on the platform at Waverley Station. But yes, there was at the back of his mind, the idea that he'd left behind a strange land. A beautiful land, of course.

'Oh, yes, beautiful.' Lynette, in the taxi they were sharing, agreed and remembered with a little stab her use of the same word to Ronan. 'But strange. Well, different. How d'you feel, Dad?'

'How do I feel?' Frank's face, in the dusky light of the taxi, was hard to read. 'Well, I'm glad to be back. I realize I've missed Auld Reekie more than I thought. But I won't mind when I have to leave again, put it that way.'

No more was said until they dropped Scott off at his mother's flat, when they arranged to have a meal together the following evening, though he and Lynette also agreed to meet earlier, for a sentimental walk in the city.

'Not going to tell us about your appointment on Saturday morning?' Lynette asked cheekily. 'Don't mind me, I'm just being nosey.'

'Maybe one day,' he answered seriously. 'At the moment, it's a secret. Hey, here's Ma looking out – quick, say hello!'

After a brief handshake with Scott's mother, a friendly, youthful-looking redhead, it was back to the taxi for Lynette and her father, with butterflies for her, she said, all the way to their tenement.

'This certainly seems to mean a lot to you,' Frank remarked when they'd paid off the taxi and were standing at the foot of the well-known stair. 'I never realized how attached you were to the place.'

'I'm not sure I even knew myself.' She stood looking up the stair towards the first landing. 'But I know I was glad we kept the flat on.'

'Let's go up, then. I'll just open the door and run up to speak to Mrs Logan.'

'No,' Lynette said quickly. 'Let's go in first, and then speak to Mrs Logan.'

'OK, just as you like.' Frank laughed a little edgily. 'Hope the key still fits, eh?'

It fitted, and slowly they stepped over the threshold of their old home.

Now I feel like Ronan, coming back, thought Lynette, looking around at all that she remembered. Except that her home hadn't changed. Hadn't changed at all. Everything was still there, so neat, so clean – Mrs Logan had done a good job. The table where they'd had so many meals, the range, the cooker, the sofa and chairs, the pictures, the television, the book shelves, Ma's handworked rug, some of her cushions they'd left behind . . .

'Oh, Dad,' Lynette said softly, as memories of her mother came rushing like a torrent over her. 'Oh, Dad!'

And as he put his arms around her and held her, she melted into tears.

Of course, she quickly recovered herself. Had to, really, as Mrs Logan was soon knocking at the door and hurrying in to greet them.

'Now is it no' grand to see you folks again!' she cried, shaking Frank's hand, hugging Lynette. 'I thought I heard a taxi and we don't get many, so I guessed it would be you. But don't you both look well, eh? And I bet Monnie's the same. Highland air is suiting you, all right!'

'Everything's looking so nice here, Mrs Logan,' Frank told her. 'We're really impressed, aren't we, Lynette? And I've got your envelope here, now—'

'Och, now I don't want paying, Mr Forester! What are neighbours for?'

'Come on, this is an ongoing job.' Frank put his envelope into her hand, at which she shook her head and said he shouldn't, she felt so bad, then rattled on.

'Now, I ken it's summer, but this flat has got very chill, so I've lit the range and put some hot water bottles in your beds. You'll no' be wanting to catch your deaths, eh? And when you're ready, come away up the stair and have a nice bit of meat pie with Bob and me. Don't be long now!'

'Oh, dear, I feel like crying again,' sniffed Lynette, as Mrs Logan bustled away. 'What can we say?'

'Aye, they were good neighbours here,' Frank murmured, walking slowly round the flat, picking up books and putting them down, switching on the radio and turning it off. 'Seems odd, we're not here any more.'

'You had to move on, Dad.'

'True, and I'm glad I did. And you are, too, eh?'

'Oh, yes.'

He gave her a long keen look, then picked up his overnight case and said he'd have a wash before going up to Mrs Logan's.

'That's a nice laddie, yon Scott, Lynette. Wonder what he's up to, back in Edinburgh?'

'Whatever it is, he's not saying,' answered Lynette, who was still wondering that herself.

At night, in her old bed with its warm sheets, she thought of Ronan, so very far away, but like the Highlands that were so clear cut when she was there and now seemed indistinct, his image was cloudy in her mind. As soon as she returned, it would be this place that lost its clarity, and Ronan would be his true handsome self. She was just all at sea at the moment, had become disorientated, which was not like her. How lucky it was she'd soon be back in Conair.

Which reminded her – how was Monnie coping?

Thinking of her sister, Lynette fell asleep.

Forty-Eight

Monnie, acting as senior warden for the first time at Conair House, was pleased with the way she was managing. She hadn't felt nervous at all. In fact, having to rely on herself, had given her confidence. Of course, she had to admit, laughing a little on Saturday afternoon, she'd only been on her own for two days. Well, to be honest, one and a half so far, but for one of those – Friday – she'd had to accept advice from Mrs Duthie, which had not made things easy.

Lord, how tactful one had to be! How did her father cope, then? Monnie herself was soon tired of Mrs Duthie telling her what to say to those laddies who left wet towels on the bathroom floor, and shouting 'door', when Monnie could hear the bell perfectly well and had already come running. Then there was the perpetual problem of the hostellers' kitchen and the way they left the stove . . .

'Now if I was you, Monnie,' Mrs Duthie announced, 'I would start fining 'em. Yes, I would. Anybody leaves grease on the stove, or in the frying pan – did you see it this morning? – they pay a shilling into a fines box. And in no time, you'd have money to do all sorts of things, you mark my words!'

'I really don't think the young folk would be willing to pay a shilling for not cleaning the frying pan.'

'Teach 'em a lesson. You tell your dad what I said, my dear. I'm surprised he's not thought of it himself.'

Monnie, rolling her eyes, hurried off to her father's office, where she settled down to some typing and accounts work he'd left her, and after Mrs Duthie had completed her usual whirlwind of cleaning and departed, everything was beautifully peaceful and orderly. Until, of course, the hostellers came back and then it was action stations again and time went flying by.

No Torquil, though. Although it was Friday, he had not brought her any fish. Strange. Perhaps he'd thought she didn't want any because she was on her own? Still, he might have looked in, anyway.

All had gone well on Friday night, though she'd felt a bit worried in case any of the young men decided to visit any of the young women after lights out, which, of course, was strictly forbidden. Her father had, in fact, given her specific instructions to watch out for it, reminding her that as wardens they were standing in for parents.

'They don't usually disobey the rules like that,' Monnie had pointed out, and Frank had agreed, that no one had tried it on when he was around. But with only Monnie – well, who could say what they might do?

She'd hardly slept after that sort of warning, but as far as she could tell, there'd been no nocturnal visits and when morning came, her confidence had returned. Once everyone was out for the day, she'd had time to tidy up, check the awful frying pan and so on, and think about seeing Torquil again.

Here it was, though, Saturday afternoon and she hadn't seen him, and she'd felt so sure he'd come. Thinking back, though, to last Sunday, she wondered if maybe she should have been so sure. She hadn't told Lynette, but there'd been a change in him recently, since their quarrel. A change that was hard to describe. Even to be sure was there, maybe. But he had seemed curiously watchful. Watchful of her.

She sat in the office, still working on the accounts, trying not to watch the clock, or listen for the ring of the front door bell.

Suddenly, the bell did ring and she jumped to answer it, but it was only two young people wanting to book in. She took all their details, went through all the motions, then gave them a bus timetable and pointed them on their way to Glenelg.

Peace again. Back to the office. Another ring at the bell.

And it was Torquil.

They clung together, kissing, for so long, she wondered that she had ever thought him different. This was the old Torquil, wasn't it?

She drew herself away at last, studying his handsome face.

'This won't do, you know, I'm supposed to be working.'

'And here am I thinking you are going to offer me a cup of tea.'

'Oh, well, I can do that. I'm due one anyway. But I'll have to make it in the hostel, so I can hear the bell if anyone comes.'

Making the tea in the large kitchen she'd just tidied, Monnie felt at ease, as though seeing Torquil again had freed her from her suspicions.

'You didn't bring me any fish yesterday,' she told him, setting out cups. 'Did you forget?'

'No.' He was lounging back in one of the kitchen's shabby chairs. 'I thought you wouldn't want any, being on your own.'

'You might still have come. I mean, bringing the fish isn't the only reason for coming, is it?'

She turned, ready to hand him his tea, but as her eyes met his, her heart sank. It was there again. That watchful gaze. The sort of gaze you might train on someone you didn't actually trust. Did he think that of her? That she was someone not to be trusted? That, perhaps, she was going to leave him again?

'Here's your tea,' she whispered.

'Any biscuits?'

'Chocolate digestive?'

'My favourite.'

He was so nearly the Torquil she knew, but, then, not quite. And she was sure now that she was not imagining it. There had been a change. Since the quarrel.

'Are you worrying?' she ventured. 'You don't need to.'

'Am I worrying?' He snapped his chocolate biscuit, ate half of it, still watching her.

'I think you might be. Might be worrying that I'm going to leave you again.'

'Well, you did leave me, didn't you?'

'Yes, but that was only because I was upset. And I won't be getting upset again.'

'You need not have got upset at all.'

'You know how it was.'

He shook his blond head. 'No, I do not. I only know that you walked away from me.'

Putting aside the remainder of his biscuit, he suddenly swept Monnie on to his knee, where she sat, still as a doll, while he played with her hair.

'You must admit, that was hurtful,' he murmured, close to her face. 'Leaving me, when I had done nothing wrong.'

'It was a misunderstanding, Torquil. I thought we'd agreed to say no more about it.' With an immense effort of will, she pulled herself a little away. 'And now you've brought it up again.'

'You told me I was worrying.'

'Please don't worry, then,' she said earnestly. 'Oh, please let's forget what happened and just be as we were. I won't leave you again. I can't.'

His face was still very close, his eyes never moving from her.

'You mean that, Monnie?'

'I do.

He gave a long sigh and smiled, one of his old sweet smiles. Anxiously watching, she felt him relax and knew, relaxing herself, that the storm was over.

'I'd better get back to the office, Torquil. I haven't finished the paperwork Dad left me.'

'That's all right, I have to go, anyway. Tony's coming over.'

'Shall I see you tomorrow?'

'Sure. I will look in.'

They had reached the hall and were about to embrace when the front door bell rang piercingly in their ears.

'More customers?' asked Torquil. 'Just let me kiss you.'

'Quickly, then I have to open the door.'

The kiss was brief, only a token, but important. Meant things were all right again. But were they?

'Hello, there!' she called, finally opening the door to several newcomers. 'Want to book in? Please come to the office.'

'I'll be on my way,' Torquil said, easing himself round the young people and their rucksacks. 'See you tomorrow.'

'Tomorrow,' she cried, motioning her new customers towards the reception desk, and was not surprised to find herself trembling and sighing with relief, as though she'd just walked through a minefield.

Forty-Nine

Far away, in Edinburgh, Lynette was strolling with Scott on the castle esplanade, looking down at the crowds in Princes Street and the gardens full of summer visitors.

It was good to be back, she decided, even if some heartache still lingered. At least, the morning light had cleared the night's sense of confusion, so that she'd felt herself again and up to visiting the neighbours and a couple of old friends. Her father had been seeing old cronies too, as well as arranging with the ex-colleague who was to take over temporary tenancy of the flat in the autumn. And Scott? He, of course, had been keeping his mysterious appointment, which he was still refusing to tell her about, while they stood together at the castle battlements.

'All in good time, nosey,' he laughed, shaking his finger at her. 'If things work out, I'll let you know.'

'And we're supposed to be friends!'

'We are friends, more's the pity.'

'Whatever do you mean?'

He shrugged. 'Just joking. I was sort of hinting that it would be better to be more than friends. Come on, you know that's what I would have wanted, only I missed the boat, eh? You Know Who got there first.'

'He does have a name,' she said coldly.

'Mr Allan? Or, do you want me to call him Ronan? That's reserved for you.'

'I think it'd be safer not to talk about him at all.'

'Aye, I agree. Let's go and have some tea.'

Everywhere was crowded, but eventually they squeezed into a little café in the High Street and ordered tea and girdle scones. Scott, though, could not resist going over his loss again, in spite of Lynette's obvious discomfort, which she overcame by much rattling of the teapot and hot water jug and passing of jam for the scones.

'I know you don't like me to talk about it,' Scott said earnestly, 'but it is important to me. I mean, we could have made such a great team, you and me, that's the pity of it.'

'A great team? How would we have been a team?'

Scott carefully covered his scone with jam. 'I only meant we'd be companions, as well as . . . hell, I didn't mean anything at all. Where shall we go for dinner tonight, then?'

'Somewhere cheap.'

'Are you joking?' His brown eyes were glinting. 'Look, I'm a chef. When I eat out, I like to try the menus other chefs are creating, right? Don't forget, I trained at the North British.'

'You're not suggesting we go to the North British?' Lynette

looked aghast. 'Dad would have a fit. We wouldn't be able to enjoy anything, for thinking how much it cost.'

'As though I'd let your dad pay the bill!' Scott cried. 'This was my idea, and it's my treat.' He nodded solemnly. 'And I've got contacts here who'll get us a fine meal that'd make your Mr Allan's eyes pop out, I'm telling you!'

'I thought we'd agreed not to mention Ronan. Maybe I shouldn't be here talking with you, anyway.'

'He'd be jealous?' Scott laughed. 'Don't tell him, then.'

'Of course I'll tell him! I wouldn't dream of keeping it a secret.'

'I would,' said Scott blandly.

The restaurant he chose for their dinner that evening was not one Lynette had heard of and didn't look anything special from the outside, either, being in a small lane off a New Town square. As soon as she and her father saw it was French, however, they knew what to expect and rolled their eyes at each other, as a waiter fussed over seating them and Scott disappeared into the kitchens.

'He knows the chef,' Lynette whispered to Frank. 'He's a contact.'

'Just hope Scott's not expecting me to order. Have you seen the menu?'

'He's not expecting you to order, or pay. Don't worry about it.'

'We'll see about that,' Frank said grimly. 'I'm not letting a young chap like that pay for my meal.'

'Dad, he's got contacts! This French chap is one.'

'Why couldn't we have gone to a Scottish restaurant?' groaned Frank, leaning his head on his hand and looking, Lynette thought, more depressed than just being in a good restaurant should have made him.

'Dad, are you thinking about Ma?' she asked softly.

He raised his eyes and nodded. 'Aye, it's brought it back, being home again. I mean, losing her.'

'I know. I feel the same.'

Touching his hand, she felt a glow of relief that puzzled her for a moment, until she realized it was to do with Ishbel. No need to worry, she told herself. Coming back home had made her father realize afresh what he'd lost. There would be no change to her mother's place in his heart, and at that knowledge her own heart began to lighten, so that she was almost smiling when Scott came back, full of praise for the kitchens.

'Grand stuff there!' he exclaimed. 'Have to hand it to Henri – I couldn't have put together better food myself. Now, I've taken the liberty of ordering for us already, hope you don't mind?'

'No frogs' legs, I hope,' Frank growled, at which Lynette shook her head at him.

'Oh, Dad, please! Scott's doing his best for us, you know.'

Colour rose to Frank's cheekbones and he looked apologetically at Scott. 'Sorry, laddie, I'm really sorry. I'm just a bit of an old grump tonight. I'm sure anything you choose for us will be fine.'

'Don't you worry, Mr Forester—'

'Frank, please.'

'I know it can be a bit off-putting, being in a place like this, but all you've got to remember is that the aim here is to give you the best food possible.' Scott gave an easy smile. 'So, just enjoy it when it comes. And remember, this is my treat.'

'No, no, that's something I'm not happy about, Scott. I'm old fashioned, I think if I go out, I'm the older generation, I should pay.'

'Ah, but I'm getting a deal, Frank. It won't be so much for me.'

'Are you sure?'

'Certain. Now, I'm going to call for the wine list.' Scott raised his hand. 'Don't even think about it, Frank!'

Both Lynette and Frank agreed, when they left the restaurant, that they had never had a better meal, and the wine – oh, Lord!

'My head's buzzing,' Lynette cried. 'I should never have had that extra glass. But it was a wonderful dinner, Scott. Can't praise it enough.'

'Aye, we'll always remember it,' Frank added. 'And that chef, your friend, Henri, Scott, I thought it was really nice of him to come out and say hello to us.'

'He's a good chap. We got on well when we were cooking together.' Scott was rattling coins in his pocket. 'Shall we get a taxi back?'

'Och, no,' said Frank. 'I need the Edinburgh wind to clear my head. Let's walk.'

'Just our luck, it's not windy,' Lynette laughed. 'Why, even the weather seems French tonight. Come back with us, Scott, and we'll have some more coffee.'

'Black,' said Frank.

When Scott left their flat some time later, Lynette went down the stair to see him off.

'Want to thank you again, Scott. You did push the boat out, didn't you, whatever deal you got?'

'I'm just glad you enjoyed it, your dad as well.' Scott laughed shortly. 'Though I have to admit I feel a bit like a male Cinderella at the moment. You know, going home from the ball.'

'Where's the pumpkin?' Lynette's laughter was uneasy.

'There's no pumpkin. Or fairy godmother, either.'

'Scott—'

'No.' He put his finger over her lips. 'Don't say anything, Lynette. And please don't give me a little kiss on the cheek – I don't need that.'

'I wasn't going to,' she said quietly. 'But I can say it's been a good weekend, can't I? For Edinburgh folk, seeing Edinburgh again?'

'Aye, it has. Goodnight, then. See you tomorrow at Waverley, eh?'

'At Waverley.'

Going back up the stair, she felt her head had cleared. Maybe too well.

Fifty

'Any problems?' Frank cried, when he and Lynette arrived back very late at the hostel. Monnie, who'd been on the look out for them for some time, rushed to greet them.

'No problems, Dad.' At least, not with the hostel, she added silently. 'Everything was fine.'

'You get any new people coming?'

'Oh, yes. I booked 'em all in, did all the paperwork. There's no need to worry.'

'Of course there isn't.' Lynette was collapsing into a chair in the kitchen. 'Help, I'm tired! And stiff. Feel as though I've been packed in a sardine tin all the way from Inverness.'

'Very good of Scott to drive us, though,' Frank muttered, yawning and stretching. 'Saved us having to spend the night somewhere.'

'Too right, and I'm very grateful. Monnie, any chance of tea?'

'I'm putting the kettle on now, and then you can tell me all about the weekend.'

'It was lovely and it was sad.' Lynette cast a look at her father, who was sitting at the table, seemingly lost in thought. 'Wouldn't you say that, Dad?'

'What? Oh, yes. Very sad, at times. But, you know, useful. I got quite a bit done.'

He stood up. 'Don't worry about tea for me, Monnie. I'm for my bed. All quiet in the dormitories?'

'They've been asleep for ages.'

'Goodnight, then.' He kissed both daughters, took his bag and departed. 'See you in the morning, girls.'

'Goodnight, Dad.'

Monnie, raising her eyebrows, made the tea, while Lynette shrugged and lit a cigarette.

'Don't ask me if he's all right. I don't know what to make of him.'

'Seems a wee bit upset.'

'Well, I think he is. We both were, seeing the flat again, remembering Ma, you know.' Lynette set her cigarette in a saucer and sipped the tea Monnie gave her. 'The good news is that I'm pretty sure we needn't worry about him and Ishbel any more. Now that he's been home, he's only thinking of Ma. Said it had brought her back.'

'That'd be a relief, but he seems – I don't know – sort of preoccupied to me.'

'He's working out what to tell Ishbel, is my guess.' Lynette drew again on her cigarette. 'Even when Scott took us out to a posh restaurant, he was like that. Pretty grumpy, to be honest.'

'Scott took you to a posh restaurant? Lucky things! While I've been having beans on toast.'

'Didn't Torquil bring you any fish?' Lynette smiled. 'I'm sure he called round, eh?'

Monnie looked down into her teacup. 'Yes, he came round. Didn't bring any fish.'

Lynette's eyes sharpened. 'Was he all right? Did anything happen?'

'Nothing happened. Och, I can't describe it, Lynette. In fact, I wasn't going to say anything . . .'

'About what? Is something wrong?'

'Not wrong, exactly. It's just – things aren't quite the same between us. Since the boat trip.'

Lynette leaned forward. 'Look, you've forgiven him, and if things aren't right, just give him the boot again.'

'Oh, I couldn't do that. No, it's out of the question.'

'Why? People break up all the time. You don't have to stick with someone if you've changed, or he has.'

'You make it sound so easy. Only thing is, I can't do it.'

'Do you want to? That's the point.'

As Monnie made no answer, Lynette said irritably, 'Look, do you love him or not? That's what you have to decide.'

'I did love him,' Monnie said slowly. 'Now, I just know I'm in thrall. Under his spell, Paul says. How do you get out of that?'

'Oh, Monnie!' Lynette groaned and stubbed out her cigarette. 'It's very late,' she murmured wearily. 'I'll have to go to bed. We'll talk in the morning, eh?'

'There's not really a lot more to say,' said Monnie.

The morning brought no relief from Lynette's feelings of unease. With Monnie silent and Frank lost in thought, having breakfast was like being in church, and as soon as she could, Lynette left for work and the bright prospect of seeing Ronan.

But even that, for some reason, failed her.

All the way to the hotel in the bus, she kept thinking about him and how much she loved him, but somehow the image of Edinburgh kept blurring the image, as it had that first night in the old flat. Stop it, she told herself, stop thinking of Edinburgh. Think of Ronan. Think of Ronan.

But it wasn't until she was in his office and in his arms, and they were kissing and caressing to make up for three lost days, that his magic worked and she felt the memory of Edinburgh receding.

'Oh, Lynette, you don't know how I've missed you,' he kept murmuring. 'Please don't go away again.'

'I was only away a weekend,' she said, laughing, freeing herself from his arms.

'Three days. It was a lifetime.'

'You were busy, you wouldn't have seen me, anyway.'

'I'd have known you weren't far away. That would have made all the difference.'

'Listen, I'd better get back to work. Fionola was looking very knowing, when I knocked on your door. I bet Mrs Atkinson and even the porters will be smiling about it, as well.'

'Hell, let them think what they like!' he cried. 'We're as good as engaged, after all.'

When she made no reply, he kissed her gently and ran his hand down her cheek. 'You haven't told me about your weekend,' he said softly. 'How was Edinburgh, then? Did Scott get to his appointment?'

Oh, God, I said I'd tell him, she thought, with sudden anxiety. I promised I'd tell him. Oh, what does it matter? What's a cup of tea?

But she'd said she'd tell him.

'Scott got to his appointment, all right, but he wouldn't say what it was for,' she said casually. 'Even when we had a cup of tea in town, he wouldn't say anything.' After a moment, she added, to make all clear, 'And Dad wasn't with us, so Scott might have told just me.'

'You had tea in town?' Ronan seemed not to notice what she was trying to tell him. 'I'm envious. Always enjoy tea in Edinburgh when I go there, which is once in a blue moon. Did you have a decent dinner somewhere? I expect Scott knows all the restaurants.'

'He took us to a very good French one. Owned by a friend,' he said.'

'I was sure you'd do well on that score. Scott knows his food.' Ronan glanced at his clock. 'Well, I suppose I'd better let you go, dearest Lynette. Thank God you're back.'

They kissed again and he shook his head. 'Can't help feeling sorry for Scott, you know.'

'Why?'

'Come on, you know why. Because he cares for you and you care for me.'

'You're right about me,' she said seriously. 'I'm not sure about Scott.'

'Love will out,' Ronan said lightly, opening the door for her. 'That's why there's no real point in trying to keep our feelings a secret. I don't even want to.'

She slid away, glancing back. 'I'll see you later, Ronan.'

'Make sure you do.'

Somehow, as she took up the reins again, Lynette still didn't feel right. Headachy, weary, anxious, without knowing why. It was no surprise when Fionola commented on her looks, asking her if she was all right, not getting the flu, or something?

'I thought you'd be even more full of life than ever, after your weekend away, you know. But you don't look well.'

'Don't feel it, either. It's odd, because I was happy, being back in Edinburgh – once I'd got used to it again.'

'Know what I think?' Fionola asked, nodding confidently. 'I think you're homesick.'

'Homesick?' Lynette stared. 'What are you talking about? I've been here for months. I can't be homesick!'

'You've reminded yourself of home by going back. It's obvious that's what's got to you.'

Homesick. As Lynette turned away to answer the phone, she wondered, could it be true? Too bad if it was, for she couldn't see herself going home again at any time soon.

'Coming for coffee?'

It was Scott, appearing at Reception, brown eyes dancing, generous mouth smiling. 'Come on, it's all ready and waiting, and I want to know how you're feeling.'

'A bit low, as a matter of fact. Missing Edinburgh.'

'She's homesick,' Fionola put in, smiling wickedly. 'Claims she's not, but she's got all the signs.'

'Homesick?' Scott raised his eyebrows. 'Funny you should say that. I feel exactly the same.'

'You do?' asked Lynette.

'Aye, and the best thing for it is decent coffee. Doesn't cure it, just cheers you up. If you can't have a whisky, that is.'

'I don't think I can spare the time for a break,' Lynette said with a sigh. 'I haven't been back at work long enough.'

'Just go,' ordered Fionola. 'The quicker you go and come back, the quicker I get my break, OK?'

And Lynette did go to sit with Scott out in the gardens for a while, to sip his coffee, talk about their trip, and in the end to feel the better for the break. It wasn't until she returned home late that evening that the blow fell.

'Oh, Lynette, thank goodness you're back,' Monnie cried, running to meet her. 'Something's in the wind. Dad's invited Ishbel and her family round tomorrow evening.'

'Whatever for?'

'He wants to talk to them. Well, to all of us. About something important.'

Something important. The sisters stood together, exchanging wide-eyed stares.

'And we know what that is,' Lynette said, after a moment.

'We don't really know. We could be wrong.'

'So, why doesn't he tell us first? I'm going to ask him now to tell us what's going on. Where is he? In his office?'

'No, right here.' Frank was striding into the kitchen. 'Lynette, glad you're back. You're looking tired. Need an early bed, eh?'

'What's all this about telling us something important when Ishbel's family comes?' she demanded. 'Why not tell us now?'

'Because it affects everyone. Don't ask me anything else, Lynette, I've decided what I'm going to do. Monnie, I think you and I should be in the common room. Goodnight, Lynette.'

'Goodnight, Dad,' she said blankly.

Fifty-One

They were like relatives, waiting to hear the reading of the will. Nervous, watchful, wondering what was coming.

Or, at least, Niall and Sheana were wondering, as they sat in silence in Frank's office the following evening, though Lynette and Monnie, sitting with them, were pretty certain they knew. Hoping he would prove them wrong, they kept their eyes on their father, and weren't the only ones. Niall's dark gaze was on him, too.

'Mr Forester,' he said, breaking the silence at last, his Highland voice rather strained, 'how about telling us why we are here?'

'Wish you'd call me Frank, Niall.'

Niall hesitated. 'Frank, then. Point is, we were wondering why you wanted to see us.'

Frank cleared his throat. 'I – that is, your mother and I – have something we'd like to tell all the family. An announcement, I suppose you could call it.'

At his words, a certain rigidity came over Niall and he looked at once to his wife.

'An announcement,' he repeated. 'Must be important, to call us over.'

'Yes, it's important.' Frank looked across to his daughters and back to Niall. 'The fact of the matter is that Ishbel and I have formed a relationship – a very close relationship – and we are . . . going to be married.'

Another silence fell. In the distance, they could hear a radio playing faintly, and a sudden clatter, probably of pans. The hostellers were preparing supper.

So it was true, what they'd been afraid of, Lynette was thinking desolately. And she had been so sure, after the trip to Edinburgh, that her father was not going to forget their mother and marry again. He'd said that seeing the flat again had brought it all back. By which he must have meant his love for Ma. And then he'd been so preoccupied since their return home, it had seemed as though he was rethinking what he was going to do. Yet all the time he'd been planning this bombshell.

Her eyes sought Monnie, who seemed as though she was about to cry. 'I got it wrong,' she mouthed, but Monnie made no answer, and it was Niall who broke the silence. Slowly, he raised his eyes to Ishbel, on whose cheekbones, two circles of scarlet burned.

'Mother, is this true?'

'Yes, it's true.'

'You are going to be married again? To Mr Forester?'

'To Frank, yes. We love each other.'

'How can you say that? How can you put aside my father?'

'I'm not—' she began, but he spoke fast over her, his lips trembling, his eyes bright with emotion.

'Yes, yes, you are. You are putting aside my dad, who gave his life in the war. What thanks is that to him? We have remembered him all these years and now you throw him on the scrap heap? Say you have a very close relationship with someone else, a man from Edinburgh we do not even know?'

'How can you?' Sheana cried, her green eyes fiery on Ishbel. 'How can you hurt Niall this way? Forget his father, for a stranger?'

'Stop it!' Frank cried, putting his arm round the shaking Ishbel. 'Both of you, stop talking to your mother like that. She is not putting aside your father, Niall, she is not throwing him on the scrap heap, any more than I'm throwing aside my dear Ellie, whose memory will never leave me. But your dad and Ellie are gone and we are here. The time's come to move on, and we believe our loved ones would want us to do that.'

Looking desperately towards his daughters, he lifted a hand from Ishbel's shoulder as though in appeal.

'You believe that, don't you, girls? You know I haven't forgotten your mother, but the time's right to make a new life and it's what she would have wanted. You believe that, eh?'

All eyes went to Lynette and Monnie, sitting frozen in their seats.

'I'm . . . not sure, Dad,' Lynette said at last, as Monnie gave a quiet sob. 'I – it's going to take a bit of getting used to – you thinking of marrying again.'

'But you want me to be happy? That's what you've always said. If I wanted to make a fresh start, come up here from

Edinburgh, you wanted that for me? In fact, you urged me to come, didn't you? You urged me to take this job and start again.'

'We never thought you'd want to marry again!' Lynette flashed at him. 'We've nothing against you, Ishbel, you've always been very kind to us, but we just never thought—'

'Never thought is right,' Niall said heavily. 'Sheana and me, we never thought for a minute that there was anything going on between you and Mr Forester, Mother. Never for a minute!'

'We never dreamed there could be talk of marriage,' Sheana put in. 'At your age.'

'As though people of our age never get married?' Ishbel asked, dabbing at her eyes.

'Aye, maybe they do, but we never thought it of you,' Niall declared. 'We never believed you'd want to – and I still don't believe it. I cannot believe it. I won't.'

He rose to his feet, pushing back his chair. 'Look, this has been too much for me. I'm going to have to go home.' He put his hand to his brow, which was shining with sweat. 'Mother, I'll – I'll maybe see you . . . sometime – I don't know—'

'Oh, Niall, don't go,' she wailed. 'We were going to have a cup of tea – we can talk—'

'No.' He shook his head. 'There's no point in any more talk.'

'Don't leave your mother this way,' Frank said, rising as Niall and Sheana moved to the door. 'Can't you see she's upset?'

'We're all upset,' said Sheana, taking her husband's arm. 'Specially Niall. I'm taking him home.'

No one made a move to see them out, but they all could hear the front door bang and the next moment the sound of a car starting up and roaring away. Ishbel's family had gone.

'I thought they might – you know – have been expecting it,' Frank muttered, as Ishbel collapsed back into her chair still shaking. 'You were, weren't you, Lynette?'

'We'd guessed. But then Niall and Sheana haven't been here.'

'You think it was too much of a shock, then?'

'Must have been.'

'I never thought they'd take it so badly,' Ishbel said faintly. 'Maybe I should have just quietly told them myself, Frank. We made too much of it, asking them over.'

'Aye, maybe I got it wrong. But there was no easy way.'

'It's fifteen years since my Robbie died in the war,' Ishbel went on, half to herself. 'In all that time, I've never looked at another man till you came, Frank. Then, it seemed so right. I thought Niall would understand.'

'Look, he's upset. It's all been a shock to him. After he's had a bit of time to think about it, he might come round.'

'Maybe.'

'I'll make some tea.' Lynette stood up, not looking at anyone. 'Or, maybe coffee.'

'I'll make it,' said Ishbel. 'Will give me something to do. Who wants what, then?'

'If I can't have a whisky, I'll settle for coffee,' Frank muttered, rubbing his hand over his face.

When the girls said they'd have coffee, too, Ishbel said she'd make it for everyone and left them, walking slowly, as though she were much older.

Frank, taking out his cigarettes, passed the packet to Lynette.

'How do you two feel, then?' he asked, as he lit Lynette's cigarette and his own. 'Monnie, were you crying just then? I never wanted you to cry.'

'I was just thinking of the old days,' she said in a low voice.

'You mean your mother. Do you really believe I've forgotten her? I've tried to explain how it is. I thought you'd understand.'

'Looks like our generation is not good at understanding,' Lynette said shortly, watching the smoke of her cigarette curl away.

'It was a shock for Niall. You were expecting it.'

'It was still a shock.'

'Hard to take in,' Monnie murmured.

'But if you think about it, surely you can see why Ishbel and I feel ready for a new relationship? It's natural to want companionship – and love.'

'You'll have to give us time, Dad.'

'All right,' he said eagerly. 'Take time, all you want, but don't turn away from me, eh?'

'We never said we'd do that,' said Monnie.

After they'd finished Ishbel's coffee, there were still duties to be done in the hostel, but the girls told Frank to take Ishbel home, they'd look after things.

'You're sure?'

'Oh, come on, we can do the sing-song as well as you,' Lynette said. 'And call lights out!'

'I'll be back long before then,' said Frank, helping Ishbel into her light jacket.

No more was said, except for sombre goodnights, as he and Ishbel left the hostel, and then the girls were alone.

'Better get along to the common room,' said Monnie. 'Do I look as though I've been crying?'

'No, you look fine. Well, shattered, but no one will notice.'

Lynette, studying her own looks in a compact mirror, laughed a little. 'Know what's happened to us?' she asked, snapping the compact shut. 'We've been made redundant.'

'Redundant?'

'Well, we came up here to keep Dad company – look after him, if you like – and now he doesn't need company, doesn't need looking after. Our job's over.'

Monnie's eyes were widening. 'Is that what you think?'

'Don't you?'

'I don't know. I thought there was more to being here than that. I thought we were happy here.'

'Maybe you are.'

'But aren't you, Lynette? You've got your job – and Ronan.'

'True. But things are going to be different now, aren't they?'

'I suppose so. Can't help feeling sorry for Dad, you know, and Ishbel. They're so happy to have found each other, but now it's all been spoiled.'

'They couldn't expect it to be easy. Families count for something. We have to be happy about it, too.'

Monnie sighed, then brightened. 'Thank goodness I'm going walking with Paul tomorrow. Up in the hills, everything gets put into perspective.'

'And Torquil? When are you seeing him?'

'At the weekend, I expect.' Monnie's bright look had faded. 'Look, let's see what's happening in the common room. I'm responsible for order, when Dad's not here.'

But as they hurried through the house, Monnie had one last question for her sister. 'If you're not settled here, Lynette, what will you do?'

'Do? I'm not sure. I'll have to think about it.'

In the common room, of course, there was no time for thinking, and as the girls mingled with the young hostellers, Lynette being persuaded to have a go at snooker, Monnie to play a game of dominoes, it was soothing to know they could shelve their troubles, at least for the rest of the evening.

Fifty-Two

While Monnie put things into perspective on top of the Hill of Scree above Loch Hourn, Paul a sympathetic listener at her side, Lynette was walking with Ronan on the strip of shore below the hotel gardens. She had asked him to meet her at lunchtime, when the guests would all be in the restaurant, telling him she thought they ought to talk.

'Talk?' The eyes she found so fascinating lit up. 'I hope this is going to be talk I want to hear?'

'I hope so,' she answered seriously.

'You're going to give me my answer?'

'And a question.'

The light in his eyes had died. 'Not sure I like the sound of that, Lynette.'

'Just come down to the shore, Ronan.'

'Nothing would keep me away.'

There they were, then, walking on the narrow sand, the waters of the Sound within a pebble's throw, the mountains opposite without cloud. Lynette and Ronan, however, were not looking at the scenery.

'There's a bench here,' Ronan murmured. 'Let's sit down.'

'Think I'll have a cigarette,' Lynette said, as they sat together, both checking to see if anyone was in the gardens, watching, but turning back, satisfied that they were unobserved.

'No smoking,' Ronan said firmly. 'You smoke too much, my darling. I'm going to see you cut it down.'

'It settles my nerves.'

'What nerves?' He laughed. 'You have no nerves.'

'How can you say that? I was like a jelly when you interviewed me, remember?'

'Don't remind me of that interview. Anyway, you gave no sign.' He folded her hand in his. 'Come on, then, let's talk.'

'You're not feeling too hungry? You're missing lunch.'

'As though I care about lunch when you want to talk to me.'

When it came to it, however, she was hesitating, feeling the nerves he said she didn't have.

'A piece of news first,' she told him, lightly stroking his hand. 'My dad is going to marry Ishbel MacNicol.'

'Why, Lynette, that's wonderful! You must be delighted. Ishbel's a fine person.'

'Delighted?' Lynette frowned. 'We thought he would never want to replace our mother.'

'I can understand why you'd think that, but time passes, doesn't it? Your father's been alone for years and a man needs a wife.' Ronan's grip tightened on Lynette's fingers. 'I know I do.'

'The point is, that we're not really needed now. We only came up to the Highlands to be with Dad, we didn't want him starting a new life on his own. And now he's not going to be on his own, so we can think again.'

Pulling her hand suddenly away from his, Lynette took a deep breath.

'I do want to marry you, Ronan,' she began, and as he gave a quick shuddering sigh, added quickly, 'but I don't want to live here.'

Their eyes locked together, they sat still as a pair of decorative statues, their lips parted, no words coming.

At last, Ronan moved, still keeping his eyes on Lynette, and took out his handkerchief, touching it to his brow.

'You want to marry me? You did say that, Lynette?'

'That was my answer.'

'And the question is?'

'Will you come with me to Edinburgh?'

Replacing his handkerchief in his breast pocket, Ronan stood up and began to walk up and down in front of Lynette on the bench, but saying nothing. After watching him for a few moments, she jumped to her feet.

'Ronan, aren't you going to say something?'

He stopped, looking into her face. 'What can I say? You know it's not possible for me to come with you to Edinburgh.'

'Why? Why is it not possible?'

'Because my work is here, my life is here. I can't imagine living anywhere else. I told you that once, didn't I?'

'Yes, and I know you love this place, it means a lot to you. But then you say you love me too.'

'I do love you. I want you to marry me and you've said you will.'

'I will, but not here. I want us to go to the city and make our lives there. You'd have no trouble finding a post in Edinburgh, Ronan, you'd be snapped up for one of the hotels straight away.' Lynette moved towards him, taking his hands. 'And it'd be so different there. So full of life!'

'You think there's no life here?' he asked quietly.

'Oh, yes, of course, but it's different, eh? Listen, I think this part of the world is the most beautiful I know, but it's not my world, you see. It's somewhere I can admire and enjoy, but I just feel all the time as though I'm passing through. On holiday, sort of thing.'

'That would change,' he said eagerly, taking her in his arms. 'Once you realized it was your home – and it would be, with me – you'd settle down, grow to love it as I do. Oh, God, Lynette, you wouldn't turn me down for Edinburgh, would you?'

She was silent in the circle of his arms, and he gently turned her face to his. 'Tell me, you wouldn't,' he said softly. 'You love me, you have to be with me.'

'Couldn't I say the same thing to you, Ronan? If you love me, you'll follow me, wherever I go, won't you?'

He dropped his arms and stood without speaking, his face taking on its old sombre look. He looked at his watch. 'Time to go,' he said huskily. 'We must just talk again, Lynette.'

'What will change?' she whispered, and he gave a twisted smile.

'One of us. One of us will have to give in.'

'It's not a question of giving in! It's a question of wanting – wanting to do what the other person wants.'

He shrugged. 'I call that giving in. Let's go, Lynette. I have to make some phone calls.'

'Will you have time for a sandwich?'

'I don't feel like anything. How about you?'

She shook her head. 'Fionola's had lunch, but I'd better get back to the desk with her. We're pretty busy at the moment.'

In fact, Lynette did not go straight back to Reception. As soon as she'd seen Ronan disappear into his office, she went through the glass side door into the gardens, where she lit a cigarette and sat down on a wrought iron seat. Which was where Scott found her a little while later.

'Lynette, this is a bit of luck!' He sat down beside her, lighting one of his own cigarettes and smiling happily, until he more clearly saw her face.

'Hey, you're upset. What's up? Is this why you're not at the desk?'

'I should be,' she murmured. 'But I needed something to get me there.' She dabbed at her eyes with her handkerchief. 'Thing is, I've had a disagreement with Ronan.'

'Music to my ears. Tell me more.'

'You won't like it.'

'Try me.'

'Well, some time ago, he asked me to marry him – you probably know that.'

'Guessed.'

'Today, I said yes.'

Scott looked at his cigarette. 'And? Come on, what went wrong? You wouldn't be sitting here like this if everything was all right.'

'No. What happened was that I said I'd marry him if he came to Edinburgh with me.' Lynette rested her blue eyes on Scott's closely attentive face. 'Maybe it sounds selfish, but I think I've always known at the back of my mind that I couldn't settle here. Monnie's different. She's like Dad, she loves it. But now my dad is going to marry Ishbel and there's no real need for me to be here any more.'

'Your dad's going to marry Ishbel? Good for him. And her. I hope they'll be very happy. But is that what's spurred you on, to go home?' He stubbed out his cigarette. 'Or, was it seeing Edinburgh again?'

'Both, I think. Scott, I just know I don't want to live all my life in the Highlands, but when I spoke to Ronan, he told me he could never leave.'

'Even to be with you?'

'Even to be with me. But then, it's true, I'm not prepared to stay here for him.'

Scott said softly, 'I'd go anywhere for you. You know that, eh?'

She nodded, rising, throwing away her half-smoked cigarette.

'And you know what that means?' Scott stood close. 'Means that you two don't love each other enough to do what I would do.'

Her face twisting in pain, she shook her head. 'I do love Ronan, Scott. I do. And he loves me.'

'And neither of you will do what the other one wants? Lynette, think about it.'

'Just now, I don't want to think about anything.'

As she moved hurriedly away, he stayed where he was. 'You'll see, I'm right,' he called after her. 'Come to me when you do.'

There were guests approaching, looking with interest at the chef in his whites, who was away from his kitchen, and at the pretty girl from Reception opening the glass door. Drama, eh? But by the time they drew nearer, both chef and receptionist had gone.

When Paul brought weary Monnie back to the gates of the hostel, he stopped the car and gave her a light pat on the back.

'Well done. It's a tough climb, that one, tougher than people think, but you managed well. I told you, you're a natural.'

'I feel stiff as a board already. Be worse tomorrow, I expect.' Monnie opened the car door and smiled as she slowly prepared herself to get out. 'But I'm so grateful to you, Paul. Not just for the climb, but for listening to me, bending your ear all the way to the top of the hill.'

'Nae bother, as they say. But I'll tell you something interesting. You talked about your dad and Ishbel, you talked about Lynette, but you never once mentioned Torquil.'

'No reason why I should mention him, is there?'

'He's important to you. I thought his name might have come up. After all, you've talked of him before.'

'There's nothing new to say. We are still seeing each other.'

'And everything's the same?'

'It's the same.'

He gave her a long steady look which only made her own gaze fall, until finally he sighed and switched on his engine.

'I'll give you a ring, shall I? How about Skye next time?'

'Skye? Paul, that'd be terrific!' The change of subject brought a smile to her face. 'Can we really go to Skye?'

'Sure, why not?'

When she'd thanked him again for the day, he waved and drove off, leaving her to make her way stiffly to the hostel, her thoughts already back with Torquil. It had been the truth she'd told Paul about their continuing relationship. There was nothing different to say. Nothing had changed. How could it?

As she sank into a chair in the hall of the hostel, she felt his hold over her as strong as ever. And whatever happened in the future, she could not see herself being free.

Fifty-Three

As August moved into September, Ishbel, it was clear to Frank, was losing heart. She tried to put a brave face on things, but there seemed no solution to the impasse Niall had created. He had not replied to the letters she had written, he had not made any effort to come round and 'talk', which she saw as their only hope of a settlement. And when Frank suggested they should just get married anyway, she shrank away from any such plan.

'Oh, no, Frank, I could never do that. I'd have to feel our families wanted our happiness, otherwise everything would be ruined. All our new life together.'

'I have the feeling that Monnie and Lynette are not going to put any difficulties in our way,' Frank said, trying to sound hopeful, and Ishbel replied that it would be wonderful if that were true.

Not wonderful enough, Frank knew, if Niall still held out, but at least it would be a start, eh? And one day Lynette and Monnie did put their arms round Ishbel and told her that if she was going to make their father happy, they wanted to welcome her to their family. At which, there were tears all round, and promises from

Ishbel that they need never worry – making their father happy was all she wanted to do.

Afterwards, Lynette told Monnie she was glad they'd made the move to accept Ishbel.

'Was worth it to see her face and Dad's, eh? Like sunshine after rain, and all thanks to you, Monnie. You were the one with the soft heart.'

'I felt in the end that Dad was right. Ma wouldn't have wanted him to be alone all his life. And I do believe he'll never forget her. Same as Ishbel won't forget her Robbie.'

'Now we just need Niall to come round, though I feel he'll be the sort that doesn't want to have to climb down. May take some time, and Dad and Ishbel are wanting to get wed.'

'Poor things. At least, we've done our bit.'

'Poor things,' said Ishbel, of her future stepdaughters. 'They've made us happy, Frank, but I can tell they're not happy themselves. Have they said anything to you?'

'Not a word. And I know better than to ask.'

That September Sunday afternoon when they were together at the hostel was as warm and dry as any summer's day, and Frank, feeling guilty, said maybe he should do some gardening. Monnie'd been very helpful, but now she was out with Torquil and Lynette at work, which meant, Frank groaned, it was up to him to get on with it. Not that he was much of a gardener.

'I am,' Ishbel cried. 'I'll help.'

'Och, you do too much, you need a rest.'

'I hate resting. Come on, let's find the tools. And are there any hats?' Ishbel laughed. 'It is not always that we need sun hats here, is it?'

They spent the next couple of hours weeding, stripping out dead wood, mowing the lawn and watering, feeling perfectly in tune working with each other as helpmates, and were standing together, arm in arm, admiring what they'd done, when a car drew up at the end of the drive. No one got out and for a time neither Frank nor Ishbel noticed it, until Ishbel, carrying a bag of grass clippings for the compost heap at the rear of the hostel, stopped and caught her breath.

'Niall?' she whispered. 'Is it Niall?'

She knew it was Niall, for she could see him, and of course by now had recognized his car, but she still couldn't believe he'd come at last. As he left the driving seat and came slowly up the drive towards her, she felt so dazed, so nervous, she dropped her bag of clippings at her feet and stood looking down at it as though she couldn't think what to do.

'Oh, Mother!' Niall muttered, stooping to gather up the clippings that had burst from the bag over her feet.

'Oh, Mother!' Sheana echoed, joining him from the car and moving the bag to the side of the drive.

'Not like you to go dropping things,' Niall said, brushing leaves from his fingers and fixing his mother with a long dark stare.

'Not like you at all,' said Sheana.

She was rather pink in the face and obviously feeling the heat, as she pushed back her ginger hair and gave Ishbel a wary smile.

Ishbel, seeing the smile, felt her heart leap. 'I wasn't expecting to see you,' she murmured. 'I never thought you'd come.'

'We thought we would.' Niall was looking about him. 'Where's Frank, then?'

'He was here a moment ago.' Ishbel, recovering herself a little, called his name.

'We know, we saw you both from the car.'

'We didn't see you.'

'Too busy looking at the garden.'

'Well, we've done well, haven't we?'

'Here's Frank!' cried Sheana. 'Hello, there, Mr Forester.'

'Please, make it Frank,' he muttered, looking mystified.

'Where've you been?' Ishbel asked. 'You disappeared.'

'I . . . went to put the kettle on.'

'Get you,' said Sheana. 'So useful, eh?'

He was keeping out of the way, thought Ishbel. Being tactful . . .

'Shall we all have tea out here?' she asked.

'If that's all right,' Niall said, and, her leaping heart taking wings, Ishbel said she'd go and make it.

'Want any help?' asked Sheana.

'No, no, you sit down, dear. Frank, aren't there some garden chairs somewhere?'

'In the garage, I'll get them.'

'I'll give you a hand,' offered Niall.

The four of them, wearing cotton hats and balancing in ancient basket chairs, sat on the lawn at the front of the house, drinking tea and eating Ishbel's buttered scones and melting chocolate cake, talking stiltedly, smiling edgily, until silence fell.

'I'll take this lot out of the way of the wasps,' said Frank, gathering the tea things on to a tray, and Sheana said she'd go with him. Which left Niall and Ishbel sitting together, Ishbel fanning herself with her hat, to give her hands something to do, Niall looking around as though the newly tidied garden was of absorbing interest. Suddenly, he turned to his mother.

'This is no good, is it?' he asked. 'Pretending we don't have to say anything?'

'Is it not?' she asked in alarm. 'Oh, why do we have to say anything?'

'It's all right, Mother. There is no need to worry. I have . . . I suppose I have come round to it.'

'Oh, Niall!'

'Aye, we both decided – was not just me, was Sheana as well – that we should not – you know – stand in the way of your happiness. I was upset about my dad—'

'I know, I know, I understand.'

'But, well, he's been gone a long time, and you've been on your own. We think now 'tis what he would have wanted.'

'I think so too, Niall.'

'And so, today, we thought we'd come over. We guessed you'd be here, being a Sunday, and when we saw you, with Frank, in the garden –' Niall took out his handkerchief and mopped his brow – 'you looked so right, the two of you, we . . . well, we were glad we'd come.'

Ishbel, her eyes glazed with tears, put out her arms to him and, taking her hands, he pulled her up and hugged her, which was the little tableau Frank and Sheana saw when they came back into the garden.

'Ah, look at that!' cried Frank, and Sheana nodded.

'I guess he will be all right now, Frank, for he has been in such a state, you would never believe. He never wanted to quarrel with his mother, and neither did I, come to that. My own mother, she says, you must both make it up before you do any more damage, but we had already decided. To come over.'

'Thank God you did,' Frank said fervently. 'How about you and me having a hug, too, then?'

'Welcome to the family,' Sheana said, and kissed his cheek.

'Frank!' Ishbel called, moving from Niall. 'They are coming back – the hostellers!'

'Aye, and my girls, too.'

He was already hurrying down the drive, through the crowd of weary young backpackers, home from the hills, to greet Monnie and Lynette who had arrived together. Though he had no eyes for the van that was turning to drive away, or the large Wolseley that was following it, his girls were conscious of little else. Until Frank's delight came through to them and Lynette asked, 'What's up, Dad? Swallowed the cream?'

'Come and see!'

Calling to the hostellers that the door was open, he'd be with them in a minute, Frank ushered his daughters over to the lawn, where he stopped, waving his arms like a showman at Ishbel and her family waiting there.

'Oh, it's Niall!' cried Monnie. 'And Sheana.'

'We've just had tea together,' Ishbel said proudly. 'Everything is going to be all right.'

And then the hugs began again, and the warmth generated by a family reunited surrounded the troubled sisters and cheered them for a while.

Fifty-Four

After the hostellers had cooked another of their terrible fry-ups, even on such a warm evening, the Foresters and the MacNicols prepared to have supper together in the annexe kitchen. At first, Niall and Sheana had said they couldn't stay, but Ishbel had insisted that they should, it would be nice, it would be special, to eat together for the first time. And there was cold roast beef and ham, with plenty of salad, and she could just boil up a few eggs, and fetch a ham and egg pie from her shop.

'Oh, Mother, trust you!' Niall laughed. 'Never lost for a menu!'

'I told you, this was special. I suppose we should really have something to drink.'

'Sorry, I've no wine,' Frank said. 'Next time, eh? I foresee plenty of celebrations ahead.'

'Any thoughts on the date yet?' asked Sheana.

'Tomorrow?' he suggested, with a laugh, in which they all joined.

'Seriously, it will depend on the kirk,' Ishbel told them. 'I do not want a registry office wedding. So – maybe late October.'

'Anything you say,' said Frank. 'If you want the kirk, the kirk it shall be.'

'And then what?' asked Niall. 'You move in here, Mother?'

She stopped slicing hard-boiled eggs and glanced at Frank. 'I had not got that far, but, yes, I suppose I will.'

'What about the shop?' put in Sheana. 'I should think you'd want to keep that on, it's so good. I'd love to run a shop like that.'

'Oh, yes, I'll keep it on. I can just run it from here, it will be easy enough.'

'You could always be assistant warden,' Monnie suggested lightly.

Ishbel's eyes widened. 'Why, that's your job, Monnie! I could not take that.'

'Plenty of wardens' wives do act as assistants to their husbands, you know, like the MacKays. It makes sense when you think about it.'

'Yes, but I would never dream of depriving you of your job, Monnie. Don't worry about it. Now, who is doing the dressing for the salad? We are almost ready now.'

That first meal together, impromptu though it had been, was a great success, everyone feeling relaxed because they were relieved that a possible family rift had not actually happened. In fact, by the time Frank and Monnie had to leave to prepare for lights out, there was the lovely, rosy feeling around the table that if they hadn't drunk any wine, they felt just as mellow as though they had.

'Oh, what a shame the party has to break up,' Ishbel said with a sigh, as they all left the table. 'It's been so lovely.'

'Aye, duty calls,' Frank murmured, his gaze meeting hers. 'Just when I should really be taking you home, Ishbel.'

'We'll take Mother home,' Niall told him.

'No need,' she said quickly. 'I can wait till Frank's finished his rounds, he need not be long away.'

'That's fine, then,' Niall agreed, with an understanding grin. 'So, shall we be off, then?'

'Yes, you go.' Ignoring Sheana's protests that they should help with the washing up, Lynette saw them to their car, along with Ishbel, Frank and Monnie, for there were hugs again and handshakes before they finally drove away.

'Oh, what a day!' cried Isabel. 'I don't know if I am on my head or my heels, but I know I'm happy!'

'How about you go with Dad to the common room, Ishbel?' Monnie suggested. 'While Lynette and I clear up?'

'What a grand idea!' cried Frank, and away the lovers went, arms entwined, though ready of course to untwine as soon as they met the hostellers.

'They are so sweet together,' Monnie said quietly. 'I'm so glad it's all worked out for them.'

'Feel like Cinders?' asked Lynette. 'Come on, let's get on.'

Later, in their room, preparing for bed, the girls felt the euphoria of the evening slipping away. Well, they'd known it would happen. It was second-hand euphoria, after all, and though they couldn't be more pleased for Frank and Ishbel, their joy now seemed to contrast too painfully with their own lack.

Lynette, in blue pyjamas, putting cream on her face, appeared disgruntled. 'Seems silly that Ishbel can't just stay the night with Dad,' she muttered. 'I mean, why not?'

'Why not?' Monnie, brushing her hair, paused, her expression astounded. 'You know why not, Lynette. Dad's the warden here, he has to behave correctly, or there'd be trouble. Anyway, he and Ishbel – they're not the types to jump the gun. What a thing to say!'

'I don't see that there's anything immoral in it, really. If it weren't for the risk of having bairns, I bet nobody'd think twice about having sex before marriage.'

'But you and Ronan, you've never . . .?'

'No, of course not.' Lynette's face was as dark as the night sky. 'We've never slept together. Never will now.'

'Oh, Lynette! Is it definitely over, then?'

'We've been trying to pretend that it's not, just behaving as always, but it can't go on. There has to be a decision and I've made it.'

'What?'

'I'm going back to Edinburgh.'

'I see.' Monnie slowly climbed into bed and propped herself against her pillows, keeping her gaze on her sister. 'Have you told Ronan?'

'Not yet.'

'He'll be heartbroken.'

'He knows what to do, if he is.'

'You'll be heartbroken, too.'

'I already am.' Lynette's voice cracked a little. 'But I know what I want.'

Monnie was silent for some time, her fingers pleating her sheet, her eyes staring into space. 'You know what I think?' she asked, as Lynette settled into bed and picked up the novel she was reading.

'What do you think?'

'I might come with you.'

Lynette sat up straight, dropping her book. 'Monnie, you can't do that! You love it here, you can't leave. You have your job—'

'My job . . . Look, I wasn't joking when I said Ishbel should do it. It's the obvious thing. She'd love working with Dad, and didn't you hear Sheana say she'd like to run the shop? I bet she would, too.'

'But, Monnie, I just can't see this happening. You've made your home here much more than I have – it's not necessary for you to leave, really it's not.'

'Have you thought about what it'd be like for me, living in the hostel after Ishbel's moved in? Talk about playing gooseberry! You said we'd been made redundant and that couldn't be more true for me.'

'Maybe.' Lynette leaned forward, her gaze sharp on her sister's face. 'But it's not the real reason you want to go, is it? Did you think I hadn't noticed, you never mentioned Torquil?'

Monnie looked down at her hands on the sheet. She made no reply.

'Come on, he's the real reason you want to get away, eh? He holds you, and you want to be free. That's what you told me.'

'Lynette, it's my one chance! If I stay here, I know I'll never be free, I'd never be able to give him up. But if I say I've no job and I have to go back to Edinburgh with you, he might accept it and I might be able to do it.' Monnie's grey eyes were large with emotion and hope. 'What do you think?'

'I think you're going to have to try it. You have to free yourself somehow, that's for sure.'

'I know. I have to see some end to this, I have to have my life back.'

'Well, don't say anything to him yet. I still have to speak to Ronan, remember.'

'Oh, poor Lynette!'

'Never mind me. I'm doing what I have to do. But you must wait till everything's arranged before you tell Torquil. The less time he has to think about it and you have to change your mind the better.'

'I shall not change my mind,' Monnie said fervently, but Lynette, picking up her book, shook her head.

'I'll believe that when we're safely back in Edinburgh.'

Fifty-Five

On a late September day with a nip of autumn in the air, Lynette finally promised herself that she would find the courage to speak to Ronan.

'Today's the day,' she told Monnie at breakfast after Frank had left them. 'I can't put it off any longer.'

'You've certainly taken your time about it.'

'Well, you can guess I'm not looking forward to it!'

'No, I know. OK, just as long as you tell him today and then we can make plans.' Monnie began to clear the table. 'Thank goodness it's my afternoon off, anyway. I'm seeing Paul.'

'Not climbing in Skye again?'

'No, but that was wonderful.' Monnie gave a reminiscent smile.

'Taking the ferry, just being on the magic isle, never mind getting up one of the hills! Of course, it was one of the easiest.'

'Where to, today, then?'

'That's the funny thing, Lynette. I don't know. Paul's making it a surprise. But we're not hill walking, I know that.'

'Have a good time, anyway.'

Lynette, looking rather pale, was preparing to leave for the bus. 'Wish me luck, Monnie.'

'Oh, Lynette, I will. Just wish things could have worked out differently.'

'You're not the only one.'

As Lynette went out, Mrs Duthie came in, quick to remark that Lynette was looking 'peaky', and Monnie, too. She hoped it was not the flu, then, though it was early for that.

'We're both quite well, thanks,' Monnie said coolly as Lynette hurried on her way. 'No need to worry about the flu.'

'But is it not wonderful news then, about your dad and Ishbel MacNicol? I cannot get over it, and that is the truth. Such a fine couple they will make! You must be so happy, eh?'

'We are all delighted,' Monnie said firmly, who had had this conversation before, as the news of the engagement had been filtering round the village for some time. 'Now, if you'll excuse me, I must check the dormitories.'

'No date yet for the wedding bells?' Mrs Duthie called up the stairs.

'Not yet.'

'You will be sure to tell me when it is? I shall have to crochet one of my table cloths – always makes lovely presents, my crochet.'

'You will be the first to know,' Monnie replied, sure it would be true.

After an early lunch, she was out on the drive, waiting for Paul's car, intrigued to know where he could be taking her, glad to have something else to think about, apart from what might be happening between Ronan and Lynette. And Torquil, of course.

'Not late am I?' Paul asked, when he'd driven to a halt at the gates.

'Just got here, as they say,' Monnie answered, jumping into the passenger seat.

She could see that Paul was excited, bubbling over with news that he wanted to tell, yet keeping it back until they reached wherever it was they were going.

'Why all the secrecy, Paul? You're like someone waiting for Christmas.'

'No, I've got what I want for Christmas,' he answered, smiling, as they drove away. 'Well, partly. But it won't take us long to get there and then all will be revealed. In the meantime, what news of your father's wedding plans? The whole village is agog to know.'

'You mean Mrs Duthie is. Well, it's probably going to be late October, and for their honeymoon – it's no secret – they're going to Skye. Only be for a few days, Dad doesn't want to be away from the hostel too long.'

'Though you'll be holding the fort, won't you, while he's away?'

'Oh, yes,' she answered readily, only just stopping herself from adding, 'before I go to Edinburgh.' Luckily, Paul appeared not to notice her awkward pause and she hurried on to remark that it looked like they were making for Glenelg. 'Is that our destination?'

'We're going a little way beyond Glenelg, not far from the ferry to Skye, and within reach of some good hills. A perfect place for me.'

'I can't wait to see it.'

'Nearly there. Christmas is coming! Just hope you do like it, Monnie. So far, I think we've always seemed to like the same things, haven't we?'

'We have, so if you like it, whatever it is, I'm sure I'll like it, too.'

When they had progressed a short way down a narrow country road some few miles from Glenelg, Paul turned into a private, tree-lined drive, at the end of which was a large house built of stone. There were creepers turning red. A gravel sweep before glass entrance doors. Long curtained windows, tubs of plants, wrought iron garden chairs. What struck Monnie most vividly, however, was the fact that there was a sign over the glass doors which read : Altair Hotel.

'Ta Ra!' cried Paul, stopping the car and leaping to open Monnie's door. 'This is it! This is my surprise. What do you think?'

'This is a hotel?' she asked, bewildered.

'No, this *was* a hotel. Now, it is my climbing school.'

His eyes were alight, he could hardly stop smiling at her expression, so astonished, so impressed.

'Paul! You've found it? Your climbing school? I don't believe it.'

'It's true. I've found it and I've bought it. The deal's just been clinched and I've got the keys. Apart from Jonas, my brother, you're the first person I've shown it to – want to see inside?'

'Do I not? But I really can't believe it, Paul, that you've actually bought a whole hotel. And you've kept so quiet about it, I had no idea.'

'I didn't dare to talk about it, in case I didn't get it. I tell you, I've been on pins, waiting till I could say it was mine.'

'You know, the name's familiar,' Monnie told him, as he turned the key in the front door. 'The Altair – I think it's the place Lynette came with Ronan for dinner. And very good it was, she said. Yet the hotel still had to close?'

'Sad for them, lucky for me,' Paul said cheerfully. 'Come on in, then.'

'Why, it's lovely!'

Monnie, standing in what had been the hotel's entrance hall, was admiring the white décor, the impression of light and space, the long windows over the staircase, the plain carpeted floor space. At the same time, she couldn't help thinking that no one like Lynette would ever sit behind that empty reception desk; no guests would ever take those empty chairs. Without people, there was undoubtedly a feeling of loss, of desolation, because something had failed.

Wouldn't last long, though. The way Paul was walking around, transmitting feelings of energy and determination with every step, Monnie could almost see the transformation scene from abandoned hotel to climbing school taking place and felt absurdly comforted.

'Of course, there's everything to do,' Paul was saying happily. 'I've an architect coming tomorrow for a preliminary survey, then there'll be plans to follow, builders to book, furniture to buy. I bought some of the hotel stuff – a few beds and chairs, but most of it wasn't suitable and went for auction in Inverness.'

'It's amazing that you're able to do so much,' Monnie said wonderingly, as Paul continued the tour, showing her the dining room, the lounge, the bedrooms and bathrooms.

'Only possible because of what my parents left me, and help from my backers. Oh, and courtesy of the bank, who've given me a whacking great loan. Not to mention the mortgage!'

Paul, guiding her back down the stairs to the hall, was laughing. 'I should be weighed down with worry, but I'm not. I'm just so happy, Monnie. I've found what I want to do and I've found the place to do it. What more could a fellow want?'

'I'd say you were very lucky,' she said honestly. 'You've followed your dream and it's come true.'

'That's exactly right. And this really is the perfect place, you know. The gardens go down to a little beach and there's a wee fishing village just a mile away, with Glenelg a few miles further back. But more important for me is that there's easy access to the Skye ferry, and all the climbs I'd like to use are not too far away.'

Taking Monnie's hand, Paul smiled down at her like a man on champagne, making her smile back just to feel she was joining in.

'I really do think my school will take off like a bomb. I can take a good number of people here, though the hotel's not too big, and my brother has decided to throw in his lot with me. He always was a bit bored with the law, and thinks he'll be happier being my business manager.'

Paul fell silent, still looking at Monnie, though he had released her hand. 'Thing is, we'll obviously be recruiting other staff. I was wondering – would you care to come and work here too?'

'Me?' The question was so out of the blue, she felt completely taken aback. 'Me, Paul?'

'Why not? You're going to make a wonderful climber and hill walker. I can see you doing really stiff climbs in the future and eventually teaching like me. I want to encourage women to join us and really need women on my staff, but to begin with, till you got more experience, you could work for Jonas.'

Paul's eyes, filled with the light of expectation, never left her face, but she saw their light flicker and fade when she slowly shook her head.

'Oh, you're not saying no already!' he cried. 'You haven't even thought about it.'

'Paul, I'd love to come to work for you, but I can't. I'm leaving.'

'Leaving?'

'Lynette and I, we've decided to go back to Edinburgh. Dad doesn't need us now, and . . . well, we want to go.'

'Want to go? You don't want to go.' Paul's face was suddenly pale; he was no longer on champagne. 'It's Torquil, isn't it? You're hoping you can solve the problem by running away to Edinburgh. What makes you think you can do it?'

'I have to do it, Paul. It's my only chance. If I'm going with my sister, he might understand that things have changed for me. My dad's getting married, Ishbel should have my job – I'm sure he'll see that it's best for me to go.'

'He still hasn't mentioned marriage, then?'

'We've never discussed marriage. I used to think about it, in the early days. Now I know it wouldn't work out.'

'Yet you've told me you could never leave him. What's changed, then?'

'Paul, I know I have to leave him. It will be my best chance, to go with Lynette.'

'And to think you might have worked with me,' he said, with a bitterness strange to him. 'Can you really not consider it?'

'It's not possible. Torquil might let me go home. He'd never want me to work with you.'

'Yet he sees me as no threat. Why would he care?'

'Going hill walking now and again is one thing, working with you all the time, that'd be different. And I'd never be free, would I? I wouldn't be far enough away.'

Monnie suddenly caught at Paul's arm. 'Oh, Paul, I'm so sorry! You were so happy, showing me your climbing school, just over the moon, and now I've made you sad and worried again. Say I haven't spoiled things for you? Please?'

'Of course you haven't.' His face was relaxing, he was finding a smile. 'I'm here, eh? I've found my dream, just as you said. So, let's lock up, go to Glenelg and have tea.'

But when they were in the car, negotiating the drive, Paul did say quietly, 'And let's not say another word about a certain nameless fisherman.'

'Not another word,' Monnie promised.

Fifty-Six

Having told Monnie that 'today was the day', Lynette decided that the morning was not going to be 'the morning'. No, she'd stick to Reception, working without a break so that she need not venture into Ronan's office, or even have coffee with Scott, and then have lunch and . . . yes, tell Ronan after that. Of course, he might have a meeting, or something. She might not be able to tell him . . . He did not have a meeting, she could see him any time. When the clock raced on to two o'clock, she knew she must find the courage that had deserted her and with a murmured excuse to Fionola, went to Ronan's door and sharply knocked.

'Come in,' came his familiar voice, and after a moment's hesitation, she opened his door and faced him.

'Lynette!'

At once, he left his desk and came to her, closing the door behind her and drawing her to a chair. 'Lynette, what have you been doing all day? I left my office this morning, saw you beavering away, but you didn't even catch my eye. What's happening? Is something wrong?'

'We were very busy this morning, Ronan. I didn't even have time to have coffee.'

'That's all it was?'

With his extraordinary eyes on her, seeming to act like X-rays seeing into her mind, she shook her head. 'No, it's not all. What's the point in telling lies?'

'Lies, Lynette? Who's been lying?'

'I mean, making excuses. Pretending I was busy, when . . . when I was just putting off talking to you.'

His face was taking on the sombre look she had last seen when she'd first asked him to go to Edinburgh with her, and he was sitting back at his desk almost as if they were once again in interviewing mode.

He's putting up all his defences, she thought. He knows what's coming. Get it over with, then. Tell him.

'Ronan, we've been circling round each other for days, haven't we? As though we could put this conversation off for ever.'

'Why not? Why not keep the status quo, if it means we don't have to hurt each other?'

'Because we can't go on like that, and you know it. For us to be really together, one of us has to give in. That's what you said, isn't it? But neither of us will.'

'So?'

'So, I've made the decision, Ronan. I'm going back home. I mean, Edinburgh.'

If Ronan had been trying to put up his defences, he now let them go. His face changed, his whole serious manner dissolved, and he ran from his desk to take Lynette in his arms.

'No, Lynette, no, you can't do that. I can't let you go. You mean too much to me. Oh, God, you're not serious, are you? You're just trying this on, to make me—'

'Go to Edinburgh?' she cried. 'Well, will you? Will you come with me, Ronan?'

'Please don't ask me,' he answered, kissing her. 'I know it's what you want and I wish I could say yes, but I can't do it, I can't leave this place. I belong here, it's part of me. If you love me, you'll understand.'

'But you make no effort to understand me, Ronan! I told you, I think this place is beautiful and I'd always want to come here for visits, but I'd die if I had to live here all the time. Looking at the scenery, seeing so few people, getting everything late, never seeing a film, never going dancing except to a ceilidh once in a blue moon . . .'

Wrenching herself away, Lynette faced him with tears spilling from her lovely eyes, and finished quietly, 'You need someone born and bred here, dear Ronan, someone who'll be able to share the life you want with you. I can't do it. I wish I could.'

He turned his face aside and made no answer.

'Look, be reasonable,' she cried, shaking his unresponsive arm. 'If we were to get married, we might be happy for a while and then it would all fall apart. Because we want different worlds. If you were in Edinburgh, you'd start dreaming of being back here. If I were here, I'd be homesick for the city. Can't you see, it's an impasse?'

'An impasse,' he repeated dully. 'All your talk tells me one thing. You don't love me enough.'

She drew back. 'Someone else once said that, about us both.'

'Who? Who said it?'

'It doesn't matter.' The tears she had been fighting began to roll down her cheeks. 'Because it's true.'

There would be things to discuss. Practical things, such as when she should put in her notice, but they didn't have the heart to speak of them then, and with distraught faces, they parted.

'May I kiss you goodbye?' Lynette whispered.

'We are not saying goodbye yet.'

'I'll go back to Reception then.' Her voice trembled. 'Better wash my face first, I think.'

'You look fine,' he said with a groan. 'Beautiful. You always do.'

Saying no more, she let herself out and made her way back to Reception where Fionola stared at her aghast.

'Lynette, what's happened? You look—'

'I know how I look.' Lynette glanced around at the guests in the vestibule, grateful that they weren't watching. 'All right if I just go and tidy up a bit?'

'But what's wrong? Lynette, tell me. I think you should go home, or else have a coffee with Scott, or something. Lunch is finished, he'll be free.'

'I don't want a coffee with Scott just at the moment. Look, you might as well know, I'm leaving this job, Fionola. I'm going back to Edinburgh.'

Fionola caught her breath and stared, her eyes huge on Lynette's tear-stained face. 'I don't believe it! No, it can't be true. Why? Why are you leaving?'

'I'm leaving here, I'm leaving Ronan. Look, I don't want to talk about it. I'll go and wash my face, OK?'

'OK,' Fionola repeated, still stunned, as Lynette walked swiftly away towards the cloakroom.

But she was not to get there, for Scott was in the corridor coming towards her. One look at her face made him take her arm and open the glass door to the gardens.

'This way, Lynette. You can tell me what's wrong and then you can come to my kitchen for a coffee.'

'No, I don't want to, Scott. I don't want to talk to you just yet. Later, maybe.'

'Now,' he said firmly, and made her walk with him almost to the edge of the grounds where there were steps down to the shore. 'There's a bench here where no one can see us. Come on, you poor lassie. Tell me what's happened, as though I couldn't guess.'

Fifty-Seven

'Haven't we done this before?' Lynette asked, wearily, sitting close to Scott on the bench from where they could look down at the Sound.

'What of it? Tell me what's wrong.'

'I think you've already guessed, I've just parted from Ronan.'

'You can talk to me,' he said softly. 'I'm a friendly shoulder.'

'More than that.'

'Aye, that's true. And I don't think you owe anything to our Mr Allan. If he's no' willing to do what you want, he doesn't deserve you.'

'It was too much to ask, when I wouldn't do what he wanted.'

'Face it, he's just no' the one for you, Lynette.'

'I can still feel sad about it.'

'I know. But what's the plan? You give in your notice, go back to Edinburgh?'

'That's it. Monnie and me, we're going back together.'

'Would it surprise you to know that I'm about to do the same?'

Lynette paused in dabbing her hankie at her eyes, but the look she gave Scott was wary. 'Oh, yes? Another coincidence?'

'It is, then, because I fixed this up before I knew what you were going to do. I mean, you might have made it up with Ronan, mightn't you?'

'What did you fix up then?'

'Remember I told you I had an appointment in George Street when we were in Edinburgh? Well, it was with the bank. I was negotiating a loan.'

'A loan? You kept it very secret.'

'Sure, didn't want to look a fool if I didn't get it. But, I did get it and – wait for it – I am now the proud owner of a restaurant in the High Street. I'm going solo.'

'Scott!' For the first time that day, Lynette's attention was on something other than her own troubles. 'That's wonderful news! Oh, I'm so happy for you. Does Ronan know?'

'No' yet. I'm just deciding when to tell him. Guess he'll no' be too pleased, but Hamish is good. I've trained him and he's just about ready to take over.'

'As Fionola will probably take over from me.'

'In more ways than one, maybe.'

'What do you mean?'

'Och, who cares?' Scott's face was serious. 'Listen, here's an offer. How about coming to work for me at my restaurant? My Scottish restaurant, I should say, because Scottish food is going to be my specialty. Don't look like that, I'm serious.'

'Scott, I've had a few lessons but I'm no cordon bleu. I couldn't work for you.'

'No' as a chef, though I reckon you would do well. No, I'm thinking manager. Accounts. Back room stuff that I'd be no good at, but you would. What do you say?'

'I'm not an accountant. You'd need somebody properly qualified.'

'Yes, I'll have to have a qualified accountant, I know that, but all the day-to-day stuff, ordering, managing the staff – Lynette, you'd be ideal for it. You've a good practical head, which is no' true of me, because all I want is to cook.' Scott's brown eyes were pleading. 'Come on, you could give it a go, eh? I mean, back in Edinburgh, you're going to need a job.'

'I'd say yes like a shot, if . . .'

'If what?'

'Well, if things were different between us.'

'Lynette, I promise, there'll be no strings. A strictly business arrangement is what I'm offering.' Scott paused, looking down for a moment. 'I know how you feel about Ronan, I'm no' expecting you to change just like that. But there might come a time when you do change. And if you do –' he looked up, his craggy features melting into a smile – 'I'll be there.'

'I should say I'd like to think about it,' she said quietly. 'But I don't need to. Scott, I'm going to accept your offer, and say thank you.'

'No need for thanks,' he said fervently. 'No' from you.'

'Maybe we needn't say anything about this to Ronan? I mean, for now?'

'Won't say a word. Listen, want to know what I'm going to call the restaurant? Och, you'll never guess, but I'll give you a clue. It's a place you know.'

'A place I know? I can't think. Tell me.'

'The Conair,' he answered, with a grin. 'Like it?'

'Scott, I think it's perfect. Well done.'

'Feel like a coffee now, or a nice cup of tea?'

'Thanks, but I must go back to the desk.'

They rose, aware, as they walked back into the hotel, that they had both passed over a bridge into a completely new phase.

'Feel a bit better now?' asked Scott, opening the glass door.

'In a way.' But her face had grown troubled again, as her interest and pleasure in Scott's news began to fade. 'It's going to take time, Scott, you know that, eh?'

'Aye. No need to worry, Lynette. We'll take things as they come.'

They touched hands and slowly went their separate ways.

I hope we're busy this afternoon, Lynette said to herself, returning to Reception. So that I don't have any time to think.

But then if the new job at Scott's restaurant came into her mind, there would perhaps be no need not to think of that.

Fifty-Eight

When his girls told Frank that they were planning to return to Edinburgh, he was astonished. He'd had no idea, he cried, no inkling whatsoever that they weren't happy in the Highlands. How could it have escaped him?

They had all just finished another fine meal cooked by Ishbel in the warden's flat when Lynette and Monnie had broken the news. Now, Frank and Ishbel were exchanging startled glances, with Ishbel reaching for Frank's hand and Frank shaking his head, as though what was happening was quite beyond his understanding.

'Dad, we never said we weren't happy,' Lynette said quickly. 'Why, Monnie loves it here, don't you, Monnie? And I've enjoyed being here, too. But, we have to go.'

'Why?' Frank asked blankly.

'Yes, why?' echoed Ishbel, her eyes on the girls troubled. 'It is not to do with me?'

'No, no,' said Monnie. 'Except I think it would be better for you and Dad to run the hostel on your own.'

'What do you mean, "run the hostel"? I won't be involved in that.'

'If you were assistant warden you would be. And it would be easier, if you were, as I was saying the other day.'

'Monnie, please do not talk like that.' Ishbel's colour had risen. Her hand on Frank's was tightening. 'I would never take your job from you. And your dad and I do not want you to think you have to leave the hostel. This is your home. This is where you should be.'

'No, not now. Look, I can't stay. I don't want to go into details
. . .'

'Monnie, just tell them, so that they understand,' Lynette said crisply.

'Understand what?' asked Frank.

'I think I know,' Ishbel said quietly. 'Are we talking about Torquil?'

'We are,' said Lynette. 'Monnie feels, if she came with me to Edinburgh, it would be her chance to get away from him. And she wants to get away from him, that's for sure.'

'For God's sake, you have to go to Edinburgh to give that guy the push?' Frank cried. 'What's wrong with just saying goodbye?'

'It is not always so easy,' Ishbel told him.

'It's not easy at all,' Monnie murmured.

'All right, I'll say it for you,' Frank declared. 'It will be no problem for me, I can promise you.'

'Oh, Dad, you know you can't do that,' Lynette cried. 'A father can't interfere.'

'It would be better for me to tell him and then leave,' Monnie said hastily. 'I'm going to write my letter of resignation tonight, then you can apply for my job, Ishbel. They'll be sure to give it to you. They like married couples sharing the work.'

'Would you like to apply?' Frank asked Ishbel gently. 'Work with me, eh?'

'Frank, I'd love it!'

'But what about your shop? You run it so well, you'd be a terrible miss.'

'I haven't been in to it with her, but I'm sure Sheana would take it on, and she and Niall could have the cottage too. It's no distance for Niall to drive into Glenelg for his job.'

'And maybe you could still do a bit of cooking for it,' Frank said cheerfully. 'The village wouldn't like to lose your pies, you know.'

'I'd find a way,' Ishbel agreed happily.

'Things seem to be working out, eh?' In spite of the words, Frank was suddenly serious again, his eyes fixed on Lynette. 'But what I haven't figured out yet is why you wanted to go back to Edinburgh in the first place, Lynette. Was it seeing it again, that time we went back?'

'Partly.' She was shifting uncomfortably in her chair. 'Look, I have something to tell you as well. I've split up with Ronan.'

'Oh, no!' Ishbel wailed. 'You have never given up the lovely Mr Allan? Oh, no, I cannot believe it.'

'Nor me,' Frank muttered. 'What the devil did you find wrong with him, then? Seems to me he was perfect for you. A catch some would say, eh?'

'Thanks,' Lynette said coldly. 'Why shouldn't I be the catch? The thing is, we discovered that we wanted different things. He wants to stay in the Highlands, I want to go back to the city. Neither of us will budge, so that's it. End of the affair.'

'You want the city?' Frank stared. 'But you just said how much you've enjoyed it here in the Highlands.'

'Yes, as a place to visit, to stay for a time.' Lynette lowered her eyes from her father's wondering face. 'But when it comes to living . . . Dad, I'm for the bright lights. I can't change, I wish I could, but it's just the way I am.'

'And we thought you were so happy here,' Ishbel sighed.

'I was. I mean, I am, but, as I say, not for ever.' Lynette looked up. 'You do understand, eh?'

'Looks like we'll have to.' Frank stood up. 'But I must get back to work. Ishbel, I'll see you after I've checked round, OK?' Moving to the door, he looked back at his daughters, his face seeming to crumple.

'Have you thought how much we're going to miss you?'

'Oh, don't!' cried Monnie, running to him.

'As though we're not going to miss you!' said Lynette, following.

And for a few moments, the three Foresters stood together, arms around one another, as Ishbel tactfully began to clear the table.

'Better go,' Frank said huskily, and went his way with Monnie, her lip trembling, in tow, while Lynette, after blowing her nose and straightening her shoulders, came to help Ishbel.

Fifty-Nine

Things seemed to be working out, Frank had said, and this seemed to be the case when first, Ishbel was appointed his assistant without even an interview, and next, their wedding was fixed for a date in late October.

'So, we know where we are,' Lynette told Monnie. 'I can put my notice in and arrange to leave with you after the honeymoon. We can't leave before, because you're going to look after the hostel for the time they're away.'

'That will only be for a few days. They don't want to be away too long. Especially as they're leaving Sheana in charge of the shop.'

'As Dad says, though, things seem to be working out. Except that you look as though the furies are after you. You'll really have to pull yourself together, you know.'

'It's just the strain of not telling Torquil until the last minute. I can't help worrying how he'll take it. He's so unpredictable.'

'And my big fear is that he'll persuade you to stay. When the chips are down, are you sure you can hold out?'

'Yes. I've made up my mind.' Monnie's face was pale and set. 'I know what I want to do and I'll do it.'

'Stick to that. And while we're preparing to depart, let's not forget Scott. He's got to get to work on refurbishing his new restaurant as soon as he can get away.'

'He's told Ronan he's going?'

'Oh, yes, he's put his notice in and it looks as though Hamish is going to get his job.'

But at the mention of Ronan's name, Lynette's face had taken on a closed expression and Monnie said no more. She knew her sister was finding it difficult to work out her last weeks at the Talisman, keeping out of Ronan's way, while making sure that all would go well for Fionola who was taking over her job.

'Changes all round,' she'd told Monnie with a shrug. 'It's an ill wind, as they say, that does nobody any good.'

And Fionola, it seemed, was not finding the wind that was blowing her way in the least an ill one; Lynette said she was looking more beautiful than ever. Monnie, however, could really only think of her own situation. Of when she could tell Torquil that she was leaving him. And of what he would say.

In the suddenly brilliant days of autumn, when the Highlands had never looked so spectacular and Monnie was feeling homesick for them before she'd even left, it was ironic that Torquil seemed gentler and sweeter than he'd been for some time.

More like he'd been in the early days, Monnie would have said, except that when she looked back on those early days, she'd remembered he'd been on occasion quite offhand and even uncaring. Take the first time they'd been out together, when he'd said he must meet his brother and had brought her home early. She'd been upset and he hadn't understood why, just as he hadn't understood why she'd been upset over the gulls' eggs incident.

As she had told Lynette, he was unpredictable, that was all that could be said. For here he was, being so kind and thoughtful, even losing his worrying watchfulness, so that she really couldn't fault him. Now would be the time to tell him, she decided. Why wait?

'No, no, Monnie, don't tell him yet,' Lynette still warned. 'Wait till nearer the wedding. Do some nice fell walking with Paul to take your mind off things, if he can spare the time from his climbing school. I still can't believe that he's bought the old Altair, you know.'

But Paul was too tied up with architects and builders to go fell walking, though he promised he would arrange it as soon possible.

'Oh, you bet I won't want to lose time with you if you're leaving so soon,' he told Monnie fervently. 'I'll be in touch.'

Leaving so soon? The words sounded a knell, and Monnie knew that whatever Lynette said, she would have to break her news to Torquil and put herself out of her misery. Better to let the sword fall, than have to picture it permanently poised over her neck.

Meanwhile, as she agonized over her dilemma, plans were going ahead for her father's wedding. As Ishbel had requested, the ceremony was to be in the Glenelg kirk, to be followed by lunch at a local cafe. Everything, in fact, was to be low key, though there would be a good attendance of guests, all Ishbel's friends and neighbours having been invited, even if Frank's Edinburgh cronies were too far away to attend. As long as his girls were present, he declared, they would be all he wanted, and of course both were to be present, as the wedding was to be early and Monnie could be back at the hostel in time for the return of the hostellers.

'Next day, it'll be our turn to steam away,' Lynette reminded Monnie, though the reminder brought her no cheer. In a way, it was a relief to be with Torquil himself one Saturday afternoon, when she could say what she had to say.

Sixty

They had driven to their favourite woods that were now a riot of colour, as the late afternoon sun lingered on the deciduous trees and set them sparkling against the evergreens.

'How beautiful!' Monnie cried. 'I'll always remember these woods.'

'Remember?' Torquil, having parked on a rutted pathway, turned to look at her. 'That is a strange thing to say.'

'Is it?'

'Why, yes. You sound as though you won't be here to see them.'

Her head jerked up, her hands trembled, for this was the perfect opening for her, all that she could have wanted, and it had come before he began to kiss her, when she knew she would be in danger of losing herself in the delight he gave.

'I won't be,' she brought out, not daring to look away from him. 'I mean, I won't be here, Torquil. Things have changed for me, since my father and Ishbel decided to marry. There's no place for me at the hostel now, and Lynette and I . . . we're going home.'

The silence between them stretched and stretched. His eyes on her were grave. Why didn't he speak? Monnie was desperate for his reaction, but he said nothing.

'I know I said I'd never leave you,' she hurried on. 'But, like I say, the situation's different, I have to go. With my sister. We're going home together.'

As she fell silent again, Torquil, reaching out to take her hand, spoke at last. 'You did say you would never leave me, Monnie. I believed you.'

'But I've told you how things are, Torquil. You must see, that I should go.' She looked down at her hand in his. 'After all, you've never . . . never said we should be together permanently.'

'Be married, you mean?' He smiled. 'Things move slowly in the Highlands. Who says we would not have got around to it?'

'I think we should both face facts,' she murmured, marvelling at her own bravery. 'We might not be really right for each other. I mean, I'm a Lowlander.'

'And you think I should have a Highland girl?' He gave a long deep sigh. 'Perhaps you're right. If it's what you really feel, that we are not suited, yes, you must be. It takes two to be happy, suited.'

'Yes,' she cried, breathing hard. 'Yes, it takes two.'

'In that case . . .'

Torquil started up the engine of his van and began to back out along the narrow track.

'In that case, I'll take you home.'

'Take me home?' She was mystified.

'Take you home, and let you go.' He shrugged, as they came out on to the road and turned for Conair. 'What else can I do, my darling Monnie? I cannot hold you, if you do not want to be held.'

Am I dreaming? she thought. Can it be true what's happening? He's letting me go?

'Only thing, if we have to say goodbye, I do not know if I can do that now.' He gave her a quick look. 'Shall we have one last meeting, before you go?'

· 'Oh, yes. Yes, Torquil. One last meeting.'

'On Friday?'

'Aren't you working on Friday?'

'No, I'm taking the day off. Taking advantage of this weather.'

'Well, Friday afternoon would be fine for me. Where shall we go?'

'We'll think of somewhere. Somewhere special. I'll call for you, then.'

'I'll be waiting.'

When he drew up at the gate to the hostel, she thought they would kiss and she would have to be very strong to draw away, but he only smiled an affectionate smile and got out to open the door for her.

'Till Friday, Monnie.'

'Friday. But Torquil, what about our fish that day?'

'I can bring it later. Don't worry about it.'

When she began to walk up the drive, she looked back once to see if he was waiting, but his van had already gone. Still, she found it hard to believe, that she had told him; it was done, and the sky had not fallen in. How had it happened? Had all she said got through to him? That they weren't really suited? He'd be happier with a Highland girl?

All she knew was that her head was splitting, and she was glad the hostellers were soon due back, so that she could fling herself into work and speak to no one. In fact, some were already back and had scattered boots about and dropped their rucksacks in the hall.

'Hey!' she called up the stairs. 'Come on, now! Anyone who's left stuff down here, please come and take it away.'

'You back already?' Frank asked, putting his head round his office door. 'Everything all right?'

'Fine, thanks, fine. Just sorting this lot out.'

'That's the ticket!'

Sixty-One

By midweek, the weather had begun to change. The sun was hidden behind cloud, the golden colours had faded; rain was forecast.

'Not so good for an outing,' Frank remarked, as Monnie waited for Torquil on Friday afternoon.

'We'll be all right. Probably just go for a drive.'

'I thought you'd said goodbye to him. Why go out again?'

'This is our real goodbye.'

Hope so, thought Frank, as Torquil arrived, dismissing worries over the weather. He knew the look of the sky, it would be clear again before long.

'Ideal for a trip to my special place,' he added.

'Your special place?' Frank repeated. 'Not your island again?'

'No, no. Monnie will know.'

'Take care, then.'

'Of course.' Torquil raised his hand in salute. 'Special care, for a special place.'

'And I know this special place?' Monnie asked, when they had left the village.

'Sure you do. Remember when I told you how I liked to take my rowing boat out on Loch Hourn and just sit in peace, looking at the mountains?'

'We're going in your rowing boat?' Monnie's heart was plummeting. 'I'm not sure I want another boat trip.'

'This will not be like our last one, sweetheart. This one will be very quiet, very peaceful. Just a little row on the loch so that you can think of me in my favourite place, when you are far away.'

'Odd, you've never taken me there before.'

'Well, you went there with Paul Soutar, didn't you? I never thought the time was right for you to go with me, until now.'

'Paul says the loch can be treacherous in bad weather,' she said in a low voice. 'It may not be fine enough today.'

'Trust me, it will be just what we want.'

Perhaps not surprisingly, Torquil, the fisherman, used to watching the weather, was right. By the time they arrived at the loch and parked on the narrow shore, there were patches of blue breaking up the greyness of the sky, and even a ray or two of thin sunlight. No need, then to worry, thought Monnie, who had rather hoped there might be cause to persuade Torquil not to take his boat out. After all, it was pleasant enough here, with the quiet cottages and their friendly smoke showing signs of life, even though no people were visible.

'Perfect,' Torquil was murmuring. 'The water is calm, Monnie, you will have no need to fear, and we shall not be out long.'

'The mountains seem so dark, looking down,' she said shivering.

'Ach, they are splendid and the sun will be on them soon. Come, give me your hand. Here's my boat ready for us at the jetty. Just an ordinary rowing boat, as you can see.'

He helped her into her seat, on which there was one shabby cushion, then sat down himself to take the oars.

'All right?' Lit by a smile, his face, so wonderfully handsome, made her catch her breath. It was partly this face that had held her in thrall, but there had been more to his power over her than just good looks. She had never really been able to analyse it, had only been willing to yield, until in the recent weeks, she had somehow found the strength to know she must make the break. As she nodded in answer to his question and they began to move smoothly over the water, she felt a great thankfulness that she had achieved what she wanted. The break had been made. Now all that remained was the last goodbye.

'No spin drifts to cause great waves today,' she said lightly.

They had reached the centre of the loch and Torquil, resting on his oars, was no longer smiling.

'Only from you.'

'Me? What do you mean?'

'Do you not think that you have been causing great waves for me?'

'How could I do that?' She was glancing around at the darkness of the mountains, the silent water. She had begun to shiver.

'Spin drifts upset boats. You have upset me, by leaving me.'
He leaned a little towards her. 'Monnie, people do not leave
me. I might leave them, they do not leave me. You are the first.'

'You – you said you couldn't hold me, if I didn't want to be
held.'

'Did I say that?' He trailed an oar in the water. 'That was not
like me.'

'You did say it.'

'But is it true, that you do not want to be held? Are you sure,
you want me to let you go?'

It was growing colder now, with a chill wind rising, and the
surface of the water, no longer calm, was moving in widening
ripples, slapping the sides of the boat. Aware of that and of her
situation, Monnie, her teeth chattering, was beset by fear, but
she would not answer him. She would not say what he was
waiting to hear.

'Monnie!' He was still leaning towards her, his eyes seeming
to shine, even glitter, his smile eager. 'Monnie, why are you not
answering? Are you afraid? Afraid to admit you want to stay with
me? Come on, it is all nonsense, eh, this going away? Girls do
it, I know. Play hard to get. Make men give them what they
want.'

He held out a hand to her, which she did not take.

'Is it marriage you want, Monnie? OK, we'll be married. I
am willing, very willing, and, as you know, it is what my mother
wants—'

'Torquil,' Monnie interrupted, her voice as clear as she could
make it, though she could not disguise its tremor. 'I don't want
to marry you. I just want to go away. I have to, you see, I have
to leave you, and I'm sorry, really sorry, if you're upset and
disappointed in me.' She swallowed, feeling her throat thick with
tears, while keeping her eyes fixed on Torquil, who was now
sitting back in his seat, his face blank of any expression.

'It's a shame things didn't work out,' she was desperately struggling on. 'They should have done, we were so happy, weren't
we? There were some lovely times. Oh, please, Torquil, can we
go back now?'

'Go back? Yes, why not?'

Suddenly he stood up in the boat, and for a moment looked

down at her, then he took off his jacket and threw back his head
to stare round at the mountains, seeming for a moment, in the
weak sunshine, as clear cut as the statue he had once resembled
before.

'Why not go back this way?' he whispered, and, stooping,
pulled her from her seat, so that she was standing, shaking in the
boat.

She cried out, begging him to let her go, to let her sit down,
oh, please, please, but she knew he was past listening, and was
herself numb to any surprise as, faster and faster he rocked the
boat and she felt herself falling, falling from the boat, down,
down, until the waters of Loch Hourn opened to receive her.

Sixty-Two

Darkness. Monnie had never known such darkness, all around
her. Was this how it must be inside a grave? Yet, this was water
over her and she was rising, rising slowly to the surface, gasping,
floundering. But still there was darkness and she knew she was
losing consciousness. Soon, she would sink again, sink to the
bottom of the loch and would not rise . . .

'It's all right,' she heard someone say, and strong arms were
turning her, holding her. 'I've got you, Monnie. Don't struggle,
don't struggle.'

Paul's voice? Yes, it was his, it was Paul, moving her through
the water, oh, thank God, thank God. It might have been Torquil,
come back to undo what he had done? No, never Torquil. It
was Paul.

'Don't worry,' his voice came. 'I have you, you'll soon be safe.'

I'm safe now, she wanted to tell him, feeling him so close, his
wonderful hands beneath her shoulders, taking her with him as
he swam, until gradually the water became shallow, they were
swimming no longer and he was carrying her from the loch to
the shore. It was true, she was safe.

'Poor girl,' he was whispering, as he laid her on the strip of
sand. 'Oh, my poor girl – thank the Lord, you're all right.'

And there were people around, people from the cottages, helping her cough up water, taking off her sodden jacket, wrapping her in blankets, giving her something warm and fiery to drink. Best of all, there was no more darkness, only the light of the day she had thought she would never see again, and Paul, in a soaking shirt, smiling down at her, as someone threw a blanket round him too and handed him a flask.

'Come on,' he said gently, when he'd drunk from it. 'There's a lady here – Mrs MacIntyre – wants to lend you some dry things, then we must get you home. You will be shocked, we must take care.'

'Aye, come along, dear, I'm just in this nearest cottage,' said a dark-haired, kindly-faced woman, as she helped Monnie to her feet. 'I've a lovely wee fire going, we'll soon have you nice and warm. What a thing to happen, eh? But the young man was able to swim back and you were saved anyway – what a blessing!'

'He swam back?' Monnie was wavering on her feet. 'Where is he? I want to see him!'

'No, Monnie, no!' Paul cried. 'I'll speak to him. You go with the lady.'

'I must see Torquil. I must see him for myself. Where is he?'

He was sitting on the shore, only a short distance away, a blanket round his shoulders, his face very pale, his yellow hair dark with moisture on his brow. As Paul and Monnie came to him, he coughed and shivered, but made no move to look at them, or to speak.

'Surprise, surprise, Torquil, here's Monnie,' Paul said grimly. 'I bet you didn't expect to see her again.'

'I do not know what you are talking about.' Torquil had put his hand to his mouth. He was breathing fast. 'It was an accident what happened out there. Monnie will tell you herself, won't you, Monnie?'

At last, he turned his gaze on her, but she did not flinch.

'I know what you wanted to do, Torquil.'

'It was no accident,' Paul said roughly. 'I was watching from the shore, I saw it happen.'

'And what did you see? Monnie fall in? That was nothing to do with me. It was a sudden squall.'

'There was no squall. You were standing up in the boat, you were rocking it, for God's sake! You made Monnie stand, too, and you watched her fall, and then you swam away and left her!'

'I tried to see her, but I could not, the water was too dark. In the end, I had to give up, save myself.'

'Fine, we'll let the police decide what the truth is.' Paul put his arm more firmly round Monnie. 'As soon as I see that this poor girl is well, I'm making the call.'

Torquil's eyes flickered, he opened his mouth to speak, but Monnie, unloosening Paul's arm took a step forward.

'It's all right, Torquil, you needn't worry about the police. I am not going to press charges. I don't care if you say it was an accident, as long as I never see you again.'

She turned to look at the water, pointing a shaking finger. 'Whatever I felt for you is buried out there in that loch, where you told me once you liked to sit and think peaceful thoughts.' She laughed weakly and turned to Paul. 'Can we go?'

'Give me a moment.' Paul, his face white, his expression hard as stone, put his hands on Torquil's shoulders and dragged him to his feet. 'I just want to speak to this fellow first.'

'And say what?' asked Torquil.

'Say this. If Monnie doesn't want to be involved with the police, I'll do what she wishes for now. But that won't stop me writing a full account of what I saw, and of speaking to all the people here, for I guarantee someone else will have seen what I saw and back me up. And if you do not leave this area and remove yourself to some place where no one here will see you again, I will persuade Monnie that we should tell the police what happened and ask them to investigate.'

'You're asking me to leave my home?' Torquil asked incredulously.

'No, I'm telling you. Have I made myself clear? I mean what I say, Torquil, and tomorrow morning I shall be round at your mother's to see what plans you've made. I've heard that it's possible now to go to Australia for only ten pounds. That might be something for you to think about.'

As Torquil stood, transfixed, and the people at a distance stared, Paul put Monnie's arm in his and they moved slowly back towards

Mrs MacIntyre, who drew them into her cottage and quietly closed the door.

Some time later, on the drive back to the hostel, Monnie, dressed in borrowed jersey and trousers, turned to Paul. 'How did you know?' she asked. 'How did you know where to find me?'

Hunched over the wheel of his car, Paul gave a long shuddering sigh. 'I didn't know, I guessed. What happened was that I was desperate for us to have that last walk together. I had found some time to spare and thought I'd come over, see if you were free. But your dad said you'd gone out with Torquil, gone to his "special place".'

'His special place,' Monnie repeated softly. 'Oh, God.'

'Well, I didn't know where that was, and anyway, what could I do? But for some reason, alarm bells were ringing in my head, and as I drove away, I remembered you'd told me once that he liked to go to Loch Hourn and sit in his boat. Without really knowing what I was up to, I turned round and drove to the loch.'

'And you saw us?'

'I saw you. In the boat. I took out my field glasses and watched. Next minute, I saw him make you stand, I saw him rocking the boat, and then I . . . well you know what I did.' Paul tried to laugh. 'I've always been a strong swimmer, but just then I think I could have qualified for the Olympics. I went cleaving through the water like some sort of shark and, thank God, I was in time.'

'Paul, what can I say? You saved my life.'

'I had to, Monnie. If anything had happened to you, I – I don't know what I'd have done.'

There was a silence between them then until they reached the end of the hostel drive, where Paul stopped the car.

'You must go in, Monnie, have a hot bath, try to recover. I don't think you were actually in a near-drowning state, because I reached you fairly soon, but you may feel delayed shock symptoms and need to have the doctor check you out.'

'First, I must tell Dad what's happened. I don't know what he'll do.'

'He'll want to go after Torquil, but I'll tell him what we've decided. If you're sure you don't want to involve the police?'

'I'm sure. I just want him away, out of my life. Paul – will you come into the house with me?'

'I want to, I want to ring the doctor.'

They exchanged long tender glances, then Paul suddenly drew Monnie to him and held her close.

'Oh, Monnie – do you have to go away? Couldn't you stay, come to my school, work with me? Please, think about it.'

'I don't need to think about it.' She pulled a little away, looking at him with clear grey eyes. 'I'm free now, you see. I'm truly free. I have no feelings for Torquil, he's gone completely from my mind. I'm myself again.'

'Thank God,' Paul said hoarsely. 'Will you come, then? To my school? I don't ask anything of you, you'll still be free, but if . . .' He stopped and she kissed him lightly on the lips.

'I understand what you're saying, Paul. I will come to your school, and we will work together. And – just take it from there. Will that be all right?'

'All right? More than all right!'

Their kiss then was shared, a long, deeply satisfying kiss, that told them more about the future than any words, and when it was over, they left the car and walked up to the hostel's front door, arms entwined, almost like the lovers they would become.

Sixty-Three

Frank's wedding to Ishbel, at the end of October, provided all the balm needed to calm the village rocked by stories of what had happened on Loch Hourn and Torquil MacLeod's mysterious departure. There was talk that he had tried to drown the warden's younger daughter, or, that it had all been an accident, but one thing was for sure, he hadn't tried to rescue her – that had been left to nice Mr Soutar. Sure, whatever hysterical Agnes said, everybody knew those boys of hers were wild ones, Torquil as well as Tony, and if Torquil had taken himself off, it was no loss to Conair.

Everyone invited to the kirk on that fine, autumnal wedding day, had therefore relaxed and taken comfort from the joy that flowed so clearly from the happy couple. If there were bad things that happened, there were good things too, and nobody needed the reception champagne (a present from Mr Allan at the hotel, would you believe?) to feel a sense of well-being again.

And how sweet it was to see young Monnie fully recovered from her ordeal and so calm and serene, as her father's eyes followed her, and other eyes, too – and how good it was to know that she would not be leaving the Highlands she'd come to love, but staying on to work for Paul Soutar.

Sadly, goodbyes would have to be made to the lovely Lynette, who also had eyes following her – cheerful brown eyes belonging to Mr Allan's chef, who was departing to start his own restaurant. Very upsetting, no doubt, for Mr Allan, who was already upset, the talk went, because Lynette was leaving, but then other rumours had it that he would find consolation with the beautiful Fionola, now in charge of Reception at the hotel. Seems she already had a new young assistant – rather plain, it was said, but a nice, willing girl who would be no threat to anyone, 'And would never ever wear red,' Lynette had been heard to remark, but no one knew what that meant.

The time came at last for Ishbel, lovely in blue, and Frank, still in his best suit, to leave the little cafe for Niall's decorated car and the short trip to the Skye ferry. Everyone ran alongside for as long as they could, cheering and waving, until the car was out of sight, and then turned away, feeling the little feeling of let down that always comes at that time.

Monnie and Lynette, who had been the last to hug their father and Ishbel, were in fact now shedding a few tears, joined by Mrs Duthie, who said she always cried at weddings, never ask her why, and also Sheana, who said really she should be opening up the shop. But then everyone said, no, no, come and have a cup of tea and a little more wedding cake. Hadn't Ishbel made it herself and was it not the best ever?

'Talking about opening up the shop, I should be back at the hostel,' Monnie told Lynette, over the teacups. 'I'm in charge until the honeymoon's over, remember.'

'And then you'll be moving to Paul's climbing school, when I thought you'd be coming back with me tomorrow, to our old flat.'

Lynette sounded a little sad, but suddenly gave a broad smile. 'No, I'm really happy for you, Monnie. It'll be perfect for you over there, to be with Paul and to stay in the Highlands. I know that's what you really wanted.'

'And you've got what you really wanted, too. The bright lights, eh? Plus a new job and a new admirer.'

'Scott?' Lynette smiled. 'We'll have to see how that works out. Just as you'll be waiting to see how things work out with you and Paul. It's odd, really, how our lives have moved along parallel lines, eh?'

'Both making mistakes first, you mean?'

'And being giving second chances.'

The two sisters hesitated, then clung together, dashing more tears away as they moved apart.

'The main thing is that you're all right,' Lynette said huskily. 'Oh, Monnie – if you hadn't been—'

'I am, though. And so are you and Dad and everyone we care about. We did the right thing, coming to the Highlands – even if you are going home again.'

'I wouldn't have missed it, though,' Lynette said quietly. 'I've learned a lot.'

Monnie nodded. 'Better get back,' she whispered.

'Want a lift?' asked Paul, appearing at her side. 'Car's at the door.'

'So is mine,' Scott told Lynette. 'All ready for tomorrow?

'Always ready for tomorrow,' cried Lynette.